Because of Blake

CHRISTINE LAYNE

Edited by NICE GIRL NAUGHTY EDITS
Edited by D.P. Lehan
Cover Designer COFFIN PRINT
Formatting Christine Layne

FROM THE AUTHOR

Because of Blake

Christine Layne

Because of Blake is a full-length, stand alone that features strong language, mature situations, and explicit sexual scenes. Reader discretion is advised, and this book is intended for readers age 18 and up.

Trigger Warning List:

Death of loved one

Grief/Trauma

Anxiety/panic attacks

Depression

Mention of Suicide

This book is dedicated to my husband—

My very own Blake.

Chapter One

I jump as my cell phone trills in my pocket, barely managing to keep my afternoon coffee in its mug. Even after three years and countless ringtones, the sound still rattles me. It's an inconspicuous reminder of that one life-changing phone call, and my heart races every time it rings.

Seeing my best friend's name on the screen, I relax, sagging against my chair. "Hello, Michelle."

"Hey, Mags. What are you doing?"

"Sitting at the table, enjoying a cup of coffee. You?"

"Nothing. I was wasting my Sunday afternoon on social media when I remembered I have an actual friend to talk to."

A smile creeps across my face as the image of Michelle pops into my mind. Snuggling under a blanket with her phone in one hand while the other twirls her long, blonde hair between her fingers is how she wastes time.

I waste mine drinking coffee with my wavy brown hair tied into a messy bun.

"So, Mags, I need to know if you're going to send the post office a change of address, or if I'm going to keep getting your mail until we die?"

I smack my forehead with my palm. "Oh my gosh, I'm so sorry. I'll do it this week."

She laughs. "It's alright, Mags, I'm just giving you shit. Moving is stressful. I don't blame you for forgetting. Speaking of, how's the new house?"

"Coming along." I take a sip of my coffee, letting my gaze float around my new kitchen, still littered with the moving boxes I should be unpacking. Swallowing down my drink, I get up from the table to continue on the box of dishes I started earlier. "The kitchen is almost unpacked."

"How much do you have left to do?"

"A lot." I sigh. "It's taking longer than I thought it would."

"Mags, you've only been there a week. Give yourself some grace. Like I said, moving is hard, especially when you leave behind a house you've lived in for a decade."

My bottom lip works its way between my teeth, and my toes wiggle against the tile floor. The house isn't the only thing I left behind. All the memories are there, too. I wonder how long it'll take before they're replaced with new memories, new experiences. How long do I have before I forget?

Michelle clears her throat. "What about the kids? Aren't they supposed to be helping you?"

I blink my eyes and shake my head to clear it. Setting down a stack of plates wrapped in newspaper, I peek through the patio door into the backyard. "Oh, yes. They're a lot of help when all they want to do is play in the Slip 'N Slide."

"Those little shits."

"Michelle!"

She laughs again, probably happy to get a reaction from me after my silence a moment ago. "Easy, Mags. You know I love them. In fact, they haven't had a sleepover with Aunt Michelle in a while. Let's set one up."

"We'll see. They start school soon and we haven't been supply shopping yet."

"School? Already? It's only the middle of August."

"And school starts the 23rd." As I unwrap the plates and load them into the dishwasher, I take a breath, huffing it out with puffy cheeks. "I go back to work tomorrow."

"Oh, yeah. Part-time, though. I bet it feels good knowing you won't have to see that intern you like so much every day. What's her name?"

"Abbey." Her name comes out tight. "Yes, that's one of the perks, but I'm looking forward to more time with the kids, and having a day to myself here and there." Which reminds me, I should call my therapist and set up an appointment now that I'll have a couple weekdays off. *Maybe I can kill two birds...* "Michelle, can I come to–"

The patio door slides open. "Mom, can we have popsicles?" Dylan, my nine-year-old son, asks as he pokes his sopping wet dirty blond head inside, dripping water all over the floor.

"Sure, sweetie. There're some in the freezer in the garage, but towel off first, please." I roll my eyes. "So, Michelle, can I–"

"Put me on speaker, Mags. I want to say hi."

With a groan, I press the speaker icon. "Say hi to Aunt Michelle, Dyl-pickle."

"Hi!" He doesn't even glance in my direction as he rushes across the room, disappearing into the garage.

I laugh and turn off speaker phone, grabbing some bubble-wrapped glasses from the box. "So much for that."

"What a punk. Where's Syd?"

Glasses in hand, I crane my neck to see around the backyard, glimpsing my eleven-year-old daughter, Sydney, lying in the grass under a tree with her nose in a book. "Take a guess."

"I don't remember reading so much when I was her age."

Sydney has always been a different type of kid. As a young child, she preferred to play alone, using her imagination in some wild ways, but as she's grown, she's gained an affinity for reading. Instead of creating the worlds on her own, she escapes to ones created for her. It's a big thing we have in common.

Dylan comes careening back through the room with two popsicles in his hand. He's out the door before I even turn around. "Well, I guess you're not talking to the kids."

"Whatever," she says quietly, though I can hear the disappointment. "So, you go back to work tomorrow, but school doesn't start for another week and a half. What are they doing while you're at work? Your nanny still coming?"

I pull out the other glasses left in the box and pick at the tape on the bubble wrap. "No. As much as I love her, I can't ask a woman of her age to drive across town."

"Mags, Littleton is what, twenty-five miles away? It's not a long drive."

"For you or me, no, but this woman is like eighty. I don't want her driving all the way out here, especially in the winter. Plus, the kids are getting older. We probably wouldn't need a nanny much longer, anyway."

"You're actually thinking of letting the kids be home alone? For a whole day? *You?*"

My grip tightens on the glass in my hand, popping a couple of bubbles. I hate the implication in her voice. Yes, I may be a bit on the overprotective side, but these are my kids, and I know firsthand how accidents happen when you least expect them. "Not yet. They're still too young."

"How old do they have to be to legally stay home alone?"

"Colorado doesn't have a minimum age for it, but I'm not ready for them to be home by themselves. The school system has a summer program for kids whose parents work, so they'll do that until school starts."

"Oh, I bet Sydney's going to love it, being the social butterfly she is," Michelle's words drip with sarcasm.

"Well, she doesn't have a choice. I can't send Dylan to the program and let Syd stay home." With the last of the glasses loaded into the dishwasher, I break down the box they had been in, pinching the edges of the cardboard between my fingers. "I'm sure she could handle it, but I don't know how Dylan would fare."

"Oh, please. You know he'd just be on that damn Xbox all day."

"Exactly. At least this way, I know they're getting outside and doing activities, all while being supervised." I drop the flattened box onto the floor and run my hand over my head, stopping when my fingers get twisted in my bun.

"I don't envy all the motherly anxiety you have, Mags. I'm not saying there's anything bad about being a mom, but I'm glad I never did it."

A chuckle escapes me. Kids were never in Michelle's plan, and as hesitant as she was when we first met, she's fallen in love with mine. They love her equally as much. She's like family, hence the name Aunt Michelle. I knew I'd miss having her as a neighbor, but I didn't realize there would be such a big hole in my life without her living next door.

Speaking of being neighbors. "Hey, what's a good day for me to come get the mail?" I need to make an appointment with my therapist, and since her office isn't too far from Michelle's house in Aurora, maybe I can make one trip instead of two.

"What? No, I'll bring it to you. I need to see your new place!"

"Oh, right." I walk to the table, picking up my cup and swirling the remaining coffee. "Well, I'm off Tuesdays and Fridays now."

"How about this Friday? So I can stay late if I want."

"Sure. Will Tom be with you?" I tip my cup and swallow down the last few drops of caffeinated goodness, albeit cold now.

"Pfft. He's such a workaholic; I doubt he'll be around. Besides, I want girl time. Maybe we can scout the neighborhood for any hot neighborly prospects you might have."

I roll my eyes. "Michelle, you know I don't date." A smirk dances on my lips as I think about what my online profile would look like. A nice picture of myself with my wavy brown hair cascading around my shoulders as I sit on my deck with a book in one hand, a mug of coffee in the other. The details, though, are where I'd rake in men by the thousands. I can see it now.

Thirty-five-year-old, widowed, suburban mom of two, employed part-time as a paralegal at the same firm for over a decade, with no other ambition, seeks man who–

My stomach drops. Betrayal creeps up my spine as my husband's face jumps into my mind, his shining hazel eyes staring at me. I always told him his eyes put my plain old blue ones to shame. He never agreed, and I miss hearing him say mine were the most beautiful eyes he'd ever seen.

I press my fingertips into my eyelids before glancing at my empty mug on the table. Another cup of coffee wouldn't be bad, would it? "Even if I was ready, I wouldn't date a neighbor. It's too weird. I may be single, but I'm not on the market."

"The only reason you're not on the market is because you won't allow yourself to be. Charlie's been gone three years."

A tightness forms in my chest. "And I'm still grieving."

"I'm not saying you should be over him, but don't you think you should be able to move forward by now? Even just a little?"

"No one gets to tell anyone how to grieve. It's a personal experience which is different for everyone, and this is how I do it." I bite back the edge to my tone, but it still comes through.

Michelle takes a deep breath. "Okay. Speaking of Charlie, how are your nightmares? Better since you moved, or worse?"

I pick up my mug, twirling it around on the table. "The same. I still have them, like, four or five times a week."

"Well, that's better than every night like they used to be, right?"

"Yeah. I guess what they say about time healing wounds is true." I stop twirling the mug. "At least for some wounds."

"See? You're getting there, and I think meeting someone would help. It would give you a distraction."

I tilt my head from side to side, stretching the now tense muscles. "Okay, thanks for the pep-talk, Michelle."

She sighs, but doesn't say anything more about me finding a man. "Will you text me your address?"

"I thought I did when I put the offer in so you could Zillow-stalk me?"

"Yeah, but that was months ago and I don't feel like searching through the messages."

My chuckle eases my stiff shoulders. "Okay, I'll see you on Friday."

"Bye, Mags."

I send Michelle a quick text with our address, receiving the thumbs up and kissy face emojis back. All our talk about the mail reminds me I should go check ours. Even if I haven't given the post office our change of address, the Realtor, mortgage company, and all our utility providers have the new one. There might be something important in there I've been neglecting.

Grabbing my keys, I set my mug in the sink and poke my head into the backyard to tell the kids I'll be gone for a few minutes. They wave me off like it's no big deal, and deep down, I know it's not, but my stomach always clenches when I think of them being alone. They're old enough. They're not stupid. I'll be gone all of five minutes, but the things that can happen in those five minutes have panic bubbling in me.

I force myself to the front door. As I stand before it, I employ my breathing and focus technique. A grounding thing for when my brain goes into overload and I can't recover. Acknowledging a number of things I can see, feel, hear, smell, and taste allows me to refocus and bring my anxiety down a few notches. My therapist taught this to me early on in our meetings. I really do need to make an appointment.

Once my heartbeat is back to normal, I open the front door and step outside into the warm, August air. I inhale deeply, realizing I've been stuck in the house all day, aside from helping the kids set up the Slip 'N Slide. Getting outside, even for only a few minutes, calms me. It's almost as if the fresh air breathes life into my lungs.

Four houses sit between ours and the community mailboxes at the bottom of the hill. I come to an abrupt stop before the mailboxes as a guy with a dog approaches from the opposite direction. My walls go up in an instant. This will be the first solo interaction I've had with a neighbor since we moved in. Sure, I've waved at a few of my surrounding neighbors, even exchanged pleasantries with a couple, but my kids have always been around, giving me an excuse to cut the conversation short.

Small talk is one thing, and one I don't particularly enjoy, but it doesn't lead to questions about where my husband is. Up until now, I've been able to skirt around any detailed conversations. This time, I'm alone. Completely defenseless. *Shit.*

As this guy gets closer, I size him up. He's easily a half foot taller than me, maybe a couple inches more, and he's built like no one I've ever met. Even in the loose, athletic clothing he's sporting, I can tell he's in great shape. Broad shoulders, nice biceps, toned calves. This guy should be on magazine covers, not walking his dog in a suburban Colorado neighborhood.

His mouth ticks up on one side as he meets my gaze. "After you," his deep voice rumbles, suddenly making me aware of my staring.

"Oh, um, thank you." I turn my gaze toward the mailbox, hoping he didn't catch me drooling. I can't remember what number is ours. My eyes jump from box to box, my brain a jumbled mess. It's seemingly turned to mush after being overstimulated by this hunk of a dog walker.

"Is something wrong?" he asks, kneeling down to calm his Irish Setter who spotted a squirrel across the street.

"I... I don't know which one is mine. We just moved in, and I can't remember which number they told me at closing." I turn to this stranger for confirmation I'm not a complete idiot, and I'm met with a warm, closed-lipped smile.

"Well, it's not number eight, that's mine."

I feel heat flooding my cheeks, so I turn away quickly. "Thanks. I think it's number seven, then." I put the key into the lock and turn it successfully. *Thank God.*

"Good guess," he says, standing back up and removing his Rockies baseball cap to run his hand through his dark brown hair. With the hat off, I see his hair matches his eyes. His deep brown irises invite me in, and I lose myself in them after only a few seconds.

I shake my head to break the spell. "Yeah, I'm sure it was only beginner's luck."

"You say you just moved in? Welcome to the neighborhood. My name is Blake Averson. I live in the corner house in the cul-de-sac." He hikes his thumb over his shoulder, then pats his dog on the head. "This here is Oscar."

"Nice to meet you. I'm Margaret, er, Maggie Hansen."

He replaces the ball cap, casting a shadow over his eyes again, but not before I catch him eyeballing me from my head to my wiggling toes. I notice his gaze lingers a moment on my left hand, sans wedding ring. "Good to have you here, Maggie. You and your, uh, kids? Husband?"

A lump forms in my throat at the word husband. "Kids," I say, all too quickly.

One corner of his mouth quirks up. Not fully up-turned, but enough to hint he's pleased with my answer.

I clear my throat. "And what about you? Wife and kids?" My heart picks up speed a bit as I anticipate his answer. Why do I care?

"Nope. Oscar and I are living the bachelor life."

I chuckle, brushing a piece of stray hair behind my ear and watching Blake's eyes follow my movement.

"Well, if you need anything, feel free to knock on my door. I'm no contractor, but I've been known to do a household repair every now and then."

"Thank you, Mr. Avers–"

"Blake, please."

"Blake. You're very kind." We stare at each other for a moment, my mouth curving awkwardly before I pull myself out of my stupor. "Well, I need to get home before my kids report me as a missing person." My nervous laugh sounds so stupid.

"I'm sure I'll see you around, Maggie." There's a gruffness in his tone as he says my name, almost like gravel, and it sends an exhilarating chill up my spine. He tips his hat, and I give a polite smile as I turn to walk away, fighting the urge to look over my shoulder to see if he's watching me.

Thank God Michelle wasn't here. She would've certainly cracked some lewd innuendo and I'd be spending this entire walk explaining to her why she's insane.

Mr. Averson... I mean, Blake is much too young for me. By five years, at least. And even if there was the slightest chance he was interested in me, I'm not interested in him. Am I?

I shake my head. No, of course not. I'm holding strong to my "not on the market" comment from earlier. I don't have the time, energy, or desire to dive back into the dating pool.

But that's not really true, either.

I'm only working part-time, so I actually have the time, and from what I've seen of the apps, it doesn't take much work to find a date. The only question is if I have the desire, and I wouldn't know what that felt like if it bit me on the ass.

While Blake is certainly nice to look at, that's *all* he'll be. A hot neighbor I can ogle.

Chapter Two

My hand cramps and I drop my pen onto my desk. I'm writing too fast. As much as this paperwork needs to get done, there's no rush. I glance at the clock.

Shit, it's almost noon? Okay, maybe a little bit of a rush.

The affidavits were piled high when I arrived at my desk this morning. Apparently, the person appointed to cover for me, didn't. I've been working my butt off playing catch up, and although I've made a good dent, I still have a full day's worth of paperwork sitting in front of me. Being a part-time paralegal might be harder than I thought.

This one's almost done. I'll finish it and then take lunch.

As I put the final touches on my hurried, yet precise notes, my stomach rumbles. Finished in the nick of time. Clicking the button on my mouse, the icon for "OUT" turns gray. I sling my purse over my shoulder, shut down my computer, and exit my cubicle just as Abbey turns the corner from the mailroom.

Her ruby red lips purse and her penciled-in eyebrows furrow as she eyes my bag at my hip. "Where are you rushing off to?"

"Hi, Abbey," I say as pleasantly as I can. "It's lunchtime. My stomach's begging me to eat something. I've been working so hard today, I haven't even taken a break, so I'm ready for one."

"I didn't ask for your life story." She raises her perfectly manicured hand.

"Okay," I draw the word out.

"Did you enjoy your little vacation?" She flips her bleach blond hair behind her shoulder and folds her arms across her chest.

Vacation? Only someone in their mid-twenties would think of moving as a vacation. "I moved, Abbey. It wasn't exactly a picnic." I adjust my purse strap on my shoulder. "And I'd better get moving now. I've still got plenty of work to do this afternoon."

"Yeah, sorry I couldn't get to your stuff last week." Her tone sounds anything but apologetic.

"It's alright." I grit my teeth, trying my hardest to keep my professionalism, but my words still come out tight. "I'll just be busy Wednesday and Thursday."

Her eyebrows come together so closely, I'm worried the pencil will smudge and leave a uni-brow. Okay, maybe I'm hoping it will. "Well, that's the price you pay for working part-time." She huffs, walking past me, grazing my arm with hers.

With a deep, cleansing breath, I steel myself to walk through the office and out the door. The warmth of a Colorado August greets me, a glorious change from the frigid air-conditioned office, but as I step away from the shade of the building and into the parking lot, the sweat builds on my skin. It's like crossing a not-so-glorious desert.

Opening my car door, I'm met with self-cleaning oven temperatures even though I parked under the giant oak tree in the middle of the lot. This is ridiculous. I love summer, but even I have my limits. I sit in the car with the door open, blasting the A/C for a minute or two until the air coming from the vents cools. Putting my hands on the dash, I let the cold air run down my shirt sleeves and into my damp armpits. I'm sure I look sexy right now, but who do I have to impress?

Yes, I dress professionally and wear makeup for work, but it's the only time. When I'm not working, I prefer a natural look. Maybe a little mascara and lip gloss, but not always. I'm not trying to attract anyone, so what do I care if I don't look the epitome of sex all the time?

Like Abbey. I let out a deep exhale. *Abbey.*

I'm glad I'm part-time, since her internship will most certainly turn into a full-time position at the beginning of the year. I'll be stuck with her and her smug, snotty attitude. She thinks she's so much better than me because she'll be applying to law school next year. Like I didn't consider law school myself.

Getting my bachelor's degree in criminal law, I interned here at Fisher & Sons the summer right out of college, and I've loved every minute of it. I had, at one point, thought about going to law school, but when I saw the insane hours and stress the lawyers went through, I canned the idea. I've kept my position as a paralegal, and I'm good at it.

Abbey will make a phenomenal lawyer. She's the right amount of bitch for the job. As annoying as she may be, she's smart and had outstanding accolades when she applied for our internship. I have to give credit where credit is due.

Doesn't mean I have to like her, though.

My body finally cools enough to be comfortable, so I cut the engine. Sliding the driver's seat all the way back, I roll down the windows and take in the sounds of summer. Birds chirping away in the tree branches above me. Bugs buzzing through the air. In another month, autumn will officially be here and, although the heat is sweltering, I'm not ready to say goodbye to these warm summer days.

With a sigh, I open my insulated lunch bag to retrieve my strawberry salad and French bread. I've always preferred bringing my lunch to save money, and I could very well eat in our lunchroom, but I'd rather be outside and slightly sweaty than freeze in the overactive air conditioning.

And in the car, I can listen to my music.

I turn up the stereo, cranking the deliciously powerful guitar riffs of Rise Against, and stare aimlessly out of the window. My husband, Charlie, always hated this band. I used to play it on purpose to annoy him. He got me back with some of his awful music tastes, but I miss the way we tortured each other. All in the name of fun, of course.

Grimacing, I pinch my eyes shut as my nostalgia dissipates, and I feel the sting of Charlie's absence. To placate the tears pricking my eyes, I stuff my mouth full of dressing-drenched spinach, and pull out my phone for some riveting rounds of Candy Crush.

An ad for a dating app pops up after a difficult level, and as I wait for the "X" to appear, Michelle's words from yesterday ring in my ears. Is it time for me to meet someone? What would it be like to swipe through all those profiles? Do people really have any luck finding worthwhile partnerships on these things?

My curiosity begs my finger to hit "Get", but I shake my head and close the ad. Even if it was only in jest, I can't entertain the idea. Sure, three years is a long time to be alone. It's only natural the compulsion to find companionship surfaces every now and then, but that's all it is; a compulsion. It's not something I need, and certainly not something I'm looking for.

Even if I was ready, would I be able to compete in the dating world?

I don't intend for it to happen, but thoughts of women like Abbey pop into my head. Hair perfectly curled and pinned to frame their faces which are painted like runway models while they sip cosmopolitans in their tight skirts and low-cut tops. Their immaculate manicures would beckon men who are probably Adonises in their own right.

Adonises like Blake.

BEEP! BEEP! BEEP! The alarm on my phone sounds, making me jump and alerting me to the fact my lunch hour is over. I pack up my containers and head back into the office. When I step inside, Abbey's chatting with our receptionist. She doesn't notice me as I walk by, but I take a second to scrutinize her appearance.

She's always dressed to kill, her makeup fiercely applied, and her stature radiating confidence. She'll dominate her opponent in the courtroom. Based on her body language, she probably dominates the dating game, too.

I skulk away, not sure why my legs are suddenly heavy like lead. The love of my life is gone, yes, but I found my one and only, and I wouldn't trade the time we had together for anything. Not even a chance at new love.

"The house is beautiful, Mags." Michelle gazes up at my vaulted ceilings as she walks down the stairs after we tour the upper level.

"Thanks, but I didn't do anything to it. The previous owners updated it before selling."

"Yeah, but you found it and snatched it up." Michelle walks into the kitchen and takes a seat at the table. "So, how are the neighbors?"

I shrug and open the fridge to retrieve the iced tea. "The ones I've met are fine, I guess." As I turn away from the fridge, I groan. "The woman across the street, though." I roll my eyes. "She's a piece of work."

Michelle laughs as I fill her glass. "How so?"

"She came over the day after we moved in with a huge gift basket in her arms. Apparently, she's the head of the welcoming committee. After rambling about the neighborhood, she told me" –I place my hand over my chest and raise my nose into the air– "she 'must have me over for coffee and cakes so we can get to know each other.' Ugh, I've been avoiding her ever since."

"Why? Knowing your neighbors isn't a bad thing." Michelle points to herself. "Case in point."

"You're the exception." I sit down across the table from Michelle, sighing before taking a sip of my tea. "She had the air about her that screamed nosy. I know what getting to know people like her entails, and I don't like it, or all the questions that come with it."

"It's been three years, you're not used to it by now?"

"Never." I keep my gaze on my glass as I swirl my tea before meeting Michelle's eyes.

She presses her lips into a flat line, but swallows down her argument and says, "Okay, so you've got neighbors who are 'fine,' and one who you'd like to forget. Anyone else? This is a big neighborhood, Mags."

I take a long drink of my tea, swishing it around in my mouth. "I met a guy who lives in the cul-de-sac. Blake."

Michelle wiggles her butt in her chair. "Ooh, Blake. He sounds hot."

"Hot doesn't even begin to describe him. This guy is gorgeous."

"Even better. How many times have you seen him?"

"Just once. On Monday after we talked, I went to check the mail and he was walking his dog." I fight a smile and ignore the ache between my thighs as I picture Blake and recall our conversation. "We chatted at the mailbox."

Michelle groans and hangs her head a moment. "Chatted? Come on, Mags. You've got to give me more."

"There's not more. We exchanged introductions, he welcomed me to the neighborhood, and offered to come help me with anything I need fixed."

Michelle's eyes widen. "He invited himself over?"

"Not for dinner, or anything. Just if I had a problem I couldn't handle myself. You know, household issues."

"Like fixing your pipes?" Michelle waggles her eyebrows.

"Not *those* pipes." I roll my eyes, but my cheeks heat all the same. "But yes, I suppose if a sink or something needed to be looked at, he'd come help."

"So, do you want me to go break something?"

I bark out a laugh. "No, thank you. If I need something fixed, I'll call a professional."

"Why, when there's a hot guy offering to do it for free?" Michelle almost sounds offended.

"Well, for one thing, I don't know how handy Blake is. He might not know what he's doing at all, and I'll still end up having to call someone. And asking Blake into my home poses all kinds of other issues I'm not ready to deal with. I don't want to send him any wrong signals."

Michelle frowns. "Asking him to change a light bulb would send the wrong signal?"

"I don't know. He could see it as an invitation for more, and I don't want, or need, to have those kinds of conversations." I lean forward, putting my elbow on the table and plopping my chin into my palm. "It's easier if I call a professional."

Michelle crosses her arms and sits back in her chair. "Okay, fine. You're making all the sense, but I don't have to like it. Mags, you should be getting out there. New house, new city, new chapter, which could include a new man."

"I don't need a new man, and I wouldn't know how to go about it, anyway." Michelle opens her mouth, but I put my hand up. "I know what you're going to say, but even if I was ready to 'get back out there,' I'm not going to use my *neighbor* as my guinea pig." I make an X with my arms, uncrossing them as I wave them through the air. "The subject is closed, Michelle."

Chapter Three

The kids' first week of school is always a stressful transition, but I welcome the chaos all the same. With my part-time schedule, I now have two full days during the week completely to myself. It's bliss.

I love my kids, and I love spending time with them, but as a single parent, I don't get much alone time. I should have done this three years ago, but I wouldn't have survived mentally. I needed the distraction. Now, things have settled, and I'm ready to take back my life, or at least part of it.

The month of September brings Dylan's tenth birthday. Suddenly, my baby is in the double digits and I'm elated and devastated at the same time. He's gone from my quirky, happy little guy to my quirky, happy, ten-year-old man. Next thing I know, he'll be asking for the keys to my car.

We celebrate on Saturday with a simple celebration, just the three of us. Dylan gets to pick our meals and activities for the day. He chooses pancakes for breakfast, waffles for lunch, and breakfast burritos for dinner.

I'll need to double my workouts this week. Maybe doubling is a little much. An extra walk or two wouldn't hurt, though.

I give him the gift of a new bicycle and Sydney picks him out new clothes and shoes. They go for a bike ride while I wash the new clothes because Dylan *has* to wear them to school. The kids are gone for a while, which blows my anxiety through the roof.

They've gotten lost. They've been kidnapped. Maybe run over. I should go look for them.

My heart pounds in my chest and I'm on the verge of hyperventilating, so I employ my calming technique again. As my heartbeat slows and I start breathing normally, I decide to do something more relaxing than wallowing in my irrational mom fears.

I make myself a glass of iced tea, blindly grab a book from my to-be-read pile, and take a seat on the front porch to wait for the kids to get home. Our house faces east, so by the afternoon, the front is shaded nicely. As I snuggle up in the cushy patio chair and raise my book to my face, I catch a glimpse of Blake walking Oscar up the street. I can barely see over the porch railing, but I know it's him. I'd recognize the man anywhere. Plus, Oscar is a dead giveaway.

I haven't run into him since the day at the mailbox a few weeks ago, and to be honest, I've been hoping I wouldn't. Not that he isn't great to look at, and he was insanely charming when we met, but the fact I'm attracted to him scares me. It's something I haven't dealt with in a long time, and I wouldn't even know where to start.

I slink down in my chair, my nose almost touching the book as I eyeball Blake over the top of the pages. My attempt to hide is futile, though.

He spots me and crosses the street, walking up my driveway to stop at my porch steps. "Hey, Maggie. How are you doing? "

He remembered my name? A flutter rushes through me and I lower my book onto my lap. "Hi, Blake. I'm good, thanks. Just waiting on my kids to get back from their bike ride."

"Ah, that must have been them I saw on the street behind us. Blondish boy on a black and orange bike? And his sister with hair like yours?"

I nod as my tension ebbs. "That's them."

"So, did everything go okay with the move?"

"Yes, I think we're good, thanks for asking." I hold his gaze a moment, his dark brown eyes never leaving mine, and I have to swallow down my racing heart. "How are you?"

"Never better." Blake's gaze trails down my body and pauses on my bare feet, my toes wiggling. As his gaze floats back to my face, he does a double take of the book in my hand. "Sorry, to interrupt you. I'll let you get back to reading. That looks like a good one."

"Oh, no problem. I haven't even started yet." I lift the book and see the cover for the first time since I grabbed it. My cheeks instantly redden as I'm put face to face with a Fabio wannabe and the scantiest clad woman I've ever seen, passionately embracing in a magical forest clearing. I snap it shut and lay it face down at my side.

Blake's deep chuckle rumbles through the air. "I don't read much romance, but maybe I could learn a thing or two from leading men like that." He winks and my stomach flips. "Are you a big reader?"

I nod, tucking a piece of hair behind my ear, and let out the breath I didn't realize I was holding. "Sydney, my daughter, and I are both big readers. My son, Dylan? Not so much." He and Charlie have that in common.

"Dylan sounds like me."

An awkward silence settles between us. I don't know what to say. My book certainly isn't getting brought up again, and I don't want to be the mom who can't stop talking about her kids, so I sit here, smiling politely and staring at Blake. He follows suit, though his gaze bounces around as he adjusts his baseball cap. Different than the one he had on during our last interaction, but still the Rockies.

"So, you like baseball?" *Duh, Maggie.*

He nods, his mouth quirking up. "I do. Me and my buddies get together for a couple games a year. It's a fun reason to get out of the house, y'know?"

"Actually, I don't. I've never been to a baseball game." Sports have never been my thing, and Charlie never pushed it, so the only times I paid attention was when someone invited us to a Superbowl party or a Stanley Cup Playoff get-together.

Blake's mouth drops open a moment, before curving up into a calculating smile. Like the wheels are turning inside his head with an idea. "Well, you should check one out sometime. You might enjoy it."

"I don't know the first thing about baseball."

"I'd be happy to teach you everything I know. Maybe I could take you to a–"

My kids come careening into the driveway before he can finish, saving me from what sounded like Blake asking me to a baseball game. Possibly even as a date.

"Mom! This bike is so fast!" Dylan shouts as Sydney pulls up next to him. "Ha ha! Beat you!"

Sydney rolls her eyes. "Yep, you sure did."

"You guys had fun, though?" I ask with a shaking voice, and as they nod, their eyes land on Blake. "Oh, um, guys, this is... Mr. Blake. He lives in the cul-de-sac. Blake, this is my daughter, Sydney, and my son, Dyl–"

"You have a dog!?" Dylan squeals and leaps off his bike toward Oscar.

Blake laughs. "Yeah. This is Oscar. You can pet him, he's friendly."

Dylan squats down, tentatively petting Oscar, who nuzzles into Dylan's hands. It isn't long, though, before the two of them are wrestling. Blake undoes Oscar's leash, allowing him and Dylan to run around the yard, barking and laughing.

Blake watches them play a moment before turning to Sydney. "So, Sydney, how are you liking the new house?"

She shrugs. "It's fine."

"And school? What's your favorite subject?"

"School's okay." She shoots me a sideways glance and flicks her eyes to the ground. "I like English class best."

"Yeah, your mom said you're a reader. What's your favorite book?"

"I don't know."

"She's read the entire Percy Jackson series at least a dozen times," I chime in.

"No, I haven't." Sydney rolls her eyes, again. "Can I go in and have a Coke?"

"Sure, sweetheart."

"It was nice to meet you, Sydney," Blake says, nodding as Syd disappears into the house. He shoves his hands in his pockets and turns to me. "She's a tough cookie to crack, huh?"

I laugh. "Hey, you got more out of her than I do lately."

"Well, then I'll call it a win." He turns to the yard where Dylan and Oscar are still rolling around. "Hey, buddy, I hate to say this, but I've got to get home. Can I have my dog back?"

"Awww, but we were having fun." The whine out of Dylan is like nails on a chalkboard.

"Next time, buddy," Blake says, patting his leg for Oscar to come.

Next time? He's planning on hanging out with us?

"Mom, why can't we have a dog?"

Blake turns his head to meet my gaze. "Not a dog person?"

My mouth runs dry. "No. I love dogs, but I was always wiping my kids' butts, so I didn't want to clean up after a dog, too." I feel the redness filling my cheeks. *Smooth, Maggie.* Talk about poop to the hot guy.

Blake chuckles. "That's a good reason." He gives a little wave as he and Oscar head down the driveway. "See you guys later."

My entire body relaxes, melting into the patio chair with the relief of dodging an awkward conversation. I've turned down a good number of men in the last three years, but that doesn't mean it's become any easier. There's some level of guilt accompanying the word "no." It may have something to do with their sad, puppy dog faces when I reject them, or some societal obligation cemented into my subconscious, but I made my decision and I'm sticking to it.

Still, this tightness in my chest tells me rejecting Blake will be the most difficult yet.

I shrug it off and walk Dylan inside. Not two minutes later, the doorbell rings, and my heart leaps into my throat. I swallow it down only to have it pound in my chest as I imagine Blake standing on my porch. It makes sense, right? He was just here, a very vulnerable moment interrupted by my kids, so he's come back to finish asking the question I thought I'd escaped. I whip open the door without looking through the peephole. No need to since I know who's out there.

"Oh, Maggie. I'm so glad I caught you at home!" my neighbor, Joanna, from across the street says, her eyes lighting up.

I smile, but it's tight. "Hi, Joanna."

"I haven't seen you much since you moved in. Thought maybe you were avoiding me." She laughs.

Because I have been. "We've been busy. It's all go, go, go when you move."

"Oh, I know. Speaking of, how is the house? You all settled in?" she asks, peeking over my shoulder to eyeball my entryway.

"Yep." I shift my stance to block her view. I know it's not a big deal, but nosiness irritates me. "We're unpacked, the kids started school, and I think I'm getting used to working part-time." *Shit.* I shouldn't have said that last part.

"Part-time? How wonderful. Do you work certain days, or shorter hours?"

I feel my fake, cheery expression drop slightly. "Days. Mondays, Wednesdays, and Thursdays."

Joanna's eyes gleam as they widen momentarily. "Oh, perfect. I don't have any plans on Tuesday. Why don't you come over for a coffee, hm?"

Well, crap. My avoidance tactics have been all for naught, and I think I've exhausted every excuse in the book. "Sure," I say, reluctantly.

"Fantastic. How about you come over around nine?"

My eyes widen. "In the morning?"

Joanna chuckles and waves me off like I've said the most ridiculous thing in the world. "Well, you can't very well have coffee at nine at night."

Tuesday morning, I cross the street to Joanna's house, my stomach wrenching. I hate this song and dance of meeting new people. It always ends up in the same place; with them pitying me and my kids, while I fume at the universe for cheating us out of happiness.

I take a deep breath, exhaling slowly, before pressing the doorbell. The chime barely finishes before Joanna whips the door open. It's like she was watching out the window for me.

"Maggie, hi. Come on in." Joanna steps aside to allow room for me to enter. "Don't you look nice." She turns to close the door, and I roll my eyes.

I'm sure I look *very nice* in my plain white t-shirt, stylishly frayed jeans, and Converse sneakers. "So do you."

She scoffs at my compliment and runs her hand over her perfectly positioned "messy" bun. "No need to lie. I know I'm a hot mess right now." Her button-down, pink blouse side-tucked into her perfectly creased black slacks begs to differ. "Let's go sit in the living room, shall we?"

Joanna ushers me through the foyer and into a spacious room which isn't lacking in the style department. White wainscoting covers the lower half of each wall beneath navy blue and white striped wallpaper, as accents of cream and gold are spread throughout the décor. Two large Ficus trees flank the patio door, which opens up to a large deck.

Taking seat on an oversized, white couch, she pats the cushion next to her. "Have a seat." She pours coffee into a mug. "How do you take yours?"

"Oh, um, lots of sugar and cream, please." I almost can't take my eyes off this exquisitely decorated room. And I thought my house was nice. "This is beautiful, Joanna."

"Thank you. I worked hard on it. Such is the life of an interior decorator."

"Is that what you do?" I sit down and take my mug from her, lifting it up to smell the heavenly aroma.

"Mhm. It's so much fun. I could come over and do a consult for you, if you'd like. We could give your house a makeover." She beams at me like a child waiting for their parent to say it's okay to have ice cream before dinner.

I shake my head and take a sip of my coffee. *Good God, this is delicious!* "It's nice of you, but I think moving was a big enough change. How long have you been decorating?"

We chat for several minutes about how flexible and lucrative Joanna's job is. She tells me about her husband, Mark, and his job as a financial planner, including the many wonderful opportunities it provides. While I don't mind having the conversation geared toward her instead of me, the bragging about her and Mark's sensational life grows tiresome.

"This coffee is excellent, Joanna. Where do you get it?" My question isn't only a change of subject, I'm genuinely curious for the future of my taste buds.

Joanna's eyes widen as she looks at me over the rim of her mug, the corners of her mouth turning up before she answers. "Mark and his co-workers are part of some coffee trading group. It's international, so we get coffee from all over the world at prices you wouldn't believe. I'd be happy to send you home with a bag." She furrows her brow. "But you have to have a grinder, since we buy strictly whole bean. It's the only way to do it."

"Ah, I see. I don't have a grinder, but thank you for the offer." Suddenly, the bag of pre-ground grocery store coffee sitting in my cabinet seems inadequate.

"Oh, I wish I'd known. I could've included one in your welcome basket." Joanna sips the last of her coffee and sets her mug on the table. "So, Maggie, I noticed it's just you and the kids in the house. What's the story there?"

I nearly choke on my drink. She jumps right in, doesn't she? "I'm a single mother, Joanna."

While I know exactly what Joanna is asking, the death of my husband isn't something I like to talk about. Over the years I've learned to give vague enough answers to skirt the elephant in the room. So, until someone comes right out and asks where Charlie is, I'll play dumb.

Joanna purses her lips, glancing down at her lap. "Where's Mr. Hansen?"

I'm taken aback at Joanna's forwardness. It's slightly relieving to know I won't be exhausting myself by trying to circumvent the story, but it doesn't make the words any easier to say. I swallow the lump in my throat and avert my eyes to my coffee mug, running my finger around the rim. "He passed away."

I hear Joanna gasp. "I'm so sorry. When?"

"Three years ago."

She places her hand on my knee, and I brace myself for the onslaught of pity-filled words about to stream from her mouth. "That's been a long time. Though, I know it probably doesn't seem like it." She removes her hand and pours herself another cup. "You know, if you're interested, Mark has some co-workers who are single."

Not what I expected, but not any better. "Thank you, but no. I don't date anymore." I raise my head to meet Joanna's gaze, expecting to see disappointment, but instead, I find her brow furrowed in contemplation.

"Why not?"

"I, uh, haven't had any luck the few times I've tried."

"Maybe you haven't found the right guy."

I clench my jaw. I found the right guy sixteen years ago. "It's also exhausting."

"Well, what about someone in the neighborhood. Blake Averson in the cul-de-sac is single, and he's right down the street."

My stomach flutters. "What? Joanna, no. Blake is a neighbor, that's all."

Joanna smiles slyly. "Now, Maggie, there's no need to be embarrassed. I may be forty-five years old and married, but I'm not blind. Blake Averson is a bonafide catch. I've known him for years."

"You have?"

"Yes. He and Mark hang out a few times a month, playing pool or watching some sport on TV." She rolls her eyes before fixing them on mine. "But men like Blake don't stay single for long. You'd better snatch him up quick."

Is she saying Blake is a player? I should've known with his looks. I sigh. "Joanna, I'm not trying to snatch him up. He's too young for me, anyway."

"This isn't high school, Maggie. Blake turned twenty-eight in June, plenty old enough."

He's only twenty-eight? Great, even younger than I thought. I shake my head. "Like I said, I don't date anymore, and even if I did, I wouldn't start with my neighbor."

"I just wanted you to know there are options out there."

Indignation flares in me, and I set my mug down on the table rather roughly, the porcelain clattering against the glass tabletop. "Thank you, but I'd appreciate it if you left my personal life to me." I stand abruptly and run my hands down my thighs. "I really should be going. Thank you for the coffee."

Joanna opens her mouth to protest, but must be able to read my irritation, because she zips her lips and walks me to the door. We exchange pleasant, albeit forced "goodbyes" before I turn and walk away. Maybe I should feel bad about being so curt. She was only trying to help, I'm sure, but it was unsolicited advice and an intrusion on my personal life. I'm certainly not going to hold it against her, but I won't be seeking out Joanna for any more coffee dates.

Chapter Four

Three weeks later, Sydney's birthday arrives. Her best friend, Kelsey, spends the night and the two of them stay up way too late having a teen romcom movie marathon and doing each other's makeup. They talk and giggle and eat snacks, as shown by the aftermath of wrappers in my living room.

They have fun, though, and that's what matters. After last week when Sydney told me she thinks all the girls at school hate her, my mom heart sank. Middle school is rough enough without the added stress of not having any friends, so I'm glad she was at least able to have fun with Kelsey.

Sunday afternoon, the girls run out of movies, so they switch to experimenting with more makeup. Dylan escapes into the basement, and as much as I'd love to see myself in bright pink eye shadow and mauve lipstick, I don't think I can handle another giggle fest. I haven't been able to work out the last two mornings, so I decide to go for a run. It takes a lot of breathing and a round of my grounding practice to convince myself the kids will be fine for a half hour, but I manage to quell my anxiety enough to head out the door.

After all, I have my phone and I'm only making laps around the block.

Late September is still warm in Colorado, though not as nice as August, so I slip into a pair of Lululemon leggings and a racer-back tank top. After one lap, I text Sydney to see how they're doing. She responds with an eye roll emoji and confirms they're fine, so I keep going.

In the middle of my fifth lap, my phone dings and my heart leaps into my throat. I hop under the shade of a tree, frantically tapping my phone screen to see what emergency is happening at my house.

They tried to cook something and lit the house on fire. Someone tripped down the stairs and cracked their head open. Dylan snuck some candy and is choking.

A hundred worst-case scenarios play out in my head as I try not to hyperventilate. When I get my messages open, I all but pass out.

SYDNEY: *Can Kelsey stay for dinner?*

I sag against the tree trunk and clamp my hand over my mouth, shutting my eyes tight. I'm so close to vomiting right now it's not funny. In all the years I've been a mother, I've never been able to not think the worst will happen, and it's only been intensified by Charlie's death.

"Maggie? Are you okay?"

My eyes pop open and my head whips up to find Blake and Oscar standing on the sidewalk. His face is rife with concern and his chocolate eyes are locked on me.

I must look worse than I thought. I swallow and push off of the tree. "Hi, Blake. Yes, I'm fine. I was out for a run and got over-heated."

His eyes soften, but the worry in his features remains. "Should I get you some water?"

"What? No, you don't have to do that. I'm heading back home. It's just around the corner."

"You're going to walk the rest of the way, right?" He arches an eyebrow and gives me a one-sided smirk, sending butterflies through my stomach.

Don't throw up, Maggie. "Of course I'll walk."

He drops the eyebrow and his eyes narrow. "Maybe I should walk with you, just to be safe."

The butterflies dissipate, and I let out a feathery chuckle. "You don't have to. I'll be fine."

"It's no trouble. I'm going the same way you are. Come on." Blake waves me on, and I have no choice but to join him.

As soon as I'm on the sidewalk, Oscar makes circles around me, tying me up in his leash. When he jumps up to lick my face, he knocks me off balance, and I tumble into the grass, landing on my ass with a hard thud.

"Oh shit," Blake says as he kneels down and quickly unties my legs. Once I'm free, Blake's gaze crawls up me, lingering a moment on my chest before landing on my eyes. His irises darken and he clears his throat. "I'm so sorry, Maggie. Are you okay?"

Chuckling, I roll to my side before standing up. "I'm fine, thanks." I twist my body to make sure I am actually fine and brush the dirt from my butt. As I turn around to face Blake, his head pops up, meeting my gaze before flicking away as he swallows.

He was looking at my ass. I bite the inside of my cheek to keep from grinning. Maybe I should buy some more of these leggings.

Blake clears his throat, rubbing the back of his neck. "You okay to walk?"

I nod as Blake and I fall into step. Although my stomach flips every time I look at him, it's a welcome change from the heart pounding panic of Sydney's text. As I focus on quelling the butterflies that keep returning, I realize neither of us are speaking. The silence kills me. We've spoken a few times in the last three weeks, and every time it's been easy, but right now I can't think of anything to say. This is incredibly awkward.

Why, though? I'm not trying to date him, so why do I have to worry about what I say? At this point anything would be better than this. "I should've worn shorts today. I'm sweating like a pig in these leggings." I cringe at myself. On second thought, that was worse than the silence.

Blake chuckles. "Yeah, September can be deceiving. The air is cooler, but the sun keeps things pretty warm. Shorts would be more comfortable, but they probably don't look as good as your leggings."

I whip my head up to look at him in his wide eyes.

"Uh, I mean, those are nice leggings. High end, right?"

I nod, but his pink cheeks give me an urge to be bold. "Yes, they are, and it's nice to know they look good from behind." As the flirtatious words leave my mouth, a pang of guilt hits my gut. *Stop flirting with him. He's not Charlie.*

Blake chokes on his inhale, and I want to giggle, but the moment is gone. "Where are the kids?"

I suck in a breath and release it slowly, not allowing panic to take over again. "At home. Sydney had a birthday sleepover and I had to get away from the giggling."

He chuckles. "And let me guess, Dylan is tucked away on the Xbox?"

"You nailed it."

"To be fair, pretty much every time I've talked to Dylan, the Xbox comes up."

My mouth ticks up. Blake certainly pays attention to details. He's learned more about my kids through the few conversations we've had in two months, than any of the men I've dated since Charlie. Considering most of them lasted less than a week, it's not surprising, but it's refreshing all the same. "Well, thanks for indulging him."

"It's no problem. I kind of enjoy it."

I look at him as I scratch my cheek, dragging my fingers down my jaw. "You enjoy listening to a ten-year-old talk wildly about video games?"

Blake shrugs. "I play online with my friends, so I get where Dylan's coming from. Depending on the game, it can get pretty intense with tournaments and stuff, though the ones I play aren't for Dylan, yet."

"Why?"

"There's a lot of violence. Blood and guts type games. I'd offer to show you, but something tells me you're not a gamer."

I realize my nose is scrunched up, though I don't mean to be rude. With a shake of my head, I relax my features. "No, not a gamer myself, but I've played a lot of Mario Kart with Dylan. I'm not too shabby."

"Mario Kart, huh?" Blake tilts his head down to look at me. "That's one of the few games I play that doesn't involve death and dismemberment. Maybe you and I should have a tournament sometime."

My stomach churns. I'm thankful Blake can't see my toes moving wildly inside my shoes. I run my hand over my head, steadying myself for the pained look on Blake's face when I turn him down.

I open my mouth, but am interrupted by Joanna's husband, Mark, calling out from up the street. "Hey, Blake! The game's about to start. Hurry up!"

Blake groans. "I forgot I told Mark I'd watch the football game with him. Broncos are playing the Patriots. It's a big deal." An exasperated huff comes through his lips. "Especially if you've got money riding on it, which Mark does."

"Well, it's a good thing I live right across the street. You don't have far to go."

He shrugs. "Even if you lived on the other side of the neighborhood, I'd walk you home. Mark can wait."

I turn away to hide my red cheeks. Blake is a sweet man, for sure. A sweet *neighbor*, I remind myself.

As we reach my house, I'm surprised he follows me to the porch. "Thank you for seeing me home. I would have made it on my own, though."

He hikes his shoulder to his ear. "I know, but I liked having the company. Oscar isn't exactly a conversationalist."

I chuckle and look at my feet. When I lift my head, I meet Blake's intense gaze, and my mouth goes dry. I have to clear my throat to speak. "Well, I should get inside and drink some water. Have fun with Mark."

"Thanks, I'm sure I will." He rolls his eyes, but settles them back on me with a wink, which has my stomach flipping. "But I've got to take Oscar home first."

"He doesn't get to watch the game?"

"Joanna's not a dog person." His tone holds more than a bit of irritation. "Enjoy the rest of your weekend, Maggie."

"You too." I watch him walk down the street toward the cul-de-dac. As he reaches the sidewalk leading to his house, he turns and waves. I raise my palm up, shaking it slightly, and let out the biggest breath I've ever held.

Chapter Five

"Mom! We need Halloween pumpkins!" Dylan shouts, while we're watching *The Nightmare Before Christmas* and noshing on popcorn and root beer floats.

The kids are on fall break, and I've taken the week off so I don't have to worry about them being home alone. They much prefer to be home than at the school program, anyway, but I wouldn't be able to concentrate at work knowing they were on their own.

"Oh, my gosh. You're right! We'll get some after the movie." I beam at my son who settles back down, tossing some popcorn into his mouth while his sister rolls her eyes. Sydney pretends not to be interested in the movie, but I not only glimpse a smile, I also catch her watching it and lip syncing to the songs.

Later, at the local garden center, Sydney informs me she doesn't want to trick or treat this year.

I can't believe my ears. I know she's growing up, but I thought I'd get another couple years of trick or treating before she went full teenager on me. "Really, sweetheart? You don't want to go at least once in the new neighborhood?"

She shakes her head, her wavy brown hair, which matches mine, flipping into her face. "No. I'm too old."

This is a sudden change, even for an almost teenager. "But you've always loved Halloween. What's with the one-eighty?"

She shrugs, looking away and dragging her toe through some dirt.

"Syd?" I crane my neck to try to meet her gaze.

"The other girls at school were talking about going to parties. They said trick or treating was for kids."

Ugh, my heart. I turn so I'm in front of her and I squat down. "Look, if you want to trick or treat, then you can. You don't have to answer to anyone else, only yourself."

"But what if someone sees me? I'll get made fun of for being juvenile."

I scrunch my forehead as I contemplate a way to work this out. "I think I have an idea."

Her eyes flick to mine, her focus suddenly strong.

"You can use me and Dylan as an excuse. He's your little brother and he's so excited, but your mom insists you go as a family. Blame it all on me."

I see Sydney fighting the grin I'm putting on her mouth. "Okay, fine. But I'm not dressing up."

"Deal," I say, and shake her hand, glad to get one more year.

"Look!" Dylan shouts. "Mr. Blake is picking out pumpkins, too!"

I raise my head to see Blake walking through the pumpkin patch. He's wearing a form-fitting, long-sleeve t-shirt with a small logo on the pec, and the way his arms are crossed makes his biceps much more pronounced. I swallow deep as he turns his back to us and I get a great view of his butt. His jeans are doing him more than justice today.

My grip on the pumpkins tightens as my eyes follow him. He seems to be pacing more than perusing, but he looks sexy either way.

Maggie! Stop thinking like that!

"Mom, should we go say hi? Isn't he like, our neighbor?" Sydney's lack of enthusiasm cuts through my gawking.

At first, I think she's right. It's the neighborly thing to do, but then anxiety twists in my gut. Practically every time Blake and I interact, he hints at asking me out in some way. Carving pumpkins would be an easy one. The kids would jump at the opportunity for someone other than me to help.

I swallow down my heartbeat thumping in my throat. "Um, no, sweetheart. We don't have to. We've got what we need, let's let him shop for his pumpkins." I hike the oversized squashes onto my hips and jut my chin toward the checkout.

Besides, the last thing I need is to say something embarrassing about my giant, round gourds.

When Halloween comes, I'm over the moon we get to go as a family one more time. Dylan dresses as Captain America and I'm supposed to be The Scarlet Witch, the red-headed superhero from the Marvel movies Dylan adores. Though I'm not sure my makeshift costume is very convincing. Honestly, I forgot to go shopping, so I threw it together from things I already had in my closet; a red halter top, black leggings with knee-high boots, and a fire-burst headband I wear when I work out. The only thing I had to purchase was a cape, and I got it at the thrift store. I'm sure Dylan would have preferred me to buy an actual costume, but this will have to do.

Sydney happily goes with us, though she keeps to her conviction and goes sans costume. We walk up and down the block, stopping at the cul-de-sac when Sydney complains about the cold.

"Can we do these houses and *then* go home?" Dylan pleads.

I give Sydney the puppy dog eyes, and she caves. She's doing her best impersonation of an angsty teen as we make our way around the circle of houses, coming to the last one; Blake's house.

Dylan tugs on my arm. "Come with me. Please?"

I'm going to need all my reinforcements for this. "Okay, but only if Sydney comes, too." I glance at her to see a huge eye roll, making me laugh.

"This is so embarrassing," she says, hiding her face in her hands.

"Oh, come on. He's probably not even home." I'm sure he's out partying.

Dylan bounds up the steps while I drag Sydney with me. As we ascend to the porch, I notice there aren't any pumpkins. What was Blake doing at the pumpkin patch, then? I don't have time to wonder, because not three seconds after Dylan rings the bell, Blake opens the door. My breath catches in my throat before I can say "trick or treat."

Blake pushes open the screen door and freezes as he locks eyes with me, his dark brown irises sparkling in the porch light. "Hey, Maggie." There's a nervousness to his tone, which confuses me until I drag my gaze from his to look him over.

He's wearing overalls with a plaid shirt underneath. I bite my lip as I stare at how well the overalls fit him in the hips, but I tear my eyes away to get a look at the rest of him. A straw hat sits on top of his head, shadowing his face, but even under the scarecrow makeup, I see his cheeks tinge pink.

"You dress up for Halloween?" How incredibly cute is he?

"Yeah, every year. Speaking of..." He puts a huge handful of candy into Dylan's bag.

"Wow! Thanks, Mr. Blake."

"Anything for my favorite Avenger." Blake turns to Sydney. "What are you dressed as?"

"A moody teenager." I snicker and Sydney rolls her eyes. "She's very dedicated to the character, you see."

"Mom!"

I laugh out loud, and Blake hands her a full size Hershey's bar. "Well, that kind of dedication deserves a prize."

"Thanks," she says, and stalks down the porch with Dylan bouncing alongside her.

Blake turns his gaze back to me, his eyes drinking me in from head to toe, lingering a moment on the dangerously low neckline of my halter before meeting my gaze again. "Scarlet Witch?"

"Wanda Maximoff, in the flesh." I do a small curtsy, immediately feeling like an idiot. "I'm glad it's obvious. I was afraid I wasn't pulling it off."

"I think I have a new favorite superhero." His tone is husky and it makes me blush.

I bite the inside of my cheek, flicking my gaze from his. "I sort of thought you'd be at a party. Isn't that what young, single people do?"

Blake chuckles. "A lot of them do, yeah. My buddy throws one every year but I don't go. I've never been a big party guy. Don't get me wrong, it can be fun, but it's also exhausting. Besides, if I don't pass out this candy, I'll end up eating all of it. I'm saving myself a stomach-ache, really."

I laugh and watch Blake's eyes soften. Something in the air changes and a shiver goes down my spine, but not from the cold. I swallow and say, "Where are all your pumpkins?"

"Excuse me?"

"We were at the garden center the other day and saw you in the pumpkin patch. Thought maybe you were getting some for decorations." Great, now I sound like a stalker.

"Oh, um, no. I was working."

"You work at the garden center?"

"No, but I work with them." He reaches his arm up and rubs the back of his neck, flicking his gaze away from mine. "I'm a landscaper. We were there to pick up an order and I was waiting for the owner."

"You're a landscaper?" I try not to sound incredulous, but I can't help it as I glance over the railing at Blake's barely landscaped yard. "I would've never guessed."

He shrugs. "It pays the bills."

"That's what matters." An awkward silence takes over, the electricity from a moment ago is gone. I killed the mood by bringing up work. *Smooth move, Maggie.* "Well, thanks for the candy. Happy Halloween."

"Wait, you didn't get any." Blake turns to grab something off his entry table. When he comes back, he offers me a full-size Twix.

I gape at him. "How did you know this was my favorite?"

"Come on, Maggie. It's everyone's favorite." He winks, and just like that, the electricity shoots back through me.

"Well, thanks." I put my hand up to wave, but it's too quick and I seem too eager, so I pretend to scratch my shoulder instead. I must look like a fool. "I'll, uh, see you later."

"See you, Maggie."

Chapter Six

The weekend before Thanksgiving brings our first big snowfall of the season. Not only is it over a foot deep, but it's also the wettest, heaviest snow I've seen in a while. Years ago, I would have bundled up my children to build snow-forts and snowmen while Charlie shoveled. Now, they aren't interested.

Dylan would be if he had someone to play with, but since Sydney can't be bothered to do "kid stuff" anymore, he'd rather play Xbox. I should really encourage him to bring a friend over, or maybe I should get him into a sport this spring. He's an energetic kid, and a natural when it comes to agility, but I'm so far from the sporty type, I wouldn't know which one to get him into. Charlie would've been the one to do those things.

It stops snowing in the late morning, so I suit myself up and head out to shovel. After about ten minutes, I take a break. I drive the shovel into my measly snow pile and toss my coat onto the trunk of my car inside the garage. It may only be thirty degrees out here, but moving heavy snow with the sun shining will warm you up in no time.

Maybe I should buy that snowblower Charlie always wanted.

A hollowness settles in my chest as I think about the multitude of conversations we had about it. Charlie argued since he was the one in charge of snow removal, it should be up to him if we bought one. I told him he was young and shoveling was good exercise. In truth, I didn't want to spend the money. I was always the frugal one, even though we didn't have to be.

After his death, I hired high school kids on our street to do it. Now I'm the one doing it and I realize I should have let Charlie spend the damn money.

I pick up the shovel and resume my slow, but steady excavation when I see a figure moving down the street. As I lift my head, I find Blake trudging through the snow. His body a stark contrast against the bright white terrain, he heads in my direction with a shovel in his hands.

Surely, he's not coming here. But even as I try to justify the reasoning behind his trek, I find myself hoping he is. Would it be such a bad thing?

"Hey, Maggie. Want some help?" he asks with a hopeful look in his eye as he scratches at the scruffy beard covering his face.

It looks good on him, and my mouth runs dry. "Hi, Blake. Um, I would love some help, but you don't have to."

"I know, but it's the neighborly thing to do, right?"

I look up and down the street. There are a few other people out shoveling, all by themselves. "I've never had a neighbor offer to help me shovel."

"Well, then let me be the first," he says, and stomps up the driveway to join me where I left off.

We work side by side for some time. The snow seems to get heavier every minute the sun beats down on it, and when we're done with the driveway, I stand to stretch my back.

"You okay, Maggie? Need a break?"

"I just need to stretch a bit. This is killing my back." God, I sound so old.

"So take a break. I can finish the sidewalk."

"No, I'll help. Give me a minute."

"I don't mind. I mean, your sidewalk is nothing compared to mine. Having the corner house means I have the entire walk in front of and on the side of my property." He juts his chin to the porch steps and I reluctantly sit down. With a warm smile, Blake resumes shoveling.

As I arch my back and bend from side to side, I watch Blake work. The man is a machine. He took off his coat a while ago and now I've got a front-row view to the show. Even in a thermal long-sleeve shirt, I can see his rippling muscles as he scoops and heaves snow over his shoulder. Every lift has his biceps popping, his back flexing. The way his hips drive his momentum to cast the snow into the air is nothing short of virile, and that beard somehow makes him sexier.

Forget the snowblower. "So, what's with the beard? I've never seen you with one before."

"It's no-shave November."

Ah, yes. Charlie used to participate in that, too.

"Don't worry, it'll be gone here, soon."

"Oh, that's too bad."

Blake stops mid-shovel and turns to me with an eyebrow cocked. "Why?"

"I think it looks good on you." My body temperature skyrockets as Blake smiles at my compliment. The guilt of betrayal creeps into my gut, and I need a change of subject. "Is snow removal part of your job as a landscaper?"

Blake goes back to shoveling, heaving a shovelful of snow into the yard. "We do snow removal, yes. But it's usually for businesses and we use plows."

"So, you're not just showing off to get me to hire you in the future?" My intended joke must not come across because Blake stops mid-shovel, straightens, and turns to me with furrowed eyebrows. I scrunch my nose. "Not a good joke, huh?"

His features relax. He laughs, resuming his shoveling. "If I wanted to show off for you, I'd do more than shovel your driveway." The gruffness of his voice makes me shudder.

"How did you get into landscaping?" I need to change the subject before I end up taking a dive into the freezing snow to cool off.

"Just the way life played out. It's not what I thought I'd be doing."

I grab my own shovel, following him down the sidewalk to join him in the last bit. "Why? What did you want to do?"

"Well," he says, taking a break to lean onto his shovel. "I got my degree in graphic design from CU Boulder. I wanted to go into marketing, but my dad wanted me to go into finance, so I added a minor in business management, thinking that would satiate him." Blake tenses and picks up the shovel. He scoops a rather large mound of snow and heaves it with a deep grunt.

"It didn't?"

Blake turns to me, and I see pain in his eyes. "That's a story for another time."

"Oh, okay." Silence takes over, and I toss a couple shovelfuls to the side. "So, landscaping was the obvious replacement to a marketing job?"

Blake laughs, though it's a bit stilted. "No. If I had gone to Chicago or New York like I'd planned, I'd probably be doing something in my field, but I love Colorado and decided to stay. The landscaping job was supposed to be temporary." He scoops the last bit of snow from the sidewalk and turns in my direction, his broad shoulders squared and his chest heaving with deep breaths. "There, all done."

I stare up at him, a heaviness in the air, and I have to clench my thighs. "Thank you, Blake. That went a lot faster than me doing it by myself."

"No problem. I'm happy to help."

My gaze flicks to his house, where the driveway and sidewalk lay still covered in snow. As guilt settles in my gut, I have to ask, "Can I come help you with yours?"

"What? No, Maggie, you don't have to."

"I know, but you worked hard on mine. Besides, it's the neighborly thing to do," I tease.

A slow grin spreads across Blake's face. "Well, then I'm glad you're my neighbor."

I'm grateful for the biting cold keeping my cheeks red. "Let me tell the kids where I'll be. Hold on." I put up a gloved finger and turn back into the garage. As I open the door to the house, I find Sydney right where I left her on the couch with her book. "Hey, Syd. I'm going to help Blake shovel. I'll be back in a little while."

She shakes her head without looking away from her book. "You have weird ideas on dates, Mom."

"Sydney!" I gape at her. This is as far from a date as anything could be, and why she would think that is beyond me. "I'm returning a favor. He helped me shovel, so now I'm helping him."

"Okay, whatever."

"Will you guys be okay?" I huff. "I'll be right down the street and I have my phone. I'll shut the garage door, but if you need anything give me a call and–"

"Mom!" Sydney rolls her eyes. "We'll be fine. Go do your weird 'not' date. Sheesh." She scoots down farther into the couch, pulling the blanket to her shoulders.

It's my turn to roll my eyes before shutting the door. Once I'm outside, I use the keypad to close the garage, grab my shovel, and join Blake on the sidewalk. "Okay, I'm ready."

"Kids okay?"

"They'll be fine," I say, but part of me is reeling inside at the millions of things that could happen while I'm gone. Ninety-nine percent of which are highly improbable, but the pit in my stomach is still there.

Blake nods, but doesn't say anything as he heads toward his house. In fact, we don't say a word as we trudge through the snow.

I chew on the inside of my cheek, wanting to fill this void between us. Blake seems like he needs to hear something encouraging. The words are on the tip of my tongue, but I know where they will inevitably lead to. "I know how it feels to have someone be disappointed in your life choices."

Blake's head whips up to look at me, his eyes searching mine for an answer.

"My father-in-law wanted us to move to Boulder after college because he lived there, but we didn't want to. So, we ended up in Aurora."

"Does your father-in-law still live there?"

My stomach drops. *It's okay. He's asking about Charlie's dad, not Charlie.* I swallow down my pounding heart and shake my head. "No. He passed away three years ago."

Blake's eyes become sullen. "Oh. I'm sorry."

"It's alright, thank you." I inhale deeply, realizing I'm not out of breath from the anxiety bubbling in my gut. This snowy trek is much more arduous than I expected. Though Blake doesn't seem to have any trouble. "How tall are you?"

He glances over at me, a slack look on his face. "Uh, about 6'3". Why?"

"Because I'm little miss struggle bus over here, and you're gliding through these drifts effortlessly." Even at 5'7", I wish I had a couple more inches for this excursion.

"You want me to carry you?" Blake asks, a playful look in his eyes.

I have no doubt in my mind he could carry me. The image of Blake whisking me into his strong arms and hiking through the neighborhood threatens to put a smile on my face, so I shake my head. "No, but could you slow down?"

His deep chuckle sends butterflies through my stomach.

We reach his house and begin with the sidewalk. He tackles the long way around the side of the house, and I work on the shorter part in front. When it's time to start the driveway, we stand next to each other and stare at it a minute.

"Do you want some water or something?" Blake asks.

"Water would be wonderful, thank you."

He nods and treks up the drive, using his footprints from earlier as a path.

As I wait, I stretch my back and shoulders. I'll be sore tomorrow, but it's worth it. Not only am I doing a nice thing for a nice neighbor, but I'm getting to spend more time with Blake. This isn't a get-to-know-him-better-so-I-can-date-him sort of thing. More like an I-enjoy-his-company thing. He's a sweet man, who happens to make me feel like a teenager with the way he looks at me, and I relish in the feeling. There's no harm in it.

Is there?

Before I can decide, Oscar leaps into me, knocking me into the snow pile at the corner of the yard. I go butt first and sink all the way in so my arms are sticking up in the air. My feet come off the ground to put me in an exaggerated V. I'm completely stuck.

"Oh, shit! Oscar!" Blake shouts and rushes to my aid. "I'm so sorry, Maggie. Here." He shucks his gloves and grips my ribs right under my armpits, pulling me out of my snow prison. "Are you okay?"

His hands linger on my ribs as he waits for my answer, and I swear his fingers press into me. Before I can think too hard on what it feels like being held by him, I process what happened and burst into laughter.

Blake's expression moves from concern, to confusion, finally settling on amusement and he laughs with me. We spend several minutes like this, until my sides hurt. When our laughter quiets, our gazes meet. The delight in Blake's melts away to something more serious, more intense, and my mouth runs dry as I realize his hands are still on me.

"I could use that water now," I say quietly.

Thanksgiving comes and goes. It's not the big family holiday it used to be. If I'm being honest, it never has been. The only family my kids have ever known to be around for holidays is my father-in-law, but with him and Charlie gone, it's just us.

I don't go all out like Charlie used to, either. Since I've been a vegetarian the majority of my life, I go to the deli and get some carved turkey for the kids, mashed potatoes, and all the other normal Thanksgiving sides, but I don't bother cooking. It seems like a waste of time. There's only three of us, and we'd end up throwing away a lot of it. Besides, I don't know the first thing about cooking a turkey.

Thanksgiving may be a bit of a bummer, but the weeks leading up to Christmas are even worse. Heading into December, I find I'm falling into my habit of retreating inside myself. Christmas was Charlie's favorite and he always decorated the house from top to bottom to the smallest detail. I haven't put out the Christmas decorations since he died. It's never felt right.

Holding my chin high, I tell myself this year will be different. I'm not going to hide and ignore the holidays like I have for the last three years. I've already started in the right direction by accepting an invitation to Joanna's Christmas party.

Shit, that's next weekend, isn't it? Ugh.

A heaviness settles in my legs and I have to shake them to ease the feeling. I'm not big on parties, or get-togethers in general. Michelle has a holiday party every year, and as nice as it is to see old friends, I haven't been able to go without Charlie. Too many questions. Too much pity in people's eyes. I've already told the kids we'd go to Joanna's and they seem excited about it.

I wonder if Blake will be there? The vice gripping my chest loosens, replaced by an airy feeling as I think about seeing him again, even if it will be at Joanna's house. Normally, I'm ecstatic to escape the get-to-know-you questions and conversations, but with Blake I *want* to know more. I don't know if I'm ready to tell him everything about my life, though.

I loathe getting to know people, because it forces me to relive the hardest parts of my life. The questions about where my husband is still hurt. The words never get any easier to say, but if I want to know more about Blake, I'll have to share, too.

Keeping him in the dark won't be an option for long as it's already hard to do. All the butterflies, heated cheeks, and thigh clenching aside, Blake is easy to talk to. He has an understanding in his eyes, a warmth in his voice. It's almost like my walls don't exist when he's around, and I'm beginning to think I like it.

I shake my head to clear the warm fuzzies from daydreaming about Blake. I've got work to do.

We're in a new house, a new neighborhood, new schools, and we need a new start. My kids need me to be strong. They need to see me moving on with my life so they can move on with theirs. What better way for us to honor Charlie, than by decorating the way he always did?

Even if it is three years later.

While the kids are in school, I get in the crawlspace, my heart pounding in my chest, and find the Christmas totes. My shaking hand grips the handle of one and I close my eyes to focus on grounding myself.

I recall my therapist's words at our last session six months ago. *You can do this, Maggie. For yourself. For your kids.* She was referencing the move, but the sentiment applies now, too.

Shit, I still haven't made an appointment. Do I need to, though? My breathing techniques seem to be working since I haven't had an actual panic attack since we moved. I've had a couple close calls, but nothing I haven't been able to handle.

The tension in my rib cage eases, and I think about how I'm doing this for my kids. The image of their beaming faces as they enter the house decorated like a winter wonderland flashes behind my eyelids. It gives me a momentary burst of courage. I blink my eyes open and drop my gaze, finding a small puddle of water off to the side.

Uh oh. This can't be good. I follow the pipes and I see the small leak happening right before my eyes. *Crap.* I guess the decorations will have to wait.

I move all the totes to the other side of the crawlspace, then go back upstairs to google "Handyman Littleton CO." I get a bunch of ads, some Yelp reviews, and a couple local website suggestions. How do I know who's good and who's not?

I've never had to do this. At the old house, Michelle's husband, Tom, took care of things for us, and if it was something out of his skill level, he knew who to call. How do I know which independent contractors are legit? Even a reputable chain could charge me an arm and a leg. I know that's what reviews are for, but how do I know those aren't friends of the guy?

I rub my temple as all these questions make my head spin. The barrage of options is daunting. I could call Michelle and ask who Tom uses, but I'm an adult. I can do this on my own.

What if I pick the wrong one, though? Who's the right choice?

"Blake." His name rolls off my lips in a whisper. He offered to help with repairs, but that was months ago. Does the offer still stand?

I walk to the window and pull back the curtains. Surely, he's not home. It's the middle of the day on a Tuesday. I can't know for sure, though, unless I walk down there.

A scene plays out in my head with me nervously asking Blake for his help and him confidently accepting. I'd watch him fix the leak, his expert hands twisting, fiddling, tweaking things. He'd be quick, but precise. The leak would be fixed within minutes, and then he could use those expert hands on me. His fingers are probably rough from manual labor, but he'd be gentle as he slid his fingers up my thigh and–

I quickly draw the curtains back across the window, my cheeks flushed and an ache between my thighs. No, I'm not asking him. Not only do I feel like a stalker right now, but I don't need to indulge these fantasies. Blake is a neighbor. Nothing more. And I can't ask a neighbor I'm not paying to climb around in my cold, musty old crawlspace to fix a leak. I shake my head. I'll call someone.

Clicking the first number on the Google list, a very cheerful man answers, addresses all my concerns, and tells me he can come on Friday. I accept immediately. When Friday comes, the man arrives on time, fixes my pipes, and leaves with only charging me a trip fee. I think I've found my new handyman, and he doesn't live down the street.

Chapter Seven

"Maggie! I'm so glad you and the kids came," exclaims Joanna as she reaches for our coats.

I'm not even completely out of mine before she's tugging it off my shoulders. "Yeah, thanks for inviting us."

"Well, there's food and drinks in the kitchen. Help yourself." Joanna turns to Sydney and Dylan. "And if you kids want to make yourselves a plate and join the other kids in the basement, Mark has everything set up down there. Movies, video games, you can play pool if you want. Go have fun!" She ushers them out of the entryway.

Dylan looks back at me, unsure of what to do. I nod and jut my chin toward the basement, giving permission to leave my side. He may be ten years old, but he's still very much my little boy.

Joanna turns back to me. "So, Maggie, how have you been?"

"Fine, nothing exciting." As the words leave my mouth, I get the distinct feeling someone's staring at me, though Joanna's gaze is so intense it could be her. My eyes flit around the foyer and into the living room, which is no longer navy, cream, and white, but now a mixture of ruby red, soft mauve, and deep teal. "I see you redecorated. It looks nice."

"Oh, thank you. It was just a little something I came up with one day and voila. It's one of those problems with being an interior decorator, you know..."

I can't concentrate on what Joanna is saying. Someone's heavy gaze is definitely on me, and it's not hers. She's twirling around and waving her hands in the air, explaining her latest inspiration. My eyes flick around the living room. People are gathered in small groups, chatting while they drink and eat, but I can't find whose intense staring has me squirming.

"Joanna, do you have any more dip?" someone calls from the kitchen.

She turns away from me. "Oh, yes. Hold on, I'll be right there." As she takes small steps away, she waves her hand in the air at me. "Sorry, Maggie. Duty calls."

I'm left alone in the foyer with two choices; follow Joanna into the kitchen and endure more babbling about her décor, or go into the living room, where I'll be forced to make small-talk with people I don't know.

Neither option sounds appealing in the least, but I opt for the living room. I could use a break from Joanna, and maybe I can figure out who was staring. As I enter, my eyes roam the room, but I don't know any of these people. I suppose they could be work friends of Mark's, or clients of Joanna's. I don't know many neighbors, but I don't recognize anyone in here.

This is so awkward. I contemplate pulling my phone out of my back pocket, but I hate to be the person who stands in a room full of people, staring at their phone when they should be socializing. Even though I don't want to socialize at all.

"You look scared," a man's voice says quietly, and I whip around.

I come face to face with a good-looking guy who tips his beer bottle up to his smiling lips and takes a drink. He has dirty blond hair sculpted into the "I just rolled out of bed" look. He's taller than me, but only by an inch or so, and his pale blue eyes sparkle in the lamplight as he swallows his drink and meets my gaze again.

He holds out his other hand. "I'm David, a friend of Mark's."

"Maggie." I take his hand for a quick shake, but he doesn't let go right away.

His eyes flick down to our handshake. Our left-handed handshake where I'm noticeably missing a certain ring. "Nice to meet you, Maggie. You know, when Joanna said there were going to be some single women here tonight, she didn't mention any as pretty as you." David doesn't seem bothered by his cheesy attempt to break the ice as he takes another drink.

Even if it is a terrible line, I can't help but blush as I slide my hand from his.

A sly grin crawls across his lips. "So, you're a friend of Joanna's?"

"No, we're neighbors."

"Neighbors can't be friends?"

"Not always."

He chuckles, and glances around, his eyes landing on my empty hands clasped in front of me. "Would you like a drink?"

"Yes, very much." I turn toward the kitchen, but David steps in front of me. "I'll get it."

"No, I'll come, too," I say, determined to ensure I get the drink I want and that it's not tampered with. One can never be too cautious.

We find the kitchen fairly crowded, so David offers to get our drinks since it'll be easier for him to get in and out than for both of us. I reluctantly agree, telling him I want a bottle of water.

"Water?" He steps close to me so our faces are only inches apart. "It's a party Maggie. You're supposed to have fun."

"I can have fun and drink water, too," I say with a tight jaw.

"Okay, coming right up."

When David returns, he has a beer in one hand and a red Solo cup in the other. He hands me the cup with some foamy green liquid in it. "Sorry, there weren't any water bottles, so I got you some punch."

I frown at the cup, pursing my lips. It's not a sealed container, but in such a crowded room, it's highly unlikely he was able to slip anything in my drink. It may not be water, but punch is harmless. "Thank you."

David and I escape the bustling kitchen, settling back in the living room, where he boxes me into a corner. My hackles spike, but as David sags against the wall, I release a breath. *Not everyone is a creep, Maggie.*

"So, Maggie, what do you do?"

"I'm a paralegal downtown at Fisher & Sons."

"That's quite a drive from here, isn't it?"

"It is." I take a sip of my punch, the strength of the flavor sitting heavy on my tongue. It's thick, sweet, and creamy, but I manage to swallow it. "But I only work three days a week, so it doesn't bother me."

David takes another sip of his beer, his lips curling as he eyeballs me over the bottle. "You know, I could talk to a buddy of mine who works at Gunther, Olsen, and Brooks. It's a bigger firm and closer to here."

"Oh, thank you, but I like my job. They're very good to me."

David gives me a dismissive nod. "I'm sure they are, but at a bigger firm, you could get more hours, which means more money."

"I'm aware, but I like working part-time. It gives me more time with my kids and–"

He nearly spits out his drink. "Kids? You've got kids?" The tone in his voice is blatant disappointment.

"Yes, I have two kids. A ten- and twelve-year-old. They're downstairs in the basement, which is why I'm not drinking alcohol tonight," I say, holding up my cup and taking another sip. This one goes down easier.

"Right. Makes sense." David runs his tongue across his bottom lip before his eyes move up and down my body. "So, do you do anything besides work?" He changes the subject from my kids quickly and I see through him. I've met plenty of men like David. Attractive, charming, intelligent, but not interested in my life, only in getting into my pants.

I contemplate walking away right now, but I'm struck with the notion of my only options being Joanna or standing alone. I can endure David for a few minutes while I enjoy my punch. When I'm finished, I'll make an excuse and head downstairs to hang out with the kids.

David continues to talk, mostly about himself. He tells me about the lavish vacations he's taken to Fiji, Hawaii, and other such tropical places. He talks about his numerous promotions at work and the frivolous ways he spends his money. The conversation revolves around him in every aspect, only diverting to me when he pauses to sip his beer.

I'm growing tired of listening to David when a headache strikes me. I close my eyes and rub my forehead.

"Maggie, are you okay?" David asks, but not with concern, more like eagerness.

"I'm fine, thank you. Just a little headache."

"Do you need to lie down? I can take you upstairs and find you a room." He places his hand on the small of my back, and even though it makes my skin crawl, I stand firmly in place.

Maybe he did spike my drink after all. I open my eyes to look at him so he knows I'm serious. "No, I don't think that's necessary."

"Are you sure? I've been known to cure a headache or two in my day." His eyebrows bob up and down in the most disgusting manner.

Luckily, I've learned how to deal with men such as David. "What exactly are you insinuating?"

"Excuse me?"

"Are you proposing you and I go upstairs and have sex? Because if you are, then I have to say it's wildly inappropriate." David takes a step away, removing his hand from my back. "And for you to assume that I, let alone any woman, would go upstairs and have sex with a man she just met, in her neighbor's house during a holiday party, which her children are attending, tells me you have very poor standards for the women you date."

"So, is that a no?"

I sigh heavily. "Enjoy the party, David." I turn and storm off toward the kitchen.

The kitchen has cleared out, thank goodness. Everyone has filtered out to the covered patio, basking under the propane heaters. Walking to the counter, I set my cup down firmly on a bare spot, and let out an exasperated groan. With a shake of my head, I close my eyes and try my hardest to forget the conversation I just had. I try to forget the audacity of David. I try to forget the fact I'm stuck in a rut and even if I'm able to let Charlie go for one minute, I'll probably never find a man who isn't an utter jerk–

"Is the party so bad?"

I spin around to see Blake leaning against the fridge, a beer in his hand, and a warm smile on his still bearded face. It's thicker than before, but it's being maintained nicely.

"Blake, hi," I say, though it's more of a whisper, my tension easing at the sight of him.

"Sorry, I didn't mean to scare you."

"It's alright. I didn't know you were here." *But I'm glad you are.*

"I think I got here right before you and the kids."

"Really? I didn't see you."

"Well, you got ambushed by Joanna right off the bat. Then you were talking to that guy, and I didn't want to interrupt." There's a slight irritation to his tone on the last bit.

I roll my eyes. "I wouldn't have minded."

"I'll remember that for next time." The depth of his voice sends butterflies through me. As I fight the urge to rub my thighs together, my head throbs again. I rub my forehead and shut my eyes. "Are you okay, Maggie?"

"I have a headache. I haven't eaten dinner yet, so…"

"Well, drinking on an empty stomach will do that." Blake points to my cup.

"Oh, no, this is punch," I say, tipping my cup to the side.

"No, the red one is punch. The green one is some concoction of Joanna's she makes every year." Blake motions to the counter with the drinks and I see a bowl of green punch and a bowl of red punch, both clearly labeled as "Alcoholic" and "Non-Alcoholic."

Now, I'm even more pissed than I was before. "Asshole!" I blurt out in a loud whisper.

"Excuse me?" Blake's eyes widen.

"No, sorry, not you. The guy I was talking to earlier." I see Blake tense as he shifts his stance. "Some friend of Mark's. Another self-involved prick, who apparently didn't listen when I said I didn't want any alcohol tonight."

Blake narrows his eyes. "You said you wanted punch and he brought you that?" He inhales, his chest expanding and his shoulders squaring. "Maybe I should talk to him about his listening skills."

I laugh and shake my head. "He's not worth it, Blake." Based on the reaction he's had to David's treatment of me, I'll omit the proposition to have sex. I don't need to start a fist fight in the middle of Joanna's party, though Blake could level David in a heartbeat. There's something incredibly sexy about a man wanting to defend my honor. I can do it myself, but it's nice to know someone has my back.

"Well, sit down," Blake says, turning to get into the refrigerator. He hands me a bottle of water. "Drink some water, I'll make you a plate."

No bottles, huh, David? "What? No, Blake. You don't have to do that."

"I don't mind. Sit down and relax, some food and water should help your headache." He walks to the counter and piles finger foods and appetizers on a paper plate. He reaches for the cocktail weenies.

"Oh, none of those, please. I'm a vegetarian."

He turns his head over his shoulder. "Really?"

"Mhm. For years now. I eat fish every now and then, but mainly I'm an herbivore."

"Interesting," he says, and turns back to the food.

"That's it? I'm interesting?"

"What?" As he finishes piling food onto the plate and places it on the counter, he stares at me with a blank expression.

"Most of the time when people hear I'm a vegetarian, they either think I'm the healthiest person on the planet, or look at me like I'm insane."

Even underneath the beard, I see Blake's warm, core melting smile, and I have to take a sip of water to cool myself off as his eyes dip down, scanning the part of my torso not hidden by the counter. "Well, I can see you're pretty healthy. For an insane person, that is."

I laugh, nearly spitting out my water.

Blake hands me a napkin. "Here. Now eat something."

"Thank you." His kindness fills me with longing as I wipe my chin. His lack of attempt to take me upstairs is refreshing, although I wouldn't mind so much if Blake proposed the idea.

Maggie, stop it.

Blake turns back to the counter to make himself a plate of food, and I watch him intently. The broadness of his shoulders, the way his back muscles move as he breathes, the curve where his waist meets his hips. Now my head is spinning and the throbbing has settled elsewhere, much farther south.

He opts to stand on the opposite side of the counter facing me, leaning over it to eat. "So, what are your plans for Christmas? Traveling? Family?"

I shake my head. "It's just me and the kids. You?"

"Nope. Oscar's the only one I have around. My buddy's wife always invites me over, so I'll go over there for dinner or something, but I always feel like the fifth wheel."

I suddenly feel the urge to invite him to our house. At least there he'd complete our set of wheels, but it's an absurd idea so I stop it by putting more food into my mouth. As I chew, I realize my headache is gone. So, no Roofies after all. What a relief. "You were right. Food and water did the trick. My headache is cured."

A grin spreads across Blake's face. "If I'd have known curing beautiful women's headaches was so easy, I would've become a doctor."

The compliment has my toes struggling to move in these tight flats. My cheeks instantly heat, and I turn my head to look at my food. "So, uh, you've still got the beard I see." I raise my gaze to find him still staring at me. "What's with that? I thought you were going to get rid of it."

"Well," he says, rubbing the back of his neck. "Someone whose opinion I value told me they thought it looked good on me."

The sheepish grin he gives me makes me feel like I'm going to spontaneously combust, so I quickly shove some food into my mouth.

"Maggie, you alright?"

"Mhm."

He clears his throat. "Uh, I saw a handyman van in your driveway yesterday. Everything okay?"

"Yes." I steel myself and raise my head to look at him. "There was a small leak in the crawlspace. It was a quick fix, and the guy only charged me a trip fee."

Blake leans toward the end of the counter to throw his paper plate in the trash, but keeps his gaze on mine the whole time. "You know, my offer still stands. I'm a handy guy, and I don't mind helping with things."

I sigh, setting my cream cheese filled celery stick on my plate. "Thank you, Blake. I really do appreciate the offer, but I would feel terribly awkward asking you to fix my house for free."

"Who said I'd do it for free?" His mouth curls into a grin as he cocks an eyebrow. "I'm sure we can work out some kind of payment." When his eyes flick to my mouth, he meets my gaze again, wide-eyed and frozen still. He swallows deeply. "I'm so sorry. That came out way more suggestive than I meant it to."

I let out a hearty chuckle, though it does little to thin the innuendo thickened air. Blake and I stare at each other a moment, both smiling awkwardly, but not breaking eye contact. His eyes are so soft. So inviting. I want to dive into them, lose myself in their deep, chocolaty warmth.

As I let myself fall into this strange spell, Sydney appears from around the corner. "Mom, Dylan's tired, and I'm bored. Can we go home?"

"Huh?" I blink myself out of my stupor as I turn to my daughter. "Sure, sweetheart. What time is it?"

"Eleven-thirty."

"Oh, geez. Go get your coats. I'll be right there." I turn to Blake with apology in my eyes. "Sorry, we have to go."

He shakes his head. "No problem. Actually, can I leave with you? Walk you guys home?"

"Blake, we live across the street."

"Yeah, but it gives me an excuse to leave, too."

As we enter the foyer and Blake ducks into the closet for our coats, Joanna appears, quite obviously drunk by the way she leans against the wall. "Maggie! You're not leaving, are you?"

"Yes, the kids are tired. Time for bed."

"Oh, yes. Well, thank you for coming." She uses the wall as a brace to inch her way closer to me. "So, meet any nice men tonight?" She nudges me on the arm, a knowing look on her face.

"Oh, well, um–"

"Maggie, which coat is yours?" Blake pokes his head out of the closet. Joanna's eyes grow so wide, I feel like her eyelids are going to peel back.

"Oh, it's the brown one, there," I say as I point. "What were you saying, Joanna?"

"Well. Um, I... I'm sorry. I didn't know."

"Didn't know what?" I ask, fighting the smirk threatening to cross my lips.

"I didn't realize you were–"

"Hey, Joanna." Blake exits the closet with our coats. "Thanks for the invite. I'm going to leave with Maggie and the kids, then I need to let Oscar out." He helps me into my coat and slips into his own. "Tell Mark I'll hit him up for pool or something next weekend."

We bid Joanna a good night and leave her standing in awe in the entryway. I'm sure I confused the hell out of her by being with Blake since I told her there was nothing between us. There still isn't, but the idea of her wracking her brain to figure it out makes me chuckle.

"Mom, can you hurry up?" Sydney whines, as she stands, shivering in the cold.

"Oh, my gosh Syd, here." I toss her the keys. "You two go on ahead." I turn to Blake. "Sorry. I never knew a twelve-year-old could have so much attitude."

"Already a teenager, huh?"

"Yes. I thought I'd have another few years."

"She seems like a good kid, though," Blake says, extending his arm in a gesture for me to walk first.

"Oh, she's a great kid. Smart, clever. I'd even call her funny if it weren't for the sarcasm."

He chuckles, sending butterflies through me. I love the way he always asks about my children. Normally, if someone, especially a man, asks about my kids, I go into overprotective mother mode and assume the guy is a pedophile. I don't feel that way with Blake. He seems genuinely interested, giving me his full attention, but checks in on my children, which makes me enjoy his company even more.

He stuffs his hands in his coat pockets, hunching his shoulders a bit. "Thank you for giving me an excuse to get out of there. You're saving me from having to listen to drunk-ass Mark talk about politics. I hate that stuff."

"You're welcome. Thank you for walking us home, though based on the expression on Joanna's face, you and I are going to be the topic of the rumor mill."

Blake laughs, deep and rich. "Yeah, and Joanna is good at that. But, I guess if there's going to be rumors spread about me with someone, I'm glad it's you." He nudges me with his shoulder, and tilts his head to the side to look at me, those big, brown eyes softening in the moonlight.

I feel warmth rush to my face. "Blake," I say, utterly embarrassed, but flattered. "Ditto."

"You know, there's a way to keep us from becoming a rumor?"

"Oh, yeah? How?"

"Let me take you to dinner."

My breath catches in my throat. I'm silent as we reach my porch and I take the first step up, turning to face him. "Blake, you're very sweet, and I'm flattered—"

His body goes rigid. "I feel a but coming on."

"I don't date."

"Oh." His shoulders sag and his brow furrows. "Can I ask why?"

"I have my reasons."

"Okay."

The hurt in his voice and the disappointment on his face are heart wrenching. Almost enough for me to want to take back my words, but I steel myself for the onslaught of pleasantries coming my way. He'll say he understands and tell me goodnight, but not before saying he'll see me later. I won't see him again, though. We'll avoid each other at all costs. The idea rips my heart to shreds.

"Well, can we still be neighbors?" There's an endearing hopefulness to his tone.

I nod. "Of course. I'd like that."

"Me too." Blake shivers. "Okay, it's freezing, and I do have to let Oscar out. I'll talk to you later, Maggie. You and the kids have a Merry Christmas."

"Thanks, you too." As I watch him walk down the snow-covered street, I'm relieved at how well our conversation went, though there's a surprising hint of remorse lingering on my tongue. Maybe I shouldn't have said no?

CHAPTER EIGHT

The new year comes and I ring it in curled up on the couch with Dylan fast asleep in my arms and Sydney in her room. New Year's has never been my favorite holiday, but Dylan gets excited to stay up late every year, even though he never makes it.

As the ball drops and fireworks go off all around us, I lean down and kiss Dylan on top of his head. I sit back up, my eyes landing on our Charlie Brown Christmas tree and a pang of guilt rips through my gut for not decorating more. A tree is the most I've been able to manage for the last three years. Dylan still believes in Santa, so I have to have one, though it's always bare. I know my kids aren't surprised. They've stopped asking about it.

I'll try again next Christmas.

January and on into February are brutally cold, even for Colorado. The temperature never gets above twenty-five, which means other than going to work and school, we stay inside. It also means I don't get to see Blake. The most we've interacted since before the new year is a wave as I drive by while he's out walking Oscar. There's no sense in freezing my butt off for the chance to talk to him, but I miss our conversations all the same.

It snows several times, and I keep watching for Blake to come help me again, but he doesn't. For one thing, the snow accumulations are an inch or two. I'd feel ridiculous if someone had to come help me shovel so little. Plus, the timing is all wrong. Instead of snowing on a weekend, it seems to only snow during the week, and Blake works full-time.

With a shake of my head, I remind myself I turned him down, so it doesn't matter. Still, I don't like the emptiness in me when he's not around.

To force myself to ignore what I'm feeling, I throw myself into my job. The new year always brings new cases, and when Abbey comes down with the flu in early February, I take over her paperwork, too. She's a little more than angry when she comes back to find I've successfully finished everything without breaking a sweat. I'd be lying if I said it doesn't make me walk a bit taller through the office.

One morning, on my way back from the copy room, I have to pass Abbey talking to our receptionist. I wish there was another route I could take. Ever since she was sick, she's been extra pissy with me.

"You should totally come with us. It's a lot of fun," Abbey says over the receptionist desk, smacking her gum before turning her chin over her shoulder. "Maybe Maggie wants to come, too."

I stop in my tracks. "Come to what?"

Abbey spins around, leaning against the desk and picking at her manicure. "Me and some friends are going speed dating for Valentine's Day tonight. You're single, right?"

Yes, but I didn't turn down Blake so I could pick up some random guy at speed-dating. "Thank you for the invite, but I'll have to pass." My words are clipped, but my tone is pleasant. I think.

"Okay, suit yourself. But you never know, you could find your knight in shining armor."

I fight the urge to roll my eyes. "Why would I need that?"

A malevolent grin crosses Abbey's lips. "So you could have some company on your high horse."

My jaw clenches and I grip the stack of copies in my hands so tight, I feel like my nails are putting holes in the paper. Two can play at this game. I lift my chin and straighten my posture. "Then there wouldn't be any room for me to carry your load." I stride off, but not before seeing Abbey's mouth drop open. I smile.

"Come on, Sydney. It'll be like old times. Remember how much fun we used to have sledding?" I'm pleading with my daughter to be a kid for a little while so I can take Dylan to the neighborhood park. "There's a fantastic hill."

She purses her lips. "It's too cold."

"Syd, it's forty degrees and the sun is out. It's perfect."

Winter is always hard for me. Aside from the obvious turmoil of the holidays, being stuck inside when the weather is bad really takes a toll on my mental state. I like to be outside. When it's zero degrees and snow is blowing sideways, I keep my butt in the house, but today is too nice to pass up.

"I'll go for an hour."

"Hour and a half."

"Fine," Sydney huffs.

I wrap my arm around her and squeeze. "Thanks. Now, let's get suited up!"

At the park, Dylan and I take turns going down the hill, and it only takes a few attempts to get Sydney to go down, too. Even though I'm freezing my ass off, our laughter warms my insides. For a moment, I forget my kids are almost teens and I'm reminded of sledding when they were young.

Charlie was a daredevil sledder. He'd do all kinds of crazy stuff and scare the daylights out of me doing it. If I wasn't so afraid my tears would freeze to my face, I'd let myself cry, but I don't want icicles hanging off my chin, so I choke back the tears and focus on my happy kids.

"Mom! Your turn!" Dylan squeals, handing me the rope to the sled.

"I think I'm done, guys."

"No, do one more, Mom!" Dylan pleads.

"Yeah, Mom. This was your idea, anyway," Sydney says as she folds her arms.

My daughter will unravel me completely one day, which might be today. I take the sled from Dylan and line it up in one of our tracks. If I'm going to do this again, I'm going for an easy, pre-made trail. I drop into the plastic seat and count down for Dylan to give me a push. As I get to "one," Sydney also grabs on and helps Dylan propel me down the hill.

I hold my breath.

This is way too fast, and I'm way too old for insane stunts like this. As I'm going through the multitude of outcomes, I see Blake walking Oscar through the park. It's been a couple weeks since we've spoken. Between all the breaks from school and the crappy weather, I haven't had a chance to see him.

My staring only lasts a second before I reach the bottom of the hill, hitting a huge pile of packed down snow and flying into the air. The sled goes one way and I go another, rolling across the frozen tundra like a giant, screaming snowball.

I finally stop, my face buried in the snow, and I laugh. I'm laughing so hard, I don't notice two strong hands grip my arms to roll me over. As I settle onto my back, I'm put eye to eye with Blake's gorgeous, bearded face, but whereas I'm laughing, he's not.

Trying to stifle my laughter, I press my lips together and watch the worry melt from his face. He lets out a light chuckle and shakes his head. "You're nuts, Maggie Hansen." Rising to his knee, he lifts me by the elbow to sit up. "I don't think I've ever seen such a move."

"I bet you never thought I'd be into extreme sports, huh?"

With a tilt of his head and that adorable warm smile, he says, "Color me amazed." He holds my gaze for longer than a standard moment, and I'm no longer freezing. His gloved hand reaches over and brushes snow from my face, his finger lingering on my cheek.

This effect Blake has on me is terrifying, in a way. Right now, my heart is going to burst from my chest with a million butterflies carrying it away. I'm so warm, but not in a lying-on-the-beach-in-Mexico sort of way. I'm warm on the inside. It's radiating from my core, and I wish I could say it was adrenaline from my awesome sledding jump, but deep down, I know the warmth comes from Blake's attention.

My children choose that moment to arrive. "Mom! Are you okay?" Sydney asks as she drops to her knees at my side.

"I'm fine, sweetheart. It was actually fun."

"That was like the stuff Dad used to do!" Dylan yells, the excitement in him palpable.

I swallow and turn back to Blake. "Thanks for rushing to my aid, but I think I'm good."

"Well, in that case, let me have a turn." Blake hands me Oscar's leash, and jogs across the snow to retrieve the sled before heading up the hill. Once at the top, he waves to us and settles into the plastic seat. He pushes himself off, flying down what looks like the same path I took. My suspicions are confirmed when he hits the bump and sails into the air, though he manages to keep his butt in the sled. It hits the ground, bouncing around, and gracefully slides to a stop.

Dylan claps and jumps up and down as he cheers for Blake, much in the way he used to cheer for Charlie. It's heartwarming, but sad at the same time, and I'm reminded of why I can't get involved with Blake. No matter how fun he is, or how cute he looks in his winter hat, or even how a touch from his gloved finger burns on my skin, he'll never be Charlie.

I stand up, brushing the snow from my pants and clearing my throat before Blake and I exchange the sled for Oscar. "Good run, Blake. I give you an eight out of ten."

He gapes at me. "Only an eight? Even though I stayed in the sled the whole time?"

"This is extreme sledding, remember? Only bodily endangerment experiences get perfect scores." I turn to my children. "It's time to go home. I need some hot chocolate and ibuprofen after all this action."

The kids groan, a surprising response from Sydney, but they give in as I'm sure they're freezing, too. They say their goodbyes to Blake and head off.

I turn to say goodbye, but I'm stopped by Blake's intense gaze on me. The longing in his eyes was there when he asked me to dinner, and it's there now. My nerves cling to each other, on the verge of breaking if he even mutters the word "date."

His mouth opens, but closes right away. "Guess I'll see you later, Maggie." The depth of his voice as he says my name gives me all the chills, but not in a bad way.

I nod and walk away, focusing on the snow crunching under my feet instead of my pounding heart. I'm not sure what's going on. I should be relieved we got through an entire interaction without him trying to ask me out, but I'm not. My chest is tight, and my legs feel so heavy it's like they're pulling me deeper into the snow with each step. I think I'm actually disappointed he didn't say anything, and that scares the shit out of me.

Chapter Nine

"Bye. Thank you again for all your help," I say to my handyman as I see him out the door. This makes the fourth trip from him in the last three weeks. I'm beginning to think my house is a lemon.

With each call to him comes a pit of guilt in my stomach as I remember Blake's offer to help with repairs. He even repeated it at Joanna's party. I made myself clear on why I wouldn't ask him, and I'm sticking to it.

It's not just the guilt of not accepting his offer of handy work, it's also the bizarre disappointment I felt when he didn't ask me out in February. Ever since that day, the few quick interactions we've had are rife with tension. All from me. He's always so cool and calm while I'm reeling inside over my decision to reject him. I'm worried it'll get the best of me, and I'll say yes if he asks again, so I avoid Blake.

The weather helps in my efforts.

Spring in Colorado is a fickle thing. It seems like our springtime yields more snow than our winters, but it's mixed with wind and rain and temperatures yo-yoing unpredictably. In some respect, it's nice because it offers the opportunity to get out of the house without having to bundle up completely, but some days can be so miserable, they leave you wishing it was still January.

But as the middle of March approaches, the warming weather coaxes me outside, which increases my chances of running into Blake. As a result, I opt to read on the back deck instead of the front porch, and only check my mail when I'm coming home from work so I can pull up to the mailbox and make a quick getaway. I even limit pruning my flowerbeds to mid-day Tuesdays and Fridays so I don't chance Blake walking Oscar in the afternoon.

It's exhausting.

The kids' spring break comes in the middle of March, and we kick it off by having dinner with Michelle for my birthday. Of course, it's at Michelle's and my favorite Mexican restaurant, though today I skip the margaritas.

"Are you sure you don't want one?" Michelle lifts her margarita to her lips, moaning in delight as she takes a sip.

"I'm sure." I glance at my kids sitting in the booth with us. Dylan next to me and Sydney across from me with Michelle. "Besides, I've spent one too many birthdays regretting my decisions."

Michelle laughs. "I guess that's what happens when you share your birthday with St. Patrick!"

Bile creeps up my throat as I recall the taste of beer mixed with green food coloring. "He can have it."

"Hey, kids. Are you guys done with your food?" Michelle asks, picking up her purse. They nod and she hands each of them a five-dollar bill. "Why don't you go hit up the arcade games while we finish and pay?"

My children's eyes light up as they take her money. Though my heart thumps in my chest, I nod in permission for them to go. I can see the arcade room from our booth and it's nowhere near the front door. "Syd, keep an eye on Dylan!" I call out at the last second before settling back into the booth.

"So, Mags. How's it going?"

I lift my gaze to meet Michelle's, seeing the curious concern in her eyes. "I'm fine, Michelle."

"Okay, but... And don't be mad I'm saying this, but you always say you're fine. April is almost here."

I sigh at the heaviness in her tone. April is one of the harder months of the year. Particularly, the 24th.

Charlie's birthday is April 24th, and it's heartbreaking *not* celebrating it. My therapist told me to do something small like have Charlie's favorite dinner, or dessert, or watch his favorite movie, *School of Rock,* but those things made me feel guilty he wasn't here to enjoy them, so I stopped.

The lead up to Charlie's birthday creates this swirling tempest of emotions, which ruins my ability to function around people, so I cut myself off. Aside from my children and the occasional call from Michelle, I'm a hermit. I even work from home.

This year has been different, though. I haven't felt the crushing weight of anxiety building. "No, I mean it. I'm fine. Things are different now, with the new house and working part-time. I think I'm going to be okay."

"You think? What does your therapist say?"

I purse my lips, flicking my gaze away from Michelle's. "I actually haven't seen her since before we moved."

"What!? Why?"

"Things happened. I was so busy with the move and getting the kids settled into school that it slipped my mind. I've thought about it a couple times, but haven't felt the need to see her. I've been doing better."

Michelle stares at me, disbelief saturating her features.

"What? I *am* doing better."

Her eyes flick between the two of mine while she reads me. If there's one person who knows me better than I know myself, it's Michelle. She huffs a breath and throws her hands up. "Okay, if you say so." She leans over the table, taking my hands in hers. "But please call me if something goes south. You know I'll never judge you."

"I know." I squeeze her hand. "And I promise to call if I need anything, but I don't think I will. I haven't even had a second thought about April coming. Honestly, I wouldn't have even thought about it except I got an email about the kids' spring conferences." I crane my neck to check on the kids who are sucked into some game involving zombies.

Michelle settles back into her seat. "Ooh, conferences. Are you worried?"

"No. My kids are good students. I'm sure the conferences will go smoothly, and so will the month of April. I'm not worried at all."

That is, until the conferences actually happen.

I stroll into the middle school at 3:55 p.m. on the Friday before Charlie's birthday, five minutes early for my 4 p.m. appointment. I have Sydney's today. Dylan's was on Tuesday and went swimmingly. He's an excellent student, albeit overly energetic, and has a big heart for all his friends. I was one proud mom.

I step into Sydney's classroom and am greeted by her teacher, Mr. Henshaw. "Hi, Maggie. Nice to see you, please have a seat." He motions to a plastic chair in front of his desk, and I sit. "Let me start by saying, Sydney is a pleasure to have here, but I think I told you in the fall, too."

"Yes, you did, but it's always nice to hear."

As he shuffles the papers on his desk, he repeats everything I already know about Syd. She's a brilliant child with a bright future, and she has no problem speaking her mind. Her grades are impeccable. She excels in English, shows above-average skills in math and science, and is taking an interest in history.

My mom heart is swelling with pride, until Mr. Henshaw says something that rips it out. "You and Sydney's father must be very proud."

My chest constricts, stopping my heart altogether. I thought I could handle this, but the facade I've put on is nothing more than a glass mask, and it's shattering.

I spend the rest of the conference with a pleasantly fake smile on my face. My hands sit in my lap, wringing each other so tightly I'm surprised my bones don't snap. My outward facade may be one of a beaming mother, but inside, my guts twist.

I thank Sydney's teacher and go home. Once I'm inside, I burst at the seams, sagging against the door and sliding to the floor. I don't know how long I'm here sobbing, but it's long enough for Sydney to come looking for me. When she rounds the corner, she stops in her tracks. I raise my red-rimmed, tear-filled eyes to meet hers and I see the concern on her face.

Without a word, Sydney comes to me. She squats down, pausing a moment before wrapping her arms around me and squeezing. A few more sobs escape me, and Sydney helps me to my feet. We walk silently up the stairs, where she leads me to my room and puts me into my bed. As I curl into a ball with my back to her, Sydney runs a hand down my hair and leans down to kiss my head.

"I'll take care of dinner, Mom."

I sniffle, but don't turn to face her. "You can order out if you want."

"Okay." She pads across the room, but when I don't hear the door close, I peek out from the covers to see her standing in the doorway.

"Syd?"

"I want you to know I'm proud of you for making it this long."

As the door clicks shut, the tears flow out of my eyes, and they don't stop all weekend.

Once Charlie's birthday comes and goes, after the emotions swell, crest, and break, I'm back on my feet and I return to the office. It's a welcome change after working from home for a week.

Thursday afternoon takes a turn for the worse, though, when Abbey mouths off about my special treatment. Normally, I can handle these situations with grace. I know it seems like I'm getting preferential treatment, and I understand how Abbey might be upset about it, but when she spouts off the words, "Your princess attitude is probably why your husband left," I can't hold back. I spin on my heel and slap the Hubba Bubba right out of her mouth.

I'm put on a month-long leave of absence without pay.

Without work to keep me busy, and the kids at school during the day, I slip further into myself. I put a call into my therapist, but I get her voicemail. I don't leave a message.

Something about leaving a message makes me feel like a failure. It's as if I'm so inept at handling my own issues, I can't wait until my therapist is back in the office. I'll call back.

The month of May is much worse than April. Coincidentally, on the 24th. It's the day Charlie... The day my life ended with his. Coping with it consists of me eking through the month on autopilot, like every year since his death.

I wanted this year to be different. I thought a new house would make it easier. This isn't the house Charlie and I bought in our twenties. It's not the home we brought our two children into. It's not the place where we made memory after memory, so I shouldn't be reminded of him at every turn.

But I am.

It's not our bedroom, but it's the bed we shared for a decade. Every time I crawl into it, I expect to feel his body heat under the covers, to smell him, to hear his snore and wish I could put a pillow over my ears to drown him out. In my closet, the teal dress I wore on our fifth wedding anniversary always makes me cry, but I can't throw it away. Charlie literally drooled as he watched me come down the stairs in it.

My heart breaks as I realize it's not the house, or neighborhood, or city I live in. The memories are in me. No matter where I go, I'll never stop thinking about Charlie.

And I don't want to.

The week of... the big event, I completely shut myself in. I don't go out to check the mail, or water my plants, or even pick up whatever package is sitting on my porch. I stay in bed for the most part, only coming out of my room to eat, or to take care of my children's needs.

As I lie in bed, wallowing in sorrow, I hear a dog bark and my mind flicks to Blake. I don't intend to, but suddenly, all I can think about is him and a lightness flutters into my chest. I miss our conversations. While I normally hate small talk, our chats about the weather or local news always feel different. I don't itch to get away from him. His presence seems to ground me, and right now, it's exactly what I need.

And if I'm being honest, I miss the way he looks at me. The way my name sounds on his lips. He's handsome and sweet and I'm flattered to have his attention. My heart speeds up as I picture the way his mouth curves when he smiles.

Does this mean I'm ready to date again?

My heart sinks. Even if I am, I closed the door on us. I rejected Blake. He's probably found someone else by now. Even Joanna said it last year; men like him don't stay single for long. I've missed my chance.

The heaviness of guilt sets in as I realize I'm spending my late husband's death anniversary thinking of another man. Shame on me. My thoughts need to be with Charlie and remembering him right now. Not with frivolous fantasies of a younger guy.

On Friday the 26th, I'm feeling good enough to sit on the porch while I wait for the kids to get home. It's their last day of school and it's my duty as a mom to greet them. As I'm waiting, Blake is, of course, walking Oscar. I hadn't expected to see him in the middle of the afternoon, but I can't say I'm disappointed.

My heart races at the sight of him. Those broad shoulders, that tapered waist. Even his legs are toned. How can calves be sexy?

He casually strolls up my driveway and stops at my porch steps, his normal conversation spot. "Hey, Maggie. How are you? Long time, no see." The gravity of his tone is only enhanced by the sympathetic look on his face as he scratches at what I can only describe as his summer beard.

"Hi, Blake. I've had a rough few weeks, but I'm doing much better, thank you."

"Rough weeks? Anything I can help with?"

I shake my head. "It's all over and done."

His eyes narrow a moment as he scrutinizes my answer. "Good to hear. You had me worried for a while there."

He was worried about me? Butterflies race through me, but I swallow them down. "Everything is fine. No need to worry."

The concern on his face lessens, but his shoulders remain tense.

"How are you doing? Still have the beard, I see."

"Ha, yeah." He runs his hand along his jaw. "I had to trim it shorter for the summer. Does it still look good?"

"Mhm." It looks so good, I don't think I could form words if I tried.

His lips curve into his signature smile as he golds my gaze, but he blinks his way out of the trance and clears his throat. "I've been good, though. Nothing new and exciting. Work's been steady, so I guess I'm thankful for that."

Wish I could say the same.

"Something wrong at work?"

I blink at Blake, furrowing my brow in utter confusion as to how he read my mind.

"You said something about wishing work was steady."

Crap. I said it out loud. With a pinched expression, I say, "Oh, yeah, just a misunderstanding with a coworker."

He flicks his gaze to Oscar who's lounging in the yard, apparently exhausted from their walk. Blake steps onto the porch, taking a seat on the top step a few inches away from the edge of my chair. "Are you sure everything is okay?"

I sigh. How this man reads me so well is beyond me. I raise my gaze to the sky a moment before answering. "There was an incident where someone said something pretty rude and, because my emotions were already running high, I may...have...slapped her."

"You slapped someone!?" Blake's eyelids peel back. "You? Sweet little Maggie Hansen?"

My cheeks tinge pink as I shrug. "I'm not always so sweet."

"Remind me to never get on your bad side. Though, I've looked and I haven't seen one."

I let out an airy chuckle and drop my gaze to my lap. "It doesn't come out often." My eyes tentatively raise to meet Blake's. Instead of the judgment I'm expecting, all I see is understanding in his deep chocolate irises and, suddenly, all my tension melts away.

He runs a hand through his hair. "Well, I can see how that would make things awkward in the office."

"Oh, I've been on a leave of absence for a month because of it."

Blake's mouth hangs open. "A month? That's rough. You and the kids okay?"

I know what he's asking. He wants to know if we're struggling financially, which we aren't. That isn't a conversation I'm having right now, though, so I nod and tell him we're fine.

We continue talking, Blake thankfully changing the subject to the Rockies opening game he went to last month. "It was a great game. We won, which is always exciting. I still can't believe you've never been."

"Sports aren't really my thing, never have been."

"What about the kids? Have they ever wanted to go?"

I scrunch my forehead. Charlie took them to a game for Dylan's sixth birthday. I was supposed to go, but ended up with the flu and was stuck in bed. They had a great time, and I remember Charlie promising they'd go to another one, but they never got the chance.

"Maggie, you okay?"

Blake's voice pulls me from my memory and I realize my eyes are filling with tears. I blink them away, putting on a pleasant face and nodding. "I'm fine. The kids went to one game, but it was years ago."

He narrows his eyes and purses his lips a moment before saying, "Well, if you guys ever want to go, I can get tickets."

My heart leaps into my throat. Is he about to ask me to a game? Will I say yes? If I do, does that make it a date?

"They may not be spectacular seats, but I'm sure I can find three together."

My heart sinks back into my chest, as heavy as a ball of lead. Three seats. Me and the kids. Not him. "Oh, okay. Thank you."

The air between Blake and I changes, but not in a good way. It's heavier, like molasses, and it sticks in my throat. I feel the disappointment on both our sides. The only way I can think to break this tension is to ask Blake to take us to a game, but before I open my mouth, Dylan comes bounding down the street, fresh off the school bus. "MOM! Are we going to summer camp again this year?"

"Hi there, Dyl-pickle," I say, hugging him tightly, earning a large grin from Blake that has my stomach flipping. "Um, I haven't even thought about camp, but I'm sure we can still sign up if you want to go. Has Syd said anything about it?"

"Yeah! We talked about it on the way to the bus this morning and she said she wants to go again, too!"

Wow, that's surprising. I figured she'd pull the 'I'm too old' card. "Okay, Dylan, we'll–"

"Hey, Maggie," Blake interrupts, and my eyes flick to the apologetic smile crawling across his face. "Sorry, I'm going to get going. I'll see you later. Bye, Dylan."

"Bye, Mr. Blake!" Dylan squeals. "Can we go look up camp right now?"

"Let's wait for Sydney to get home, and we'll all look together, okay?"

"Okay!" Dylan skips into the house.

I stare absentmindedly at Blake walking down the street. My eyes drop momentarily to the seat of his pants and jerk away. Shame on you, Maggie! It was an innocent glance, and well worth it, but it's inappropriate. He obviously took me at my word that I don't date since he hasn't tried once since the Christmas party, and I'm not doing myself any favors in allowing this attraction to garner footing. I've made my bed and I have to lie in it.

Chapter Ten

The Saturday before they leave for camp, the kids and I go to the community pool. With summer break in full swing, the last week has been filled with daytime hikes, backyard ice cream parties, and late-night movies. I took the week off, but I'm exhausted, so sitting poolside and reading sounds blissfully relaxing. The warmth of the sun balanced with the light breeze while the buzzing of insects floating through the air soothes me.

While we're at the pool, I lounge in a chair with my book. I make sure to pay attention to what book I bring, since the smut novel incident from last year still rears its ugly head. This one is a romance, and still plenty dirty, but the cover isn't nearly as brazen.

I glance up from the pages as the main characters are about to do the deed to make sure my fully capable children aren't drowning. I need to know I have a good amount of time to get through this section. I don't want to be interrupted.

Before I can dive into the love making, I see Blake walk through the clubhouse and onto the pool deck. I almost drop my book and my jaw as I watch him slide into the sunlight, shirtless, tanned, and drop-dead gorgeous. He's got muscles in places I didn't even know existed and, suddenly, the love fest on the pages in front of me doesn't seem like it'll be enough.

Shit. I'm in trouble if that's how he looks without a shirt.

My heart leaps into my throat as he turns and walks in my direction. His aviator sunglasses hide his eyes, but the wave he gives says he's spotted me as he makes a beeline for the empty chair next to mine.

Do I wave back? Do I pretend like I don't see him? Before I can decide, he's standing in front of me, and all I've done is stare.

"Hi, Maggie. Is this seat taken?" he asks, gesturing to my neighboring chair.

I swallow deeply as I rake in his bare chest, the muscles much more defined now that he's closer. "No, it's all yours."

"Are the kids here?" He spreads out his towel and lies back in the chair.

"Yep, they're over there. See the two trying to dunk each other? Those are my angels."

Blake takes off his sunglasses, as if it's going to help him see better, and takes a quick glance at the pool before turning his head to trail his eyes from my feet to my face, pausing on my hips a moment. "Looks like they're having fun. And you're sitting here by yourself?"

"I've got my book." I hold it up, much more confident than the last time he caught me reading.

He studies the book, a sparkle in his eye. "That one doesn't look as good as the one you had last year." His lips curl into a mischievous smile, and I blush. "But, I don't want to bother you if you're reading. I can find another seat." He leans forward.

"No!" I say it too quickly, too enthusiastically. "No, it's fine. I'd rather have a conversation, anyway. I can read any time."

The smile on his face spreads into a grin. As he lies back down, his eyes travel from my face and down my torso, lingering a moment on my bikini top before going all the way to my feet. He stares at my feet for a few seconds, and I curl my toes to stop them from wiggling. He flicks his gaze back to mine. "Nice suit."

He may be passing on taking me on a date, but he's still checking me out. That's a good sign. "Thank you," I say, glancing away as my cheeks are undeniably red.

He folds his arms behind his head, his chest and biceps flexing as he does, and closes his eyes. Even with the bustle of the pool, the silence between me and Blake is deafening.

Unable to form a coherent thought, I blurt out, "Do you come to the pool a lot?" I cringe at the way my question sounds like a cheesy pick-up line.

Blake shrugs. "A couple times during the summer. I'd rather be at the lake with Oscar, but I don't always have the time, so I come here when I need a little water getaway. What about you? You like the pool?" He turns his head slightly and pops one eye open to look at me.

"Yes, I do. I'd much rather be on a beach, but they're hard to come by in Colorado, so the pool has to do."

"There are beaches at the lake."

"I suppose there are, but I'm talking about a tropical beach. You know, the ones with palm trees and little umbrellas in the drinks."

Blake laughs. Good, I was hoping he would. I don't want to sound like some kind of high maintenance diva. I do love tropical beaches, but the pool is fine with me.

"I'd love a drink with a little umbrella in it."

"Well, I don't think they serve those here. You'll have to settle for a soda from the vending machine."

"You buying?"

"I certainly can if you'd like," I say, picking up my bag and reaching for my wallet.

Blake sits up and puts his hand on mine, pushing my bag down to the ground. The electricity of his touch radiates through my body. I've never even so much as shaken his hand and now that he's touching mine ever so gently, my heartbeat speeds up. I look over to see him shaking his head. "Maggie, thanks, but I was kidding. I'd be happy to get you a soda. What do you like?"

"Dr. Pepper if they have it, Coke if not. And at least let me pay for mine," I say, holding up a couple dollars.

Blake waves me off as he walks away, and as much as I try not to, I watch his every step. Those tight swim trunks stretched across his ass don't leave much to the imagination.

After fighting with the machine, he collects our drinks and walks back toward me, all the while being watched by other women. Almost every single woman on the pool deck has their eyes locked on Blake. I can't say I blame them. As he hands me my Dr. Pepper, their eyes come to me, but with daggers in them.

"Thank you," I say. "So, do you know many people in the neighborhood?"

"I've met most on our street." He sits down so his legs hang off the side of the chair closest to me and he rests his elbows on his knees. "I don't know as many around the corner, but I've met a few when I walk Oscar. Why?"

"It seems like there's a lot of interest in you around here." It sounds more jealous than I intend. I have no claim to Blake as I made it clear he's just my neighbor after all. My incredibly handsome, chiseled neighbor.

Blake chuckles as he hangs his head, twisting the cap off his soda bottle. "Yeah, I guess I've learned to ignore it. I don't actually recognize anyone here except you today. That's part of the reason I came to sit with you, so I don't have to hang out alone, surrounded by the wolves."

"What's the other part?" I ask shyly.

He takes a sip of his Dr. Pepper, swallowing it with a delicious smirk on his lips. "So I could get to know you better." The sincerity in his deep tone makes me wish I'd taken a dip in the pool earlier.

"Well, from the looks of things, Dylan and Sydney won't be ready to leave any time soon, so we've got plenty of time. But haven't we pretty much covered what we need to know about each other? In terms of being neighbors, anyway."

Blake shifts in his chair, leaning on his side and propping his head up with his arm. "Well, maybe we should expand past the terms of being neighbors then. Take our relationship to the next level."

My heart leaps into my throat. Relationship? What a strong word to use after I told him I don't date. Maybe he's going to try again? I should show him I'm open to it. Excitement bubbles in me and I take a big drink of my soda. As I swallow, I shift my body so I'm lying on my side, facing Blake, matching his position. I flutter my eyelashes and say in a sultry voice, "And how do we do that?"

A crease forms between his brows. "Well, you said you moved here from Aurora. How long were you there?"

"Oh." The excitement dissolves, and I sigh. Not the question I was expecting. "Almost twelve years. After college, Charlie–" The mentioning of his name chokes me up, and emptiness fills my chest as I lower my eyes to the ground.

"Maggie? Are you okay?" I turn to see Blake sitting up in a crunch and looking at me intently. His eyes tell me he's concerned.

I offer him a smile, but it's forced. I don't want his pity. "Yes, I'm fine. Sorry, just a little carbonated bubble." *Oh, smooth, Maggie. Talk about belching. Okay, change the subject.* "And you? You said you were born in Chicago. Do you ever think about going back?"

"No. I'm in Colorado for good."

"Well, I'm glad you are." I wink, my heart racing, but slowing when all Blake does is smile and turn onto his back again. Ugh, I have no idea what I'm doing. I'm obviously no good at flirting.

"Even though I'm not doing what I wanted to with my life, I still love it here. And I have a good job, so that helps. Speaking of," Blake says, turning to his side to face me. "Are you back at work?"

I sigh in sad acceptance of the fact Blake isn't going to ask me out. "I go back on Monday after the kids leave for camp."

"So they are going?"

"Yes. They'll be gone for eight weeks." A small bubble of panic rises, but I wash it down with more Dr. Pepper.

"Are you worried about them?"

I look at Blake in wonderment, appreciating how well he reads me. "I am, but only because I always worry about them. I know they'll be fine. Plus, it'll be good for me to have some time to myself, although it'll be a little lonely."

"You know, Maggie, if you need some company, I'm right down the street." I'm starting to like the gravel in Blake's voice when he says my name.

Did he just... *This is it, Maggie. This is your shot.* Accept his offer to keep you company so he knows you're open to other things. "Blake, that sounds–"

"MOM! Sydney dunked me under and wouldn't let me go!" Dylan comes trotting around the deck, crying.

"Sydney!" I yell. She's hanging onto the edge of the pool a few feet beyond the end of our chairs. "What did I tell you about playing so rough?"

"Sorry, Mom. I thought Dylan could handle it now. He's ten years old, you know."

I wrap Dylan's towel around him and settle him onto my lap. I mouth the word "sorry" to Blake, who waves me off like it's no big deal. After Dylan calms down, he asks to leave. I glance at Blake, and I swear there's disappointment on his face, but he hides it with a warm smile.

"Thank you for the soda" I say, hiking our pool bag onto my shoulder. "Sorry to rush off in the middle of our conversation."

"It was my pleasure," Blake replies, sliding his aviators down his nose so his brown eyes are visible. They glint as the sun hits them just right. "We can continue our conversation another time."

My stomach does a somersault. Maybe I haven't missed my chance after all.

Chapter Eleven

June 3rd finally arrives, and I bawl like a baby watching the camp bus fade into the horizon. I know my kids will be fine. I know they're safe, but it's that damn motherhood thing forcing me to cry every time I think about them growing up. They've gone to camp for years, with the exception of the year Charlie died, but they've never done the eight-week program. I'm afraid they'll look like different kids when they get home.

I scoot into work after having to fix my makeup twice. Someone should bottle tears to use as makeup remover, I swear.

As I pass Abbey's cubicle, I glimpse her from the corner of my eye. I hesitate a split second and consider finally apologizing for slapping her. I know she was upset that day, and it was overtly unprofessional of me, not to mention just plain mean, but what she said was beyond rude. I'm giving myself a pass.

I settle at my desk and begin my day by checking my emails. I'm not even through the first one when there's a knock on my cubicle wall. Spinning around in my chair, I'm surprised to see Abbey standing in the entryway.

She's a little shrunken from her normal stature, but purses her lips as she taps her nails against her thigh all the same. "Maggie…"

"Abbey." I don't know what the hell she needs, but this weird silence from her isn't normal.

"I didn't know your husband was dead."

Is that supposed to be some kind of apology? "Well, now you do."

She huffs a breath and shifts her footing so her hip leans against the wall. "Sorry for what I said."

My mouth hangs open as I stare at her, unable to comprehend what's happening.

"I was actually going to press charges, but when I found out what was going on, I changed my mind. Losing your husband so suddenly... it must have been hard." She adjusts her feet again and begins picking at her nails. "I don't blame you for slapping me."

"Thank you, Abbey. But for what it's worth, I am sorry I did."

She presses her lips into a line, nodding curtly before turning to walk away.

Wow. That's exactly what I needed after this morning.

Abbey stops and comes back to my desk. "You know, if you want, I could help you with your makeup and stuff. Teach you how to do it if you're going on dates."

Aaaand the apology is negated. "Thanks, Abbey, but I don't date."

"Oh, okay. Well, if you ever change your mind, I'd be happy to help." Her tone sounds sweet, but bitter as she leaves.

I mean, I guess she tried? And what's wrong with my makeup? I study myself in my computer monitor screen. It's fine... I think.

Abbey's apology has my week started off right, and I breeze through the rest of the days. Even though my kids are gone, I feel like something good is coming my way and it keeps my mood lifted all week.

The feeling is ripped to shreds early Saturday morning.

I wake with a start, drenched in a cold sweat. My jaw hurts from being clenched. My pillow is soaked with tears. As I turn to grab the glass of water sitting on my side table, I see the clock. It's 4 a.m. I take a sip of water and flop onto my back, inhaling deep to calm my racing heart.

Are these nightmares ever going to stop?

They aren't always the same, but they always leave me an emotional wreck. Sometimes they're random scenes. People I don't know in situations I can't save them from. Other times, it's very specific, much like this one. The details are hazy, but I can picture Sydney's face twisted with fear, and hear Dylan's ear-piercing scream as they're pulled away from me. A chill runs down my spine at the feeling of their hands slipping through my grasp.

I sag into the mattress and close my eyes, but force them back open as the images replay behind my eyelids.

"I have to get out of bed." The sun may not even be up yet, but there's no way I'm going back to sleep.

With my endorphins pumping after a hefty cardio workout, I make breakfast, and eat in silence. This hasn't happened since last summer when the kids went to camp. It's blissful and serene, but also haunting. I don't like it. I never have.

I wish I had someone to talk to. I could call Michelle, but she won't be up yet. This is one of those times when I wish I had a partner. Charlie would have been up by now, giving me someone to pass the time with, but now it's me alone with my thoughts. A dangerous combination sometimes.

As I finish breakfast, the sun peeks out over the horizon, bathing everything in a warm sunrise glow. I decide to finish my coffee on the back patio. I listen to the birds chirping, the gentle breeze blowing through the branches, and as my heart finally thumps at a normal pace, I think, *this is more like it. Today is going to be good.*

By the time lunch comes, I've done some gardening, taken a shower, and read half of another book from my to-be-read pile. I enjoy a veggie wrap on the back patio, again taking in the sounds of summer all around.

I remember the days of the kids being little and how Charlie and I never got to enjoy a meal by ourselves. All we wanted was to get through a conversation without having to get up a hundred times to refill juice, or get another serving of mac and cheese, or wipe up the inevitable spill. Or, maybe that's what I wanted.

Charlie was almost always the instigator when it came to rambunctious behavior. He was the one making funny faces, or talking in silly voices. He'd get the kids all riled up, and I'd be the one to clean up the mess.

Now those days are gone. Charlie's gone.

With a grimace on my face and a knife in my heart, I head inside to clean up. I scrape the little crumbs off my plate and into my garbage disposal. Flipping the switch, the sound of metal grinding together makes my jaw clench. Before I can react and turn the switch, a piece of metal comes flying out of the sink, barely missing me. I let out a shriek, ducking under the cabinet before jumping up to shut off the disposal, my heart beating a mile a minute.

What the hell just happened? I grab my phone and dial my handyman while I search the floor for my assailant.

"Hi, you've reached Mr. Fix-It." *Great, voicemail.* "I'm out of town for the week..." *What!? No, no. Crap!* "If this is an emergency, you can call my buddy, Francis, at–" I hang up the phone. Call me crazy, but I don't want Francis. I've built a great relationship with *my* handyman, and I trust him. I don't know Francis. He could be shady or crooked.

But what other choice do I have? I don't know how to change a garbage disposal by myself.

Maybe I could YouTube it? I laugh out loud. *That's the worst idea you've had yet, Maggie.*

A thought crosses my mind. *Blake.* He said I could ask for his help if I needed it and, boy, do I need it.

I shake my head. I can live without it. After all, it's only a week. I groan thinking about how annoying it would be, though. Only using one side of the sink for fear of it springing a leak. And what happens if I forget and flip the switch again? What if it explodes?

"Calm down, Maggie. You're overthinking this."

I look out my front window toward the cul-de-sac at Blake's house. I can't tell if he's home, but it's Saturday and I figure worst-case scenario, I knock, there's no answer, and I'll have to go back later. As I walk down my porch steps, I hear a lawnmower start up and see Blake, shirtless, pushing his mower around the yard.

Well, at least he's home.

I cross the street while trying to figure out why my heart is pounding. Am I worried he'll say no? Am I nervous about asking for his help after not asking for almost a year? Or is this excitement about talking to him while he's not wearing a shirt again? Could be all three, I suppose.

Coming to a stop at the edge of his yard, I stand and wait for him to notice me. He glances up and waves as I give a little wave back. He cuts the mower, and as he walks toward me, I can see the sweat already beading on his skin, glistening in the sunlight. It highlights every sexy nuance of his muscles.

"Hey, Maggie, what's going on?" he asks, running his hand through his damp hair and making it stick out to the sides in the most adorable way.

"Hi, Blake. Sorry, I didn't mean to interrupt you, but I need your help." I squish one side of my mouth up toward my eye.

Blake's eyes widen and his mouth twitches like he's fighting a smile. "Sure, what can I do for you?"

"My garbage disposal just blew up and–"

"Blew up?"

"Yeah, I turned it on and there was this grinding noise, then a chunk of metal flew out at me. I have no idea how to replace one of those and my handyman is out of town for a week, so–"

"Whoa, okay, slow down. I'm happy to help. I've replaced one or two of those in my life. It's not too hard. We'll have to go to Home Depot and get the stuff. Are you going to be around this afternoon?"

"Yeah, I'm home all day."

"Alright, well, let me finish my lawn, then I'll take a quick shower and head over. Okay?"

"Great, thank you so much." I spin on my heel and head back home.

Once inside my house, I lean against the door and close my eyes. The image of shirtless Blake appears, forcing me to bite my lip and clench my thighs. Too bad he'll be fully clothed when he comes over.

My chest tightens, joined by a tingling sensation as I realize Blake is going to be in my house.

"Crap!" I start cleaning frantically. I put the dishes in the dishwasher, wipe the counters, sweep, and pick up all the stray socks and books from the living room. Then I run upstairs to do a quick check on myself.

My messy bun has become even messier after my disposal attack, so I tighten it up a bit. I decide to brush my teeth. Why, I don't know, but I had a veggie wrap with a balsamic vinaigrette and I don't need my breath to be the one thing Blake remembers about coming to help me.

Should I put on makeup? I don't usually wear any if I'm not at work, and I just saw Blake without any on, so if I put some on, he'll know I did it for him and–

Okay, no makeup. I splash some water on my face and start throwing clothes into my closet. As I'm making my bed, I realize he's not going to be in my room, so I return to the kitchen and pour myself a glass of iced tea while I sit at the table to wait. My knee bounces up and down uncontrollably as I thrum my fingers on the table.

Maybe I should've had wine instead.

There's a knock on my door, and my head whips up. This is it, no going back now. I slowly walk to the front door so I don't seem eager, and open it to a freshly washed Blake standing on my doorstep. His hair is still damp, but now it's sculpted. He's got on a gray t-shirt stretched tight across his chest, jogging shorts, and he has a toolbox in his hand. Even his beard has been shaped up.

"Hey," he says in his signature low, gravelly tone.

"Hi," I reply shyly.

"Can I come in?"

"Oh, yes, right. Sorry." God, I'm such an idiot.

He steps inside, giving me a whiff of his cologne. A musky scent, with hints of juniper and sage. It's heavenly.

"So, where is this dastardly disposal who attacked my friend?" Blake asks with a chuckle.

I laugh, waving him to follow me into the kitchen.

He sets the toolbox on the counter and bends down to get under my sink, giving me a front-row view of his ass. Disappointment floods me when, after a minute, he stands back up. "Okay, you've got a ½ horsepower unit. We'll get the same one if that's okay. We can upgrade if you want."

"No, I'm sure the same thing will be fine."

"Alright, are you driving, or should I?"

"What?"

"We have to go to the store and buy one, remember?"

"Oh, right. I can drive. It's no problem."

We climb into my car and head off down the road. My radio is turned down low, but I'm hoping it's loud enough to muffle the sound of my heart hammering in my chest. I keep my eyes on the road and my hands on the wheel. I'm so nervous right now, I can hardly think.

"I like this song," Blake breaks the silence.

"Oh, yeah, I do, too," I say. As I reach over to turn the volume up, so does Blake and our hands bump each other's. We both withdraw quickly, our awkward silence resuming. After a moment, I hear Blake chuckle, and he reaches over, turning the volume up.

I'm relieved at his ability to laugh at himself. I need to do more of that.

Blake's fingers move to the beat of each song, tapping out the drums. It's been a steady stream of Linkin Park, Queens of the Stone Age, and other such bands, and Blake seems to know every one of them. It's not until Lady Gaga comes on that he reaches over and turns down the music. "How come your radio keeps playing all the good songs?"

"It's my iPod."

"People still use those things?"

I laugh. "It's my old one from college. The power button doesn't work, and the battery won't hold a charge, so it became my permanent car device."

"Nice to know I'm in good company with great musical taste."

I check my blindspot for no other reason than to hide my heated cheeks.

"So, what were your big plans for today? You know, before the disposal explosion."

"Nothing special. Do some reading, maybe a walk. I'll probably fall asleep on the couch watching Hallmark movies tonight."

"Wait. You listen to Disturbed, but you watch Hallmark movies?"

I fight the smile threatening to spread across my face. "And what's so weird about that?"

"Nothing. You just keep surprising me, Maggie."

The smile wins and I'm grinning from ear to ear. "So what were you going to do today?"

"The same as you. Except for the reading. And the Hallmark movie. I will take Oscar for a walk, though."

I shoot him a sideways glance. "One out of three, not bad."

Once inside Home Depot, Blake walks me around to gather everything he needs. He tells me stories of repairs he's done to his home and some horror stories from his friend's experiences. At the checkout, Blake reaches for his wallet, but I stop him. I insist on paying since it's my house, and he doesn't argue much. We walk across the parking lot and back to my car, silence taking over once more. When neither of us starts a conversation, I turn the stereo back up so there's a bit more background noise.

"What's the tattoo on your foot for?" Blake's voice cuts through the music.

"What?" I glance over at him, then back at the road.

He reaches over and turns down the stereo. "The tattoo, on your foot. It's a guitar, right? I remember seeing it last year, then I saw again it at the pool last week, but I didn't get a chance to ask you about it. I noticed it again in Home Depot. So, what's it about? Any special meaning?"

Tears well in my eyes. My throat closes up. My stomach flips, but not from the euphoria of sitting with Blake. I bite my lip and tighten my grip on the steering wheel. Instead of wiggling, my toes curl in on themselves.

"I got it last year for my husband's thirty-fifth birthday. He used to play guitar in high school and through college, but gave it up as he got older. He was a big music guy. Our kids are named after his influences."

"You've never talked about him to me. Where is he now?" Blake asks, innocently.

"He... died," my voice cracks. "Three years ago, in a plane crash with my father-in-law." The tears stream down my cheeks, and I feel the drops on my leg, but I don't wipe them from my face. "It was a birthday present from my father-in-law to my husband. Charlie had always wanted to fly a plane, but wasn't disciplined enough to go to flight school or anything. So, my father-in-law pulled some strings and probably spent a pretty penny to get Charlie a chance to do it. There was an experienced co-pilot, of course, but even he couldn't stop the plane from crashing."

"Why? What happened?"

I sniffle, running my hand over my cheeks and wiping my palm on my pants. "They said it was a mechanical failure in one of the engines. It wouldn't have mattered if there were two top-notch pilots. The plane would've crashed anyway."

"I'm... I'm so sorry, Maggie. I had no idea. That's awful." Blake's immediate remorse shines through in his shaky voice.

"It's okay. Thank you, though."

"Your poor kids. That had to be tough for them."

"Which is why we moved. We couldn't live in our house anymore. Too many memories. We were all sad all the time. It wasn't a good life."

"I can imagine..." Blake's voice trails off. "So, who are your kids named after?"

"What?" I sniffle and swipe at my nose.

"You said your kids are named after your husband's influences. Who are they?"

"Well, Bob *Dylan* should be the obvious one."

Blake smacks himself on the forehead. "Duh. Okay, and Sydney?"

"That one's a little harder." I roll my lips between my teeth. "Sid Vicious of the Sex Pistols." The smile spreads and something resembling a laugh creeps through my lips. "I never understood why Charlie loved that band, but he did.

"Wait, didn't we just listen to a Sex Pistols song?"

"Yes. I put it on my playlist after Charlie..."

Blake's hand twitches, like he's going to reach for me, but rests his elbow on the armrest instead.

I swallow. "Since I was vehemently against the name Sid, we compromised on Sydney, and I got to pick the spelling."

"So, it was a win-win. Awesome."

"We always worked things out."

"Well, it's beautiful." Blake's tone is soft, caring, and it envelops me in comfort.

"What is?"

"All of it. The name origin story. The tattoo. Not just the image, but the meaning behind it. I'm sure your husband would be happy to know how you honored his memory."

I chuckle and shake my head. "He'd probably scold me for wasting my money on such a frivolous thing."

"No. I bet he'd love you even more for it."

"Can you hand me the needle nose pliers, please?" Blake asks from underneath my sink.

"Hmm?" I reply as I've not been listening to a word he's said. I've been too busy fantasizing about licking the muscles on his abdomen peeking out from under his shirt.

Blake comes out from under the sink. "The pliers, Maggie?"

"Oh, yeah, sorry. Here you go." I hand him the pliers, and he raises his eyebrows with a knowing look as he slides back into the cabinet.

I put my burning face in my hand, beyond mortified.

"Okay, I think it's good to go. Let's test it out," Blake says, turning on the faucet. He bends down to look into the cabinet. "No leaks, that's a good sign. Now, for the real test." He reaches for the switch, and I brace myself for a barrage of shrapnel, but as he turns it on, the disposal quietly churns. No metal flies out, no grinding noises, just a smooth whir.

I exhale deeply. "Thank you so much, Blake. I don't know what I would have done without a disposal for a week."

"No problem. It was my pleasure."

"I feel bad for taking up your whole afternoon. Can I at least pay you for your time?"

He holds up his hands. "No. I don't mind, really. You paid for all the materials. All I did was install the thing."

"That's still work. There must be something I can give you as a payment." In the back of my mind, a voice tells me I've stumbled onto the beginnings of a porn. He fixes my plumbing and I have to pay him somehow.

"How about you come over and watch a movie with me tonight?"

Aaaaannnnd now I'm in the porn. "What?"

"Well, you said earlier, you're probably going to fall asleep watching Hallmark movies, so instead of us watching two movies alone, why don't you come over and we'll watch one movie together?" He shrugs and shoves his hands in his pockets. It's a change from earlier today. He's been so confident and masculine, but right now, he seems downright scared.

My heart races. He did it. He finally asked me out. The elation inside me sucks all the moisture from my mouth, so I stand here with my lips parted, not saying a word.

He holds up his hands. "I'm not trying anything here, I promise. It's two neighbors enjoying a movie together, that's it. You seem tense, like you could use a little R & R."

I swallow my premature elation down. He didn't ask me on another date. He asked me to hang out like friends would. I'm such an idiot.

But he's right. Almost being impaled by what probably used to be a fork, definitely made me tense, but spending the afternoon with Blake has risen my heart rate substantially, so while I'm not sure spending more time with him is the answer, this is as close to a date as I've come since Christmas. I can't say no. "Um, sure. What time?"

"Is eight o'clock too late?"

"No, eight is fine. Should I bring anything? Snacks, or something?"

"Just yourself," he says with a wink, and my stomach flips.

"Okay. I'll see you later."

I let Blake out and shut the door, sagging against it while I take deep breaths to calm my heart. It's not a date. It's not a date. It's *not* a date. Is it? Now I am definitely putting on some makeup.

Chapter Twelve

At 7:55 p.m., I'm standing at my front door, gauging how long the walk to Blake's house is. It can't take more than a minute or two, so if I leave now, I'll be early.

Is that bad? Will I seem eager? I should wait a couple more minutes and be fashionably late. Will that send the wrong signal, though? I have no idea what I'm doing.

Shaking off the frustration of being clueless, I leave the house at 7:58 p.m. and knock on Blake's door at 7:59 p.m. Not too early, not late at all, perfect timing, I hope. As soon as I knock, I hear Oscar barking and Blake yelling at him to stop.

The door opens and Blake greets me with soft eyes and his warm smile. "Hi," he says quietly.

"Hi," I reply, returning the smile.

Oscar pushes past Blake to jump up and down at me. He licks my hands and knees as he circles in between the jumps.

"Oscar! Get down!" Blake grabs Oscar's collar. "I'm so sorry, Maggie."

"It's fine. He's just happy to see me," I say as I squat down to Oscar's level and scratch behind his ears.

"Well, that makes two of us," Blake says under his breath, but the words are clear. I don't draw attention to it, I simply soak up the warmth his statement creates in my chest. "Come on in." Blake steps back to let me inside, and I get a knee-buckling whiff of his cologne as I pass him.

The layout of his house is similar to mine, although it's slightly smaller. A staircase runs up the wall to our right. He leads me through a sitting area which bleeds into a dining room with the kitchen around the corner to the right. The kitchen opens up into the living room, which makes my eyes widen.

There's a full wrap-around couch starting on one wall, jutting out to separate the kitchen from the living room. The flat-screen television mounted on the wall is at least eighty inches and flanked on either side by surround sound speakers. Professional lighting illuminates the built-in shelving in the corners of the room with soft blue-colored light bulbs. Beautiful graphite and charcoal landscape artwork hang in various places. It's enough to tantalize the brain, but not overwhelm it.

"Blake," I say quietly. "This is...amazing."

He sidles up next to me after putting Oscar outside, his hands in his pockets. "Thanks. I put in a lot of work to make this space what it is. Nice to have someone here to appreciate it. I don't think Oscar is as impressed with it as you are."

I turn my head to find him gazing down at me with a look of adoration on his face. We stare into each other's eyes for a moment before Blake clears his throat awkwardly. "Um, would you like a drink? Water, soda? I have beer, if you'd like one."

"I'll have a soda, thanks."

"Coming right up." He disappears into the kitchen. "I got Dr. Pepper. That's your favorite, right?"

A flutter rushes through me at his thoughtfulness. "Um, yeah. It is, thank you."

"Do you like it in a glass or straight out of the can?" His head is ducked into the refrigerator as he asks, and my eyes can't help but stare at his ass.

"The can is fine."

"Okay, suit yourself," he says, handing me a frosty soda. "Cheers." He clinks his bottle against the aluminum can in my hand as I crack it open.

"What are we cheers-ing to?"

He gives me a sideways look and one side of his mouth ticks up. "To neighbors becoming friends."

My heart skips a beat. "I'll drink to that," I say, then tip my drink to my lips. "So, what are we watching tonight?"

"Well, I was going to watch this documentary on black market trading, but we can watch something else if it's not your style."

I scrunch my nose. "Doesn't sound like something I'd watch."

"What about superhero movies, then? The new Marvel one is out, and you had your Scarlet Witch costume down pretty good last Halloween." He rakes me over, as if recalling my outfit.

I must have made quite the impression. "Oh, that was all Dylan's idea."

"Well, it was a great idea." He stares at me a moment before blinking a few times and taking a drink. "Those movies kind of have everything. Action, suspense, romance." His voice cracks on the last word and he turns his gaze to the floor.

I pinch my lips, not wanting to embarrass him further. "Sure, sounds good to me."

I take a seat on the couch, right in the spot where it curves so it cuddles me. Sitting all the way against the back, my feet barely hang off the edge of the over sized cushion. Blake settles down a full cushion away. He's far enough to emphasize the fact he's "not trying anything," as he said earlier, but close enough I can see him from the corner of my eye.

"What about Oscar? Weren't you two supposed to watch a movie tonight? I don't want to steal his place."

Blake frowns. "You want Oscar in here? After his antics on the porch, I figured he should hang out in the yard."

I shake my head. "I don't mind."

"Okay." An easy grin spreads across his face. Then, as if he realizes he's smiling, he blinks and furrows his brow. "You asked for it."

I laugh as he gets up to let Oscar inside. Oscar jumps onto the couch and settles on my other side so he's not impeding my nearness to Blake. I pull my knees up, tucking my feet to the side to nuzzle them under Oscar. When Blake sits back down, he presses play on the remote, and as the epic intro music to the Marvel brand starts, I relax a bit more. I've watched so many of these movies with Dylan, this is almost comforting, but I miss snuggling with my baby.

Maybe Blake would snuggle with me.

That will definitely send a signal. One I'm ready to send, but I'm not sure Blake wants, so I'll have to be content to snuggle with Oscar for now.

Halfway through the movie, Blake pauses it and stands up, "I'm going to have another beer. Do you want another soda?"

I shake my head. "No, thank you. One is enough."

Blake disappears into the kitchen, and I hear bottles clinking, the snap and spurt of the cap being shucked, then he's back at the couch. This time, though, he's on the cushion next to mine. Still far enough away to be nonthreatening, but close enough if I reached my hand out, I could touch his. I won't, but I could if I wanted. My toes wiggle so much under Oscar's soft coat, he gets up and settles onto another cushion.

Blake arches an eyebrow at Oscar, and hands me a bottle of water. "Here. Water's better than nothing."

"Thank you." My cheeks heat and I turn my gaze down to Oscar who's fallen asleep. Traitor.

The movie resumes and soon explosions and acrobatics ensue, keeping the room anything from silent. It's entertaining, to say the least, but my attention is elsewhere.

As the credits roll, Blake turns and asks, "So, what did you think?"

I don't really know how to answer. I was only watching the movie part of the time. I was more focused on Blake in my peripheral vision. He fidgeted with his beer bottle a lot, shifted his position on the couch at least once every ten minutes, and when he sat down between the cushions, he was as stiff as a board. I couldn't tell if he was looking at me since I was trying not to look at him, but there were a few moments I thought I saw his head turn.

"It was good," I say, hoping it's enough to convince him.

"Still not your style, huh?"

"What? No, it was good. I've watched a lot of these with Dylan. I enjoyed this one." What I saw of it, at least.

Blake nods silently.

I hope he believes me. I look over at the clock, it's 11:46pm. "I should get home, it's late."

"Oh yeah, sure. I'll walk you home." A twinge of disappointment hangs in his words.

"Blake, you don't have to do that. It's all of four houses away."

"Which means I won't have far to walk back. Besides, my mom would roll over in her grave if she knew I let a woman walk home alone in the dark."

"Oh, I'm sorry. I didn't know.""Don't be." He puts a hand up. "It's been a long time. But she raised me right, and I'm going to honor her by doing what I was taught. So, come on, I'll walk you."

The walk up the street is the most thrilling minute of my year. Blake walks close enough for our arms to brush every so often. At first, I think it's because the sidewalk is too narrow, but after the fourth time, I realize it's intentional. Or maybe I hope it is.

When we arrive at my house, I walk up the porch steps while Blake stands at the bottom. Before I put the key in the lock, I turn around. "Thank you. Tonight was fun. I definitely feel more relaxed."

"Good, mission accomplished." He shifts his stance, puts his hands in his pockets, and drops his head slightly. "Um, maybe we could do it again next weekend?"

"What?"

"Unless you have plans or something. I've never seen a Hallmark movie, remember?"

I'm shocked. He wants to do it again? So maybe it *was* a date. "Well, um, sure. I mean, I don't ever have plans, so I'd love to be your first time."

Blake snorts out a chuckle, but swallows it and pinches his lips into a line like he's fighting a smile.

My cheeks burn, probably glowing bright red. Good thing it's dark. "I meant, your first Hallmark movie."

Blake lets out the hearty laugh he was holding back, but it doesn't feel aimed at me. More like with me, though I'm not laughing. "Sounds good, though I'm not sure how I'll explain a Hallmark movie on my watch list."

"What do you mean?"

"I share my account with a friend of mine, so when he sees what I'm watching, I'm sure I'll hear all about it."

"Well, then I'll bring one." I fold my arms, confident in my solution. "That way, you don't have to worry about it."

"You have them on DVD?"

"Even better... VHS."

"Seriously!?"

Now it's my turn to laugh. "No, not really. I wanted to see your reaction, that's all. I'll bring the movie and the drinks."

"No, Maggie. You don't have to-"

I put my hand up this time. "Nope. You're hosting. And besides, I have a feeling you might need a few drinks to get through one of these movies."

Blake takes his hands out of his pockets. "Alright, deal. Same time?"

"Perfect."

"Goodnight, Maggie."

"Goodnight." As I open the door, I glance behind me to see Blake still on the bottom step, watching me walk inside. It isn't until I shut the door and look out the peephole, I see him turn around.

CHAPTER THIRTEEN

T he next day is Sunday and I sleep in. Like, actually sleep in. When I finally roll over and look at the clock, it's almost nine.

I can't believe I slept this late!

Although, slept is a strong word. Even though I had a wonderful night with Blake, a nightmare still came in full force. I was up for a while afterward, but when thoughts of Blake entered my mind, his image coaxed me back to sleep.

Blake. I'm still reeling from our night. I mean, all we did was watch a movie, but I enjoyed being with him. Our walk home was nice, too. My skin still tingles in the places our arms touched.

I wonder what it would feel like if we touched other places?

As I clench my thighs together, my heart sinks when Blake's voice echoes in my mind, n*eighbors becoming friends.* That's all he wants to be.

He didn't make a move last night. If the movie thing was a date, why didn't he kiss me goodnight? And even if the movie wasn't a date, why didn't he ask me on one? He had plenty of opportunities, and I'm fairly sure I made my interest clear.

Didn't I?

I sigh, my body sagging into the mattress. Blake's the nicest, most genuine man I've met in a long time. He also happens to be the handsomest, and I bet dating him would be amazing, but I have to face the fact that *I* shut the door on us. Our movie night was nothing more than a way to blow off some steam. He helped me with a house issue, and we hung out afterward. As *friends*.

The buzzing of my phone on the side table interrupts my pity party. "Hello?"

"Hey, what are you doing?" Michelle asks.

"Laying in bed."

"Are you sick or something? You're always up before the crack of dawn."

"No, not sick. Just tired and feeling lazy. No kids, remember?"

"Oh yeah. They're at camp." She sounds excited. "Well, how about we hang out then?"

"Yeah, but not today. I've got some things to do, and since I didn't get up at the crack of da–"

"Before the crack."

"Right, before. I've got to get going."

"Well, how about dinner tomorrow night? You're off on Tuesday, right? We can go get Mexican and have margaritas. My treat."

Spinach enchiladas do sound good. "Sure, sounds great. I'll text you when I'm off work."

"Yay! Okay, see you then. Bye, Mags."

I've got to get out of this bed and do something to take my mind off Blake. I think I'll start with a workout. That will at least get my blood pumping and maybe give me the energy to get my day started.

Monday brings work, which helps ease my obsession over my neighbor. I dive into my paperwork, grateful for the distraction. I'm even happy to hear Abbey back to her old self, with her endless complaints, so my mind isn't flooded with thoughts of Blake.

At the end of the day, I'm feeling much better. Even if I think Blake and I will only be friends, I can at least accept it. He's still a nice guy and having a friend who's only a few houses away wouldn't hurt. When Michelle was my next-door neighbor, she and I used to hang out all the time. Granted, she's a married woman, whereas Blake's a single man, but it's harmless.

Isn't it?

I take out my phone and text Michelle I'm leaving work. She responds that she's running late and will meet me at the restaurant, which means I'll have at least twenty minutes to munch on chips and salsa before she gets there.

The server checks on me for a third time, asking if I need anything besides water, when I see Michelle walk through the door.

"Sorry, I got held up," she says, plopping into the booth.

"No problem, but can we order?"

Michelle nods and tells the server to bring us both house margaritas with extra limes, and our favorite appetizer of more chips, but with queso this time.

"So, what's new with you, Mags? What have you been up to lately?" Michelle asks, picking through the chip crumbs I've left in the basket.

"Not much. Enjoying a quiet house." I pause a moment, pursing my lips. "That's not true. I miss the kids."

"I bet you do. Are you sleeping okay without them at home?"

I snort. "When do I ever sleep okay?"

"Alright, I'll rephrase. Are you sleeping any worse without them?"

"No, not really any worse, but certainly not any better. I was hoping when I went part-time and had more time for myself, the nightmares might ease up, but they haven't. I guess moving wasn't the answer."

"Speaking of, how's the house? Things okay there?"

"Yeah, it's been fine. The spring was rough, though. Lots of issues. The handyman I found is great, although he went out of town this week and my garbage disposal blew up on Saturday."

Michelle gasps. "Oh no. What did you do?"

"Well, do you remember that guy, Blake, I told you about?"

Michelle's eyes widen. "The hot one who walks his dog a lot?" she asks as her lips close around the straw of her water.

I roll my eyes. "Yeah, him. I know I said I wouldn't ask him for help, but I didn't have a choice this time. He came over, took me to Home Depot, and replaced it for me." "So, he did fix your pipes!" Michelle takes her drink from the server, who's trying hard to contain his laughter.

In utter embarrassment, I order my meal. Michelle orders hers and we sit in silence a moment while we sip our cocktails. I wiggle my toes in my shoes as I contemplate telling her the rest of the story. "He and I actually hung out afterward and watched a movie together."

Michelle nearly spits out her drink. "What!?"

"It wasn't anything special." I pick up a chip and stir the queso with it. "He asked if I wanted to watch a movie, and I said yes. What's the big deal?"

She dabs her lips with her napkin. "The big deal is, you hung out with a *man*. And a hot one, at that! This is huge for you. I thought you were off relationships after Charlie."

A lump forms in my throat at the mention of his name. I swallow it away with some tequila. "It was just a movie. It's not a *relationship*, Michelle." *Though that's what Blake called it.*

"Sounds like the start of one. Do you want it to be?"

I bite my lip, nodding. "I think I'm ready."

"Think?"

"I mean, the feeling of betraying Charlie is still there, but it's much more muted when I'm with Blake. He's got this way of bringing down my walls. Like, he can read me no matter how much I try to cover. At first, it was scary, and I didn't want it, which is why I said no when he asked me out."

Michelle's eyelids peel back. "He asked you out!? When?" She leans over the table, smacking me on the shoulder. "Why didn't you tell me?"

"Ow." I rub the spot, but keep my eyes on hers. "Back in December, and I didn't tell you because I knew you'd go on about how I should get back out there. I wasn't ready then."

"But you are now?" Michelle sits back against the booth and folds her arms.

"Yeah, I am." A smile creeps across my lips, but falls when I think about our movie night not being a date. "But I think I missed my chance."

"Why?"

"Because I told him no in December, and he hasn't once tried to ask me out again."

"You just said he asked you to watch a movie with him."

"Exactly. We watched a movie, as *friends.* His words. It wasn't a date and he didn't ask about going on one. All he did was invite me over to watch another movie."

Michelle groans, her head dropping back so she's looking at the ceiling. "Mags, come on." She lifts her head to meet my gaze. "Even if the movie wasn't a date, why would he ask you to do another one if he's not into you?"

I shrug. "Maybe he's being nice? He knows the kids are gone for a while, so he was just trying to give me something to do."

"Yeah, him." Her eyebrows bob as she takes a drink of margarita. After she swallows, she sighs. "Mags, this guy seems like he'd be great for you, and from where I'm sitting, it sounds like he's interested. Have you tried asking him out? Maybe he doesn't want to push, but if you take the lead, he'll bite."

"I haven't actually asked him, but I've been flirting." I crinkle my nose.

"What's that face for?"

"My version of flirting is what Sydney would call 'cringe.'" I drop my elbow onto the table, resting my chin in my hand. "I have no idea how to flirt, so I bet Blake doesn't even know I'm doing it."

"Then come out and say it!"

"But what if he's not interested anymore? What if he's just being a good neighbor?"

"Then you enjoy having a hot guy friend and move on. But you need to try, or you might miss out on something wonderful."

I chew on my lip, sitting back up, my hands falling to my lap. "Okay. I'll say something next Saturday."

"Good. Now where the hell is our food?"

Tuesday morning brings a whirlwind of thoughts. I wake up with the sun, a late start for me due to the margaritas from the night before, but I instantly replay my conversation with Michelle. I'm glad she thinks Blake would be good for me, since I think so, too.

I close my eyes and take a second to imagine what being with Blake would be like. How his strong arms would wrap around me, what I would smell or hear as I'm snuggled against his firm chest. My heart picks up speed. I know what his voice sounds like, but what would his breath feel like on my neck? What would his lips feel like pressed against my own? How would he taste?

The butterflies come so fast, I almost vomit.

This sort of reaction is something I haven't felt in over a decade. Charlie was the last man to elicit it from me, and I haven't met anyone else who's come remotely close. Until now.

A thickness forms in my throat as I recall Charlie's and my first date. We were broke college sophomores, but he pooled his money to take me to a fancy Italian restaurant. He tried his best, but he spilled wine all over me, dripped spaghetti sauce on his shirt, and accidentally tripped a server when he got out of the booth. After that, all our dates were take-out.

Some people might think it's silly, but it's how we fell in love. He gave me his time and attention instead of trying to impress me with flashy things.

Blake's the same way. Aside from being the hottest man I've had a chance with, he's also the most genuine. The only one I've opened up to in years. Letting my guard down around him is so easy. I've shared information with him which people at work don't even know. Like the story of my tattoo.

As refreshing as it is, it scares me. I don't usually get this far. The guilt of betraying Charlie rips apart my stomach if I have the slightest attraction to a guy. I know Charlie isn't coming back, but I haven't allowed myself to be intimate with a man, physically or emotionally, because my conscience smacks me upside the head. Everyone says Charlie would want me to be happy. He would want me to live my life, but would it include sleeping with another man? Would Charlie be happy knowing I'm replacing all the memories of him with *new* memories of a *new* guy?

I don't think so.

We never had that conversation. I never wanted to think about a life without Charlie, and I'm sure he didn't want to talk about me being with anyone else. We probably should have, though. It would make things easier right now, but it's not something you think will ever happen.

Maybe it's a good thing Blake and I haven't gone on an actual date. What if it's amazing and it replaces the memory of my first date with Charlie? What if I fall so hard for him, I let my memories of Charlie fade away? I'm afraid of losing Charlie forever.

I can see it happening. Blake's almost too good to be true. When I told him about Charlie, I heard genuine compassion in his voice. He actively listened to my story of the tattoo and why we moved. He seemed like he actually cared. He even sounded concerned about the kids having to deal with it.

And I've never once felt uncomfortable in his presence. Nervous? Yes, but scared of him? No way. Sure, he may eyeball me like a tasty snack every now and then, but I've never felt like I should keep my guard up. He's never given me any indication of foul intentions, and he's always been the perfect gentleman.

I need to find out how he feels, even if it's not the same way I do.

A heavy sigh escapes me. This is all so confusing and scary, but maybe it's a sign of me being onto something good. The worthwhile things in life involve risk.

Am I willing to risk the total embarrassment of being rejected by Blake? Or worse, am I willing to risk having to face every anxiety I've had for the last three years if he *is* interested in me?

I think the answer to both of those questions is yes, and I owe it to myself to find out. I can picture myself and Blake in a relationship. I just hope he can, too.

Saturday finally arrives and I'm a bouncing ball of nerves. I want eight o'clock to come so badly, but at the same time, I don't want it to come at all. I've been thinking all week about how I'm going to ask Blake out, and I've got nothing.

I don't know how to do this. Charlie asked me out in college, and I never had to worry about it after that. The dates I've been on since Charlie died were set up by Michelle. I don't know the first thing about this process. Should I be blunt or coy? And what the hell does being coy even mean?

Ugh, I'm out of my element.

Two workouts, a long shower, an even longer walk, marathon cleaning of my kitchen and my bathrooms, then finishing with vacuuming does nothing to ease my anxiety. On the one hand, it takes my mind off the time, but it only makes it go faster and I'm not sure that's what I want.

At six-thirty, I'm sitting at my kitchen table pushing around my dinner with my fork. I can't eat, I'm so frazzled. Maybe I should have another glass of wine.

Crap! I'm supposed to bring the drinks tonight!

I dash out to the liquor store, but end up having to go to three to find the beer I want. When I get home, it's nearly seven-thirty and I still have to pick out a movie to take. I thumb through my selection of Hallmark classics, trying to find one that's not too cheesy. Like that's possible. There are so many I love, but I don't know if they're good for Blake's first time.

Should I pick a holiday themed one? Or your basic big city gal falls for the country boy trope? I mean, they all sort of follow the same plot. I'm overthinking this.

Just grab one, Maggie.

I put entirely too much effort into choosing a movie and end up being a few minutes late to Blake's house. When I knock on the door, I'm expecting to hear barking, but I don't. My stomach drops and my heart hammers in my chest. He probably forgot and made other plans because this *isn't* a date. I've worked myself up for nothing.

Before the tears can well in my eyes, the lock clicks and the door opens to reveal Blake with relief in his eyes. "Hey. I thought maybe you forgot."

I hike a shoulder to my ear. "Sorry, I couldn't decide which movie to bring."

He chuckles. "Are there really that many to choose from?" He steps aside and extends his arm in a gesture for me to enter.

"Oh, you have no idea. And I had to make sure I picked the right one for your first time," I say, stepping past him and into the entryway. This time, I purposefully take a deep inhale of his cologne, and it's still just as intoxicating. "Though, I was expecting Oscar to greet me, again."

"Oh no, after last week, I learned my lesson. I put him outside before you got here."

I pout. "I was kind of looking forward to my couch buddy."

"If you want him crowding you, I'll let him in here in a minute." He leads me around the corner to the kitchen. "What did you bring to drink?"

I set the six-pack on the counter and hand a bottle to Blake, taking one for myself. "I hope you like it. It's one Charlie and I used to drink together." I feel the sad smile creep across my lips, then the guilt hits my gut. Is it wrong of me to share our beer with another man?

Blake keeps his kind, brown eyes on mine, comforting me from a distance. "I'm sure I will." He pops his bottle cap off and holds his hand out for mine. After our drinks are opened, he walks toward the living room with me following behind. "So, how was your week?"

"It was fine. Work was busy, which is good. And I got a letter from the kids. It made my day." My sadness melts away at the thought of their handwritten letters.

"I bet it did. How are they doing?"

I love how he asks about my kids. "They're having a great time. They always do. I miss them every year, but they love it so much, I can't not let them go."

"That's what a good mom does." Blake's eyes soften into mine. A moment passes and he clears his throat. "Have a seat. I'll let Oscar in."

With my drink in hand, I sit in the curve of the couch again, my feet dangling off the edge of the cushion. Oscar comes careening around the couch to leap onto my lap. I laugh as I struggle to get him to settle next to me. Once he's calm, I glance at Blake, who's looking at me like I belong right where I am.

My lip twitches, but instead of asking him out, I sip my beer. "How was your week?"

"Pretty boring. Just work, really." He rubs the back of his neck. "My birthday was the 13th, so me and a couple friends had drinks at the bar. Nothing special."

"Well, happy belated birthday. If I had known, I'd have got you a card or something."

He shrugs. "Thanks, but it's not a big deal. I've never been big on my birthday, and year twenty-nine isn't anything to write home about."

Blake pops in the movie and takes a seat, sitting on the cushion right next to me. Not close enough for us to be touching, but close enough for me to notice. It may be something harmless, a coincidence, but to me, it's a sign of him wanting me. Or at least wanting to be close to me.

As the movie wears on, it becomes clear Blake is not a fan of Hallmark movies. I have to laugh as he points out all the cheesy lines, the cliches, and even has something to say about the romantic kiss the main characters finally share. "Really? That's the big climax? The kiss everyone knows is going to happen?" He sighs, though I think it's more of a groan. "I think I need another drink. Do you want one?"

"You know what? I will have another, thank you." As he leaves the couch, I giggle to myself. If he hates this one, then he definitely won't like any of the others.

When Blake returns, he hands me my drink, but doesn't look before he sits and ends up sitting so close to me, I feel his body heat on my skin. Again, it might be an innocent oversight of his, but to me, it's purposeful.

The movie ends and Blake lets out a sigh of relief. "Well...that was...a new experience for me. You actually like watching these?"

"I do. I know they're cheesy and predictable, but they're happy. Everything works out in the end and everyone gets what they want. I don't know, it helps to ease the pain of real life, y'know?"

I turn to look at Blake, who is already looking at me with sympathy in his big brown eyes. They soften as he smiles, and I can see him taking in the features of my face. He's trying to read me.

"I get that," he says, the gentle tone of his voice creating a warmth in my chest.

With a sharp exhale, I turn back to the TV. "Charlie always hated them too, it's okay."

"Well, at least I know Charlie and I have two things in common. Hatred of Hallmark movies, and love for this beer. It's really good, thank you for bringing it."

"You're welcome, I'm glad you like it."

We sit for several moments, simply looking at each other. Maybe it's the romance lingering in the air, or maybe it's the alcohol, but something prevents me from turning away. The deep brown irises of Blake's eyes pull me in. They blanket me in comfort and whisper everything will be alright. He has the Hallmark movie of eyes.

Ask him right now, Maggie! My mouth opens, but no sound comes out, so I shake my head and glance at the clock. "It's late, I should go."

"Yep, I'll...uh, I'll walk you again."

The walk home is the same as last week. We walk side by side, our arms brushing with every step. Now I *know* this is intentional.

When we get to my house, I start to climb the steps, but I stop on the first one, which puts me at eye level with Blake. "Thank you for another fun night. Sorry you didn't enjoy the movie," I joke.

"It's okay. Now I know to avoid them, so thank you."

I laugh, but it's shaky as I drop my gaze to the ground, dragging my flip flop across the concrete to keep myself from wiggling my toes. I lick my lips. "Blake, I was wondering..."

"If I want to do the same time next week?" Blake asks, a hopefulness to his tone. "Absolutely."

"What? You want to do this again?" Emotions war within me. My heart wants to sink, since it's not technically a date, but the idea of spending more time with him sends me reeling.

"Well, I certainly don't want to watch another Hallmark movie, but I'd like to watch something with you. If you want to, that is. I thought maybe we could make this a weekly thing, until your kids come back, of course."

Excitement wins the battle, bubbling within me. "That sounds good, but are you really okay giving up your Saturday nights to watch movies with your neighbor? Wouldn't you have more fun hanging with your friends?"

Blake shrugs. "There's six other nights I can do stuff with them. Saturdays are for you."

My heart flutters, my mouth going dry. There's no way I can stop my toes from wiggling now. "Alright. Saturdays it is," I choke out.

"Awesome. We can switch who chooses the movie every week and–"

"I promise no more Hallmark movies."

A deep chuckle rumbles out of Blake. "Thanks. I'll see you next Saturday. Or maybe out and about this week." He takes a step, narrowing the gap between us. "Goodnight, Maggie." He tips up on his toes to lean forward, and kisses me gently on the cheek, his scruff brushing my skin. The sensation of his lips on me shoots a wave of heat through my body. The kiss only lasts for a second or two, but it feels like eternity. As he backs away, the expression on his face is one of accomplishment, but his eyes burn with longing.

My heart is about to leap out of my chest. My whole body is on fire and my stomach is doing double gainers. I'm doing my best to control my breathing, but it's attempting to stop completely. I manage to squeak out a quiet, "Goodnight."

Once inside, I lean against my front door and put my hand to my cheek. I close my eyes and the tears fall happily. I can't wait to tell Michelle all about this.

Chapter Fourteen

"**S**o you chickened out?"

"I didn't chicken out, Michelle." I drum my fingers on my kitchen table as I tuck my phone between my shoulder and ear so I can take a drink of my lunchtime coffee. "There wasn't a good time to ask."

"Mags, you're telling me you sat through a ninety-minute movie, and you never had a chance to say 'Hey, Blake, want to go get sushi sometime?'"

A laugh escapes me. "Is that what you're having for lunch?"

"Yeah, you jealous?"

"Extremely." I sigh, rolling my eyes and letting them land on my plain, boring grilled cheese sandwich and carrot sticks. "The timing never felt right."

"Then forget asking and jump his bones. You don't have to worry about birth control anyway."

I run my fingers along my hysterectomy scar. "Thanks for the reminder."

"I'm just saying, you're thinking too hard about this. Dive in. You might be surprised by what happens."

"He did ask me for another movie night." I drag a carrot stick through the hummus. "I'll give myself one more chance to say something."

Michelle groans. "Mags, *that* was your chance."

"What was?" I ask as I snap the carrot between my teeth.

"Him asking you for another movie. You should have suggested having dinner or something beforehand."

I smack my forehead with my palm. "Oh, my God. You're right. Why didn't I think of that?"

"Well, worse comes to worst, you can use it tomorrow when he walks you home again. Unless you find your spine and ask him earlier."

Swallowing my carrot, I chew on my lower lip, furrowing my brow and wiggling my toes.

"What's on your mind?" Michelle's voice breaks the silence.

"Why didn't he ask me to dinner?"

I hear Michelle's breath bleed through the phone speaker. "Mags... I don't know. Maybe he's treading lightly to make sure you're okay with it? You did turn him down, remember?"

"Of course I remember." I push my plate of food away and pick up my coffee. "Or maybe he just wants to be friends."

"I doubt it."

"Why?"

"After everything you've told me, I'd bet a million bucks he's into you. He probably wants to be sure so he doesn't get hurt again."

"I didn't tell you... everything."

"Ooh, something else happened?"

I swirl my coffee, a smile creeping onto my lips. "He kissed me," I say quickly before tipping my cup up for a drink.

"What!? Oh, Mags, you've gotta give me more."

"It wasn't anything big, a goodnight peck on the cheek." I put my palm to my face where Blake's lips touched my skin, the feeling lingering as I recall the moment.

"This changes things. I'd bet a hundred million bucks he's into you."

I drop my hand back to the table, drumming my fingers again. "What if it meant nothing?"

"Seriously, Mags?"

"I can see the look on your face right now." The image of Michelle's one-sided smirk with one eyebrow arched pops into my mind.

"Is it the one I use to judge you with? Because that's the one I'm making." She sighs. "No one kisses someone else for no reason. This isn't Europe, where they kiss each other hello and goodbye."

"Maybe his parents were French."

Michelle laughs. "Okay, but what on Earth could possibly make you think the kiss meant nothing?"

"Well, this afternoon, I went to get the mail, and I saw him walking Oscar down the other side of the street. He waved, but then he just went home."

"So?"

"So, any other time, he would've crossed the street to talk. He didn't this time." I expected him to jog across the street and at least say hi. It would have been nice for him to scoop me up in his arms and swing me around in the air. Maybe plant his lips on mine while he pushes me up against the mailbox–

"Maybe he had to take a dump."

I nearly spit out my coffee. "Thanks for that, Michelle."

"I'm just saying, there are a ton of reasons he didn't come chat. Needing the bathroom is an obvious one, but maybe something for work came up."

"He's a landscaper. That's not exactly a job where emergencies happen."

"Okay, maybe his mom called."

"His mom died."

"Jesus, okay." Michelle draws out the syllables. "Mags, what is this about? Why are you trying so hard to play this down? Is it because of Charlie?"

I shift in my chair. Even though I'm not under Michelle's scrutinizing gaze, I can imagine how she'd be looking at me right now. "I keep wondering how he'd feel about the situation. There's a lot of guilt associated with all this."

I picture him watching me with Blake and I feel how much it would hurt him. Not that either of us believed in those sorts of things. We weren't religious and didn't have much thought on the afterlife, but with years of beliefs being drilled into us through our parents and society in general, it's hard not to think about.

"Mags, Charlie would want you to be happy. I mean, I'm sure he wouldn't be sitting on the sidelines, cheering Blake on as he's balls deep inside you, but if Blake makes you happy, then Charlie would be on board."

I chuckle at Michelle's lewdness. "Why do I tell you things?"

"Because if you didn't, you'd never get out of your head." She sighs. "Mags, I know you're scared. This is a huge step for you, but I think this is a defense mechanism."

"I'm trying to stay rational. I don't want to read into things too much. What if I'm taking all these little instances and making them into something bigger than they are?"

"And what if they're exactly what they sound like?"

My heart flutters at the notion. It's like I shook my Magic 8 ball after asking if my crush likes me, and all signs point to yes.

Saturday night I'm standing on Blake's porch at 7:50 p.m. I'm early, but I don't care. I want to see Blake. I want to dive in like Michelle said. Okay, maybe I'm not going to throw myself at him, but I at least want to test the waters and ask him to dinner.

Start simple, and go from there.

When I knock on the door, Oscar begins barking, and I hear Blake yelling something. It's taking him longer than normal to open the door. Oscar is nowhere in sight when he does.

"Sorry," Blake says, hiking his thumb over his shoulder. "I had to put Oscar out. I didn't want him jumping all over you again..." His voice trails off as his eyes rove up and down my body. "You look... nice."

"Oh, thank you." I hadn't even given two thoughts as to what I'm wearing. It was such a hot day, I put on my favorite summer dress. The halter top style is comfortable enough to wear around the house on really hot days, but nice enough to go out in public. "I threw this on because it was so hot today."

Blake swallows. "Yeah, it is, um, was– It *was* really hot." He clears his throat. "Come on in."

I can't help but smile as I cross the threshold. As Blake follows me into the kitchen, I set a six-pack of beer on the counter.

"So, what are we drinking this week?" Blake asks, tapping his palm on the tops of the beer bottles.

"Oh, nothing special. I asked the clerk what was good and he suggested this. I hope it doesn't suck."

"I'm sure it will be great." Blake takes two bottles and grabs an opener from a drawer. Cracking both open, he hands me mine and our fingers graze slightly, sending shock waves through my body.

"Cheers," he says, clinking our bottles together.

"And what are we cheers-ing to this week?"

Blake's eyes soften, the irises growing darker as he tilts his head to the side, and says, "To new beginnings."

I nod as we both take a sip, assuming he's talking about our movie nights becoming a new thing, but part of me wonders if he means something else. Maybe "hopes" is a better word for it.

I take my normal seat on the couch, waiting for Blake to sit right next to me, but he doesn't. Instead, he sits a full cushion away. My heart sinks.

"Um, can you let Oscar in?" I could really use my snuggle buddy right now.

"Oh, yeah. Sure thing."

After Oscar dashes through the door and we have our ceremonial greeting, he snuggles up next to me, taking up the gap between me and Blake. I'm trying my hardest not to read into things, but it feels like the universe is telling me to keep my distance.

Blake presses play on the remote and we settle in to *just* watch the movie. "I hope you don't mind, I picked *The Gray Man*. I don't think it's scary or anything, but maybe suspenseful. Is that okay?"

Why not? I'm living in suspense right now. "I'm sure I can handle it."

Halfway through the movie, Blake goes for his usual second beer and Oscar follows, going to the back door and barking. Blake lets him out, but the whole time Blake's gone from the couch, all ninety seconds, I fight back the intrusive thoughts.

Blake kissed me... On the cheek, but it was a kiss all the same. Another fact is he keeps making movie dates with me. Are they *dates,* though? If they aren't, then why did he kiss me? Pity? Too much to drink? Maybe it's something he does with people he's more familiar with?

I have no idea, but the more I think about it, the more I talk myself out of asking him to dinner.

When Blake returns, he sits right next to me. Like, *right* next to me. Almost as close as Oscar was. Part way on my cushion, part way on his own, the heat from his body radiates off him, warming my right side. Hints of sage and juniper waft across the air, tantalizing my senses, as he gets comfortable.

We sit like this for some time, but I notice Blake is pretty rigid, not his usual relaxed self. His thumb picks at the label on his bottle and he seems to be chewing on the inside of his lip. Something is quite obviously bothering him.

And I'm not waiting for the movie to end to find out. "Blake, are you alright?"

"Hmm?" He glances over at me, then back at the TV, blinking several times. "Yeah, I'm fine. Why?"

"Well, you seem a little tense. You're destroying that label pretty quickly and you've sighed at least a dozen times in the last ten minutes. Is something wrong?"

He sighs again, but this one is the biggest yet. "I wanted to talk to you... about... last week." His voice wavers. "You know, when I walked you home?" He's not looking at me at all.

Oh no... "Okay, what about it?" Please say anything but the word "mistake." I don't think it's humanly possible, but my heart races even faster. I know my breaths are short, but I'm trying my hardest to control them. If he even so much as mutters the word, I'll burst into tears.

"Well, I want to apologize. I shouldn't have kissed you–"

There it is. I don't even hear the next words to come out of his mouth as the crushing defeat of rejection weighs me down. Here I thought I was being wooed by the sexiest neighbor I've ever seen, the first man I've been interested in since Charlie, and now he's telling me he shouldn't have kissed me? A heaviness settles in my body, like the couch cushions are sucking me down into oblivion.

"Then why did you?" I ask meekly, interrupting whatever Blake is saying, but not looking at him.

"What?"

I turn to him, my throat closing up as I steel myself for the heartbreak I'm about to receive. "If you shouldn't have, then why did you kiss me?"

Blake's eyes widen, then close tightly. "No, that's not what I meant–"

"Then what did you mean?" I need answers, now.

"I meant, I shouldn't have kissed you like that." Blake opens his eyes, a fire of need burning in his irises. "I should have kissed you like this."

Suddenly, Blake's hand is behind my head and his mouth is on mine. His lips press gently, parting my own so his tongue can find its way inside. The kiss lasts for several moments, taking me to the clouds, when he pulls away all too soon and presses his forehead to mine.

He closes his eyes, as do I, and he says, "*That's* how I should have kissed you."

"Yes," I whisper, "that would have been better."

I hear Blake exhale, and I know he's smiling.

"Blake?" I wait for him to acknowledge his name. "Kiss me again."

He doesn't waste a second. As his lips press against mine, and his scruffy beard grazes my skin, his hand keeps my head steady. His other hand snakes around my waist and he lowers me onto my back. He's careful not to crush me with his weight, but I feel the need to be crushed. My arm raises, my hand grabs his shoulder, and I pull him over onto me.

His lips leave mine and trail down my jaw to my neck, then down across my collarbone. My head dips back and I'm lost in the moment. It's been so long since I've been kissed like this, touched like this. The reality of how it feels is overwhelming, but more so is my desire to keep feeling it.

Blake pulls away, leaning on his arm so he can look me in the eye. I see traces of passion and longing, but also a reverence filling me with warmth. "Are you okay with this? We can stop if you want."

I shake my head. "Kiss me again."

Blake follows directions so well. His kiss ignites something in me I haven't felt in a long time. It's bringing up the craving to be touched in places I haven't been touched in years. I still don't know how far I'm willing to go, but I'm ready to find out. I run my hand down his back and around his waist, pinching the hem of his shirt and tugging gently.

He smiles against my lips and raises up to remove his shirt. Coming back to me, his warm chest presses against mine as his lips claim my own, and I am on fire at every single point of contact. His bare skin on me sends an electric shock through my body and I suddenly can't touch him enough. My fingers trace every ridge of every muscle across his broad shoulders, down his back, up his ribs, and over his firm chest. Finally, when my hands stop, they're on the button of his pants.

My breath hitches as I realize what I'm about to do.

With a brief break of the kiss he says, "Here, let me." He sits up, undoes his pants and slides them off, leaving himself in his underwear.

Hm, he's a boxer brief guy. And they're straining to keep him contained.

Lifting me upright, he kisses me again, and runs his hand up my back to stop on the tie of my dress at the base of my neck. He pulls the fabric string, undoing the bow, and slides the dress down my torso, exposing my breasts.

I'm expecting him to pull away and take a look, but he doesn't. His mouth never leaves mine. His hands, however, furiously explore my body. *My body.* Even though I work out almost every day, this thirty-five-year-old body has birthed and breastfed two babies. It's not exactly in its prime anymore. Though I'm thankful it's dark in the room, I still tense at the idea of Blake's disappointment in seeing me naked, and I curl in on myself.

He must feel my tension because his hand runs down my side, stopping at my waist and squeezing gently. I relax. He wouldn't be doing this if he didn't want to. I let the moment take me as my head dips back and Blake's lips run down my neck and shoulders, but I giggle at his facial hair tickling me.

Stopping, he pulls back. "You okay?"

I nod, trying to stifle my laughter. "Your beard. It tickles."

"I'll shave it tomorrow."

"No, don't." I reach my hand up to run my fingers through its short length. "I don't mind being tickled."

With a sensuous smirk, Blake resumes kissing my body, moving his head lower. His kisses trail my collarbone and come back to the middle of my chest before he moves even farther south to nestle between my breasts. With gentle kisses he moves across one, taking my hardened nipple in his mouth. A tiny gasp escapes my throat as his tongue swirls in a smooth, circular motion. His other hand leaves my back and cups my other breast, his fingers finding my nipple and mimicking his tongue.

When one hand leaves my breast, it slides down my side, his thumb hooking into my doubled over dress at my hip. He pulls slightly, as if testing the waters. I don't object. Without letting his lips leave my breast, he somehow slips my dress from my hips to my ankles. I kick it to the floor without a second thought.

As his hand runs back up my leg, it makes a turn above my knee and settles between my thighs. I don't know if he can tell how wet my panties are, but I certainly can.

Releasing my nipple, he kisses my body all the way back up to my ear. His breath is hot and heavy against my skin. It feels like desire and lust. I like it.

He takes the lobe between his teeth. "Please, Maggie, may I?" His usual low, gravelly voice sounds strained by self-control.

I hesitate. Not because I don't want Blake in this moment, but it's been so long.

"Maggie? You okay?"

"It's just... It's been a long time." My embarrassment surprises me, but I can't help it.

Blake leans over, putting his finger on my chin and turning my head to meet his comforting gaze. "It's okay. If you're not ready, we can stop. But you have to make the call." His eyes flick to my mouth and back to my eyes. "Are you ready?"

All or nothing, Maggie. An airy, "Yes," comes out of my mouth.

Blake trails kisses down my neck. His hand pushes my panties aside and he slides a finger inside me, moaning deeply as another finger slips in. "You're... really ready."

"For you," I whisper.

With another moan, Blake lays his thumb on my clit and all his fingers begin twisting and moving in such a way, I lose my mind. Blake's mouth finds my nipple again, and between the swirling of his tongue and the pulsing of his fingers, I don't know how much longer I can keep my composure. Not that I'm doing a great job in the first place.

Pressure builds in my abdomen, my back arches, and as my body shakes with release, Blake's mouth comes back to claim mine. As we kiss, he nudges my legs apart and settles between my thighs, his erection teasing me. I didn't even notice him take off his boxers.

He leaves my lips, trailing kisses down my jaw. I lie here, waiting with agonizing patience for him to push inside me, but he doesn't. I lift my head to meet his gaze. "Blake, what's wrong?"

"I, uh, I need to grab a condom."

I *really* don't want to wait for that. "Are you clean?"

His brow furrows, but he nods.

"Me too. I haven't been with anyone in three years."

There's a brief flash of something resembling sympathy in his eyes, but he blinks, and it's gone. "I'll pull out. If that's okay?"

I nod and wrap my hand around the back of his head, pulling his mouth back to mine. My breath hitches when he presses himself into me, but we both let out strained moans as our bodies become one. Then, slowly, Blake raises himself and begins moving his hips. My hands hold on to his broad shoulders as my legs wrap around his waist, and I hook my ankles behind his back. My head dips backward as my body arches with pleasure.

"Maggie," Blake grunts. "Maggie, look at me."

I tip my head forward and my eyes meet his. They lock instantly and his gaze doesn't waver for a second as his thrusts speed up. He smiles, which prompts me to do the same, but our eyes never leave each other's. That is, until our gyrating hips get the best of me, and I can't do anything but let my head fall backward as I cry out his name.

A loud groan escapes Blake as he tenses, shudders, and pulls himself out of me, finishing on my stomach. His head hangs for a moment, his hair tickling my chest. He shivers slightly, and tilts his head up to look me in the eye. Adoration spills from his irises.

My chest heaves with exertion, as does his. Pressing a sweet kiss to my lips, he pushes off of me and heads to the bathroom. Emerging a few seconds later, he brings a handful of tissues to wipe away his mess from my skin. Tossing them in the small wastebasket next to the couch, Blake leans down and hands me my panties.

The smug expression on his face as he dangles my underwear from his finger makes me blush. I don't know why, though. We just had sex on his couch, so why the sight of him holding my panties embarrasses me, I'll never know.

After putting on his underwear, he lowers his body to rest on his side, cradling me in his arms. Neither of us says a word for some time. We simply lie together, Blake's fingers making small circles on my hip.

"How are you doing?" he asks, forcing me to pop my eyes open. I hadn't noticed them closing.

"I'm... I'm great. How are you?"

"Wonderful." He exhales, hard. "I don't want you to think I intended for this to happen tonight."

I pull away from him a bit. "Didn't you, though?"

"What? No." His words are laced with shame. "I certainly intended to kiss you properly, but I never thought we'd end up having sex on my couch. I could have at least given you the courtesy of my bed."

"I don't think I could have waited that long." This bedroom honesty spewing from my mouth keeps surprising me.

He props himself up on his elbow and looks down at me. His brown eyes shine in the glow of the movie credits now rolling. There's a tenderness in them I haven't seen before. In fact, no one has looked at me this way since Charlie, and it makes my mouth go dry.

My eyes instinctively glance at the clock on the wall and then come back to meet Blake's, which now almost appear hurt and afraid. "Please don't say it's late and you have to go."

"What?"

"You always leave right after the movie." He swallows hard. "Please, not tonight. Stay with me?"

Stay? He wants me to stay? "Blake, I don't know if–"

"Please?" His voice cracks. "If you want to go home, I won't stop you, but it kills me to know you're all alone in your house. I hate watching you shut the door." He closes his eyes. "I hate coming back here without you."

I place my hand on his cheek and he turns to kiss my palm. "Will you stay?" he asks into my hand, his tone filled with longing.

His plea warms me, making my answer an easy choice. "Yes."

Without a word, Blake scoops me up and takes me upstairs. He sets me on his bed gently and turns to the dresser, opening a drawer and rifling through the clothes.

"Sorry I don't have any pajamas or anything, but this shirt is super soft," he says, as he turns around. He stops in his tracks, holding the shirt in his hand while his eyes trail up and down my body, making me squirm.

"What?" I ask, wrapping my arms around my chest to hide myself. He's getting a good look now. I'm sure he's disappointed.

"You're the most beautiful woman I've ever seen."

What a line. I roll my eyes, but can't help blushing at the compliment. "Thank you."

"I mean it, Maggie. When I look at you, I lose myself. I want nothing more than to touch you right now. You...you have an effect on me I can't control."

My eyes lower from his face to see his chest expand. His muscles tense as he speaks, and the front of his boxers grows tighter with each passing second. I raise my eyes back to his where desire blazes, burning a hole through me.

I lick my lips and say, "Then come here and touch me again."

CHAPTER FIFTEEN

I wake the next morning alone in Blake's bed, rolling onto my back and flopping my arm across my forehead. The sunlight filters in through the curtains, soft and bright. I turn my head to see the clock. It reads 6:45 a.m.

Where is Blake?

My mind instantly gives way to intrusive ideas of Blake having second thoughts. He's had me, seen me thoroughly exposed, and now he doesn't want the awkwardness of kicking me out of his bed.

Do I go look for him?

That's probably what he wants. Me getting out of bed is a natural segue to me leaving. I don't know if I can take rejection right now. I should stay in bed and wait for him to come back, but I really have to pee.

In his main bathroom, I take in as much as I can without snooping. He keeps the bathroom very clean. Come to think of it, the whole house is pretty tidy for him being a bachelor.

That's a nice attribute.

Stepping out of the bathroom, I come to my senses and go downstairs. If I need answers, I'm not getting them alone in the bedroom.

I find Blake in the kitchen, leaning against the sink counter, wearing nothing but a pair of sweatpants. I drink him in from the doorway. His disheveled brown hair hangs down, kissing the corners of his eyes, which are focused on his phone in his hand. The slight stubble covering his chin shadows his strong jaw as he lifts his mug. It reads "Caffeine is my spirit animal."

My giggle announces my entrance, and Blake stands straight up and sets his mug down, nearly spilling it. "Hey, Maggie, good morning."

"Good morning," I say shyly, raking over his bare chest. My eyes follow the curve of his collarbone and down his pecs. I bite my lower lip as I drag my gaze over his abs, stopping where those deep V muscles meet the waistband of his pants. The sight of him shirtless hasn't gotten old and even now, after everything we did last night, it leaves me breathless.

I realize I'm staring, my cheeks flushing, so I yank my gaze up to his, only to find him staring, too. I'm still only wearing his t-shirt and my panties. I feel a bit awkward, but the way his eyes dip to my bare thighs while his Adam's apple bobs calms my nerves.

He clears his throat. "Did you sleep okay?"

As I nod, my lips part to let my mouth hang open slightly. I didn't have any nightmares. It has to be a coincidence, right? I mean, Blake isn't the reason for my great sleep, is he? I guess multiple orgasms could do the trick.

"Maggie? You okay?"

My hand flies to my mouth, and with a curt nod, I glance away.

"Sorry to leave you up there, but Oscar started barking at like six o'clock to be let out, and I didn't want to wake you."

"Oh, I didn't even hear him. Guess I was sleeping good," I say, eyeing a stool at the island, not entirely sure I should take it.

"I'm glad you slept well. Have a seat."

He didn't ask me to leave right away. That's a good sign. I sit down, keeping my posture straight and laying my hands in my lap.

"Are you hungry? I make a pretty mean omelet." His cheerful expression falls a bit. "Do vegetarians eat eggs?"

He has a great memory. "Some do, but I don't. It's a texture thing with me. They're fine when they're in something, like cake, but I can't do them as a main dish." My heart pounds in my chest. This is usually when I get push-back. *How do you live like that? Eggs are fine. There's nothing wrong with eating meat. You're so weird.*

I've come to terms with my dietary choices. I made them a long time ago, grown used to it, and now I don't even have a second thought about how I eat. My kids eat whatever they want because I refuse to push my lifestyle choices onto them, but I live how I want. Normally, I don't give a rat's ass what someone thinks of it, but right now, my nerves are on high alert at the thought of Blake judging me.

"How about waffles, then?"

I swallow down my heart, the pounding slowing to a normal beat. "Maybe some coffee first. I had a late night."

"I take full responsibility." He winks, and I melt. He might as well pour me into the mug. As he slides the mug across the island counter and I reach for it, our fingers graze. Considering the things we did last night, I feel silly such a small touch sends butterflies through me.

"So, what are your plans today?" I ask, changing the subject to find out what my next move should be.

Blake shakes his head, but keeps his eyes on mine. "No plans, except you." The grit in his voice makes me squirm, like always, in my chair. He smiles, and I'm beginning to think he does this on purpose.

"I think I'll take those waffles now."

"Coming right up."

Blake's waffles are delicious. Maybe it's because I'm starving, or maybe because I'm imagining licking syrup off his chest. Other than me moaning in delight over my food, we eat in silence. It would be awkward if I wasn't so busy stuffing my face. When I'm done eating, I drink my last bit of coffee, and wipe my mouth with my napkin.

"Those were really good. Thank you," I say as I get up to put my dishes in the sink.

"Glad you liked them."

I set my dishes down, turning on the water to rinse my plate, when Blake's hand slides down my arm, coming to rest on the back of mine. He steps closer, pressing his body against me and wrapping his other arm around my waist. Nuzzling his face into my neck, his beard scratching against my skin as his hot breath runs down my collarbone.

He gently sways our bodies from side to side. "Thank you for staying the night."

"You're welcome." My eyes dart across the counter. "I guess I should go home, though."

Blake sighs, and I feel his shoulders slump. "You don't have to, unless you want to. Do you want to go home?"

"I... I don't know."

Blake kisses my shoulder, moves up my neck, and presses his lips to my ear. "Let me help you decide." His strong arms wrap around me tightly, one hand gripping my waist, the other lowering itself to squeeze my inner thigh. "Do you want to go home, *now*?"

"No," I whisper.

"Good, because I'm going to need my shirt back before you do."

I spin myself around to face him, my hands splayed across his warm chest, his arms still wrapped around me. "Then you're going to have to take it."

Blake's response is a low groan as he puts his hands under my thighs, lifting me up. I wrap my legs around his waist and kiss him. I'm not entirely sure how he does it, but he carries me up the stairs to his bedroom in this position. It's kind of hot.

Setting me on his bed, he pulls the shirt off me. I lean back onto my elbows, my legs twisting together as I squirm under his gaze. For as much as he's seen me naked in the last twelve hours, I'm still uncomfortable for some reason.

Blake's eyes trail my body several times as he pulls his bottom lip between his teeth.

"What?" I ask, nervously. He's staring too long. It makes me wonder if he's rethinking things.

"I keep waiting for you to disappear when I blink."

I pinch the bed sheet between my fingers. "I'm not going to disappear."

"Good." Blake climbs over me, locking his mouth on mine. His lips part my own and his tongue finds its way inside.

Blake's hands travel up my sides, stopping to cup my breasts, and his fingers twist and flick my nipples, making desire settle between my thighs. He runs a hand down, rounding my hip and squeezing my ass, groaning as he does. His mouth moves down my chin, my neck, my collarbone, then stops to take a pebbled nipple between his teeth.

I let out a wispy moan and grip his shoulders, my fingers digging into his taut muscles.

Sliding off my panties, Blake runs a trail of kisses around my breasts, ribs, and stomach. With his tongue in my bellybutton, his hands gently brush my thighs and push them apart. I feel his fingers run along my wetness, softly caressing before slipping inside me. One, then two, swirling and pulsing as his other hand mimics the movement on my breast.

I twist my fingers into his hair and whisper, "Blake."

"Fuck, I love how my name sounds on your lips," he says quietly against my stomach. "But I want it louder." He pushes another finger inside me, hooking them and twirling my clit with his thumb.

I can't do anything except arch my back and buck my hips into him. My moans grow louder, I'm almost yelling his name as he waits for the crest to break before pushing himself inside me. A strained groan emanates from his throat as he begins thrusting. His steaming breath floats across my skin with every exhale, and it feels incredible.

"Oh, God. Fuck, Blake!" I shout as I succumb to yet another orgasm.

I tense around his erection, my fingers digging into his back, and I shudder against his chest. Blake gives a few more quick pumps before pulling out, finishing on my stomach again with a groan of release.

Kissing my collarbone, he lifts himself from the bed and heads to the bathroom. He brings back some tissues and very gently wipes my stomach.

"You know, you don't have to do that," I say.

"Do what? Clean up my mess? Yes, I most certainly do," he says, turning to toss the tissues into the wastebasket.

"No, I mean, pulling out... you don't have to."

Blake stops mid-step on his way back to the bed, his eyes wide. "Why? Don't tell me you're in the market for another baby."

I laugh. "No, definitely not." My laughter subsides and I turn my head to look at the sheets, twisting them between my fingers. "Even if I was, I couldn't have one."

Blake settles on the bed next to me. "Why not?"

"Because after Dylan was born, I had a hysterectomy."

"Is that what this is from?" He runs his fingers lightly across my scar.

I nod. "Getting pregnant with Dylan was harder than with Sydney. We struggled so much that I finally went to the doctor, which is when I found out about Dylan."

"Was something wrong?"

"Not with Dylan, but with me, yes. After he was born, I had a lot of... issues. I went through several doctor visits, and birth controls, before they discovered cysts and a fibroid. The doctors didn't even know how I got pregnant in the first place."

"Wow, how scary."

"It was. There was nothing they could do except remove everything. But we had our two happy, healthy kids, so it wasn't a huge deal." I tilt my head up to see Blake's reaction, my nerves clenched to the brink of snapping, but when I'm met with a look of pure sympathy, I feel every muscle in my body ease.

"Maggie, I'm glad it all worked out, but why are you telling me this?"

"Well, two reasons." I prop myself up onto my elbows to be eye level with him. "One, I want you to know you don't have to pull out. Not that it's an effective birth control method in the first place. And two" –I take a deep breath– "because, I don't want it to be an issue down the road. I need you to know now I can't have kids, so if that's something you want, then you and I can't–"

Blake grabs my shoulder and squeezes. "Maggie, look. I really appreciate you telling me. It does ease my mind knowing my lack of responsibility in the prophylactic area won't turn into a sticky situation."

"It's turned into a sticky situation a couple times now," I say, nodding down at my stomach and laughing.

Blake lets out a light chuckle, running his fingers down my arm. "Touche. But this is a heavy conversation to have right now. It's a little soon, don't you think?"

"It is, I know. But, this is the closest I've been to anyone in the last three years, and I need to know if me not being able to have kids is going to be a problem before we get too involved."

"That's fair. Okay, how about this? I promise to keep this information in my mind and give it some real thought. Then later, when this" –he moves his hand back and forth between us– "becomes serious, we'll have a healthy conversation about it."

When it becomes serious? Not if? "Deal."

The tension in the air lifts, and we both exhale. I hadn't planned on having such a heavy conversation so soon, but it just came out. I knew I wanted to get the information out in the open, and honestly, I thought it was going to be much tougher. Blake has a way of easing me, which seems to come effortlessly for him. It's liberating, in a way.

Blake's hand lowers to my hip, his fingers making circles and giving me goosebumps. "So, what do you want to do today?"

"Whatever you want."

Blake scowls. "Maggie, I asked what *you* want to do. I'm guessing you don't get asked that very often, especially with two kids. I can't imagine they ever come to you, begging to do something you want to."

"No. They don't, but Michelle always asks what I want to do. We usually end up doing what she wants, but she always asks."

Blake laughs and shakes his head. "Alright. If you could do anything you wanted right now, what would it be? Money is no object, time is no issue, and there are no consequences to your actions. What's the first thing that comes to mind?"

I don't even hesitate. "Take a nap."

Blake laughs heartily. "What? A nap, that's all?"

I turn onto my side and look Blake in the eye. "I never take naps. Not even when the kids were little and took their naps. I've always done something. Cleaned, read, worked out, I never rested unless I had to."

"Okay, nap it is then. Scoot over." Blake pulls the blankets up, letting them gently settle over our bodies. He pushes me to my side and cuddles up behind me so my back is against his chest. He's so warm.

"Blake, you really don't have to–"

"Shhh. Go to sleep. I'm right where I want to be."

I wake sometime later to find Blake still nuzzled against me. I have no idea how long we've been asleep. I can't see the clock from here, and if I turn to look, I'll most certainly disturb him. His breathing is so calm and rhythmic, I can't bear the thought of waking him. I'll lie here until he wakes up. But I want to look at him.

The last day has been incredible. *He's* been incredible. Almost too good to be true. He's been caring, affectionate, charming, not to mention, a generous lover. What else could a girl ask for?

Torn in my decision to satisfy my visual desire and let my sleeping prince rest, I twiddle my toes.

"Will you stop thinking so loud?" Blake groans.

Crap, did I say something? "What?"

His deep chuckle rumbles from his chest and right through me. "You're moving your toes around. I've noticed you do it a lot when you're nervous."

"I'm not nervous," I lie. "And when have you seen me do it?"

"Any time we've talked on your porch when the weather's nice. You never wear shoes when you sit outside to read. The pool a few weeks ago. Also, when we went to Home Depot and you had flip flops on."

"Okay, okay. I get it, you're observant." I turn myself to face him and our noses barely touch.

"Hello, beautiful." He kisses me gently. "How long have you been awake?"

"Not long. A few minutes, maybe. I can't see the clock so I really don't know."

Blake turns over with a groan. "Shit, it's almost noon."

"What?" My eyes widen. "We've been asleep for three hours?"

He rolls back over, putting his nose to mine again. "Time flies, I guess. Lunch?"

"You're not sick of me yet?"

"Never." He pulls me in for a quick kiss.

"Well, as nice as lunch sounds, I need to take a shower. And I have no clothes here."

"Not true." A grin spreads over his face. "You have the dress you wore yesterday."

"And my underwear from yesterday, too. I'd like to have clean ones."

"Okay, I get that. But my shower is oversized. It can fit two people comfortably. *Very* comfortably." His eyebrows bob.

The image of a dripping wet Blake pops into my mind. Water running down his body in rivulets, highlighting every defined muscle. I fight the urge to rub my thighs together. "That's awfully tempting, and I'd love to see your over sized shower sometime, but I'd like to go home and use my own. If that's okay?"

He nods. "Of course. How about you go home, shower and get ready, and I'll do the same. Then I'll come get you and we can go have lunch? Unless you have plans."

I shake my head.

"Fantastic," Blake says, kissing my forehead. "I'll see you in an hour?"

Chapter Sixteen

Blake kisses me goodbye at the door, and I walk home, relieved he didn't insist on walking me himself. He offered, several times, but I turned him down. It's only four houses, in the middle of the day, and I need all the time I can get to think.

The short walk home, the flight of stairs to my bedroom, the shower, and everything afterward are filled with nothing but Blake. Every little thing reminds me of him and our time together. Not that it's hard to do since it happened so recently, but I can't get him out of my head.

His smile, his laugh, the tone in his voice when he whispers my name, it's all sending delicious shivers up my spine. Even in the heat of the shower, which I've turned up to scalding, I feel his hands on my skin, his lips on mine, his presence inside me, and it gives me goosebumps. I can't wait to feel him again.

Once out of the shower, I prep myself for lunch. Should I wear makeup? Would that be too formal? How should I wear my hair?

I can't imagine he's taking me to a five-star restaurant for lunch, but we're probably not going to Taco Bell either. I settle for some light eye makeup, lip gloss, and a flat iron to my hair. Nothing special, but enough to boost my confidence.

In my closet, I delve into another dilemma. Dress? Shorts and a tank-top? It's too hot for jeans.

Shorts win almost instantly, and I choose a dressy tank top that shows enough cleavage to entice, but isn't too revealing. As I examine my appearance in the mirror, I notice I'm almost glowing. I feel like a new person. *Blake* has made me feel like a new person.

Then the guilt hits me. All these things I'm obsessing over with Blake is how I used to be with Charlie. Even after flirting for our entire sophomore year of college, dating for the next two, and eight years of marriage, I always wanted to look my best for him. I thought about him constantly and he never failed to give me butterflies. He was my person. My one and only, but now, instead of thinking about him, I'm thinking about Blake.

The doorbell rings, ripping me out of my guilt fog, and I pull the front door open without a second thought.

"Oh, Maggie, I'm glad I caught you at home," Joanna says, excitedly.

"Hi, Joanna." I hope the disappointment in my voice doesn't shine through. "How are you?"

"I'm great. Here." She hands me an envelope. "It's an invitation to the neighborhood block party next Saturday. We throw one every year, I hope you can come."

"Thank you. It sounds like fun. Too bad the kids will miss it."

Joanna's mouth opens, but her words are cut short to the roar of Blake's silver Toyota Tacoma pulling into my driveway. He cuts the engine and steps out of the cab, walking to the porch without taking his eyes from mine.

Blake tears his gaze away from me for all of three seconds to acknowledge Joanna. "Hey, Joanna, how's it going?"

"Oh, uh, hi, Blake. I'm good, thank you for asking." The confusion in her voice is almost comical.

"Maggie, are you ready to go?"

"Yes, let me grab my purse and keys." I lean inside to gather my things from the entry table. Once I lock my front door, I step by Joanna. "Thank you for the invite, Joanna. I'll see you on Saturday."

"Okay, uh, yeah, sounds good." Her eyes watch intently as Blake opens the truck door for me. She returns his wave as he crosses the driveway and gets in the driver's seat.

"Did she invite you to the block party?" Blake asks as he backs out of the driveway.

"Yes. We missed it last year since we weren't living here yet. Sounds fun."

Blake nods, grunting quietly.

"It's not fun?"

He sighs. "I don't know. I mean, I guess it's fun. Mostly, it's people in the neighborhood getting drunk and lighting fireworks. Kids seem to enjoy it. I usually take Oscar somewhere to get him away from the noise. It freaks him out."

"I didn't even think about that."

"Plus, it's our movie night, or did you forget?"

"You want to keep doing movie night?"

"Of course. I need to learn to love those Hallmark movies, don't I?" He laughs. "But we can go if you want."

"I'd love to see some fireworks, but we don't have to go if it bothers Oscar. Movie or not, I'm happy to be anywhere with you."

Blake reaches over and takes my hand, giving it a gentle squeeze. "So, do you like Greek food?"

My mouth salivates at the mention of it. "Yes, very much."

"Great."

We have lunch at a small, family-owned Greek restaurant. It's delicious and I eat entirely too much. Blake says he likes my healthy appetite as he finishes the food on my plate, which I'm too stuffed to eat.

He holds my hand as we drive home, gently caressing my skin with his thumb. I'm lost for a moment in sheer joy when I realize we're going the opposite direction of our neighborhood.

"Where are we going?"

"A surprise." Blake grins.

He pulls into the parking lot of a driving range.

"Golf? Do I look like a golfer to you?" I ask, jokingly.

"To be fair, no one really *looks* like a golfer."

I'm suddenly very uncomfortable. Not only am I not a golfer, but I'm not good at sports in general, and I'm so full of Greek food, I feel like one of those punching bags for kids that pops up every time it gets knocked down. This isn't exactly a fun surprise.

As if he can sense my unease, Blake says, "I was thinking more along the lines of that." He points across the parking lot.

"Minigolf?" The weight on my shoulders lifts. "I can do that, I suppose."

Blake and I spend the next hour laughing at each other's horrible aim, stealing kisses when we can, and competing for who can get the most strokes in. I'm winning. Technically, I'm losing, but I'm winning with the rules we set.

On the last hole, as I'm lining up a shot I will most certainly miss, Blake comes up behind me. He cradles me in his arms, hands resting on mine holding my putter, and takes practice swings with me.

"Where was this help on hole number one?" I ask.

"I'll tell you a secret," he says, his hot breath running down my neck. "I'm not a golfer, either." He plants a kiss on my cheek.

"Obviously not, if you think the object is to get the most strokes in."

"I only did that because it wouldn't be fair if we played by standard rules."

"What wouldn't be fair?"

He runs his hand up my arm to my chin, turning my head to face him. "I wouldn't have been able to concentrate on my game with you standing right there. Those long, sexy legs. The way your ass looks in those shorts." His eye flick down to my chest. "And don't even get me started on this shirt."

I puff my chest out, pouting as I ask, "What's wrong with my shirt?"

"Let's just say, if you would've bent down to pick up your ball, it all would've been over for me."

"A little cleavage would've riled you?"

Blake pulls me closer, and I feel him harden against my thigh. "I'm already riled."

"This is a family establishment, sir," I say, trailing my finger down his jaw.

"Then we'd better leave before I get in trouble."

"Hold that thought." I turn away from him and line up my shot, making sure to wiggle my hips a few times as I do. Blake groans behind me and I swing. Hole in one. My first one of the whole game.

I turn back to Blake with a smug smile on my face. "What was it you said about my shorts?"

With a growl, Blake stomps down the green to retrieve my ball. He comes back to me, grabbing my wrist and tugging me toward the exit.

"What about your turn? We're not finished yet."

"I'm about to finish," Blake says, as he drops off our equipment and pulls me to the parking lot.

I giggle the whole way to his truck. I can't believe something as small as my outfit is affecting him so greatly, but I'd be lying if I said I didn't like it.

When we reach his truck, I expect him to unlock it and open my door like he's done every time we've gone somewhere, but he doesn't. Instead, he whirls me around and pins me against the passenger door, crashing his mouth onto mine with a passion much too strong for public.

I give in, though. I can't help it. Blake's intense affection has me acting like a teenager all over again.

His tongue slides across my lips, begging for entrance. When I open my mouth, his tongue finds mine, swirling and dancing together. Our hands roam without restraint, mine gripping his taut shoulder muscles and digging my fingers in. As I wrap one leg around his waist, Blake presses his hips to mine and groans into my mouth. I tip up on my toes so his cock hits my wet apex, and I want nothing more than to grind against him. When his hand runs under my shirt to cup my breast, my nipple pebbles under his palm, and I slide my leg between his to rub my thigh against his erection, whispering his name.

Blake tenses and grunts. He stops kissing me, pulling away to press his forehead to mine. "Sorry."

"For what?" I ask, breathlessly. "Stopping our make-out session? It's probably for the best. Things were getting a bit intense for the minigolf parking lot."

"Too intense."

"Should we go home and finish what we started?" I take my bottom lip between my teeth and run my toes up his calf.

Blake presses his lips into a flat line. "I think I already did."

My expression goes from sultry to surprised in one second. Did I make him come in his pants? All while fully clothed? I cup his cheek with my hand and raise his head to meet my gaze. His eyes hold a world of embarrassment, but I kiss him gently. "So, I win again?"

He laughs, his whole body shaking. "I think I won that one, but I'll be sure to tie things up when we get home." He plants one more kiss on my lips before unlocking the truck and letting me in.

The afternoon, and honestly, the last twenty-four hours couldn't have been more perfect. As we pull into our neighborhood, Blake stops at the stop sign at the top of the hill, but doesn't move for much longer than a standard pause.

"It's not going to turn green," I joke.

"I'm not waiting for it to turn green," he says flatly, staring straight ahead.

"Then what are you waiting for?"

He swallows hard. "I'm waiting for the courage to ask you if I'm dropping you off at home."

"Why do you need courage for that?" I crane my neck to look at him, but he keeps his gaze straight through the windshield.

"Because I don't want your answer to be 'yes.'"

"Why not?"

He licks his lips and his eyelids lower. "Because it's not even five o'clock, and I'm not ready to leave you for the day."

"You're not sick of me yet?" I reach over, laying my hand on his thigh and squeezing.

He turns to me, locking his smoldering brown eyes on mine, and my stomach flips. "Never."

"Well, I do have work tomorrow. Don't you?"

"Yeah, but I'm not going to bed for a few hours. There's still plenty of daylight left. Do you have a reason to go home? Like, something you need to do there?"

I shake my head. "No, I'll probably lay around and read or something. Why? Do you want me to come over again?"

Blake turns to me with pleading eyes. "I do, as long as *you're* not sick of me."

"Not by a long shot."

Chapter Seventeen

Thursday afternoon I'm sitting at my desk when my phone chimes, a million butterflies rushing through me upon seeing Blake's name.

BLAKE: *Hey, what are you doing?*

ME: *Working. You?*

BLAKE: *Wondering when you go to lunch?*

I glance at the time. It's 10:47 a.m.

ME: *I'll go between 12 and 1230. Why?*

BLAKE: *Because I'm coming to get you.*

My brow furrows.

ME: *Aren't you working?*

BLAKE: *Our next job fell thru so I've got the afternoon off.*

Strange. Why wouldn't they move another job up? I shrug it off since it's beneficial to me at the moment.

ME: *Ok. Text me when you get here and I'll come out.*

> **BLAKE:** *Ok.*

The next hour and twenty minutes are excruciating. I'm so excited to see Blake, my stomach is flipping, but that makes it difficult to concentrate on my work. My production isn't nearly up to par as normal. That's why when my phone chimes at 12:11 p.m., I all but jump from my chair.

> **BLAKE:** *I'm here, but can I come in to use the bathroom? It was a long drive.*

I giggle and hit reply, telling him to check in at the front desk first. Since I have an extra minute, I finish the affidavit I was working on and file it. I clock out, sling my purse over my shoulder, and have to use all my self-control to not skip through the office.

All the warmth pulsing through me freezes over, though, as I reach the corner to the foyer and hear Abbey giggling. I peek around the corner to find Abbey, all dolled up as usual, flipping her hair and laying her hand on Blake's arm.

I clench my jaw.

Blake has his back to me, but he's standing ramrod straight with his arms folded. His head bobs every now and then in response to whatever Abbey is saying.

She's doing her due diligence to keep his attention on her. One hand on her hip, the other either waving in the air as she talks, or touching Blake in some way. She's licking her lips and batting her eyelashes nonstop. It's enough to make my blood boil.

I'm about to stomp into the room and slap her again, when my heart suddenly sinks. What if her tactics work? What if Blake decides he's got a chance with a younger, hotter woman and leaves me behind? There's only one way to find out.

With leaden steps, I enter the foyer and sidle up next to Blake. "Hey."

Abbey turns a fiery glare on me and opens her mouth, but shuts it tight when Blake slides his arm around my waist and kisses my temple. "Hey, yourself. Ready to go?"

I nod, allowing Blake to usher me out the door. The look of utter confusion on Abbey's face is a small consolation for the turmoil eating away at my gut.

Once we're outside, Blake takes my hand and lifts it to his lips. "So, where do you want to go?" I give a half-hearted shrug, and he furrows his brow. "Hey, what's up?"

I sigh, not ready to hear the soul-crushing words of rejection, so I shake it off. "Nothing. I rushed through a whole bunch of affidavits and my head is spinning a little. I'm good. How about subs? There's a deli around the corner."

At lunch, even though I tried to move past the Abbey incident, I'm quiet and Blake notices. "Maggie, are you sure you're okay? You haven't said much and you're picking at your sandwich more than you're eating."

I pinch my lips together, unsure if I want to hear the answer to this question. "What were you talking to Abbey about?"

"Abbey? The chick in your office?" Blake arches an eyebrow. "That's what this is about?" He shrugs and takes a bite of his sandwich, talking out of the corner of his mouth. "She did most of the talking. About herself."

"Oh? Did she tell you about going to law school?"

He nods. "And landing the internship because of her grades and accomplishments, and her vacation to Fiji last year, and how she was a beauty queen in high school." He rolls his eyes. "Honestly, I don't know how you listen to her all day without going crazy."

I fight the smile threatening my lips. It's refreshing to know Blake finds her as insufferable as I do, and only after a few minutes of talking to her. "I thought maybe you'd find her impressive."

Blake sighs and sets his sandwich down. "Maggie, you have nothing to worry about. Women like Abbey are like those giant, chocolate eggs you get at Easter."

I furrow my brow. "What?"

"They're hollow."

"Oh." I let the smile take over my face.

Something in Blake's eye satiates my nerves, and my whole body relaxes. My appetite returns as the heaviness in the air lifts, and we finish our lunch with more pleasant conversation. Neither of us bring up Abbey again.

As I watch Blake drive away after dropping me off, my heart feels lighter. I don't know why I was so worried. Blake's a grown man who's perfectly capable of making choices for his life, and he chose me. I walk into the office a little taller.

I'm not at my desk more than a minute when Abbey stops by. "Maggie! Was that guy your boyfriend?"

I spin in my chair to see a look of pure disbelief on her face. It makes me sit straighter and raise my chin. "Yes. Why?"

"I thought you didn't date."

"Well, things can change, Abbey."

She purses her lips and fans herself with her hand. "Talk about going from zero to sixty, that guy was something else. Congratulations on landing him."

I set my jaw, trying to stay professional. "Thanks." I guess.

"Makes me wonder if someone like you can get a guy like him, then someone like me has nothing to worry about. Maybe I've set my standards too low." Abbey stares past me, not talking to me anymore. She chews on her lip a moment before shaking her head. "Anyway, keep a tight leash on that one, Maggie. You never know when someone else is going to come along and take his attention." And with that shining bit of advice, she leaves me alone in my cubicle to reel in the notion that I won't have Blake forever.

"We don't have to go to the block party. We can take Oscar somewhere instead," I say, checking the time on Blake's microwave clock.

It's almost six. Blake and I have been discussing the block party all week, going back and forth on whether we're going. Both of us keep saying we don't care and we're making no headway. Now it's Saturday and we *have* to decide.

"No, it's okay. I told you we'd go. I'll put Oscar in his crate in the basement with a blanket over it. He has a white noise machine. He'll be okay... I hope." Blake's concern over his canine companion is endearing.

"As long as you're okay with it. Are we supposed to bring anything?"

Blake shrugs. "What did the invite say?"

"Shit. I never even looked at it," I say as I rummage through my purse, frantically searching for the envelope Joanna handed me a week ago. "Oh, good. I still have it." I slide the invitation from the envelope and read it. "And please bring something to share." I purse my lips, staring at Blake for a solution.

Blake points to the sky. "Wait, I have something." He pulls a bag of plain Lay's potato chips from his pantry and a six-pack of beer from the fridge.

"My hero," I say, placing my hand on my chest and batting my eyelashes.

Blake walks from the kitchen to meet me at the couch. He leans over me, resting his hands on the back, staring down into my eyes. "All in a day's work, ma'am."

"Ouch. Ma'am?"

"Just being polite," he says, bending his head down and putting his lips to mine.

Our kiss grows stronger by the second and, suddenly, Blake's hand runs under my shirt and over my breast, squeezing gently.

"You're not being very polite now," I say against his mouth.

"I'm not always a hero," he growls, keeping his hand where it lies.

"We don't have time. The block party already started."

"I'll be quick."

"Please don't be."

The block party isn't actually held on the block. Instead, it's hosted in the park next to the pool. It's quite the grand event, and I would expect nothing less since Joanna heads up the committee. Balloons and streamers hang from endless folding tables littering the park, and children's laughter mingles with loud conversation as the din thrums through the air. Everyone seems to be having fun, and I'm not dreading it with Blake by my side.

I walk to the HOA table to greet Joanna. Blake parts ways with me and takes our offerings to the food tables.

"Maggie! Hi, so glad you came!" Joanna says loudly, eyeing Blake as he walks away. "And with Blake Averson. How long has that been going on?"

"Hi, Joanna. Um, about a week."

"A week, is that all? Huh. We all thought it was longer. After the Christmas party last year, everyone started saying you two–"

"Uh, Joanna, I'm really hungry. I'm going to get some food and we'll catch up later, okay?" I don't even wait for her response before I'm walking toward Blake. I meet up with him, hook my arm in his, and nudge him toward the food.

"Joanna?" he asks with a knowing grin.

"Uh huh. Keep walking."

We pile a couple of plates with food. A hot dog and plain Lay's potato chips for Blake, and a bunch of sides for me. Vegetarians are very rarely considered at these types of events, but I've grown used to it.

Once we have our food and drinks, Blake searches for a place to sit. "Well, there're two choices. Either at the table between drunk Mark and his drunk buddies, or over there under a tree."

"The tree, please."

Settling down into the grass, I welcome its coolness. July is always so hot, and while evening is closing in, the heat hasn't wavered. At least we found some shade.

"So, what did Joanna say this time? More interior decorator advice?"

"She wanted to know about you and me. How long we've been...together. She said *everyone* thought it was longer, which means people have been talking about us."

"Does it bother you? To be the talk of the town?"

I shake my head. "No. I'm used to being talked about."

Blake furrows his eyebrows. "Why?" he asks, but instantly relaxes his face and says, "Charlie's death."

My head turns so quick, I'm afraid my neck will snap. I stare at Blake, wondering how he knows all the answers. "It's one of those things. When you walk into a room full of people and it goes silent. When you come around a corner and someone stops in the middle of their sentence to say hi, but never resumes their conversation. Certain topics are danced around or avoided completely. It's not malicious, though. People's hearts are in the right places."

"Even now? Talking about our relationship behind our backs is having their hearts in the right places?"

My breath catches in my throat. "Relationship? What a big word," I say with an exhale. "Is that what you think we have?"

"Well, yeah. I mean, I know it's only been a week, but I like you a lot, Maggie. I'm not on the market, not looking for anyone else. Are you?" There's a twinge of panic in his voice.

"No, not at all. I guess I'm out of the loop. I've only ever been with one other man."

"You really haven't been with *anyone* since Charlie?"

My throat closes up and my mouth is suddenly dry. I take a large drink of my beer and swallow hard. "I've gone on several dates, mostly blind ones, but they never worked out. The longest I've 'dated' anyone is maybe two weeks, and I'm being generous."

"Why didn't they work out?"

I give Blake a sideways glance. "You really want to know about me dating other men?"

He bristles and licks his lips. "I don't need details, but I'm curious why a gorgeous woman like you has been single this long."

I roll my eyes, but Blake's compliment makes me blush. "Just one of those things, I suppose. If the date got further than dinner, which wasn't often since most of the men I was set up with gave me a reason to say goodnight well before dessert, it didn't go past them dropping me off at home. Even the one 'relationship' I had for two weeks never went further than a goodnight kiss. That's probably why he stopped calling me."

"Jerk."

"Would you have waited that long for a woman to go further with you?"

Blake locks eyes with me, grabbing my hand firmly. "I did, and I would have waited longer."

With a giggle, I look away. "Well, I'm glad you're patient. Not all guys are. So, after a while, I stopped going on dates. The guy at Joanna's Christmas party was the closest I got to one in the last couple years."

"They guy who tried to get you drunk when you said no?" Blake's shoulders noticeably tense. "That guy?"

"Yeah, but I saw through him pretty quick. Dealing with a long streak of men like him, I quit dating altogether." I take another sip of my beer and fiddle with the label. "Which is why I was so hesitant about you."

"Me? What did I do to make you hesitate?"

"You didn't do anything wrong, it was all in my head. After I told you 'no' in December, I had a hard time figuring out if you were still interested in me. Had to convince myself you were." I pick at the blades of grass, plucking one by one and tossing them aside. "Still have to."

"Maggie..."

"It's fine. Obviously, I know you're interested. I guess I'm wondering... why?"

"Why? Why not?"

"Because I'm seven years older than you? Because I'm a mom of two almost teenagers? Because I'm boring? All I do is work, read, and watch Hallmark movies."

Blake chuckles at my last point.

"I guess I'm wondering what someone like you, sees in someone like me?"

"Does this have anything to do with me coming to your office on Thursday?"

I give a dejected nod. My bottom lip goes between my teeth while my toes not only wiggle, but my entire foot moves. "It's just... After you were in the office and I saw you talking to Abbey, I felt inadequate. I can't compete with women like her."

"I think the correct way to say it is women like her can't compete with *you*." He leans his arms on his knees, tilting his head down to look me in the eye. It's all business in those deep brown pools. "Look, I don't want to be with Abbey. I want to be with you, and I am. Okay?"

A smile creeps across my lips, but even I can tell it looks sad.

"Come here." Blake scoots back to rest against the tree, wrapping his arms around me and pulling me into his chest. "Do you remember the first time we met? Last year, at the mailbox?"

How could I forget? "Mhm."

"I knew right then you were someone I wanted to know. Not necessarily that I wanted to date you, but that you were worth knowing."

"How?"

"Because you didn't immediately look at me like a fresh piece of meat." He inhales, my head rising and falling with his chest. "Too many times I meet a woman and the first thing she does is flip her hair, or puff out her chest, or eye-fuck me into oblivion. Like Abbey did on Thursday. You didn't do any of those things."

I dip my chin down to speak out of the corner of my mouth. "You obviously didn't catch me drooling."

Blake laughs, a deep rumble echoing through him before settling and running his hand down my hair. "I like you, Maggie, because you're real. You don't act a certain way, or wear certain clothes, or change yourself because you think I'd like it. You're you, honest to goodness."

I nuzzle deeper into Blake's chest. His heart thumps as he explains the reasons he waited for me to decide I was ready. My eyes dart across the ground while Abbey's words about someone else catching Blake's attention repeat in my mind. "It's been so long. I don't know the rules of the dating game anymore."

Blake pushes me up to sit so we're facing each other, and he brushes a piece of hair behind my ear. "There aren't 'rules' to dating, per se," he says, making air quotes with his fingers. "We can make up our own."

"Like what?"

"How about rule number one, we don't let Joanna, or Abbey, or anyone else invalidate our relationship."

There's that word again. I think I'm beginning to like it. "I don't think either of them meant any harm. Abbey may be a bitch, but I don't think she meant to be this time, and Joanna's just a gossip."

"Regardless, I don't give a shit what anyone thinks, or who wants to judge us. I like you and you like me. That's enough, isn't it?"

"Of course," I assure him, my eyes flicking back and forth between the two of his. "What's rule number two?"

Blake takes my chin in his hand, his thumb caressing my skin. "We don't ever lie to each other. I want you to be open and honest with me, even if it's something ugly or unpleasant. I'll do the same. We'll help each other through the hard stuff."

My eyes widen at his vulnerability. "That's a good rule."

He leans in for a kiss. "Can I be honest with you right now?"

I swallow hard and nod.

"I fucking hate these block parties."

I let out a chuckle of relief, but hope it comes off playful. "We can go if you want."

"Nah, you said you wanted fireworks. We can stay." He tightens his grip on my waist, pulling me closer.

I press my lips to his. "You're all the fireworks I need."

CHAPTER EIGHTEEN

The next three weeks go by much too fast. While I'm ecstatic my children will be home soon, it also means things with Blake will change.

We've been spending all our free time together. Dinner almost every evening, aside from the nights I meet Michelle, day dates on Saturdays and Sundays, sleepovers Friday and Saturday nights. It's enough to wear a girl out. But I'm not tired yet.

When my kids come home, though, my time with Blake will be cut. Drastically. For one thing, I don't know how they're going to react to me dating someone. I haven't brought anyone home to meet my kids in this sort of capacity in the last three years. Me doing it now could be jarring.

In the same respect, I don't think I'll be comfortable having Blake spend the night for a while. I mean, I love falling asleep in his strong embrace, but I think it would be terribly awkward for my kids if Blake sleeps in their dad's spot.

But what if my nightmares come back without Blake around? I haven't had a single one in the five weeks we've been together, so maybe it would be worth having him spend the night. If not only for the nightmares, for the sex.

My breath hitches. There is no way I'll be comfortable enough to have sex while my kids are in the house. My inability to keep quiet aside, my kids know my door is always open if they need me. What if Dylan has a nightmare and comes running to my room, only to see Blake and I naked in the throes of–

Don't even go there, Maggie.

I need to focus on the here and now. Blake and I have plenty of time left to be together. I can worry about the rest later.

On the Friday before the kids come back, in the late afternoon, Blake takes me to the lake, where he and Oscar go for walks. It's a beautiful area filled with trees and tall grasses. The light from the low sun glimmers on the surface of the lake, and later, the sunset will turn everything orange and pink. Blake said he has a surprise for me, and I'm beyond excited to see what it is.

We walk for some time when Blake finally stops. "Here we are. My favorite spot." He sets his backpack down and ties Oscar's leash to a tree.

"It's gorgeous," I say, taking in the scenery.

"It sure is," Blake says quietly. I turn to find him staring at me and not the lake.

I roll my eyes. "I was talking about the landscape."

"I wasn't."

I turn back to the calm, serene water. "I can see why you like this spot so much. It's pretty secluded and the view is breathtaking."

"Yeah, it's a great place to sketch, too."

"What do you mean?"

"I used to come here and draw. I've always loved doing it, and this place gave me inspiration." The tone in his voice sounds sad as he shoves his hands in his pockets.

"I didn't know you could draw." I furrow my brow. "I guess you did say you went to school for graphic design."

"Well, the two don't always go hand in hand. A knack for graphic design doesn't mean you're inherently good at other media."

"Did you do those ones in your living room, though?"

He nods.

"Do you still do it?"

"No." He looks at the ground, kicking at a rock. "I got too busy with life, and then I ran out of paper."

I laugh. "Sort of a silly reason to stop.""I guess I didn't do it for so long, I lost sight of the joy. I lost my confidence, and never picked it back up."

"Well, it's never too late. You obviously have a gift if those drawings in your house are any indication."

"Yeah, I guess." His gaze lingers on his feet, his toe digging into the dirt. "I hung them there because I was proud of them, but now they remind me of what I gave up. I was thinking of taking them down."

"Don't. They're beautiful. You'll find the joy again one day, I'm sure of it."

"Thanks." Taking his hands from his pockets, he says, "You ready for your surprise?"

I bounce up and down on my toes. "Yes, please."

Blake squats down and unzips the backpack. He removes a blanket, wrapped in which are two long-stemmed glasses and a bottle of wine. After spreading the blanket on the ground, he takes out five small Tupperware containers and two packages of plastic utensils.

"Ta da," he says happily. "Romantic picnic for two... well, three." He opens one of the containers and places it in front of Oscar, who gobbles up the food.

A smile of appreciation spreads across my face so quick I don't even realize it's there until Blake smiles back. "This is wonderful. Thank you."

"It's nothing special. Some grilled chicken for me, a hearty salad for you, and some garlic bread. But there's wine."

"It's perfect." I take a seat on the blanket.

"Bon appetit."

After we've eaten, and had a couple glasses of wine, Blake clears our dishes. He starts a game of fetch with Oscar, throwing a ball into the brush before lying down on his side. He pats the ground in front of him, so I lie facing him, both of us propped up on our elbows.

"Thank you," I say.

"Don't mention it. I love picnics."

"No, not the picnic. I mean, this was great, but thank you for everything. This whole summer has been the best."

His chin raises, and if he wasn't lying down, he'd probably have perfect posture. "You're welcome. You know, you've made this a great summer for me, too. Sure, I haven't gotten as much sleep as I used to on the weekends, but it's been worth it." He winks at me, and I can't help but giggle as I blush. Oscar comes back and drops the ball at our feet. Blake sits up to throw it again. "When do the kids come back from camp?"

I sigh contentedly. "I pick them up next Friday."

His head whips around to look at me, his eyes wide. "Oh, wow, like *next* Friday? As in a week from today?"

I nod.

"So this is, like, our last hurrah."

I laugh. "You make it sound like we'll never see each other again."

"Well, I mean, once the kids are back, I'm guessing we won't be spending as much time together, not to mention less sleepovers."

Has he given this as much thought as I have? "True. There will be a transition period, for sure. I still have to figure out how I'm going to tell them about us."

His head jerks back. "You haven't told them yet?"

"No. I didn't want to do it through a letter or over the phone while they were at summer camp. This is in-person information. I need to be with them so I can gauge their reactions."

Blake rubs Oscar's ears, coaxing him into dropping the ball so Blake can throw it again. This time, it goes sailing. "And how do you think they'll react?"

"I really don't know. I mean, they like you a lot. Dylan is always saying how cool Mr. Blake is. But they never met any of the men I went out with. I don't know how they'll react to a man in their life again."

Blake nods as his lips tick back and forth and his eyes dart across the blanket. "And if they don't take it well? What does that mean for us?" There's fear in his voice.

"Well, if they're hesitant, then I guess…" –I look into Blake's eyes. They're pleading, begging me not to say it– "I guess we'll have to move slower. They'll need time to adjust."

Blake exhales deeply. "Jesus, give me a heart attack, why don't you."

I giggle. "Sorry." I take his hand in mine. "I'm not about to give you up. If my kids aren't happy about us dating, they'll have to learn to live with it."

Blake leans in and kisses me softly. The kiss continues until it isn't soft anymore. It grows hungrier by the second as he scoots his body against me. His hands start roaming, as do mine and, suddenly, his lips are kissing other places. My jaw, my neck, trailing the collar of my shirt.

"If this is our last weekend alone, I'm going to have to up my game, aren't I?" Blake whispers against my neck.

"Yeah, you will, but not here."

"Why? There's no one around." He slides his hand up my leg, settling between my thighs.

I let out a quiet moan at the feeling of his hand massaging me. My head falls to the side, and I find Oscar sitting, waiting patiently for us to acknowledge him. With what little breath I have, I manage to say, "But Oscar is watching."

Blake laughs, kisses me on the lips, and removes his hand. "I guess I'll have to take you home first."

The next morning, I wake up before the sun, an unusual occurrence when Blake spends the night. I can barely make out his face in the dark, but his rhythmic breathing tells me he's sound asleep. I don't move a muscle. He doesn't need to be up when I am.

Lying in bed, my mind picks up our conversation from yesterday. Blake and I listed some big changes coming when the kids get home. I'm mainly worried about them accepting him as my boyfriend, but I think he's more scared of losing our time together. It's a valid concern, but not one I'm dreading. We'll still be able to see each other.

But we won't be having sex all the time. My heart sinks at the thought. *Come on, Maggie. You went without sex for three years; you can handle a break now and then.*

As my mind swims with thoughts, I become aware of my toes wiggling. I don't want to disturb Blake, but lying here is driving my anxiety up the wall.

A workout will help.

I slip out of bed without bothering Blake, and head to the basement. A quick flip through my exercise app has me deciding on yoga. It's not super intense, which will allow my mind to work through all these thoughts. Although, my slinky camisole and shorts set aren't ideal, they'll be fine for this sort of workout.

About halfway through the video, I'm feeling much better. The thoughts and emotions ebb while my body gets a good stretch. I inhale deeply and move into downward dog, exhaling all my anxiety through my lips.

"Practicing new positions for bed? If so, I like that one." Blake's voice cuts into my concentration, and I yelp.

"Blake, you scared me!" I collapse onto my knees, turning my head over my shoulder to look at him before moving back into my stretch.

"Sorry. I woke up and you weren't in bed, so I decided to come find you." His gaze is fixed on me, desire blazing. "I'm glad I did."

My cheeks heat as he glides past me, dragging his fingers up the back of my thigh and over my ass. "You can't be down here if you're going to distract me."

He raises his hands in the air. "Okay, okay." Taking a seat on the couch, he leans back and puts his hands behind his head. "So, you do yoga?"

"Yes, I do yoga." I breathe in and out, and move into warrior one. "It helps clear my head."

"What needs clearing out?"

"Stuff from our conversation about the kids from yesterday."

"Oh," Blake says, sounding dejected.

I lean back into reverse warrior. "I know I said the kids will have to adjust, but we're going to have to make some concessions."

"Like what? I know you probably won't be spending the night at my house and there won't be any random, middle of the day sex." I hear a throaty groan from him as I pinwheel out of my stance and back into downward dog. "Speaking of…"

"No distracting me, remember?"

"Fine." He huffs and folds his arms across his chest.

"You're right, I won't be spending the night at your house, but you won't be spending the night here, either."

"What? Why?"

"Well, for one thing, I'm worried it'll freak out the kids to have another guy in their dad's spot, but also, I can't be quiet." As I move through into warrior one on my other leg, I glance at Blake, whose smug expression gives me an idea. I take a big breath, puffing out my chest.

Blake groans, running his hand down his face to scratch at his beard. "Okay, no sleepovers, but is that, like, forever?"

"No, of course not. Once the kids adjust to you being around, you can stay whenever you want, but sex will have to wait." As I release my breath, I bend in reverse warrior again, glancing at Blake over my shoulder. "Which means we need to take advantage of this week."

Blake's mouth curves into a mischievous grin as he gets up from the couch. He sidles up behind me as I move through my vinyasa into downward dog for the last time. His hips meet the back of my thighs, and he hardens against my ass. When his hands grip my hips, pulling me closer, I gasp.

"Then yoga needs to be finished."

Chapter Nineteen

Sitting in my car at the summer camp headquarters, I anxiously await my kids' arrival while my toes bounce around in my shoes wildly. I've come up with so many ways to tell them about me and Blake, but keep scrapping them for what I believe to be better ones. The only thing all my plans have in common is to wait until I've buttered them up with their choice of dinner and Friday night entertainment. It's my only hope.

I jump at the sound of Michelle's ringtone. "Hey, Michelle."

"What's wrong? You sound out of breath. Are you with Blake?"

"Ha ha. No. I'm waiting for the summer camp bus to drop off the kids. I was deep in thought when you called and scared me."

"Oh, sorry. Speaking of Blake, when am I gonna meet him?"

My heart speeds up and again my toes wiggle in my shoes. "Um, I don't know. He works all week, and now that the kids are coming home, I'll be with them a lot."

"Mags, this isn't, like, some big deal you have to prepare for. It's me, and maybe Tom. Come on, I wanna meet this gorgeous man you've been hiding. I need confirmation he's real."

I haven't been hiding Blake. I've spoken about him every time Michelle and I have talked, but I'd be lying if I said I haven't been avoiding the issue of them meeting. "Oh, he's real, let me assure you. But, I also have to introduce the kids to the notion of us being a thing first."

"They don't know!?"

"Ugh, no." I drop my face into my other palm. "And I'm freaking out about telling them."

"Well, I don't have any advice in that area except for you to stop overthinking this. You said the kids like this guy, right?"

"Mhm."

"So, it's probably not as big of a deal as you think. They're also older now. I bet they'll handle it just fine."

I drum my fingers on the steering wheel. "I'm sure they will, but I can't help worrying about them resenting me and Blake for trying to replace their father."

"Mags, they won't think that because it's not what you're doing. It'll all work out, you'll see."

The camp bus makes its appearance, giving me a chance to get out of this anxiety-inducing conversation. "Michelle, the bus is here. I have to go. I'll talk to Blake and see what his schedule is like. I'll let you know."

"Okay, Mags, don't keep me waiting forever. I'd like to meet him in his prime and not, you know, when he's eighty-two."

"Bye, Michelle."

I get out of the car and stand off to the side, avoiding the group of parents already congregating right in front of the bus stop. Dylan comes off first, then Sydney. They both look like they've had enough camp for a while. Their hair is greasy, hanging down in front of their sun-kissed faces. The bags under their eyes make it seem like they haven't slept in weeks, but their faces light up at the sight of me. It makes my heart swell.

"MOM!" they yell in unison. While normal for Dylan, it's a nice surprise to have Sydney be happy to see me.

"Hi, guys!" I say, scooping them both into my arms. "Oh, I missed you both. Did you have fun?"

Sydney nods while Dylan yawns.

"Okay, well, let's go. You can tell me all about it in the car."

They inundate me with stories about their summer. I get to hear all about the lake and how much fun it was to swim in. I learn Sydney was an expert at arts and crafts and Dylan excelled in pretty much every outdoor activity. Both kids agree that while breakfast was the best meal of the day, it came in second to the s'mores at the campfires.

"I'm glad you two had so much fun. Are you sad to be back home with me?" I ask, glancing in the rearview mirror.

"No, Mom. I missed you a lot. Did you get our letters?" Dylan asks.

"Mhm, I did. Didn't you get mine?"

"Yeah, we did," Sydney chimes in.

"Okay, good. So, do you think you'll want to go again next year?"

Sydney shrugs, and Dylan lets out an enthusiastic, "Yes!"

Both kids request a home-cooked meal for dinner, as they've been living off camp food for eight weeks. I make one of their favorites, spaghetti, with meatballs on the side, of course, and we sit around the table stuffing our faces until we can't possibly fit any more into our stomachs.

"So, Mom, how boring was your summer without us?" Sydney asks.

It catches me off guard. I hadn't expected either of them to ask about me. "Well, sweetheart, I did the usual stuff. I worked, I gardened, read. Nothing too fun." Except sleeping with Blake, that was a lot of fun.

"You really didn't do anything? Geez, Mom, you need a life," Sydney says, rolling her eyes.

"I have a life, Syd, thank you."

"Mom, can I go play Xbox?" Dylan asks.

Do it now, Maggie. Get it over with. "Um, in a minute. I actually have something I need to talk to you about."

Both kids stare at me in confusion. The last time I said I wanted to talk to them, we moved. And before then, I told them their dad was gone. Hopefully this conversation isn't as traumatic.

"Over the summer, I... well, something happened, and I need to know how you two feel about it."

"What?" Sydney asks, and I can hear the fear in her voice.

"Nothing bad, dear," I assure her, placing my hand on hers. At least I hope not. "The week after you two went to camp, Mr. Blake, from down the street, and I... started dating."

"What's dating?" Dylan asks.

Oh, my sweet, innocent baby.

"It means they kiss and hold hands and stuff," Sydney clarifies.

"Ew." Dylan scrunches up his nose.

I hope that's all she thinks it is. "Thanks, Syd. I wanted to tell you both and see what you thought. Does it bother you for me to date Mr. Blake?"

Dylan thinks for a moment, wrinkling his nose. "No. I like Mr. Blake. He's nice and he has Oscar. Are you guys getting married?"

My eyes widen, my heart leaping into my throat. "No, Dylan. It's only been a few weeks. We're very far away from marriage. Right now, Mr. Blake and I are getting to know each other and spending time together. Having fun, that's all."

"Okay. Can I go play Xbox now?"

"Sure, sweetie," I say, shaking my head.

He bounds across the room, not giving a second thought to me and Blake. I turn my eyes back to Sydney, who has been quiet. My heart hammers in my chest. "So, what are your thoughts, Syd?"

She purses her lips while her eyes wander around the room. "I mean, I guess I don't care. Blake's cool. He's younger than you, though."

"That kind of stuff doesn't matter when you get older." *But, thanks for the reminder.* "So, you're really okay with it?"

"Yeah, Mom. It's cool. Are we supposed to call him 'dad?'"

My entire body goes rigid, and I have to fight to gingerly shake my head. "No, that's not what's going on."

"But he's going to be spending the night here and stuff?"

"No. Not for a while, at least. And I won't be spending the night down there, either. He'll be around for dinners and on weekends, though."

She shrugs. "Whatever." Getting up from the table, she grabs a soda from the fridge, turns to me and says, "If he makes you happy, Mom, then go for it. I'm going upstairs to call Kelsey."

Smiling at my beautiful, old soul of a daughter, I blow a breath through my lips with such force, I whistle. Michelle was right; I was overthinking things. I take my phone out to text Blake.

ME: *Crisis averted. They gave us their blessing.*

BLAKE: *You told them already? Good. Glad it went well. Should I come over?*

ME: *Lol, no. It's their first night back home. They need some time to relax.*

BLAKE: *I'm kidding, I know they need some mom time. Maybe lunch tomorrow?*

ME: *Sounds perfect.*

BLAKE: *Cool, I'll call you in the morning. Have a good night.*

ME: *Thx, you too.*

Chapter Twenty

The two weeks after the kids get home are filled with day trips to the museum, pool visits, and evenings with Blake. Surprisingly, even though he hasn't spent the night once since the kids came home, I haven't had a single nightmare. Just having him in my life must be enough to quell my nighttime anxieties. He may not sleep over, but he makes it a point to come for dinner every night. He says it's important to be present, but I think he's trying extra hard to impress my children.

The last Friday night before school starts, Blake comes to our house, his arms lined with grocery bags.

"What's all this?" I ask as he steps over the threshold.

He greets me with a kiss. "Just a little surprise for our Friday night dinner."

"You're cooking?"

"I thought we'd try something different." He winks at me and enters the kitchen. Setting the bags on the counter, Blake spots Sydney on the couch with her nose in a book. "Hey, Syd. What are you reading? Same one or something new?"

Sydney holds up the book. "New," is all she says before lowering it to cover her face once more.

Blake looks at me, and I shrug. He grimaces, strides into the living room, and takes a seat next to Sydney. Their voices are low, but whatever Blake says must stir something because not two minutes into their conversation, Sydney's laughing.

I watch as she points to the pages in her book, explaining it to Blake and he listens intently. His attention is hers and hers alone. My heart swells. He breaks through her barriers as easily as he does mine, and I couldn't be more thankful for him.

After a few minutes of banter, Blake gives Sydney a nudge with his shoulder and returns to the kitchen. He gives me an incredulous look. "What?"

My cheeks hurt from the wide grin stretching them. "You're amazing, that's all."

Blake says nothing, but gives me a peck on the cheek. He whips up a surprisingly delicious meal of pasta primavera with grilled chicken on the side, salad, and he brought cheesecake for dessert. My hero.

After dinner, the kids disappear to their respective hideaways, leaving me and Blake on the deck to finish the bottle of wine we opened. The sky glows with a gradient of pinks, oranges, and reds as the setting sun kisses the mountains, and the breeze tickles my skin as it keeps the August heat at bay.

Blake's chair is right next to mine, his arm around my shoulders, fingers lightly brushing the skin of my bicep. He tilts his head down and whispers, "So, the kids are gone. Want to make out?"

"I'd love to, but–"

He sighs and his fingers stop, hanging limp against my arm. "I know. I wouldn't want them catching us either, but I miss you, Maggie. It's only been two weeks, but it's been *two* weeks. I miss having you in my arms at night, I miss waking up to you in the morning." He turns his head so his lips are pressed to my ear. "I miss hearing you scream my name when I'm inside you."

A shiver goes up my spine, my panties instantly soaking. "I miss you, too."

"Any chance we could get a night together?"

I exhale, contemplating. Michelle would be happy to help, I'm sure, but now's not the time. "They just got back from camp. I'd hate to send them to a sleepover so soon. Plus, school starts next week, and they'll need time to get back into the routine." I feel Blake's posture slump against me. "But your house is close, and the kids are old enough to handle being on their own for a bit. How about this? I'll come down to your place for dinner tomorrow night. I can't spend the night, but I can stay for a couple hours, at least."

His eyes light up. "Really? Fantastic."

"Then, after a few weeks of school, when the kids and I get back into our routine, I'll see about them maybe having sleepovers with friends one weekend and we can have a night together."

"I'll take whatever I can get," he says with an enthusiastic kiss to my temple.

"Syd! I'm leaving!" I call out from the front door. I've gone over the rules with Sydney several times since telling her and Dylan I'm going to Blake's for dinner. I'm sure she knows them, but I have to do my due diligence in making sure she remembers them.

"Okay, Mom, sheesh," Sydney says, stomping down the stairs.

"Dylan is downstairs. I have my phone and you have Blake's number too, right?"

Sydney nods, and I can tell she's fighting an eye roll.

"Good. Remember, lock the door after I leave, no friends over, no using the stove–"

"Mom, I know. I'm thirteen, for crying out loud."

I point my finger at her, narrowing my eyes. "Not yet, you're not. Still have a few more weeks."

She gives in and rolls her eyes so hard I'm afraid they'll get stuck.

"I won't be too late. Probably around ten, or so. You can let Dylan play video games the whole time if you want. Call if you need anything, okay?"

"Okay," she says in her snottiest tone.

"Love you, sweetheart." I kiss her on the head.

"Love you too, Mom."

The nerves chewing on my stomach as I walk to Blake's house negate the hunger I felt not ten minutes ago. I promised Blake I wouldn't eat after lunch so I'd be hungry, and until now, I've been starving. I know my children are responsible. I know they're safe. I know they're only four houses away, but I always feel nervous about leaving them. Accidents happen.

I take the longest, deepest breath imaginable before ringing the doorbell. I have to settle my stomach. If I don't eat whatever Blake has for me, I'll never hear the end of it. From myself, not him. He's much too gracious to rub my face in anything.

The door opens, revealing Blake wearing a chef's hat, a white apron, and seemingly nothing else.

"Good evening, miss," he says with a smirk. "Your table is ready."

The tension eases from my shoulders, and I giggle as I step inside. "Are you... naked under there?" I pinch at the edge of the apron.

He swats my hand away. "Ah ah. No dessert before dinner."

"Okay, fine." I put my hands up in defeat.

When Blake's hand brushes the small of my back, the nervousness in my gut dissolves. As we enter the kitchen, I inhale the heavenly aroma of whatever he's cooking, and I'm suddenly starving again.

"I hope you're hungry." He pulls a dish from the oven, plates the food, pours a glass of wine, and sets both in front of me. "Bon appetit."

"Looks good. Smells great. What is it?"

"Well," he says, but starts laughing. "It was supposed to be homemade eggplant parmesan, but I fucked it up. So, this is eggplant parm from Luigi's. Hope you don't mind."

I take a bite, the familiar, but delicious flavor hitting my tongue, and I savor it a moment. "I don't mind at all. Honestly, I'm here for the view." I lift my wineglass to my lips, eyeballing him over the rim.

He lifts his glass and asks, "The kids okay?"

I almost choke on my drink, but I compose myself. "They're fine." My confident tone is more for me than him, but I'm sure I'm the only one doubting it.

"Well, it's only a couple hours. No big deal, right?"

My fingers wrap around the stem of my wine glass, clenching so my nails dig into my palm. There are so many things that could happen in only a few hours. Each one makes my heart rate climb. I shut my eyes, breathing deep, though it's shaky.

"Maggie? What's wrong?"

Not now. Not here. I need to calm down.

I open my eyes, not looking at Blake right away as my gaze darts around the room, searching for five things I can see. I can't find any. My focus is blurred, foggy, like I'm in a cloud. With my grounding technique off to a horrible start, I shut my eyes again and there isn't enough air to fill my lungs.

"Maggie, what's going on?" The sound of Blake's chair scooting on the floor hits my ears. Then, I feel him turn my chair. "What's the matter?"

"I... I can't... focus. The kids..." It all comes out in broken syllables.

"Shit. What do you need?"

"Five... five things I can see..."

"Maggie, open your eyes." It's an order, not a request.

I do as I'm told, and open my eyes to find Blake kneeling before me, his face directly in front of mine. My focus steadies a bit, but he's still blurred. All I can make out are his dark eyes under that chef's hat and his facial hair.

"Look at me. I'm thing number one." As the words leave his lips, my eyes adjust and hone in on his features. His eyebrows are drawn together, the crease between them deep, and all the color is gone from his face, but he's there. "Okay, now find four more."

With a small nod, I let my gaze float away from him and I locate four other objects close to me. The next step is touch. I release the hem of my shorts clenched in my fist and slide my hand into Blake's. After a gentle squeeze, I use my other hand to find three more physical things I can touch. As I move through the rest of the steps, I use Blake to start them off. His ragged breath is the first thing I hear. The delicious scent of his sage and juniper cologne hits my nose before anything else.

My heart rate slows to a normal pace. The trembling in my hands subsides. There's still tension in my shoulders, but I have one last step; taste. I throw my hands around Blake's neck and pull his lips to mine. Our kiss deepens, his divine tongue finding mine, and his arms wrapping around me for a rich embrace.

When he pulls away, our chests heave. He puts his forehead to mine, but I lower my eyelids. He whispers, "I'm sorry. I didn't mean to..."

"It's okay. Not your fault."

"Are you alright?" His voice is low, comforting and smooth.

I nod.

"Do you want some water or something?"

I gingerly shake my head and open my eyes, locking them on Blake's shining brown irises. "I want you."

"Right now? Really?"

"More than ever."

Blake stands, tosses his chef's hat across the room, and sweeps me into his arms. As we ascend the stairs, I cling to him, my heart racing with the anticipation of feeling him again. I need him. More than just sexually. Sure, the last two weeks were hard, and hopefully, *he'll* be hard on me tonight, but after what just happened, I need to feel him with me.

As soon as we get in his room, Blake shuts the door and pushes me against it, his mouth on mine within seconds. One hand twists into my hair as the other slides up my shirt, cupping my breast. His fingers slip inside my bra and roll my nipple between them. I'm already soaking my panties.

I lift one leg and wrap it around his waist. Both his hands come down under my thighs to pick me up before carrying me to his bed and gently setting me down. As he stands, he removes my shirt and tosses it aside. Climbing over me, he reclaims my mouth, and presses his hips into mine. He's hard against my thigh and it sends a wave of lust through me.

I'm suddenly pawing at the apron like a maniac, needing skin to skin contact. As I untie it, he tears it off and plants kisses along my jaw and down my neck, making a beeline for my breasts. My bra comes off and one nipple is sucked into his mouth. I drop my head back, arching my body as Blake undoes my shorts and slides my panties off with them.

His hand comes up my leg and finds it way between my thighs. When his fingers run along me, he lets out a low groan. "Damn, I've missed you," he says with my nipple still in his mouth.

"I've missed you too, can't you tell?" I joke, though it comes out in broken whispers.

His mouth makes its way back to mine and our tongues dance for several moments while his fingers move inside me. I'm moaning and groaning so much, I sound like a damn cow. Hopefully, it doesn't turn Blake off.

His mouth leaves mine and settles on my ear. With gravel in his tone, he says, "Maggie, I'm still hungry."My bliss is broken as I realize my panic attack interrupted our meal. That will certainly be a conversation worth having, but not right now. "Oh, do you want to go back downstairs?"

With his fingers still inside me, he takes my earlobe between his teeth. "No. I'm hungry for you."

He pulls back and locks eyes with me. There's a question in them, but I don't know exactly what it is. I can tell he wants permission for something, but my brain is such a jumbled mess of sexual frustration, I can't even begin to imagine what he wants. Honestly, he could do whatever he wants to me right now and I'd go along with it.

With a smile, he starts placing kisses on me. My cheek, my jaw, down my neck to my shoulder, moving over my breasts gently kissing both nipples, then to my stomach. Lingering in my belly button a moment, he continues moving south until he's kissing the crease of my inner thigh.

"Oh," I say, finally understanding what he meant by being hungry.

His breath is warm on my skin as he chuckles and parts my thighs. His fingers don't leave me as his tongue descends to meet them. The swirling of his tongue on my clit, coupled with the pulsing of his fingers is enough to turn me into a puddle.

My entire body tenses as my back arches and my head dips back. I can't manage words, just clicks and moans. The pressure builds in my belly steadily as my fists grip the bed sheet.

Blake's other hand slides up my side and his fingers twiddle my nipple between them. It's all over. My thighs clench against Blake's head as I'm set on fire with release, screaming his name.

His tongue and fingers speed up momentarily, then slow to a steady rhythm. Blake lays kisses on me all the way back to my face. Putting a hand behind my head, he pulls it up to meet his gaze. There's soft satisfaction in it, but I also see a hint of desire. He's not done yet.

"More?" he asks.

I slide my hand down and take his erection in my palm, pumping him a few times. "Yes. I want my dessert now."

Chapter Twenty-One

September marks the kids' first two weeks of school being over, and we've only now settled into our routine. The early mornings of getting ready for school, ensuring lunches are taken care of, and me commuting to work are exhausting, but we get through it. And not a moment too soon.

Both of my children's birthdays are in September, three weeks apart. Charlie and I didn't plan it that way. It's coincidence.

The day before Dylan's birthday, Blake calls. "Hello there. How's my favorite girl?"

"You have more than one?"

"But you're my favorite."

I laugh, running my hand over my head and down my ponytail. "You're too much."

"What are you up to? Anything exciting?"

"Nope. Sitting at my kitchen table, trying to decide on lunch." My coffee is almost gone, but I really want some more. "You?"

"About to eat lunch."

"Well, we make a very exciting pair, don't we?" I swallow down the last of my coffee, and get up to make another cup.

"More exciting when we're together. What are we doing this weekend?"

I suck in a breath between my teeth, making a hissing noise. "Dylan's birthday is tomorrow, and he requested to have some friends for a sleepover this weekend."

"Oh, and I guess I'm not invited?" Disappointment hangs in his words.

I bite my lip as I mull it over, testing the percolator on the stove to ensure it's cooled enough to touch. "I don't have an issue with you coming over, but as a parent, I wouldn't be comfortable with my kid being at a friend's house and his mom's recent boyfriend hanging around. Especially if I hadn't met him."

"Point taken. Okay, I'll stay away."

"And just to warn you, Sydney's birthday is the twenty-fifth, and she also requested a sleepover." I fill the percolator and set it back on the stove to heat.

"So, I'm Maggie-less those weekends, gotcha." Blake is silent for a moment. "You said Dylan's birthday is tomorrow? Can I come for dinner? I'd like to wish my buddy a happy birthday."

"He would love that, but be advised, he gets to pick what we eat and it's almost always breakfast."

"I love breakfast."

Ooh, I think I know what I'm having for lunch. Coffee goes perfect with breakfast food. "Good." I tuck my phone between my shoulder and cheek to get in the fridge, pulling out the Greek yogurt and fresh berries I washed yesterday. My lip works its way between my teeth as I hesitate to ask my next question. "How do you feel about Mexican food?"

"Maggie, how does anyone, anywhere feel about Mexican food? It's one of my favorites."

"Good, because Michelle wants to meet you and she always wants Mexican and margaritas."

"Ooh, *the* Michelle? Should I be worried?"

I roll my eyes, but crinkle my nose. He might be onto something. "Not worried, but you'd better bring your A-game because she'll be bringing all the questions."

"I think I can handle it. So, when is this happening? How long do I have to prepare?"

"She wants to do it Friday."

"Like, this Friday? Wow, okay." Blake chuckles, but it sounds nervous. "Give me some notice, why don't you."

The percolator bubbles, so I turn off the stove and pour my fresh, hot coffee into my favorite oversized mug. I take a big sniff of the comforting aroma, and turn back to my yogurt I've forgotten about. "Sorry, I've been putting it off."

"Why?"

"You'll see when you meet Michelle." I lick the spoon clean after I serve my yogurt.

"Are you eating something?"

"No. Well, yes. I licked a spoon. Could you really hear that?"

"I'm very attuned to the sounds your lips and tongue make." He groans, quietly, but I hear it. "Alright, Friday it is. Dinner, I'm guessing?"

"Yeah, but Michelle's always late, so there will definitely be appetizers."

He chuckles, but it fades, and he falls silent.

"Blake? Are you there?"

"Huh? Yeah, I'm here. It's just... I'm wondering about... the kids."

I pinch the bridge of my nose, grimacing. Ever since my panic attack at dinner, Blake's been extra attentive. We had a conversation about what happened and why, which helped in its own way. The weight I carry lessened just by knowing he understands. Blake became my safety net that night, and I'm forever grateful he did.

"I've already got someone to stay with the kids." Dylan's teacher's daughter is seventeen, CPR certified, an honor student, and I've met her several times when she's helped Dylan's teacher with school functions.

"Alright, sounds like you've got everything taken care of. Except for one thing. Whatever happened to our kid-free night you were going to set up?"

I drop my face into my palm. "I'm so sorry. I completely forgot. And since the kids are having sleepovers for their birthdays, it might be a while. I'm sorry, Blake."

He chuckles, though it's not his usual lively laugh. "It's okay, Maggie. We'll figure it out. It's not like I don't ever get to see you, I just don't get to see you naked." He clears his throat. "Okay, now I'm picturing you naked, and after those lip-smacking noises, I'd better go before I can't get out of my truck and go back to work. I'll see you tomorrow."

Blake places his hand on my bobbing knee. "Maggie, will you calm down. It'll be fine."

We've been at the restaurant for twenty minutes now waiting on Michelle and Tom. I knew she would be late, but I wanted to get here so I could have a margarita before she showed up. *Speaking of...* I pick up my drink, slurping the last of it through the straw.

"Slow down, Maggie. We've got a whole dinner to get through."

"Exactly what I'm afraid of."

"Hey!" Michelle waves from the entrance as Tom follows behind her, his eyes glued to his phone.

"Here goes nothing," Blake whispers and scoots to the edge of the booth as Michelle reaches the table. He stands and extends his hand. "Hi, I'm Blake. Nice to finally meet you, Michelle."

Michelle's eyes widen a split second as they trail Blake from head to toe and back again. She takes Blake's hand, tilting her head to the side, and says, "You, too." She leans to look past Blake at me. "You didn't tell me he had beard like some sort of hot lumberjack."

I drop my face into my palm, pressing my fingers into my eyes before meeting her gaze again as I shake my head.

She nudges Tom to get his attention. "This is my husband, Tom."

Tom clears his throat and stuffs his phone into his pocket before shaking Blake's hand. "Hey, man."

With a roll of her eyes, Michelle slips out of her jacket and slides into the booth. "Sorry, we're late." Her eyes fall to my empty glass before flicking to Blake's full water glass. "Started without me, I see."

"Hey, you made us wait."

"Well, that's one more drink you have to have." Michelle flags the server down and orders margaritas for herself, Tom, and me, then looks at Blake with raised eyebrows.

"None for me. I drove and promised Maggie I'd get her home safely."

Michelle gives him an approving nod. "Responsible. I like that." She turns to the server. "Just the three, thanks." After the server leaves, Michelle turns back to Blake. "So, Blake, Mags here told me you're a landscaper. What's that like?"

"It's actually great. I'm outside, working with my hands, and I get to create beautiful things."

Michelle folds her hands under her chin and leans onto the table. "I bet Mags can attest to how skilled your hands are."

I nearly choke on my breath, glaring at Michelle, who winks at me.

Blake reaches over and takes my hand, squeezing it before turning to Michelle. "So, what do you do?"

As the conversation flows easily, the margaritas helping move things along, the four of us fall into step like we've been doing this forever. Our food comes as Tom and Michelle, well, mostly Michelle, talk about their jobs, inviting Blake and I into the conversation more than I thought she would.

"How are the kids, Mags?" Michelle asks, taking a break from her meal to sip her drink. "Did they have fun at camp?"

I nod. "They're good. Camp was fun. They've pretty much fallen back into their lives, though. Dylan still wants to play video games all the time, but he has asked about having friends over."

"And Syd?"

I sigh. "She seems to be doing better than last year. She actually asked if she could invite a few girls from school to her birthday, but her attitude still needs some improving."

Michelle turns to Blake. "You better buckle up. Teenage girls are quite the rodeo from what I've heard."

"Actually, Sydney seems really receptive to Blake. He gets more out of her than I do sometimes."

Blake shrugs. "All I do is talk to her."

"Charlie was always good at getting her to open up, too..." My thoughts wander back to when Sydney was six and she found a dead rabbit in the backyard. She was so upset, sobbing uncontrollably. I couldn't get her to tell me what was wrong, but Charlie did. He sat her down and coaxed it out of her. Then, he made everything better. He never told me his secret, though I suspect it was a matter of being a great father.

"Maggie?" Blake's voice pulls me back to the table, where everyone's eyes are on me.

I duck my head a moment. "Sorry, I got distracted. What were we talking about?"

"About Blake being the Sydney whisperer," Michelle says. "What about Dylan? How do you fare with him?"

"Dylan's easy. Bring up the Xbox and he can talk for hours." We all laugh at Blake's comment, because it's true. "But, I've got some ideas on how to get both of them out of their shells."

"Oh?" I ask. This is the first I'm hearing about this.

"Sure. I can take them to baseball games, or to the lake. I even thought about setting up a night where it's just me and the kids. Maybe like once a month? You and Michelle can get together and I can have some time to hang with them."

At first, listening to Blake list all the ways he can connect with my kids creates a lightness in me. It amazes me how much he cares. Then, all I can think about is how Charlie isn't here to do those things, and my heart pounds the lightness out. He's not the one making these memories with my kids, Blake is. As endearing as all this talk is, I have to wonder how long it will be before Blake replaces Charlie.

The beginning of a panic attack takes root in my chest, cementing me to the booth. I lose focus on the conversation as the roaring in my ears grows. I don't want to ruin dinner, but the tequila makes it hard to concentrate.

I'm losing control of my thoughts, when Michelle asks, "So, Blake, I need to know if you're sticking it to Mags because she's a good lay, or if you're in it for the long haul?"

I gasp as I'm torn back into the present, and I notice Blake almost choke on his food.

He uses his napkin to hide his obvious struggle before setting it on the table. "Wow, the server was right. The food is hot." He clears his throat and raises his gaze to meet Michelle's. "Well, I'll be honest. I'm a lazy man, and I find dating tedious and exhausting. I was lucky enough to find an amazing woman right down the street, who not only happens to be beautiful, but also everything I could ever want in a partner." Blake turns and locks his big, soft brown eyes on mine. "So, to answer your question, I'll be 'sticking it to Mags' for as long as she'll have me, which I hope is a long time."

Although my cheeks heat, the words "a long time" ring in my ears. I didn't consider a time frame in regards to dating Blake. How long will this go on? How far will it go? Those are questions I don't think I'm ready to answer yet.

The panic bubbles through my gut once more, and I flutter my eyelashes so I don't shut my eyes. I attempt a smile, but my mouth keeps turning down. I'm losing my resolve, my anxiety threatening to bring this dinner to an early end.

Blake's gaze drifts over my face, his eyes narrowing for the briefest of moments before he leans over to plant a soft kiss on my lips. He's what I can see. What I can feel, hear, and smell. His lips on mine complete the steps of my grounding technique, and the tension melts away as I melt into him. When we pull away from the kiss, I look over at Michelle who's fallen into a swoon. Blake has won her over.

"Alright, well, that's it. Mags, you have to marry this man."

"Michelle!"

"What? I can't let you lose a man who looks at you like that."

We all laugh, though my laughter feels stilted. The seriousness in Michelle's tone negates the joking nature of her words. I've barely come to terms with being ready to date again, and the idea of marriage forms a pit in my stomach.

As if he knows, Blake squeezes my hand, bringing my anxiety to a grinding halt. "Let's not rush things, okay, Michelle?"

Our conversation returns to normal. We finish our dinner, and another margarita, before leaving. Outside on the sidewalk, Tom separates himself and goes back to his phone, while Michelle, Blake, and I say our goodbyes.

"Bye, Tom," I say, eliciting a glance and a wave.

Michelle rolls her eyes. "Sorry, some big emergency or something at work, so I've lost him until it's over."

"Hey, Maggie, I'll go get the car." Blake extends his hand in front of me to shake Michelle's. "It was really nice to meet you. Hopefully it isn't the last." His eyes shoot over her shoulder. "See you around, Tom."

"It was nice to meet you too, Blake. Can't wait to do it again," Michelle says.

Blake bends down to kiss my temple. "I'll be right back."

"Mags, I have only one word for you," Michelle says as she eyes Blake walking across the parking lot. "Dayum!"

"Really, Michelle?" I lay my face into my palm.

"What? That man is hot, hot, hot."

"Your husband is right behind us."

"So? I bet he'd agree with me." Michelle turns and takes my hand. "But seriously, Mags, Blake is great. He's just like you said. He's charming, smart, funny, and he has it bad for you."

I blush. Why, I don't know, but Michelle's words resonate with me at this moment. "Thanks." I wrap my arms around her, pulling her into an extended hug.

In this second, Blake pulls up to the curb and rolls down the passenger window. "Hey, don't get too handsy, Michelle. Maggie's my girl."

Michelle and I giggle, but hers halts as she lays eyes on Blake's truck. "You didn't tell me he drives a truck." She pulls away to lock eyes with me, a strange look in hers. "Promise me one thing before you get into his vehicle."

"Okay, what?" I draw out the syllables, my brow furrowing.

Michelle swallows hard. "Promise me you'll pull into some secluded park or something on the way home, and hump like rabbits."

"Oh, my God! Okay, bye, Michelle." I all but push her away and climb into the truck.

"Please, Mags!" Michelle calls out, holding her hands up as if begging. "Please let me live vicariously through you!"

"I'll call you later," I say, and roll up the window.

"What was that about?" Blake asks as he drives away from the restaurant.

I bite the inside of my cheek, contemplating telling him, but I say, "Just Michelle being Michelle."

The drive is mostly silent as I replay dinner. It ended up being much better than I expected. Michelle's filter stayed mostly on, and if it weren't for my near panic attack, I'd say dinner was a wild success.

Still, the idea of Blake replacing Charlie is a huge thing I need to come to terms with. If that's even possible. Thinking about it now has my core temperature on the rise, so I tuck it away for future processing, and turn to Blake.

I drink him in as he drives, his handsome profile backlit by the setting sun. I take in everything about him and let my senses be soothed. The only bad thing about him driving is I can't taste him. And I need to.

Michelle's words echo in my head. The ones about Blake having it bad for me have etched themselves into my brain while her suggestion for a pit-stop floats around. As we top the hill into our neighborhood, I make a snap decision.

"Don't take me home yet. Go to your house, but pull in the garage."

"What? Why? Don't you have to get home to the kids?" Blake's tone is full of confusion, but laced with curiosity.

"It's Friday, still early, and I have a sitter. I don't have to be home right away."

"Alright." Blake does as he's told, passing my house and pulling into his garage. "We're here. Now what?"

"Close the garage door."

He narrows his eyes, but reaches up and clicks the button. We stare at each other as the door lowers and the light dims.

"Maggie, why are we sitting out here in the dark?"

Do it, Maggie. I unbuckle my seatbelt and climb over the console into Blake's lap. He sucks in a breath, but allows me space to straddle him. My butt hits the steering wheel, honking the horn, and I bury my burning face into Blake's shoulder.

His deep laugh shakes both of us as he pushes the adjustment button on the side of the seat and the chair slides backward. "What are you doing?"

"I need to feel you," I mumble into his collarbone.

"I'm here." He nudges my head up and as I sit back to look him, the garage door opener light clicks off, but not before I glimpse those big, soft brown eyes. His hand cups my cheek, his thumb caressing my heated skin.

The embarrassment melts away at his touch and, suddenly, my body burns with desire. I put my lips to his and, soon, the kiss deepens and Blake's hands are on me, running all over in a frenzy. It takes some adjusting, but our clothes come off and we "hump like rabbits" in the dark of Blake's garage.

Chapter Twenty-Two

"Blake, I'm so sorry." My jaw quivers as I say the words.

He's silent a for moment. All I hear is his breath. "Maggie, it's okay. How could you have known Sydney would get sick? There's always next weekend, right?" The hopefulness in his voice makes my heart sink even more.

I finally remember to set up a sleepover for Sydney and Dylan so Blake and I could have a kid-free night and, of course, Sydney comes home with a fever. She's not dying, but she's certainly not well enough to spend the night at someone's house. "Depends on if she shares it with me and Dylan. I won't know for a few days, so I'll have to keep you on standby."

"I'll take my chances."

I chuckle, but it's stilted. "No. I would feel so bad if we made you sick. I don't want to be the reason you miss work."

"I'd suck it up and go in sick."

"That's even worse! You'd be miserable. Plus, it would take you even longer to get better because you wouldn't be resting." I sigh. "It's just better if we keep our distance until I'm sure we aren't contagious. I'm sorry. I know you were looking forward to this."

"Maggie," I can almost picture the forgiveness on his face from the tone in his voice. "Of course I was looking forward to it, but I'm not blaming you for anything."

"I know, but it's been such a long time since we've had a night together." It's been weeks since our quickie in his garage, and while it did help ease the tension, it also gave me a taste of what I was missing. Now, all I can think about is Blake's hot touch, his intoxicating smell, and his sweet lips on mine. It's torturous having him so close, but unable to feel him. "It's beyond frustrating. Sexually, that is."

Blake laughs and it sounds like he's choking on his lunch. "Well, we've done a few dinners at my house. We can do another one. Once Sydney is all better, of course."

I purse my lips, drumming my fingers on my kitchen table.

"Maggie?"

"Hm? Oh, um, yeah. We could do that, I guess."

"Don't sound so excited about it."

I groan. "Sorry. I mean, don't get me wrong, I love our dinners together..."

"But?"

"But I always want more. I want more time to talk, more time to cuddle, more time to... you know." All this arm brushing, finger grazing, and skin caressing drives me crazy, both mentally and physically.

"Scream my name at the top of your lungs as I make you come." The confidence in his voice has me clenching my thighs. I don't just want to touch him, I want to *touch* him.

No. Scratch that. I *need to* touch him. "Yes. But I also want to be with you. I'd like to fall asleep in your arms and wake up next to you."

"Well, then we have to wait until you can coordinate a sleepover." Blake is silent for a beat, but I can hear him licking his lips. "Or I can spend the night."

My stomach drops. It was only a matter of time until it came up, though I was hoping it wouldn't. Sure, not having our hot, passionate grope-fests is tearing me up inside, but sex while the kids are home is a no-go for me. Of course Charlie and I used to do it. It's part of life with kids, but it was different with Charlie. He never made me scream the way Blake does.

There's the stabbing guilt again. *Sorry, Charlie.* "I don't know if that's an option just yet." The despondency in my voice drags me down.

"We don't have to do anything, Maggie."

I scoff. "Do you really think we can sleep next to each other and keep it PG?"

"Probably not, but if that's what it takes to be with you, then I'll do my best to only think about old men in Speedos."

The laugh escaping me is loud and sharp, but genuine.

"Maggie, you know I'm not going to push you to do something you're not comfortable with, but I miss our nights together, too. Think about it, okay?"

Blake shows up on my doorstep Thanksgiving morning with all the supplies I told him to bring, which was the turkey. The kids haven't had an actual Thanksgiving turkey since Charlie died. Being a vegetarian, I don't know the first thing about cooking one, so I made sure Blake did. I'm in charge of everything else.

This is the first time Blake has set foot in my house in weeks. Since our conversation when Sydney was sick, it's been nothing but a barrage of cockblocking events day in and day out. Sydney was not only sick for a week, but she was kind enough to share it with Dylan, who was then also sick for a week. Then, Sydney decided to join the school play, which meant tryouts and rehearsals, and when I had to pick up a couple extra days in the office to help with a huge case, all my time was taken.

Poor Blake was left on the sidelines, but he never complained.

"Where should I put this?" he asks, holding up the turkey.

"We might as well get it started so it can cook all the way." After I kiss him hello, I wave him onward into the kitchen.

Dylan sits at the table, slurping the milk from his cereal out of the bowl. He wipes his face with his pajama sleeve and turns to Blake, a wide grin spreading across Dylan's face. "Hi, Mr. Blake!" He jumps up from the table and wraps his arms around Blake's middle.

Blake lifts the turkey up to keep Dylan from bashing his head into it. "Hey, Buddy. How's it going? Are you up early to help with the food?"

Dylan pulls back, looking up at Blake with confusion on his face.

I chuckle. "No, Dylan has already called dibs on the basement."

"Yeah, I'm so close to beating this awesome skateboarding game. I've unlocked almost every secret! Wanna come see?"

"Well, I promised your mom I'd help her cook." Blake leans down, acting like he's going to whisper, but he doesn't. "But maybe later, I'll sneak away and we can play some, okay?"

"Deal," Dylan whispers, high-fiving Blake and running off to the basement.

With a laugh, Blake stands up and hands me the turkey.

I arch my eyebrows. "You're crazy if you think you're getting out of this."

"Had to try." He shrugs. "So, what's first?"

Blake and I prep all the food. We whip it out in no time, but decide to make another pot of coffee to be sure we can last until dinner. I take a sip, leaning my back against the counter. As Blake and I eye each other over the rims of our coffee mugs, I can't help but smile.

"What?" he asks, arching an eyebrow.

"I was just thinking about how long that beard has stuck around."

With a smirk, he brushes his fingers along his jaw. "Well, someone said they like it, even though she giggles every time I kiss her."

"Not every time." I take a much bigger sip of my coffee, savoring it as I eye the mess on the counter. "Food prepping is a lot more work than I remember it being."

"Well, it's all done. Now, all we have to do is wait for the turkey to finish."

"I still have to make pies."

"Ooh, that's my favorite part. Not making them, but eating them." Blake smacks his lips.

"Well, in order to get some, you've got to get your hands dirty."

Blake's eyes flash, darkening as they lock onto mine. "I don't mind getting dirty with you."

I blush and smack the back of my hand on his chest. "PG, mister." I set my coffee down and pull out my cookbook. "I have the stuff to make a pecan pie and a sweet potato."

"I've never had either of those."

I gape at him. "You're kidding? Well, you're in for a treat. I've been told my pies put all others to shame."

"I'll vouch for that. Your pie is the best I've ever tasted."

My cheeks go full candied apple red. "Shh. Blake. There are children present."

"Not anywhere I can see." The words come out husky, full of lust, and if my kids weren't in the house, my panties would be on the floor.

I huff, steeling myself. "Either way, we've got pies to make. Keep it in your pants."

Making the pies with Blake is one of the best experiences I've ever had. He listens intently to my instructions, only messing up when I tell him a teaspoon of vanilla and he uses a tablespoon. Oh well, a little extra vanilla never hurt. We laugh and joke, teasing each other and making a gigantic mess.

I put the pies in the fridge while we wait for the turkey to finish, and I turn to Blake. "We've got quite the mess to clean up." Wiping my hands on a towel, I eye the flour and sugar and baking powder dusting my countertops. "Where do we start?"

"I know the perfect place." Blake takes two strides, closing the gap between us and pinning me to the cabinet. One of his hands wraps around the back of my head, losing itself in my messy bun, and the other snakes around my waist as his mouth crashes onto mine.

At first, I want to push away, scared my children will walk in on us, but then, I'm consumed by the kiss. It's all I want, and I don't give a damn who sees. My hands grip Blake's shoulders, pulling him to me, and I hook one of my ankles around his. Our hips press together, his hard length against my thigh. His hand on my waist moves lower to cup my ass, and I feel myself losing my composure. If he so much as grips my inner thigh, I might come.

"Get a room, you two." Sydney's voice breaks the moment, and I shove Blake away. We separate quickly, Blake turning to face the sink and me slouching against the counter.

I look from Blake to Sydney, my eyes wide and my heart racing. Breathlessly, I say, "You're up early."

She rolls her eyes. "Mom, it's like one o'clock. Geez, how long were you guys making out?" She crosses the kitchen to the fridge and grabs a soda. She eyes Blake up and down. "You okay, Blake?"

He doesn't speak, only nods. Before he lets go of the counter, I notice his white knuckles, and I have to swallow. I had no idea what kind of tension he was holding in.

Turning around, he leans against the sink counter. "Anxious to try the pies. I hear your mom makes them better than anyone."

Sydney nods. "She's the best."

Blake slides down the counter to bump hips with me. "Well, then maybe I should call her 'Magpie.'"

My heart stops with my breath as my stomach drops into my feet. I watch Sydney's eyes grow wide as they flick from Blake to me. The air in the room changes, ices over, and we all freeze. Sydney knows what's happening, but Blake doesn't.

I watch the look on his face go from playfulness to confusion to concern within seconds. "Maggie, did I say something wrong?"

Tears well in my eyes, so I escape up the stairs to my room and slam the door. How dare he call me that. It's not a name for him to use, it's Charlie's, and I won't allow it to be appropriated.

Give him a break, he didn't know. I flop onto my bed, the tears streaming down the sides of my face.

There's a knock at my door, but I don't look up. "Maggie?" Blake says, opening the door and stepping inside. "Can I come in?"

"You're already in."

"Okay, can I come sit with you?"

I nod. He crosses the room and sits beside me, the bed dipping with his weight. "I'm sorry about what I said down there. I had no idea that was Charlie's nickname for you."

I sit up, turning to him with furrowed brows.

"Sydney explained."

I flop back down and sigh. "It started as a joke before we were even dating, before I had ever baked a pie. A mutual friend hosted a Friendsgiving the week before Thanksgiving, and we were both invited. We had met a couple times through this friend, and we were amicable, flirtatious even, but nothing serious, yet. When dessert came, I went for the pecan pie first. As I was eating, I gushed over how good it was and how I wanted to learn to make one. Charlie heard me talking and started calling me 'Magpie.'" My throat closes up as my tears flow faster. "The nickname stuck and when I finally got my recipes down, Charlie added to it. I became 'Master Magpie,' but no one's called me that in four years."

"Until me?"

I nod. "I'm sorry I freaked out. Hearing Charlie's nickname for me out of another man's mouth was jarring. Not your fault, though."

"As long as you're okay now. You scared me down there."

I take his hand and squeeze. "I didn't mean to."

"It's alright." He leans down and kisses my forehead.

My eyes dart across the ceiling, my racing heart doing laps around my ribcage. "Blake?"

"Hm?"

"Will you stay the night?" I still haven't had any nightmares, but after this, I don't want to chance it. Having Blake next to me will ensure I sleep soundly.

He pulls back, a glimmer in his eye. "Really? I'll have to go put Oscar in his crate, but then I'll be back."

"Why don't you bring Oscar?"

"Yeah?"

I nod. "He's welcome here, too."

"You're really okay with me staying the night while the kids are around?"

"I've missed you, and I really think I need you tonight. But I can't promise any *adult* time."

A grin, wider than I've seen in a while, spreads across his face. "Any time with you is worth it."

Chapter Twenty-Three

"We could put this garland here, on the stair railing. And then this little snowman could go here..." Blake says.

I'm fighting my hardest not to wiggle my toes while I watch Blake hold decorations up, giving them the eye test of whether they'll look good. We haven't even been home fifteen minutes and already he's picking out spots for all the new Christmas knick-knacks he purchased. It's building an anxiety in me I've been ignoring because I thought I could handle this. Maybe I was wrong.

"Maggie?"

"Hmm," I say, not looking at him.

"Did you hear me? What do you think of putting this Santa sign over here?"

"I'm sure it's fine." I still don't look up.

Blake sighs. "Are you sure you're okay with this?"

"I told you I was." It comes out much angrier than I intend.

"Then why don't you come here and help me. Get off the couch, move around a bit. It might help you relax."

"I'm fine."

"Then why are your knees bobbing?"

Shit. I fought my toe wiggles so hard, I didn't even pay attention to the movement in my legs.

"Maggie, what's going on?"

"It's just... this is all so... fast," I say between breaths. "These are big changes." I squeeze my eyes shut, suddenly unable to focus. My chest heaves with each inhale as I can't seem to fill my lungs.

The day after Thanksgiving, Blake asked me when we decorate for Christmas and it took everything I had not to break down. Last year, I told myself I was going to stop being so pitiful and decorate again, but I used the leaking pipe as an excuse. So, when Blake brought up the idea of getting new decorations, ones without Charlie attached, it sounded doable.

Blake squats down in front of me, rubbing my knees with his thumbs. "Come on, Maggie. Use me. Ground yourself."

I shake my head. "I'm okay."

"I'm here." He kisses my forehead. "I know this is hard, I get it, but–"

"How could you possibly get it?" I ask, popping my now tear-filled eyes open. Blake's eyes widen.

"You have no idea how this feels. You couldn't." I push him away and get up from the couch. "I haven't put Christmas decorations up in four years for a reason, and it's a good one." I turn to face him. "Now you're here, wanting me to change, pushing me to do something I'm not ready for."

"Which is why I asked," Blake says softly. "Why I wanted to do this together, so I could help you through it. Rule number two, remember?"

I sniffle and wipe away a tear. "You want me to be honest? You want that right now?"

"Of course I do." His tone is pleading.

"Okay, I'll be honest." I fold my arms, squaring my shoulders. "I don't want to do this. I don't want to replace all of my and my kids' Christmas memories with new ones. I don't want to push Charlie out."

"I'm not trying to push Charlie out."

"Aren't you, though? You suggest we get all new decorations, pay for all of them, come here and think you can put stuff wherever you want. You've made this into *your* thing, not *ours,* when it's always been Charlie's."

Blake's mouth drops open, but no words come out. The hurt in his eyes is hard to look at, but right now, I don't care.

"I think you should leave," I say, turning my head away.

"Maggie, please. I never wanted–"

"Please, Blake. Go home."

He lets out a deep, defeated exhale, but says nothing as he grabs his coat and walks out the door. I crumble onto the floor into a blubbering pile of tears, shaking with anger and fear.

The hours tick by, but I don't move from my kitchen table. I haven't eaten or drank anything. Pretty much all I've done is cry since Blake left. All the decorations he bought are still in the bag by the front door. I don't have the strength to look at them, let alone throw them out.

How dare he come here and try to make our Christmas into his.

The lock on the front door clicks, and I wipe my face, trying to save it in front of my kids.

"Mom! We're home!"

Relief washes over me at the sound of Sydney's voice. My children are home safe. They come into the kitchen after tossing their backpacks on the floor, but when Syd furrows her eyebrows at me, I'm suddenly tense again. She's so damn intuitive.

"How was school, guys?" I ask in my most un-shaky voice.

Dylan chimes right in, "We had snacks and movies all day!"

I smile at his whimsy. "Good, Dyl-pickle. And, Syd, how about you?"

"Same," she replies, opening the fridge. "What's for dinner? Is Blake coming over?"

My breath catches at his name. "I– I don't know. We didn't talk about it."

She turns her head out of the fridge, an incredulous look on her face. "Talk about it? You never talk about it. He just shows up."

"Well, maybe you don't hear us talk about it." I'm being snippy.

"Mom, can Trevor come over to play video games?" Dylan asks, either unaware of or ignoring the tension in the room.

I groan internally. "Yes, sweetheart. It's winter break, after all." I'm glad Dylan found a friend, but I'm not prepared for guests. I can't punish him for my bad mood, though. "I'll call his mom in a minute. Why don't you go put your school stuff away."

"Yes!" He bounds across the kitchen and upstairs, his feet pounding the steps as he ascends.

Sydney takes a seat at the table, opens the can of soda she got from the fridge, and purses her lips. "So, what's with all the Christmas stuff by the door?"

Crap. I didn't even hide it. Couldn't is more like it.

"Oh, um, Blake wanted to decorate for Christmas. He wanted to surprise you guys after school, but I told him no."

"Why?"

"Because Christmas was your father's thing. I couldn't let Blake take that away."

Sydney fiddles with the soda can tab. "To be fair, you kind of took it away first."

"What?"

"You haven't put out Dad's Christmas stuff since he died."

"I know. I didn't want all of it out reminding us he wasn't around. I didn't want to upset you guys."

"Mom, we don't need reminders Dad's gone. We know. It doesn't matter if his corny snow globe with the creepy Santa inside isn't on the mantle, or if his favorite song doesn't come on the radio, or if you stop making his favorite dinner, we will always know Dad isn't around."

Her words bring the threat of more tears. When did I get such an astute daughter?

"I think it would be nice to have Dad's Christmas stuff out. It helps us remember things. Like the one year he tried spraying the tree with that fake snow stuff and got it all over the place?" She looks past me like she's picturing it in her mind. "You were so mad at him, but it was so funny seeing him covered in that stuff."

I laugh through my watery eyes. "It was funny, after the fact."

"So, can we put his stuff out this year?"

"I don't know, Syd..."

"How about we each pick one thing of his to put out? Then we'll do all of Blake's new stuff. It'll be like mixing new memories with old ones."

A warmth fills my chest as I stare at my brilliant daughter. "Great idea, Syd." My toes start wiggling under the table. "But I don't think Blake will be coming back."

"What? Why?"

I raise my gaze to the ceiling, blinking back the stinging tears. "Because we had a fight and I sort of threw him out." I'm almost too embarrassed to tell my thirteen-year-old about it.

"So, call him and apologize." She says it like it's so easy.

"It's not so simple, sweetheart."

"Why not? Call him, tell him what a jerk you are, and why. He deserves to know why Christmas is so hard."

"He knows. I told him."

"Good. So then he'll forgive you, come up for dinner, and we can all decorate together. Easy peasy." Sydney gets up from the table, hands me my phone, and walks to the door. "Call him, Mom."

"Will a text suffice?"

She rolls her eyes. "Whatever," she says, leaving me in the kitchen alone.

I stare at the phone in my hand. Biting my lip, I unlock the screen. I open up my text messages and the very top one is Blake. He was the last person to text me, telling me he was on his way to pick me up to go shopping for the Christmas stuff. That was the text that started this mess. If he wouldn't have–

No Maggie. This was all you. It wasn't Blake's fault.

ME: *I'm sorry.*

As my trembling fingers type the message and hit send, I suddenly realize I'm unprepared for him not to respond. He always responds, right away. What if he doesn't this time? What if he's mad at me? He has a right to be.

BLAKE: *Don't be.*

My entire body sags into my chair.

ME: *No, I absolutely need to be. I was a jerk.*

BLAKE: *I understand. I know this is hard for you. I wanted to help, that's all.*

His sincerity shines through, even in text, and all I want is to be in his warm, affectionate embrace.

ME: *I know.*

BLAKE: *Are you ok now?*

ME: *Yes. Would you like to come back for dinner? I totally understand if not.*

BLAKE: *I'll be there at 6. Pizza?*

ME: *Sure, thx.*

ME: So, *are we good?*

BLAKE: *Maggie, we were never bad.*

The doorbell rings at six o'clock sharp. I open the door to find Blake standing on my porch with two large pizzas in his hands.

I smile apologetically and say, "Hi."

He smiles back and repeats, "Hi."

We stare at each other for a moment until a gust of icy wind blows through the doorway. "Come in, sorry." I take the pizzas from him, and he removes his coat, placing it on the rack.

Blake turns to me, puts his hands in his pockets, and his eyes briefly fall to the bag of Christmas decorations and the tote sitting next to them. A puzzled look comes over his face as he looks to me for confirmation.

"Sydney made a suggestion. The three of us pick our favorite Charlie decoration to put out, then we put all your decorations up together. So, we're not replacing Charlie, we're making new memories around the old ones."

"She's a smart kid."

"I don't know where she gets it from," I joke.

Blake removes his hands from his pockets, leans down, and plants a kiss on my cheek. "From you."

After dinner, Blake and I sit on the couch, enjoying a glass of wine and watching the kids fight about how to wrap the garland around the staircase banister.

"So, am I re-invited to Christmas dinner?" Blake asks.

"You were never uninvited."

"Well, after this afternoon, I wasn't so sure."

I swirl my wine, watching the legs drain down the sides of the glass. "I'm so sorry for everything. I was out of line.""No, Maggie. You were trying too hard to guard yourself, but you don't have to with me, okay?"

"Okay." I'm not very convincing, but Blake seems to accept me at my word.

"So, do you want me here for lunch or actual dinner on Christmas? When do you guys do presents and stuff?"

"I was thinking about that." I turn to him, licking my lips. "Why don't you come for dinner on Christmas Eve and stay the night?"

Blake narrows his eyes. "Spend the night? Where will the kids be?"

I laugh. "Here. I thought if you spend the night, then you'll be here for waffles or whatever in the morning. We can do presents when the kids get up, then have Christmas dinner. You know, spend the whole holiday together."

"I love the sound of that. Should I bring Oscar?"

"Of course. We have gifts for him, too."

Blake leans over and kisses my temple. Keeping his lips on my skin, he says, "You're too good to me."

"I'm too good to your dog. I could be nicer to you."

He moves his lips to my ear and whispers, "You could make it up to me after the kids go to bed."

I nudge him away with my shoulder. "Behave, mister." Though I'm not sure I could behave myself if Blake initiates anything.

Chapter Twenty-Four

Christmas Eve dinner is a wild success. We have pizza, again, but it's alright because I have Christmas Day dinner all planned out. It will be a feast fit for kings. I'm perfectly fine being able to relax tonight and not worry about cleaning up or doing dishes.

Blake and I sit on the couch, him cradling me against his chest, while the kids lie on the floor, watching our traditional Christmas Eve movie, *A Christmas Story*. Dylan has his arm over Oscar, snuggling with him, and Sydney looks like she's about to fall asleep. Blake's fingers brush the skin of my arm, only stopping every so often when I take another sip of my wine.

When the movie finishes, Dylan sits up. "Can we open our presents tonight?"

"Ha ha, no, honey. Tomorrow."

"Please? Just one?" Dylan pleads.

"They could open the ones I brought," Blake offers.

I turn to him. "You didn't have to do that."

"Of course I did."

"Okay, we can all open one present tonight. The rest are for the morning," I say, pointing my finger at Dylan and flicking it between the kids.

Sydney rolls her eyes and Dylan jumps up, Oscar hot on his heels. He runs to the tree and pulls Blake's gifts, handing one to Sydney.

She gently shakes the box. "Feels empty to me."

"Just open it," Blake says with a chuckle.

Sydney casually peels the paper, finding a plain cardboard box taped shut. She bobs her shoulders at Blake, who nods for her to continue. Sydney cuts the tape with her fingernail and opens it. Inside is an envelope. She sighs and slides her finger under the flap.

"This is a lot of work," she says jokingly. She pulls a gift card from the envelope and flips open the cardboard covering. Her eyes widen immediately. "Holy cow!"

"What is it?" I ask.

"A hundred-dollar gift card to Barnes & Noble! Thank you, Blake!"

"You're welcome."

I turn to Blake, who has a smug look of satisfaction on his face. "That's a lot of books."

"You'd rather her be into makeup and boys?"

"Ha, no. Not yet." I turn back to the kids. "Okay, Dyl-pickle, your turn."

Dylan wastes no time in ripping the paper from his gift. The box is fairly big and my mind races with possibilities for what's inside, secretly praying Blake didn't go too crazy trying to win my kids over.

Dylan finally gets the tape off the box and flips the lid open. "What? No way! A skateboard!"

I shoot Blake a fake scowl.

He kisses my temple. "This is a replacement for the Xbox," he says out of the corner of his mouth. He pulls away, and I stare at him in wonderment as he turns to the kids. "Merry Christmas, you two."

"Thank you, thank you!" Dylan squeals.

"Alright, now it's bedtime. Santa won't come if you guys are awake." I wave my hand in the air, ushering the kids out of the room. Dylan pats his leg for Oscar to follow. He slept in Dylan's bed on Thanksgiving, so now it's protocol whenever he and Blake spend the night.

Blake leans close to my ear and whispers, "They still believe in Santa?"

I chuckle. "Sydney? No. Dylan? Yes. Sydney is a good sport and keeps up the charade, though. She'll go in her room and read until she falls asleep."

"You've got some pretty cool kids, you know that?"

"I do, thanks. How about we finish our wine and open our presents?"

"Oh, I didn't bring you anything," Blake says matter-of-factly.

I elbow him in the side. "Jerk. I got you something."

"Ow. Ha, you know I'm kidding, right? Of course I got you something."

"I know." I down the last of my wine and hop off the couch to grab Blake's gift. I hand the bag to him and take my seat, crisscrossing my legs. "I hope you like it."

Blake pulls the tissue paper out and reaches into the bag. When he pulls out his gift, he looks to me with wide eyes, though they sparkle with excitement. "Maggie... what is–"

"I think you should start sketching again. You said you miss doing it and I could tell by the look in your eyes you want to. So, I got you a sketchbook and some pencils. I don't even know if they're the right kind, but I asked the guy at Hobby Lobby and he said–"

Blake leans over and kisses me before I can finish. "This is perfect. Thank you," he says against my mouth.

He places the items back in the gift bag and gets up from the couch. I watch him walk to the closet and dig through his coat pockets. When he finds whatever he's looking for, he comes back to me and takes his seat. In his hands is a small ring box.

"Merry Christmas." He places the box in my hand.

My heart flutters. My stomach drops. Only one thing could be in here.

"Go on, open it."

With a deep swallow, I pry the box apart. Inside, I don't find a ring, I find two. And they aren't any old rings, they're mine and Charlie's wedding rings. They've been fused together and mounted on a tiny river rock with the words "Now and Forever" engraved on it.

My hand flies to my mouth, my jaw trembling, and through my watering eyes, I see a flicker in Blake's shining irises. "Blake..." I say, my voice barely above a whisper. "How did you–"

"Sydney. She snuck the rings to me one night while you were in the bathroom. I was hoping you weren't going to miss them. I sent them off to this company that makes commemorative keepsakes and voila. Do you like it?"

All I can do is nod in appreciation of the most thoughtful gift I have ever received. Blake has outdone himself. Not only has he given me a beautiful, one-of-a-kind present, but he honored my marriage to my late husband at the same time. He could have given me something to showcase our relationship. He could have made this gift all about him, but he made it about me and Charlie.

Though, now I can't wear it ever again. I shove the thought out of my mind, throwing my hands around the back of Blake's head and pulling his lips to mine. "Thank you," I whisper. "I love it."

As Blake spoons me in my bed, his fingers trace circles on my hip. His chest expands into my back with each breath and his body heat is keeping me warm and comfortable.

"Maggie," he whispers into my ear, "do you want to–"

"I already told you no, sorry. We can't have sex while my children are right down the hall."

"Okay, fine." He rolls onto his back and sighs. He's really being patient about this. "What time do the kids get up in the morning?"

"Depends on how late Syd stays up. Dylan will be up early out of anticipation, I'm sure. But I'm guessing we'll be able to sleep until seven."

"Better than I expected." Blake rolls back to his side and props up on his elbow so he can look at me. "I hope I didn't overstep my bounds with the gifts."

I turn over to face him, cupping his cheek with my hand and caressing his beard with my thumb. "No, absolutely not. You did a great job. Thank you." I lift my head to kiss him. "It amazes me you thought to give me something to honor my marriage to another man."

"Maggie," Blake's tone is suddenly very serious. "I told you I'm not trying to take Charlie's place. I know he'll always be in your heart, and I want you to know I respect what you two had. That's what your gift is about."

I run my hand through Blake's hair, pushing it to the side of his face. "You're the best boyfriend anyone could ever have, and I'm glad *I* have you. But doesn't it bother you Charlie is on my mind most of the time?"

Blake shakes his head. "No. Charlie may be your past, but I'm your present, and hopefully your future, too."

"That's the cheesiest thing you've ever said," I say with a laugh.

Blake doesn't laugh. He keeps his serious expression. "I mean it."

My eyes flick between the two of his, conviction burning in them. "How is it you can stay so level-headed, knowing you have to share my heart?"

"Because I love you."

I jump up to sit. My eyes widen and my lips part. "You... what?"

"I love you, Maggie. I've known it for a while now, but I didn't know how, or when, to say it."

My jaw trembles as I say, "Blake... I–"

"Don't say it back."

"What?"

"Don't if you're not ready. I know it's soon for these feelings to come out. We've only been together six months, but I feel like I've known you for so much longer."

"It does feel longer, doesn't it?"

Blake nods. "And I want it to keep going. I love you, and as much as I want to hear those words from your gorgeous mouth" –he runs his finger across my lips– "I don't want it to be forced, or said for my benefit. I want you to mean it. Okay?"

"Okay."

Blake leans in to kiss me. "Merry Christmas," he whispers against my mouth.

I give into the kiss. I let Blake's tongue inside and I melt into him. His hand grips my waist, inching our bodies closer. So close, in fact, I feel him harden against my hip and it takes everything I have not to tear his clothes off.

Maybe I should. The man not only gave me an incredible gift, but he also gave me his heart. He deserves something, right?

I reach down between our bodies and run my palm down the front of his pants. He groans into my mouth as his hand makes a beeline for my inner thigh. I jerk away, but keep my hand on him. "I can't be quiet when you touch me, you know that." I swallow deep. "But I can if I touch you."

Blake's eyes flick between mine.

"I know you've been holding in some really strong feelings lately, and I want you to know how much I appreciate your patience. Let me do this for you, please?"

The confusion in Blake's eyes melts away, replaced with a hungry need, and he nods.

I put my lips back to his and slide my hand into his sweatpants. His breath hitches as I grip him, but soon, he's thrusting into my palm, matching my rhythm. He's doing a good job keeping his hands from reaching certain places, and I know he's struggling as his moans get a little louder, his breathing heavier, ragged.

When his fingers graze my ribs and shoot back down to my hip, I take pity on him. "Go ahead," I whisper against his mouth, and without hesitation, his hand is up my shirt and pulling down my bra.

As soon as my nipple is between his fingers, it hardens, and I know I can't last much longer. If this continues this way, I'll break my rule and never forgive myself. So, I grip Blake harder, pump him faster, and move my lips to his ear. I take his lobe between my teeth and whisper his name.

He comes almost instantly. The tension in his muscles releases, and I mentally pat myself on the back for a hand-job well done.

"Merry Christmas," I whisper, and kiss his forehead.

Chapter Twenty-Five

"Come on, Maggie. We're going to be late."

I step out of the bathroom, placing the back on my earring. "And that bothers you? I seem to recall you not wanting to go in the first place."

"I don't want to go, but the sooner we get there, the sooner we can leave."

"Blake, this is a New Year's Eve party. It doesn't matter what time we get there, we won't leave until after midnight."

He nods and purses his lips like I've given him new information. "In that case, take your time."

I laugh and cross my bedroom to my closet.

Blake lets out a small groan. "Do you have to get dressed?"

"I do if we're going to Joanna's. Plus, it's like fifteen degrees outside."

"It's a short walk."

I scoff at Blake's joke, pulling a black dress from the hanger. It hits slightly above the knee, has a deep V-neckline, and hugs the curves of my body perfectly. I've been waiting for an occasion to wear it, but never had one until now.

"Will you zip me up?" I turn my back to Blake and lift my hair.

Very gently and excruciatingly slow, Blake tugs on the zipper. His fingers graze my skin as they rise up my back, giving me goosebumps. Once the dress is secure, I drop my hair and fluff it out. I turn from side to side, checking myself in my mirror.

"Fuck, you're hot," Blake says, wrapping his arms around my waist and kissing my neck.

"I thought you liked me better without clothes."

"I'll take you any way I can get you." His kisses grow hungrier, and his hands start to roam.

"Now *you're* going to make us late."

"Worth it."

"The kids are downstairs."

Blake sighs, resting his head on my shoulder. "I know." He lets go of me and runs his hand through his hair. "Okay, let's go."

I know he's frustrated, but this isn't like the other night. It's different, the kids are downstairs watching TV, not in their rooms, asleep.

Across the street at Joanna and Mark's New Year's party, the kids settle in the basement while Blake and I do our best to avoid prying eyes. We've been the talk of the neighborhood, according to Joanna. Either she has nothing else to talk about, or no one has ever heard of two neighbors dating.

It's ridiculous.

Later in the night, Blake and I are cornered by Mark, who's obviously drunk. "And don't even get me started on the presidency. Fuckin' democrats. They're gonna ruin everything," Mark spouts off in slurred syllables.

Blake shoots me a sideways glance with a closed-lipped smile.

"You wait and see. The market is gonna crash any day now," Mark continues.

My heart leaps into my throat at the idea. "Mark, they say that about every president. Why is this term different?"

"Because I've been watching the market trends. I've seen what's happening. Shit, don't take my word for it, ask this guy right here." Mark grabs Blake by the shoulder and rocks him around.

Blake laughs nervously. "Nah, Mark. You've got the wrong guy. I wouldn't know two–"

"What the fuck ever. If there's anyone who pays attention to the stocks and shit, it's Blake."

"Maggie, do you want another drink?" Blake turns, putting himself between me and Mark. "Maybe some more food?"

"Um, sure. I guess."

"You're a lucky lady, Maggie. A single mom with a part-time job and two kids. You've got it made with Blake here."

"Come on, Maggie. Let's go to the kitchen," Blake interrupts Mark and ushers me toward the hall, his hand on the small of my back.

"Oh, I get it." Mark's eyes widen. "You haven't told her yet."

Blake continues to put distance between us and Mark.

"It's gotta come out sometime, Blake! Better do it sooner than later!" Mark calls out as we disappear into the hall.

Blake walks toward the kitchen, but stops and pulls me into the laundry room. He shuts the door and paces in the small space, huffing as he does.

"Blake, why are we in the laundry room?"

Stopping, he looks me in the eye. "So we can get away from Mark to talk." He resumes pacing, this time with his hands on his head, fingers gripping his hair.

"Okay, so talk to me. What was all that about?"

Blake huffs some more, but continues to pace.

"Blake, talk to me." I reach for him, but he steps past me, brushing through my fingers. I press my lips into a flat line and tension settles in my jaw.

"Goddamnit, Mark," he grumbles under his breath.

"Blake. Blake, look at me," I order, the clout in my voice surprising even me. "Rule number two."

He stops, finally looking at me, his features softening. "Maggie, you know I've been open and honest with you, right?"

"Yes."

"Well, there's something I haven't told you. I was going to eventually, but I didn't know when would be the right time." His eyes float around the room, not looking at me anymore.

I bite my lip. "Okay, what is it?"

"It has to do with money."

"Oh." I lay my hand on my stomach. "I can see why you wouldn't want to talk about that. It's none of my business, anyway."

"It's quickly becoming your business."

My head jerks back. "What does that mean?"

"It means you and I are getting serious, at least I think so, and I need to tell you some stuff before it goes any further."

I swallow deeply. Whatever information Blake has is obviously big, but I can't get past the fact he used the word "serious" to describe our relationship. It makes me feel like I'm sixteen and a guy just asked me to go steady. I try to keep my expression encouraging as I fight the ear-to-ear grin threatening to appear, and nod for Blake to continue.

"Maggie, when I went to college, my dad wanted me to go into finance. Like he did, like my grandfather did."

"Yeah, I remember. You didn't want to, though." I fold my arms across my middle and lean against the washing machine.

"No. I wanted to do graphic design. I thought a job in marketing or advertising would be good enough for my dad, but it wasn't. He enlisted my grandfather to convince me."

"How?"

"My grandfather was a big investor and into finance like my dad. So, he gave me a bunch of money and taught me how to invest it. He taught me all about the stock market, when to buy and sell, all that shit." Blake licks his lips, taking the bottom on between his teeth. "I ended up making a lot of money while I was in college."

An incredulous smile creeps across my face. "That's good, isn't it?"

"Yeah, it paid for all my expenses. My art supplies, living off campus, beer. But it didn't change my mind about what I wanted to do with my life, which pissed my dad off."

"So, what happened?"

"He cut me off, other than paying for school, and we haven't talked since I graduated." Blake hangs his head.

I reach out and run my hand down his arm, gripping his hand. "I'm sorry ."Blake lifts his head to meet my gaze. "Don't be. He was a jerk. But that's not the reason I'm telling you all this."

"Okay, then what's the reason?"

"Maggie, I'm worth... a lot of money."

"What is 'a lot of money'?"

Blake scrunches his nose and says, "Three million."

My jaw drops as my eyebrows shoot to the sky. "What? Three mill– Blake, that's *a lot* of money."

"I know. It's also the reason my fiancée and I broke up."

I let go of his hand, a sudden jolt of illogical jealousy rushing through me. "You were engaged? When?"

"I proposed to Myra right after we graduated college. We dated for a while, lived together for a bit even. We were in love. Or, so I thought. After she said yes, I told her about the money, which was a lot less back then, but still quite a bit for a twenty-two-year-old. I wanted to give her a dream wedding. I wanted to give her everything." Blake's face falls with the sadness this story is bringing him. "Then things changed."

"How so?"

"She stopped looking at me like I was the rest of her life, and started looking at me as a budget. All of a sudden, it was about how much she could spend, it was about status and my bank account, not about *us* anymore. We fought about it. I called everything off, let her keep the ring, but it really fucked me up."

"I bet." This poor man. In my mind, I picture Myra to be a woman much like Abbey, and I want nothing more than to slap Myra.

"I didn't want to tell you because I was afraid of it happening again. I haven't been with anyone this serious in a long time, nor have I found anyone who I even considered telling about my money. Until you."

I brace myself on the washer. The vulnerability radiating off Blake thickens the air, so I reach out for him, taking his hands in mine and pulling him to me. "Blake, do you really think I care about your money?"

"No. But to be fair, I didn't think Myra would, either."

"Touche. Well, thank you for telling me." I bounce my toes around in my shoes. "Can I let you in on a secret of mine?"

"Of course."

"I'm worth a lot of money, too."

Blake tilts his head to the side. "What do you mean?"

My tongue juts out to wet my lips and I take a side-long glance at the door. "My father-in-law was an investment broker. He made himself a small fortune, which is why he could afford to build a mansion of a house in Boulder County. He taught my husband all his tricks and gave us all the tips. We did pretty well ourselves. We were able to pay our house off ten years early."

"That had to feel good."

"Yes, it did. But when my father-in-law died, he left all his money and everything to my husband, who left all his money and everything" –I lock eyes with Blake, arching my eyebrows– "to me."

Blake's eyes widen. "So, you got, like, double of everything?"

I nod. "My father-in-law even set up trust funds for my kids for college. If they choose to go, they'll have hundreds of thousands of dollars at their disposal. They're set."

Blake furrows his eyebrows a second before quirking one up. "So, how much are we talking here, Maggie?"

My toes wiggle so rapidly in my shoes, I'm surprised I'm not tap dancing across the floor. "Last time I met with my advisor... five million."

"Five million!? Holy shit."

"So you see, I have no reason to want you for your money. I have plenty of my own."

One side of Blake's mouth ticks up. "I was wondering how a single mom with two kids affords a house on a part-time paralegal's salary. This makes a lot of sense."

"Yes, it does. I also wondered how you could afford to live your lifestyle with the landscaping gig."

He laughs nervously again, rubbing the back of his neck. "Yeah, about that..."

"What?"

"I actually own the landscaping company."

"Are you serious? Here I thought you were an employee, and you're the owner? Why didn't you tell me?"

"Same reasons. Owner implies more money, employee doesn't. I was guarding myself." He tilts his head to the side. "We have more in common than we thought."

"It's a good thing."

Blake caresses the backs of my hands with his thumbs, and a wide grin spreads across his face. "So, you and me are, like, rich together then, huh?"

"Now who's looking at who like a budget?"

The expression on his face hardens like a rock. I've never seen him more serious. "I would never."

I tip up on my toes to kiss him. "Do you want to go back to the party, or go home? Or do you want to go thank Mark for getting us to have this conversation?"

"Ha. I won't be talking to Mark for a while. This may have been a good thing, but he's still an asshole for spilling my secrets."

"So, home, then?"

Blake pulls me in, wrapping his arms around my waist and tugging me against him. "I want to kiss you at midnight."

"Why wait?"

I intertwine my fingers behind his neck as he sways our bodies from side to side. His eyes trace my face, like he's studying me, and I watch them intently. He presses his lips to mine, gently at first, but stronger by the second until I'm pinned against the dryer by Blake's hips.

"Maggie," he moans into my mouth as his hands roam every inch they can reach.

"Hold on." I push him away and reach over to lock the laundry room door.

"What are you doing?"

"Making sure no one walks in on us."

"But, the party. What if the kids need–"

I shake my head. "It's loud enough no one will even know we're in here and I checked on the kids before Mark cornered us. They're fine and quite literally entranced by the huge explosions and karate moves in the movie. They won't be up here for a while." Walking back to Blake, I wrap my arms around his neck and pull him against me. "It might not be the most romantic place, but it could be fun."

Blake's eyes darken as they flick from my eyes to my mouth. Without a word, his lips press to mine, parting them and slipping his tongue inside. His hand runs up my back, grabs my zipper, and pulls it down. He slides my sleeve off my shoulder and kisses his way to it from my mouth before pressing his cheek to mine. "I know you don't like me to rush, but I don't think this is the right place for foreplay."

I take his earlobe between my teeth. "If you must make it fast, make it good."

With a shudder and a moan, Blake lets go of me and allows my dress to fall to the floor. He takes a quick second to rake in my body, even though he saw my underwear at home.

I lean back against the dryer again, rubbing my thighs together and biting my lower lip. My eyes trail from his pants, which are growing tighter by the second, all the way to his desire-filled eyes.

Blake runs his tongue along his teeth, unbuttoning his dress shirt, but doesn't take it off. Instead, it hangs at his sides, allowing his chiseled torso to tease me.

I reach down, undoing his belt and slacks. They slide down his legs to crumple around his ankles. My eyes don't leave his erection, taunting me from inside his boxer briefs. As I reach for him, Blake grabs my wrist and spins me around to face the dryer.

Sidling up behind me, he grips one hip with a warm palm. The other hand runs up my back, stopping between my shoulder blades and pushing me over. Once I'm in the right position, he twists his fingers into my hair and slides his other hand around to settle between my thighs.

He leans over me, his chest against my back, erection against my ass, and puts his lips to my ear. "Don't get too loud." And with that, Blake pushes my panties aside and slides himself into me.

We both gasp and my knees nearly give out, but Blake holds me up. It's been too long since we've had sex, and this not only feels amazing, but the thrill of being somewhere we shouldn't is more of a turn on than I expected.

Blake takes a second to collect himself, then starts thrusting. His hand between my thighs finds my clit and makes circles. It's all I can do to not scream his name, but it's entirely too hard. As is he. I don't know if it's been so long I've forgotten what he feels like, but Blake's cock seems to be at 110% tonight. Not that I'm complaining. As Blake picks up speed, I find it more and more difficult to control myself and I start calling out his name.

He leans down and whispers, "If you can't be quiet, I'll have to stop fingering you and cover your mouth."

That's it. I'm done. This man has made me putty in his hands, almost literally. I hold out for another few seconds before I succumb to this incredible orgasm and tighten around Blake. He thrusts a few more times, allowing me to ride this wave to its fullest extent before letting go himself.

He kisses the top of my back and around my shoulder before he pulls out, grabbing a rag on the washer to clean me up. "Sorry, Joanna," he says with a laugh and tosses the rag into a hamper.

"Call it collateral damage for what Mark did to you."

Blake laughs harder as he pulls my dress up over my hips, helping me slip my arms under the sleeves, and zips me up. He dresses himself and we both take a moment to ensure we are party presentable before I unlock the door.

As Blake pulls me to him for one last kiss, the shouts of drunk party guests counting down the Times Square Ball Drop reverberate through the tiny laundry room.

"Happy New Year, Maggie."

"Happy New Year," I repeat as Blake's lips meet mine.

The kiss is different, more personal, more intentional. It's like this experience opened us up. Not only the intimate conversation which brought us closer together, but a new sexual escapade, the likes of which I've never done in my life. It was thrilling beyond belief. Between the two events of the night, we've unlocked an entirely new level of intimacy and I'm excited to see where it leads us.

unlocked an entirely new level of intimacy and I'm excited to see where it leads us.

Chapter Twenty-Six

Valentine's Day comes and I don't even realize it until I'm getting the kids ready for school and they're both dressed in red.

"What's with the matching shirts?" I ask.

"It's Valentine's Day, remember?" Sydney replies with arched eyebrows.

I smack my forehead. "Of course. I've been so busy with work, I completely forgot."

"And did you forget me and Dylan are staying at Kelsey's?"

Oh, shit. "Yes, I did."

"And you have a date."

"Okay, okay, Syd. I get it. Now, get out of here before you're late."

Sydney giggles as she and Dylan leave the house.

How could I forget about my Valentine's date with Blake? Ever since our fight at Christmas, Blake has been extra cautious about not stepping on Charlie's toes. It makes me feel bad, but also warms me he's so understanding. I hope I didn't scare him, though. Charlie never was big on Valentine's Day, so I told Blake he was safe to plan something.

I look at the clock. What time did he say? Doesn't matter. It'll have to be at least six because of work. A new year always brings a ton of new clients and paperwork. Suddenly, my three days a week weren't enough, so I started working from home on Tuesdays and Fridays.

I pull out my phone to send a reminder text not to come before six, and he responds with a thumbs up emoji. At six on the dot, my doorbell rings. I finish inputting my last notes and rush to the door as the bell rings a second time. I fling the door open, a scowl on my face at Blake's impatience, but it drops as my eyes take him in.

He's in a tux. A bouquet of a dozen red roses hangs in his arm as he eyes me from head to toe. "That's what you're wearing?"

My gaze falls to my baggy sweatshirt and worn-out sweatpants. I dig the toe of my bright pink fuzzy socks into the floor. As I run my hand over my head, stopping on the messy bun, I realize I don't have makeup on. *Wait, why does it matter?* "Are we going somewhere?"

He runs his hands down his torso like he's smoothing out his shirt. "No. I just wanted to scare you."

I huff a breath. "So, what's with the tux?"

"What? Can't a guy get dolled up for his girl?" He shivers. "Can I come in? This thing isn't exactly warm."

"I don't know," I say, leaning against the door frame. "I need to know your intentions first."

Blake sighs, giving me the most adorable puppy dog look. "My intentions are completely dishonorable, madame." He winks, sending a thrill through me. "Now, let me in so I can show you."

I giggle and step aside to allow him to pass. As he enters I get a whiff of his cologne I adore, and I'm a puddle. "How long do you plan on wearing this tux?"

He turns his head over his shoulder as I close the door. "Depends. Where are the kids?"

"Not here. Sleeping at a friend's house. Now, how long before this thing comes off?"

"Antsy, are we?"

"Well, it's been a while since we've been together without the kids." I look up at the ceiling as I think about how long it's been since our impromptu love making in Joanna's laundry room, and realize I've been starved for this man. I run my hand down and up his back, bringing my fingers up the back of his neck and into his hair. "I've missed you."

Blake shudders at my touch, but reaches back and grabs my wrist. "Not yet." He tugs me along, guiding me to the kitchen. "Do you have something to put these in?"

I find a vase, fill it with water, and snip the ends of the roses before placing them inside. "They're beautiful. Thank you."

Blake stares at me with one side of his mouth curved up, and something in his eyes I can't quite place.

As I admire my handsome man in his fancy tuxedo, I'm suddenly reminded of my appearance. "Oh, I'm a mess. Let me go freshen up." I practically run up the stairs. I fix my hair, placing it in a not-quite-as-messy bun, throw on some mascara and lip gloss, and change into proper fitting, but still lounge, clothes. At least, somewhere in the back of my mind, I remembered to shave today.

When I come back downstairs, Blake is standing in the living room. I give him a confused look as I walk up behind him. "Too good to sit on my couch, or is the tux really that uncomfortable?"

Blake turns to me, his eyes smoldering as they meet mine. Once we're fully facing each other, he takes my hands in his. He licks his lips. "Maggie, these last eight months have been fantastic. I can't imagine how empty my life would be without you in it."

My heart leaps into my throat. Very sweet, but where is he going with this?

"I've been looking forward to this day for months. I wanted to make it perfect, something you'd remember for years to come."

I try to swallow the lump in my throat, but it's planted there. He's attempting to instill a memory in me. The tux. The flowers. Valentine's Day, the one day that isn't Charlie's.

"I have only one question for you." His voice shakes.

He's nervous. Oh, shit. Is this–

"Will you keep this a secret?"

Wait, what? "Keep what a secret?"

A wide grin spreads across his face and he leans down to put his lips to my ear. "My little show." When he pulls away, he winks at me and leads me to sit on the couch.

I sit, dumbfounded by what I'm about to see, and I watch Blake dim the lights and put on some music. My head jerks back when the song starts. Not his usual taste of hard rock, the beat of "Flesh" by Simon Curtis comes blaring through my surround sound speakers.

Blake has his back to me, standing perfectly still. Then, his hips start moving to the beat. His foot taps the carpet and as the lyrics come on, he spins around, lip syncing them.

It's all I can do not to laugh. Not because I think he's stupid, but because he's utterly adorable when he's out of his element. And right now, he's so far from his element, he's in outer space.

He takes steps toward me, the look on his face a mixture of embarrassment and worry, but as we lock eyes, his features harden with confidence. His eyes darken and he throws himself into his "little show", as it were. Slowly, he undoes his tux. The jacket comes off first and he whirls it over his head, tossing it to me as I giggle.

His shirt is next. Each button is excruciatingly slow. Right before he tears the shirt off, we lock eyes. A thrill runs through me, settling between my thighs as I watch him crumple the shirt into a ball and throw it over his shoulder.

Blake takes a large step forward so his hips are right in front of my face. I lean forward to kiss his chiseled stomach, but he puts his fingers on my forehead and pushes me away. I frown, and all he does is wave his finger in the air, all the while still mouthing the lyrics.

I didn't even know he knew this song.

He backs away slowly, keeping my gaze. Once he's across the room, he turns his back to me, and before I know it, his pants are off. I'm so taken aback by his performance, I almost don't notice the new boxers he's wearing, covered in pink and red hearts.

I can't take it anymore, and a laugh bursts from my lips. I clamp my hand over my mouth.

He turns his head over his shoulder, giving me a pouty face before spinning around. The pout drops, and desire overcomes his features. My chest rises and falls rapidly as he stalks to me again.

This time, instead of leaning forward to kiss his stomach, I reach my hands around him and grip his ass. He sucks in a breath as I squeeze, and he misses a couple lines of the song. I look up at him, my most sultry face plastered on as I lick my lips.

His cheeks redden beneath his beard, but he finishes the song, ending on a fantastic display of how well he's learned to gyrate his hips. I lie on my back on the couch and he crawls over me, resting his forearms on either side of my head. His new boxers suddenly seem much tighter than before.

I run my finger along his collarbone. "You've been holding back. Who knew you had such great moves?"

"I'm full of surprises, Maggie, my dear."

"Obviously."

His eyes search mine. "So, you liked it? It was good?"

"Mhm. Just wait until you see my panties."

Without another word, his mouth crashes onto mine with a furious passion I haven't felt in weeks. He shifts his weight onto one arm, running his other hand down my side and between my legs. I gasp at his touch. I've missed him. My head falls back, a small moan leaving my lips as I twist my fingers into his hair.

He peppers kisses down my throat and across my collarbone. When he gets to the collar of my shirt, his hands find their way to my back, and he lifts me up to sit. My shirt comes off over my head and Blake stares at me.

A little staring is good. This much makes me squirm.

He chuckles at my unease. "We've been together how long, and you still get nervous when I look at you?"

"I can't help it. You have an effect on me."

A mischievous grin spreads across his face. "I hope that's not the only effect I have on you tonight." And with that, he presses his lips back to mine, lowering me to the couch. In one fell swoop, my pants come off.

Luckily, when I changed earlier, I made sure to change into a matching bra and panties set. And I had the brains enough to make sure it was red, for Valentine's Day, of course.

Blake runs his hands down my body, his fingertips lingering on the lace covering my most intimate parts. "Is this new?"

"Mhm," I hum against his mouth before pulling away. "I've got a few surprises, too."

"Our surprises should get together."

Once again, our lips and tongues are a tangle of desire. His hands roam wildly while mine stay satisfied to trail the ridges of his shoulders and back, making a pit-stop in his hair every now and then. He feels amazing on my fingertips, and I realize how long it's actually been.

Blake spends the night at our house several times a week now, but it's never kid-free. That being said, it makes having intimate time much more difficult. Which is why I need to make this count.

I push up onto my elbows, making Blake rise. He pulls away, but I throw my hand around his head and keep our lips together. I run my hand down his neck, across his shoulder, down his ribs and graze my fingertips along the waistband of his boxers. His abdomen trembles at my touch.

Deepening the kiss, I run my palm along his hardened length. It makes me shudder with need. I weave my legs with his, my body writhing beneath him as he groans into my mouth before trailing kisses down to my breasts. My nipples harden under the lace.

His short facial hairs get stuck in the flimsy material, so he tugs down to tweak my nipple between his fingers.

As I move my hand from his cock, I press my hips to his. He tries to cover up his gasp by taking my nipple into his mouth. I'd smile, but between his expert tongue and his hard cock against my clit I can't even remember to breathe.

He makes enough space between our bodies to work his hand between my thighs. His fingers run along the thin lace barrier, and he groans. "You weren't kidding."

"I'm even wetter inside," I whisper.

Another deep growl crawls out of his throat, and he goes back to tongue twirling my nipple. He pushes my panties aside and slides his fingers into me. Slow, methodical movements at first, Blake picks up the pace with each glorious minute until I'm putty in his hands.

My head falls back against the couch and my fingers twist into his hair as I buck against his fingers.

His mouth leaves my breast and makes its way down my stomach. Stopping at my panties, he runs his tongue along the waistband. He takes it between his teeth, snapping it against my skin. "This material is pretty thin, huh?"

"Mhm," I hum, barely audible as his fingers are still inside me, working their magic.

"I want to try something. Can I, Maggie?"

I don't respond. More like, I *can't* respond.

His fingers inch in deeper and he repeats, "Can I?"

I moan and nod as fast as I can.

He chuckles and slides his fingers out of me. I open my mouth to protest when he grips my thighs and pulls my legs over his shoulders. His mouth dives onto my lacy panties. They're so thin, I can feel his tongue working through them, and once again, I'm a puddle of desire.

As his tongue lavishes me though the lace, his hands run up my sides and find my breasts. He rubs his palms over my hardened nipples, tweaking them between his fingers.

"Blake," I whisper.

He groans, not relinquishing my clit from his frenzied tongue.

"Blake," I repeat, slightly louder.

His growl rumbles through me and his tongue works even faster. I'm right on the edge, when he stops.

I groan and tip my head forward to glare at him.

His face is full of mischief as he places his fingers on the lace, massaging the very spot he was just licking. "I want you to come in your panties, Maggie." His eyes flash with darkened arousal, sending a thrill through me. "And I want to hear you. As loud as you can be. Can you do that?"

I nod vehemently, watching Blake smirk and return his mouth to my panties. I don't know what is so hot about him telling me to come, but I love it. Hearing him say the words is almost enough to push me over the edge. Almost.

I lose myself in the moment. Feeling Blake's tongue on my clit, his beard scratching my inner thighs, knowing he wants me to soak my underwear for him, and his hands all over my breasts. It's wonderful. Nothing like I've ever imagined. I'm moaning and groaning, bucking my hips against his mouth. I don't even know who I am right now, but I like it.

He squeezes my breasts and kisses my clit. "Louder, Maggie," he growls.

I grab a handful of his hair and say his name. I repeat it over and over again, breathless at first, but growing louder with each passing moment until I'm screaming it. As the crest of pleasure breaks and I shudder, Blake's hand leaves my breasts and grabs my hips, keeping me against his mouth. When I'm finally done, he rises up and slides my panties off, admiring them as they hang off his finger in the air. "Can I take these home? I want to put them on display."

I kick at him, but I'm so lost in bliss, it's barely even a nudge.

With a chuckle, he drops the panties and gently pushes my legs apart, which I allow without a fight. Not that I'd ever fight him, but I wouldn't be able to right now if I wanted.

He removes his boxers and crawls over me. Lifting me up a bit, he undoes my bra and flings it across the room. Within moments, he's inside me, moving as expertly as he did with his tongue and fingers. Only this is better, because it's him. All of him.

His rock-hard length fills me in a way I can't describe. Mostly because I'm such a puddle of orgasmic pleasure right now, my brain can't form coherent thoughts. But, also because Blake is more than a big, hard cock. So much more and I'm glad to call him mine.

Pumping harder into me, he kisses me in every place his mouth can reach. I grip his shoulders and arch my back to press my chest to his. He latches his lips onto my neck as my nipples graze his skin, and his thrusts pick up speed. His head bends down to nip at my collarbone, and I lean up to put my lips to his ear.

I whisper, "Make me come again."

That's all he needs to hear. His movements change in all the right ways. It's almost like he feels what I need, where I need it and when, and soon I'm tightening around him as I scream his name again. He holds out long enough for me to finish before ending on a few quick thrusts and a shudder as his head falls onto my shoulder.

We lie here for several seconds, drinking each other in, and it's perfect.

Blake slides himself out of me and leans over to grab some tissues off the end table to clean me up, then disappears into the bathroom.

I curl up onto the couch feeling like I've won the lottery. How did I get so lucky to find a man who not only knows what I need, but wants to give it to me? And he happens to be absolutely gorgeous.

Everything about Blake is wonderful, and it's time I start giving back to him. Starting now, I'm going to make more time for us. More kid-free time, more nights together, more uninterrupted Blake and Maggie togetherness.

Chapter Twenty-Seven

Weeks go by and my promise to myself for more Maggie and Blake time has been broken.

Valentine's Day was perfect. So was the next morning. After that, everything has fallen apart. Sydney comes home with her first ever C- on a test and is in shambles for days. She's always been proud of her academic skills, as have I, so this is a devastating blow. I have to tell Blake to give us some space.

Then, work explodes with new clients and my caseload doubles. I end up having to not only work Tuesdays and Fridays, but I have to be in the office to get everything done by my deadline of March 1st. So much for going part-time.

And, par for the course, Dylan brings home the most horrendous cold and shares it with Sydney. Magically, I don't get it, but my kids are out of commission for a week between the two of them, and much like last time, I can't allow Blake to be around us until I know we aren't contagious anymore.

This all happens in three weeks. I'm exhausted.

So, when Blake's ringtone comes echoing through the air, my heart flutters and sinks at the same time. "Hello," I say, in my most sultry voice.

"Hello? Who is this? I'm looking for Maggie."

I pinch my nose shut, changing my tone to a hoarse, nasally one. "Maggie's not here right now, Mr. Averson."

"You're a little too convincing, Danny." I can almost hear Blake shiver through the phone. "What are you doing?"

"Oh, you know. Catching up on depositions. You?" I glance at the clock, it's almost noon. He's on lunch.

"Just stepped out for lunch." *Nailed it.* "Me and the guys are getting tacos, but I thought I'd take a minute to check in with you. How's everything going?"

He misses me. He's fishing for a lead on when we can hang out. "I think everything is finally under control again. Sydney picked up some extra credit, so her grade is back up to ninety-five percent. They're both completely done with the cold and I guess I'm not getting it, knock on wood." I rap my knuckles on my desk. "And I'm about to hit send on the last of my work and head to lunch myself. I think that's it."

"Good, I'm glad things are back to normal."

"Well, almost everything." I sound more pathetic than I intend.

"That's actually part of the reason I was calling. What are you and the kids doing Friday after school?"

I think for a minute. *Friday, Friday, Friday.* I'm off on Friday. Like, actually off. No more extra shifts for me. And the kids aren't doing anything I know of. "Nothing. We're completely free."

"Good. I'm taking us all out to celebrate your birthday."

Shit. Is it my birthday already? I open the calendar on my computer. Yep, there it is. March 17th, staring me right in the face. When I was in college, I used to love sharing my birthday with St. Patrick, but those days are long behind me. I stifle a gag at the memory of how green food coloring tastes in Coors Light. "No green beer, okay?"

Blake outright laughs. "I'll take beer off the list. Besides, the kids are coming."

"Oh, yeah. You said all of us. Okay, what are we doing?"

"That's for me to know and you to find out. I've got to go, but I'll call you when I'm off. Love you, Maggie." He hangs up before I can even reply.

He never waits. Probably because he knows I won't answer. I sigh. It's not that Blake isn't amazing, and it isn't at all that I don't have strong feelings for him. It's just, saying "I love you" to a man who isn't Charlie sounds strange in my mind. I can only imagine how it would taste on my tongue if I said it out loud.

I shake my head to clear it. "Enough." I close my laptop, swiveling in my chair to grab my purse and coat. I deserve a Starbucks pastry for all my work.

Friday comes, and I'm honestly surprised my doorbell hasn't rung all day. Blake is absolutely the kind of guy who would take the day off, show up on my doorstep unannounced, and dote on me every single second we're together.

But no one has come to my door. My phone hasn't even buzzed since my happy birthday text from Michelle this morning.

I run my hand down my pencil skirt. As I was expecting Blake earlier, I made sure I was more presentable than on Valentine's Day. I check the time. The kids should be home any minute.

I'm sitting at my kitchen table, nibbling at my afternoon snack, when my phone finally dings. I pick it up so fast it nearly flies out of my hands. I'm laughing at myself as I click the messages.

My heart sinks.

> **MICHELLE:** *Hey, what are you doing?*

> **ME:** *Sitting here waiting for Blake to call.*

> **MICHELLE:** *You poor lovesick fool. Go outside and get some fresh air or something.*

> **ME:** *Did you text me to berate me?*

> **MICHELLE:** *;) No. I need Mexican food and margs, stat. My treat. You let me know when you're available and we'll make it a bday present. Cool?*

> **ME:** *Sure, sounds good.*

> **MICHELLE:** *Sweet. See you later. Now GO OUTSIDE.*

> **MICHELLE:** *In the front yard.*

My smile turns into a frown as I pull my eyebrows together. Why is she being so assertive? And why did she specify the front yard? I shrug, down the last of my tea, and head to the front door. I pause when I grab the knob, my heart fluttering a mile a minute.

Get a grip, Maggie.

I shake my head. Opening the door, I step onto my porch, but I gasp and stop in my tracks as I lay eyes on Blake standing in my front yard with Dylan and Sydney on either side of him. Sydney's holding her phone while Dylan has a Bluetooth speaker in his hands. Both of them have giant smiles on their faces.

Blake is smiling, too, but his is more mischievous.

"What are you guys doing?" I ask.

Sydney shares a look with Dylan before glancing up at Blake who gives her a crisp nod. She taps her fingers on her phone and music pours from the speaker.

He's not going to strip in my front yard, is he? I giggle at the thought, but stifle it so I don't hurt their feelings. But then, I recognize the song. It's "Shut Up and Dance With Me" by Walk the Moon. Definitely not a stripping song.

Blake begins lip syncing again as he takes steps toward me. When he reaches the porch, he extends his hand. I take it, reluctantly, and he yanks me down into the yard, wraps his arms around me, and sways us to the music. We dance the entire song in my front yard as our neighbors watch from their yards, windows, and even cars as they drive past. A few even honk their horns.

I throw my hand over my surely red face, but he pulls it away and locks eyes with me. Blake doesn't bat an eyelash. He just keeps dancing. And he's pretty good, even with his clothes on.

The song ends and Blake dips me dramatically to finish our dance. Dylan and Sydney clap wildly with Sydney jumping up and down on her toes. When Blake pulls me back, he plants his lips on mine in a tender kiss and whispers, "I told you I had surprises."

"You never cease to amaze me, Blake Averson."

"Mom, that was so fun!" Dylan comes rushing up to us, throwing his arms around me and squeezing.

"Yeah, Mom. Who knew you could move like that?" Sydney chimes in, a little more sarcastic than I'd like, but I'll take the compliment.

I ruffle Dylan's hair. "I was young once, you know. Now, you two go in and put your stuff away. Get out any homework you have for the weekend so we don't forget to do it." I eyeball Dylan mainly since Sydney is working hard to keep up her GPA.

The kids groan as they disappear through the door, and I turn to Blake, my hands on my hips. "Dancing in my front yard? Really?"

"Hey, they can't all be stripteases," he whispers against my ear and, suddenly, my cheeks feel hotter.

"Too bad." I kiss him softly. "Did you really tell Michelle to text me about coming to the front yard?"

"Nope. Sydney did." The smugness in his tone is palpable.

"Sneaky. So, was this your big plan for today?"

His eyebrows furrow. "If you think this is all I have in store for you, then you don't know me at all, Ms. Hansen." He takes my hand, tugging me toward the house. "Now, come on. You can't go out with us wearing that."

"They're after me!" Blake squeals as he jumps past me from one trampoline to another.

I laugh watching him, Dylan, and Sydney chase each other around the indoor trampoline park. They've started some game of tag with Blake being the target.

The three of them zip around, Blake narrowly escaping the kids' hands each time.

I double over in laughter as my two children corner Blake and tackle him to the ground. Dylan rushes up to me first. "Mom! Did you see? We got him good!" He fist pumps into the air and bounces away.

Sydney ambles over with Blake, patting him on the shoulder before scooting off to another play area. Blake sidles up to me and wraps his arm around my waist, kissing my temple. "Having a happy thirty-seventh birthday?"

I nod. "Thank you."

"Of course."

"No. I mean it." I turn my gaze to meet his. "Thank you for all of this. Not only my birthday, but including the kids. It means a lot to me."

"Maggie, they're your *kids*. Why wouldn't I include them?"

"I kind of thought you'd be vying for another kid-free night."

Blake sighs. "While I do love those, and I'd love more of them," –I glance away, but he puts his knuckle under my chin, turning my head back to look at him– "all I want is to spend time with you. And I know that means the kids, too. They are *the most* important people in your life, and I'm happy to share you with them. I knew that when I signed on to date you." He pulls my chin up and brushes his lips against mine.

"Thank you," I whisper against his mouth.

He deepens the kiss, and I wish he had asked for another kid-free night when Dylan runs up and tugs on Blake's arm. "Mr. Blake! This is so much fun!"

Blake presses his lips into a line, but flips his frown upside down as he turns to Dylan. "I'm glad you like it, Buddy."

Dylan turns his wide, excited eyes on me. "Can we go to one of these in California?"

"I don't know, sweetheart. I'll have to check, but if they have one close to the hotel, we can try to go."

"Woohoo!" Dylan bounces away again.

My chuckle is cut short when I turn to find a confused look on Blake's face. "What?"

"California? What's Dylan talking about?"

Now it's my turn to be confused. "The trip next week for spring break. I'm taking the kids to California, remember?"

Blake shakes his head slowly. "This is the first I'm hearing of it."

"What? No. Blake, I'm sure I told you."

"Maggie, if you had told me, don't you think I'd have tried to invite myself along?"

I lift my gaze to the ceiling, my eyes darting back and forth. He's right. He absolutely would've invited himself to go with us. *Shit.* "I'm so sorry, Blake. I can't believe I forgot." I drop my head and rub my temple. "Maybe I thought about telling you and then it slipped my mind with all the craziness of the last few weeks. I don't know. I'm sorry."

"Maggie, Maggie. It's okay. I'm not dying over it." He leans down and kisses me again. "Just next time, remember to tell me so I don't call the police when you don't answer your door."

"Promise."

CHAPTER TWENTY-EIGHT

Two days of being in California and I'm ready to go home. The kids and I have been going nonstop; sightseeing, eating, and hardly sleeping has taken its toll.

On day three I talk the kids into going to the hotel's indoor pool. Dylan loves to swim so he was an easy sell, and Sydney will take any chance to sit and read. Me? I'm happy to park my butt in a lawn chair and relax. Which I'm doing, until Sydney interrupts me.

"Mom, are you okay?"

"I'm great, sweetheart. Why?"

"You just... You seem happy."

I chuckle. "And that's a bad thing?"

"No, I didn't mean it like that."

"Then what did you mean?" I sit up so she and I are eye level.

"It's almost the end of March, and next month is–"

"Syd." I hold my hand up to her. "I know where you're going with this, and I promise I'll do better."

"You said the same thing last year, too."

Ouch. "Okay, but last year was different. I've adjusted to working part-time, we have a new house–"

"We had the house last year."

I grit my teeth. "Yes, but it was still an adjustment. We hadn't been in the house a full year and I was still having all kinds of problems with it. I was stressed about you two going to new schools, and the new neighborhood. It was a lot, even if it had been nine months." I take a breath, relaxing my jaw. "Plus, I have Blake to distract me now."

"Yeah, why didn't you invite him to California?"

Indignation flares in me. "I really thought I had, sweetheart. And, furthermore, Blake doesn't have to be in on everything we do. He and I aren't attached at the hip." My words are tight.

"Geez, Mom. Okay. I just thought it was weird you didn't bring him."

I sigh, flopping against the chair back. "Sorry, but I don't know why it's such a big deal for Blake not to come with us."

"Because he's basically a part of us, Mom."

I whip my head over to look at my daughter in utter confusion. "What?"

"Blake is, and has been, around during all our big moments. Holidays. Birthdays. He even gave me a congratulations card when I got my GPA back up. He's trying real hard to be a dad."

My heart leaps into my throat. *Dad?* She thinks he wants to be their dad? Does he? I shake my head and tuck the thought away for later.

"And I don't want you to go all AWOL and shut him out with the rest of the world when you-know-what happens."

"Sydney, I won't do that. I told you I'll do better."

"Maybe you should call your doctor. You know, just in case."

I gape at her. "I haven't seen my therapist since we moved, and things have been fine. Like you said, it's almost the end of March and I'm happy. I don't need therapy anymore."

"Okay, but it could help you get through the next couple months without having to hibernate. You know Blake will have questions, and that always ticks you off."

"Even if I have to disappear for a while, which I won't, it'll be okay. Blake understands."

"Yeah, when you tell him what's going on. Does he even know about Dad's birthday?"

"No, he doesn't. And he doesn't need to." I glance at Dylan in the pool, alone. "Everything will be different this year. You'll see." I lie back and close my eyes. "Now, go swim with your brother."

"Okay, Mom. Whatever you say."

Sydney takes her leave of me, and I'm left to wonder, is she right? Does she know me better than I know myself? I shake my head. No. Things will be different this year. I've made it this far without my therapist and without having a nervous breakdown. I haven't even had a nightmare in almost a year. I'll show everyone I'm not some frail flower who crumbles under the weight of emotion. I'll be fine.

Blake picks us up at the airport. As soon as I see him, the butterflies flutter through me. I told Sydney there was nothing to worry about.

After greeting me with a kiss and a couple high fives for Dylan, Blake throws our bags into the back of his truck, securing them with bungee cords, and climbs into the driver's seat. "Everyone buckled?" We all nod. "Okay, let's get you guys home."

The entire drive, Dylan does most of the talking. Sydney chimes in a few times, but only when prompted. I sit silently, content to look out the window while my hand is entwined with Blake's and resting on my thigh.

Once we get home, the kids grab their suitcases and hurry inside, leaving me and Blake alone in the truck. As soon as the front door shuts, Blake's hands are around me, pulling me in for a kiss much stronger than the one at the airport.

"Don't ever leave again," he grumbles.

I chuckle. "Blake, it was four days."

"Worst four days of my life."

"We went weeks without seeing each other after Valentine's Day."

"Yeah, but I knew you were right here. I could come see you if I needed to. California is a little farther away."

"Okay, fair. But I'm home now." My words are cut off by a yawn.

"Tired?"

"Extremely. We didn't stop the whole time we were there, and I barely slept. The kids crashed every night, but I stayed up to text someone who missed me." I run my finger down his cheek.

"Michelle?"

I laugh outright. "Blake Averson, you are *so* funny. Now, can we please go inside? I need a nap."

He nods and climbs out of the truck's cab. After grabbing our bags, he meets me at the front door and follows me inside where I tell him to set the bags down. We'll deal with them later. I go to find Dylan, and he's in the basement already.

"Dylan, are you okay down there?"

"Yeah, Mom. I'm playing Xbox! Can Trevor come over?"

"Not yet. I'm going to take a nap. You know where to find me if you need something."

"Okay!"

Next, I find Sydney already in her room. I tap lightly on her door. "Syd? You good?"

"Yeah, Mom. Just reading."

"Didn't do enough on the plane, huh?"

"Ha, ha. I have some stuff to catch up on for school. I want to get a head start for the next big test."

"Well, I'm proud of you. I'm going to take a nap. Dylan's in the basement, so if you guys need me–"

"Yeah, yeah. You'll be in your room. I know, Mom." I can almost hear her eyes rolling from behind her book.

I meet Blake in my room. He's already turned down the blankets and crawled in, patting the bed to invite me to lie next to him, which I do without hesitation.

I curl into him, snuggling against his chest and wrapping my arms around his middle. His chin rests on top of my head, his breath moving my hair.

I giggle, running my hand up to scratch my head. "That tickles."

"Sorry." He adjusts his position, turning his head toward the ceiling and taking some strands of my hair that get caught in his beard. "Better?"

I nod, my eyes closed, and my heartbeat falls into step with his under my head.

"See? I should've come with you guys. I could've run interference so you could get some sleep."

I sigh, no longer relaxed. "Blake, I said I was sorry. I really thought I'd told you about the trip."

"I know, and I said it's okay."

"Well, obviously it isn't if you're bringing it up right now."

"Just promise to include me in the next one, okay?"

I push back and lock eyes with him, suddenly not so tired anymore. "First of all, I haven't given any thought to our next family vacation. Second, I include you in all kinds of things we do. Things that have been just me and my kids for years, now include you."

"Maggie, I–"

"And third, if I want to take a vacation with my kids, by myself, I can. They're *my* kids, and I don't have to share everything we do."

Blake's wide eyes flick between mine, his brow furrowing as he searches for something in my gaze. He must come up empty, because his eyes fill with defeat, and he swallows. "Okay, noted." He slides his arm out from under me and scoots off the bed. "I'm going to go. You should rest."

I sigh. "Blake, I'm sorry." I rub my eyes, pressing my fingers into the lids. "I'm just really tired."

"It's okay, Maggie. I know." His words are laced with sadness as he leans down to kiss the top of my head. He runs his hand down my head, smoothing down my stray hairs, and stops to cup my cheek. "I didn't mean anything by it. You can do whatever you want with your life and kids anytime. Now get some sleep."

I watch Blake amble out of the room, a listlessness in his step as he gently shuts the door. With an exasperated groan, I flop onto my back. Tears form in my eyes as I stare at the ceiling and wish I wasn't this way.

I told myself I would be better this year. I told Sydney I would be better, and here I am, failing already. March isn't even over. Am I really going to let the overwhelming emotions which April brings turn me into a worthless pile of devastation? I have for four years now. Why did I think year five would be any different?

Chapter Twenty-Nine

I slide a chip into the salsa in front of me, sighing as I do. Michelle is never on time. I should know better than to rush out of the office. I might as well order since I know what she wants.

No sooner do I have the thought, Michelle flops into the booth. "Sorry," she says without even looking at me while she takes off her coat and settles into her seat. Her eyes land on the chips and salsa first. "Ooh, yum. I'm starving."

"So am I."

"I said sorry." She pops a salsa loaded chip into her mouth. "So, what's the haps, Mags?"

"Not much. Trying to get into the swing of things after vacation."

"Yeah, that's always a bitch. Was Cali fun, though?"

I nod. "We literally didn't stop, and I hardly got any sleep. But it's worth it to make those kinds of memories with the kids."

"I bet Blake missed you, though."

"Oh yeah. He and I texted every day and every night before bed."

"Awwwww. So, did he give you a big welcome home present?" Michelle locks eyes with me, eyebrows bobbing.

"Ha ha, no." He's messaged me a few times over the weekend to check on me, probably because I bit his head off Friday afternoon. I told him the kids and

I needed some time to adjust to being home before they went back to school today, which seemed to satisfy him.

"No? That man is absolutely smitten with you, and you're going to sit there and tell me he didn't fuck the ever loving crap out of you? I call BS."

My mouth drops open. "Crude much? While I can assure you Blake takes care of my needs, after he picked us up at the airport, we had a wonderful drive home where the kids promptly settled back into their lives, and I was so tired I needed a nap. Not an all-out sex fest."

Michelle rolls her eyes, looking eerily similar to the emoji she sends so often. "Okay, so you two took a nap together? That's cute, I guess."

"It would have been if that's what happened." I drop my gaze to the table.

"Uh oh. I know that look. What happened?"

I pinch the napkin on my lap between my fingers and twist it. "He brought up the fact he didn't come on the trip."

"Yeah. I thought it was weird he didn't go. What's with that?"

I huff and sit back against the booth, folding my arms. "I don't know. It slipped my mind, I guess. Which I don't even know how since I remember the kids asking if he was coming when we planned it. I told them I'd check to see if he could take the time off work, but I guess I never did."

"Got lost in your head again, huh?"

"Yeah, but also why does everyone think it's so weird for me to spend quality time with my kids? This is exactly what I went off on Blake about. He doesn't have to be in on everything." My words are clipped, much like how I was with Blake a few days ago.

"Geez. Okay, okay. It just seems like something you'd want him around for."

"It's not that I don't want him around. I just wish it wasn't such a big deal for me to do things without him."

Michelle stays silent, her lips pursed, and her eyes narrowed. "Why do you want to do things without him?"

"I–"

"You ladies care to order now?" The server with perfect timing chooses this moment to reappear. We order our food and drinks, and resume our conversation as he disappears once more.

"You were saying?" Michelle leans her elbows onto the table, her hands folded under her chin.

A lump takes up residence in my throat. "It feels too soon to bring him on a *family* vacation."

"Mags..."

"I know what you're going to say." I throw my hand up. "It's been almost five years. Charlie's not coming back. He'd want me to be happy." I pick up a chip and stir the salsa, staring into it blankly. "It's not that easy, Michelle."

"Why?"

"Because of Blake." I press my fingers into my eyelids. "I mean, he's amazing and I'm overwhelmed at how much he loves me, but I still have the horrible feeling of losing Charlie altogether."

"I thought you worked on that with your therapist? What does she say about it?"

I shake my head. "I haven't seen her since before we moved."

"What?" Michelle stops mid-lift of her drink to gape at me. "You still haven't gone? Why not?"

I shrug. "It kept getting pushed back. Every time I'd think about it, something would distract me."

"Well, maybe you should call her." Michelle leans back against the booth, folding her arms.

"Why? I've been making progress on my own. Sure, it hasn't been all roses, but a year ago, I wouldn't have left the kids home alone to have dinner with you."

"They're home alone? What happened to Blake hanging with them? He mentioned that when we all had dinner. Or did I have one too many margaritas?"

I shake my head. "No, you're remembering correctly. He did make that offer, but I don't need him to stay with the kids. I'm okay leaving them for a couple hours. That has to count for something."

Michelle's shoulders visibly relax, but her arms stay folded. "Okay, you're right. That's a huge step for you, but what about the next two months? How are you handling those?"

"I feel good about it." Lifting my margarita, I take a large sip to help wash down the lump forming in my throat. "I mean, last year, I made it well into April before I broke down, and even then, it was just a weekend of tears."

"Wasn't last April when you slapped your coworker and got put on a leave without pay? That's your definition of making progress?"

I groan, tipping my head back a moment before lowering my gaze to meet Michelle's again. "I'm not saying I haven't struggled, but I'm getting better. My anxiety hasn't been as bad."

"Except when it involves Blake."

"Not fair. It's not like I'm doubting our relationship, I just need to go slower with some things. Blake is always understanding."

"And does he understand what he's in store for?"

My toes wiggle in my shoes. "He, uh, doesn't have an opinion because I haven't told him."

"Mags," Michelle groans. "You need to."

"Why, when I'm doing much better? Even Sydney said I seemed abnormally happy for this time of year."

"Yeah, but she knows all it takes is one trigger to make you flip on a dime. And she knows how to handle it. Hell, even Dylan knows, but Blake doesn't. Me and the kids may be the ones who've helped you through all these years, but Blake hasn't even been told about it." She leans forward, reaching across the table to take my hand. "He's going in blind."

I pull my hand from hers. "He's got nothing to worry about."

Michelle's mouth opens, but our server returns with our food, so instead she sighs and sits back against the booth. She doesn't dive in like normal, but I do. I focus on my food, keeping my eyes on my plate to avoid her gaze.

With a heavy sigh, Michelle says, "Be careful, Mags. These next two months are always hard for you, and I don't want you to get hurt. Or Blake."

Me neither.

I spend the entire next week thinking about my conversation with Michelle. Her urging me to talk to Blake about what could happen these next two months replays in my head, but now sounds like it's coming through a megaphone. The thoughts are so loud, I have trouble concentrating at work. So much so, I have to bring some work home to finish over the weekend.

I only see Blake twice all week, but just for dinner. He doesn't spend the night which makes guilt churn in my stomach. I've been a terrible girlfriend these last couple weeks between ditching him for our vacation and then avoiding him because of the conversation I don't want to have.

That's why when my phone rings and I see Blake's face pop up, I start biting my nails. Today is the last day of March. Tomorrow is April 1st and to anyone else on the planet, I'm sure it's another April Fools' Day, but to me, it's the day that makes me feel like a fool for the way I act.

I'm already acting foolish by avoiding Blake. He deserves more than the wayside, but I don't know how to keep him around without falling into the pit of guilt I have dragging me down.

But I can't avoid him forever. "Hello."

"Wow. Don't sound so happy to hear from me." His chuckle echoes through the speaker.

"Sorry. What's up?"

"I was calling to say hi. See how my favorite girl was doing."

"I'm okay."

His tone goes from playful to serious. "Only okay? Maggie, what's wrong? You sound down."

"Nothing. Tired. This last week was exhausting."

Blake is silent. I can almost hear him chewing on my words.

"Blake?"

"Yeah, I'm here. Tired, huh? Well, why don't I pick something up for dinner and bring it over? So you don't have to worry about cooking. Would that help?"

It absolutely would, but I don't want to see him right now. "It's nice of you to offer, but not tonight. I'll make something quick."

"Maggie, did I do something wrong? Ever since you got back from California, you've been distant. Don't tell me you met someone else out there? Some super-hot surfer guy who calls everyone 'dude'."

I laugh, but it's stilted. "No, there's no one but you."

"Good. Now what's wrong?"

I bite my quivering lip, unable to tell him all the things I want to. "It's an off day. I'll be alright. How about we do something this weekend? You, me, and the kids," I offer, even though I know it's a bad idea.

"I have to wait until the weekend? Awww..." He sounds like a kid who dropped his ice cream. "I guess I can handle that. You need anything, you let me know, okay?"

"Will do."

"I got to get back to work. I'll text you later."

Chapter Thirty

Somehow, I make it through the week of working in the office. I've arranged to work from home from now until after Charlie's birthday. I learned my lesson last year, and from the way Abbey's been avoiding me, I must look like I'm about to break.

I shake my head. I don't want to think about that right now.

It's Friday afternoon. The kids will be home any minute, and Blake will be here not long after. When I offered for us to do something this weekend, he weaseled his way into spending the night tonight.

I shouldn't be so harsh. Weaseled is a nasty word for it. He's not a weasel, just a lovesick man who deserves better than me. Better than the way I've been treating him. I keep telling myself to change my behavior. To change my mindset and do better. It's easier said than done, though.

Like clockwork, at 3:15 p.m., the front door opens, and my children come strolling in. Even though they're practically teenagers, I'm still relieved they're home safe and sound. Since it's Friday, Dylan brings his friend Trevor with him. They make a snack and head for the basement. Sydney takes her stuff to her room, and then to my surprise, comes back down right away. My face must give away my shock because she stops in the entryway to the kitchen and frowns.

"What?" she asks.

I blink repeatedly at her. "Wondering to what I owe the pleasure of your company?"

With an eye roll and exasperated sigh, she crosses the kitchen to the fridge. "Do we have any Coke?"

"I think there's a couple in the back. How was school?"

"Fine. No major news. When's Blake coming over?"

My breath catches, and I chew on the inside of my cheek. "After he gets done with work. He's bringing pizza."

"Of course he is." Sydney turns around and pops the soda can open. "You okay, Mom?"

No. "Yeah, I'm fine, sweetheart."

Sydney eyeballs me with suspicion. "Are you sure?"

Who needs a lie detector with a thirteen-year-old like this? "I'm fine."

"If you don't want Blake to come over, you need to tell him."

My eyebrows shoot up. "When did I say I don't want him coming over?"

"You may not have said the words, but your body language is obvs. Tell him now, but explain why, too." She takes a sip of her Coke and leaves the room.

She's right. I should tell Blake what's going on. He'll understand, I know it. I pull my phone out to call him, but stop before my fingers tap the screen.

No. I ball my fist, my nails pressing into my palm. If I call him, he'll want to know why I've changed my mind. Then, I'll either be lying to him or having a heavy conversation, which really needs to be done in person.

But am I ready for this conversation? If he comes over, I'll no doubt have to have it.

What I need is some space to figure this out on my own, but I can't with Blake always around. If I tell him all this, though, he'll want to help. It's admirable of him, but it's my baggage, not his.

Rule number two, Maggie, Blake's deep voice echoes in my mind.

With a frustrated groan, I run my hands over my hair. This isn't getting me anywhere. I need to clear my head.

I change into my workout clothes, lace up my shoes, and go to the basement. Dylan isn't happy about me kicking him and his friend out, but they agree to find something else to do until I'm done. I open up my exercise streaming app and skip the yoga videos.

I need something more intense.

Yoga is great for releasing tension, but I have a cannonball of stress sitting in my gut and I need it gone. I choose a workout combining cardio and weights. It's a forty-five-minute video, and at the thirty-five minute mark, the trainer has us do what they call "man-makers." It's a combination of a push-up and burpee with a renegade row and an overhead weighted press. Normally, I use ten-pound weights, but the fifteens call my name.

As I finish the final rep, my shoulders killing me, the trainer goes into the cool-down. I hear a noise on the stairs. Assuming it's Dylan, I go into the cool-down without looking.

"Holy shit, that was intense." Blake's deep voice startles me.

I whip my head up to meet his wide eyes. "Blake? What are you doing here?" I ask, breathlessly. "And how did you get in?"

"It's Friday. I left my assistant manager in charge so I could take off early. One of the perks of owning the company." He shrugs and steps closer. "Sydney let me in. I thought you did yoga?"

"I do. When I need to clear my head." I step back into the cool-down move. "Yoga is good for relaxation."

"And what was the crazy shit you were just doing for?"

I grit my teeth. "For releasing stress."

Blake takes a seat on the couch behind me. "What are you stressed about?"

"I'm not even sure, to tell you the truth." With my final stretch, I finish the video and turn to face Blake. He's leaning forward, resting his elbows on his knees with his hands clasped in front of him.

The look on his face is pure concern. "So, now is a good time to talk, then? Where are the kids?"

"Um, Sydney is probably in her room, and Dylan is... I don't know, actually. I kicked him off the Xbox to do my workout. Why?"

"I really don't want to be interrupted."

My stomach drops, nausea taking over. "Okay, well, Dylan won't come down here until I come upstairs so, what do you want to talk about?"

"Us."

Uh oh. I swallow down my heart that's worked its way into my throat. "What about us?"

Blake pats the space next to him. I sit, wringing my hands together. This is it. I've done it. I've pushed him away too many times and he's fed up. *Good job, Maggie.*

I keep my gaze on my lap. "Blake... I'm sorry."

"Maggie. Don't."

Tears well in my eyes, so I shut them.

"Things have been weird for a while, and I've been wracking my brain trying to figure out what I did."

My workout was pointless. Now I'm a stinky, sweaty mess with a pit of guilt in my stomach. And it's grown two-fold. Not only for this business about forgetting Charlie and keeping Blake in the dark, but now for making Blake think he's the problem. "It's nothing you did."

"I know."

I snort, and turn to look at him, wiping away a tear. "Wow. Cocky, are we?"

He lets out an airy chuckle and drops his gaze to my hand, reaching over to take it. "I know this is a hard month for you. And next month is even harder."

"How do you know?"

"Michelle told me."

Heat creeps up the back of my neck. "She what?"

"Don't be mad with her, Maggie. She's only trying to help, and so am I."

By talking about me behind my back???

"Look, it may have been wrong of her to tell me, or for me to have asked her, but you weren't exactly being open with me."

With a huff, I pinch my lips and turn away from him, ripping my hand from his. The last thing I need right now is a guilt trip.

He reaches over, grabbing my chin and turning my gaze back to his. "Rule number two, remember?"

I melt as his deep brown irises pull me in. All the anger and all the anxiety lift from my shoulders. As I release my pinched expression and my jaw quivers, Blake runs his thumb across my bottom lip.

"Please, talk to me."

Unable to contain my emotions anymore, I burst at the seams like a water balloon exploding on contact. I bury my face into Blake's chest, my hands wrenched into his shirt as I sob.

Blake wraps his arms around me and strokes my hair. "It's okay, Maggie. I'm here."

Sydney's requests for me to explain everything to Blake ring in my ears. "That's just it," I whisper.

"What is?"

I pull away and sit up, swiping at my nose. "That's the problem. You're here and Charlie's not."

Hurt flashes in Blake's eyes, but his grip on me doesn't waver.

"Charlie isn't here to do all the things you're getting to do. He's missing his kids growing up. He's missing out on all the holidays, the family vacations, and the memories we're making. It's his birthday we should be celebrating this month, and he doesn't get to." My voice shakes, and I have to pause before I can continue. "But *you're* here. Taking all those opportunities. Stepping in where Charlie should be."

"Maggie, you know I'm not trying to–"

"Let me finish." I put my hand up. "I know you're not intending to take his place. I know that. You've more than proved it to me. But I can't help feeling guilty for letting you into these intimate moments of our lives."

"What are you saying, Maggie?"

I shake my head, my shoulders curling in on themselves. "I don't know. All I know is I've been telling myself every year will be the last time I'm like this. And every year I've failed."

Blake's hand runs up and down my back, his fingers pressing in gently.

"So, I guess what I need is... for you to go." My chest tightens as his hand stops abruptly. "Not forever. I couldn't handle that, but I do need some space and time to work through this. I need to figure out how you can fit into our lives, and keep Charlie here, too."

"Maggie," Blake's voice is tentative, unsure. "We made a rule to help each other through the tough shit. This is what that rule is for. I'm here, right now. I'll help you through all of this and we can figure it out together." He's pleading more than stating.

"No. This isn't something I can do with you. It has to be me alone. Otherwise, I'll always be wondering if you swayed my decision somehow. Talked your way into this instead of me letting you in."

Blake lets out a breath, but it's shaky and his fingers tremble against my back.

"I'm sorry, Blake. I know this isn't what you were expecting."

"I wasn't expecting anything." He brushes a piece of fallen hair behind my ear. "Hey, look at me."

I turn to meet his gaze. It's full of every emotion I could name. Hurt, confusion, worry, but also desire and adoration. It's all I can do not to fall into his arms, but I've made it this far; I can't relapse now.

"Maggie, I'll be damned if I'll let you go. I will work my ass off to keep you in my life, and if that means I have to give you some space for a while, then so be it. It'll tear me up, but I'll go through Hell and back to give you what you need." He leans forward and presses his lips to my forehead. "You let me know when you're ready. Until then, you've got my number."

As he pulls away, he stands, and my hand slips from his. I immediately miss his warmth. He walks to the stairs and pauses, his shoulders slumping as he turns his chin over his shoulder. "I love you, Maggie Hansen." And with that, he leaves.

As Charlie's birthday inches closer, time seems to creep by. Blake has texted me a handful of times to check on me, which is a far cry from his usual amount. He asks me if I'm alright and what I need. I tell him the same thing each time.

Yes, and nothing.

They aren't lies. In a way, I am alright. I haven't broken down once since our conversation three weeks ago, and Sydney even commented on how well I'm doing. That has to mean something.

The only part of my life that has changed since April rolled around is the fact my nightmares have returned. That, and the lack of Blake in my life.

I miss him. I miss his arms around me, his breath on my neck as we cuddle. His deep, velvety voice sounds in the back of my mind as his face flashes behind my eyelids. I even miss the tickle of his beard. He's the empty spot in my life and my bed, but I can't bring myself to tell him. I can't admit out loud I'm craving another man's warmth. Not when my late husband's birthday is tomorrow.

Shit, tomorrow?

I haven't been paying attention to the calendar. I guess nightmare-induced sleep deprivation does that to you.

Chapter Thirty-One

C RASH!

My alarm clock flies across the room, crashing to the floor with a sharp crack. "Fuck it. No workout today." I pull the blankets up over my head and curl in on myself.

I was a fool to think I'd make it through this month unscathed. This month, and the next, are vicious creatures which gnaw on my psyche and cut through my emotions with swift claws. It doesn't matter how much resolve I think I have; I always turn into a weakling.

The sun is shining when I feel a tug at my blanket. "Mom?" Sydney whispers.

I groan, but don't move.

She sighs. "We're heading to school. Don't worry about lunch, I made one for me and one for Dylan. Please, get up and eat something. We'll see you later." Her feet pad across the floor, and I hear her pause to open the bedroom door. "I love you."

The tears welling in my eyes finally burst forth, creating a puddle under my cheek. How can I do this to my kids year in and year out?

In the beginning, it made sense. I was a wreck after Charlie's death, and the first year anniversary of it was even worse. Sydney was only eight, but even then she knew something was wrong. She called Michelle who promptly came and stayed for two days until I was able to get out of bed, not leaving until after dinner on the third day.

But that was four years ago. This is year five. How am I still like this?

I loved Charlie, that's how.

He was my everything. And when you have everything ripped away from you so suddenly, the gaping wound it leaves doesn't heal quickly. If at all.

It would heal a lot faster if Charlie was here to help me. But then I wouldn't need healing. I have to work with what I have, and what I have is my children, my best friend, and Blake.

Reaching for my phone, I unlock the screen. I tap the messages button, my finger hovering over Blake's name. "Ugh, I can't do this." I flop onto my back and let my phone slip out of my hand.

If I do call Blake, then I'm failing to do this on my own. Sitting up, I knock my head against my headboard and sigh. I'm such a pathetic mess. I don't need to involve Blake in this right now.

My stomach rumbles. "Syd did tell me to eat something. I guess I should." I roll out of bed and head downstairs.

The toast pops out of the toaster and I butter it, sitting down at the table. I haven't been at the kitchen table more than a minute when my phone dings. Blake's picture pops up. With a deep sigh, I open the message, same as all the others.

> **BLAKE:** *Hey. Checking in. You okay? Need anything?*

My trembling fingers hover over the keyboard, but I don't type my typical response. I can't. It would be lies. I'm definitely not alright, and I do need something; him. But I can't tell him without letting pieces of Charlie fade away.

So, instead of replying, I close the app and put my phone on Do Not Disturb. The only calls allowed are the kids' school, and Sydney's cell. I finish my toast before climbing the stairs and getting back into bed.

The rest of the day is surprisingly peaceful without my phone going off every hour. Blake's not the only one checking on me. Michelle has been doing her best friend duty and texting also, but she's not as adamant about it as Blake.

I should probably let her know what's going on so she doesn't freak out when I don't answer her. I take my phone off Do Not Disturb and I'm instantly hit with several texts and even a voicemail. All from Blake. Evidently, he did not take kindly to me leaving him on "Read" all day.

The texts are all along the same lines, though they do increase in intensity as they go.

> **BLAKE:** *Maggie, are you ok?*

> **BLAKE:** *Hello?*

> **BLAKE:** *Are you ignoring me?*

> **BLAKE:** *This isn't funny.*

> **BLAKE:** *Now you're worrying me.*

> **BLAKE:** *Maggie?*

> **BLAKE:** *Please let me know you're ok.*

The last one was sent a half hour ago. I chew on my lip as I think about my next move. I should text him back, at least let him know I'm alive. That's harmless. No risk of replacing Charlie with that one. I pick up my phone, but before I can hit send, my doorbell rings. I sigh as I try to think about what I ordered from Amazon, and get out of bed.

The doorbell rings again.

And again.

Then there's a knock. More like pounding.

I know who it is. I gather myself and fly down the stairs. At the front door, listening to Blake beat his fist into it, I steel myself and turn the knob. Blake's arm stops mid-air, and his wide eyes lock on mine. They're full of fear and worry, and seem to be glossier than I remember.

Was he crying?

He stares at me a good while, his chest heaving as he collects himself and lowers his arm. No words come through his quivering jaw, just heavy, shaking breaths.

Then, his chin stops trembling and he sets his mouth into a straight line. The fear and worry dissolve from his eyes, replaced with a fury. The likes of which I've never seen. His fists ball at his sides. He looks like he's ready to pound someone's face into the dirt, but I'm not scared. Blake would never hurt me, I know that.

"Blake, I–"

"Don't," he growls, pushing past me and into the house.

I close the door and latch it, but don't turn around.

"What the fuck is going on, Maggie? I sent you a text hours ago to check on you, and not only do you not respond, but you ghost me all day? Even Michelle couldn't reach you!"

He called Michelle? Again? Indignation flares in me once more at the idea of him and Michelle going behind my back.

"If you hadn't answered the door, I would've called the cops!"

I spin around, a nasty glare plastered on my face. If it looks as angry as I feel, Blake should be backing off any second, but he doesn't. He stands with a similar glare cemented to his features. He's as mad as I am.

"The cops? Really, Blake?"

"What else would you have me do?"

"I don't know, call my kids, maybe?"

He swallows. "And get Sydney worried something happened to you? Have her finish out her school day in terror over whether her mom was alright?"

I bite my lip. I hadn't thought of that. "Blake, I told you I needed some space."

"Yes, I know. And I've been giving it to you, haven't I? I've been respecting your need for alone time. I thought maybe you could respect my need to know you're at least alive up here."

Guilt builds in my gut, and I look away.

"Look, I didn't come here to fight." His tone softens, though it's laced with irritation. "When you didn't answer any of my messages I freaked out, but I didn't want to encroach on your space. That's why I called Michelle. When she said she hadn't heard from you, and couldn't reach you either, I really freaked out. I– I was thinking the worst had happened." His voice shakes as he says the words.

Now I really feel guilty. "Blake, I'm not suicidal, never have been. I wouldn't do that to my kids." Losing one parent was bad enough, but to lose both? I shudder at the thought. "I'm sorry I worried you."

"Worried doesn't even begin to describe it. I was downright terrified."

"Sorry."

Blake walks to me, stopping in front of me and taking my hands in his. "Maggie, will you please talk to me? Please get whatever is going on in your head out so I can help you with it."

I keep my gaze on the floor, but my eyes well with tears.

"Maggie? Please? Even if it's only a few minutes, I'll listen." He tugs on my hands, pulling me into the house and to the living room.

I have no fight left in me, so I let him. We take a seat on the couch and Blake wraps a blanket around me. I glance at the clock, noting the fact we have forty-five minutes until my kids get home. We should have enough time to talk with me inevitably crying, and finish so I don't upset the kids.

Blake reaches over, taking my hand and squeezing. "Rule number two."

I meet his soft gaze, an easy grin spread on his face, and my heart melts. There isn't a single sign of anger or frustration, only love. "First, I do want to say how sorry I am for scaring you. I never meant to."

"I know, but I wish you would've told me what a hard time you've been having instead of telling me you were fine all the time."

"That's just it, though. Every time I said it, I really was fine. Ask Sydney. She even commented on how well I've been doing. Up until today." I drop my gaze, retracting my hand from Blake's.

"Because today is Charlie's birthday?"

I swallow down the lump in my throat and nod.

"Why didn't you say you were having a tough time?"

"Because I knew you'd come running up here to take care of me, and I wanted to be alone. But I also couldn't tell you I was fine, because it would've been a lie. So, I opted to do nothing."

Blake sighs. "Maggie, you could've told me it was a bad day, and told me you needed to be alone. I would've listened."

"Looking back, I know I should have, but at the time, I panicked. I chose to ignore it, hoping it would go away if I did."

"Maggie, I'm going to ask you something and I want you to be honest. No judgment, I promise. I'm just curious."

I turn my head to look at him from the corner of my eye, and I nod.

"Have you ever sought therapy over Charlie's death?"

Something resembling an offended laugh escapes me, and I fall back against the couch. "Of course I have. I went to grief counseling for months. Up until we moved here, I saw a therapist twice a week."

"You haven't gone since you moved here, though?"

I shake my head.

"What about medication? Have you ever thought about that?"

"I don't need drugs to help me cope," I bite out.

"Okay, okay." Blake throws his hands up. "Why haven't you gone back to your therapist?"

"I don't know. At first, it was because we were so busy with the move. Then, it became a hassle to find the time, seeing as how her office is across town. After a while, as I adjusted to this new life here, I guess I decided I didn't need the therapy, so I never went back."

"Maybe you should."

I sneer at Blake. "So, now you think I'm crazy?"

"No, of course not. But you obviously still have some stuff to work out, and you're not talking to me about it." The hurt in his voice is like a knife slicing through my gut. "It could be good to start up again."

The sneer fades, and my body suddenly feels as heavy as lead. "It seems like a lot of work right now."

"Okay, how about this? Today was hard, and as I understand it, the next month is even worse?"

I nod.

"So, here's what we'll do. For the next four weeks, I'll text you every day. Every day, Maggie. And you're going to tell me how you are. I don't care if it's good or bad or somewhere in between, you tell me the truth."

I furrow my eyebrows, but I keep my eyes on his.

"Then, I'll ask what you need. If you say you need to be alone, I'll leave you alone. But if you need something, anything, please tell me. I will drop whatever I'm doing and be here, okay?"

A smile creeps across my face at his words and a tear rolls down my cheek. Blake reaches over and rubs it away with his thumb as he cups my cheek, and I nuzzle into his warm palm.

He inches closer and presses his lips to my forehead. "I've missed you."

As he pulls away to look down at me, the air between us changes. His touch is like a spark, igniting my desire. I flick my eyes to his mouth and whisper his name. Suddenly, his lips are on mine, devouring me furiously. I fall into the kiss. It's an amazing feeling I've been missing for weeks, and I want nothing more than to be locked in this embrace forever.

The front door opens. "Mom! We're home!" Dylan's voice rings out from the front of the house.

Blake and I jump apart, out of breath and flushed. When our eyes meet, he grabs my hand, squeezing it gently. "I've *really* missed you," he says, his voice low and gruff.

My children round the corner, and as soon as he lays eyes on Blake, Dylan comes bounding across the room. "Mr. Blake! I haven't seen you in forever!" He leaps onto the couch and wraps Blake in a strong hug.

"Hey, Buddy." Blake eyes me over Dylan's shoulder, his gaze full of sad longing. "Long time, no see. How was school?"

"It was fine. Hey, are you staying for dinner?"

At Dylan's words, Blake shoots me a questioning glance, and I bite my lip. He nods. "Not tonight, Bud. I've got some things I need to get done. But, maybe next time?"

"Okay." Disappointment shines through Dylan's response. He turns to me. "Mom, can Trevor come over?"

"Nope. Homework first, young man."

"Aw, man." Dylan gets up from the couch and trudges away to his room, head hung and shoulders hunched.

Blake chuckles as his eyes find Sydney at the entryway. "Hey, Syd. How's it going?"

"Fine. Good to see you, Blake."

"You, too." Blake rubs his palms down his thighs. "Well, I've got to go check on Oscar. I'll, uh, see you later, Maggie." He leans over and kisses my temple before getting up and letting himself out.

Sydney waits until he's gone to come sit with me on the couch. "Mom, are you okay?"

"Yeah, honey. I'm fine."

She drops her gaze to her lap. "I was worried after this morning."

Mom guilt wrenches my stomach. I worried my thirteen-year-old. *Ugh.* "I'm sorry, sweetheart. It was a rough morning."

"Did Blake come hang out with you all day?"

"No. He had to work. He was only here for the last hour before you came home, checking on me."

"Oh." Sydney picks at the fray on her jean shorts. "Are you guys okay?"

"I think so."

"Good. We haven't seen him a whole lot lately, and I thought maybe something happened."

"No need to worry. Blake and I are fine." *I hope.*

Chapter Thirty-Two

"Why don't you tell him to stop texting you, then?" Michelle's question is valid, but the answer is dicey.

"Because I promised Blake I'd do this for him. And you didn't see his face when he showed up on my porch." I pick at the cuticle of my thumb.

"Mags, it's not like you're telling him never to text you again. If you're annoyed by it, you need to–" *HONK!* "Check your blind spot, asshole!" Michelle lets out something resembling a growl. "Sorry."

I chuckle. "Does the client you're meeting know you have a road rage problem?"

"My road rage is completely justified. Anyway, what was I saying?"

"That if I'm annoyed by Blake's texts, I should tell him." I groan, dropping my hand to drum my fingers on the table. "But it'd be so rude. He's just doing what he thinks is right. He's taking care of me."

"And that annoys you?"

"It didn't at first. I was impressed at how true to his word he was about texting me every day. It was kind of cute, and it felt good to tell him what's really going on."

"So, what changed?" I hear Michelle's turn signal clicking in the background.

"I don't know. The messages have become almost overbearing. I know what time they'll happen. I know exactly what they'll say, and I know how I'll respond. It's monotonous." My phone buzzes in my ear, but I don't even have to look. I know who it is. I huff, leaning back in my chair. "Hearing my phone ding every day at the same time, with the same message? It's giving me a headache."

"Put your phone on silent, then."

"I did, but that doesn't make it stop. I don't know why I ever agreed to this. It doesn't matter, in a week, it'll all be over." My breath stops. *In a week...*

If I had known five years ago what was going to happen in a week, I would've begged Charlie for more texts. I would've asked him to leave me a message every time I missed his call. There would have been more date nights, more cuddles, more family time. I would've done everything different.

What if this is the last time Blake texts me? What if something happens and he dies with me being annoyed with him? The guilt would eat me alive.

"Mags? You there?"

"Michelle, I have to go." The words shake as I say them.

I end the call with Michelle, my hand trembling as I set my phone down. Tears fall onto my kitchen table, making a puddle on the tabletop. My heart pounds against my sternum as I snatch my phone and type my reply.

ME: *I'm very much not ok.*

BLAKE: *What do you need?*

ME: *You.*

Thirty minutes later, my doorbell rings. I run to it and fling it open. Blake doesn't waste a second as he crosses the threshold and throws his hand behind my head and wraps the other around my waist, pulling me into his chest. I sob against him, gripping his shirt in my fists.

He holds me tight until I stop crying, then he pushes me back and wipes the tears from my cheeks with his thumbs as he cups my face.

I swallow and look up at him, my eyes flicking from his eyes to his lips. They part and his tongue juts out enough to wet them before smashing his mouth to mine. In an instant, I've gone from a puddle of tears, to a beacon of desire. I have to have Blake.

Now.

I take steps backward, tugging him through the foyer and up the stairs to my bedroom. Once inside, our clothes come off piece by piece and we flop onto my bed. I giggle at our antics, but Blake looks at me with nothing except seriousness on his face. I pinch my lips shut.

"Maggie, are you sure about this?"

"Of course I am." I put my hand behind his head, pulling his mouth back to mine.

He groans, but climbs over me as we inch higher onto my bed. His hands run all over my body, touching me in places I haven't been touched in weeks. I'm on fire at every point of contact. His fingers are like little lightning bolts, sparking as they dig into my skin.

"I've missed you so much," he whispers against my mouth.

"Me, too."

He rolls to one side and runs his hand down the length of my body, stopping on my thigh and squeezing. His fingers travel around and slip inside me. I gasp at the sensation. It's been almost two months since we've slept together, and Blake hasn't missed a beat. He still knows exactly what I want and what I need. And I'm *very* thankful for him.

I reach down and take his hard length in my hand. His breath hitches, but he moves from my mouth to my chest. As we lie here, touching each other, his tongue makes quick work of my nipples. Swirling around the peaks, flicking them every so often, Blake's tongue and fingers moving in unison has me on the edge in no time.

I grip his shoulder with my free hand, my other pumping him faster as I tighten around his fingers and call out his name.

He slows his rhythm and backs away to pull himself from my grip. Climbing over me, he settles himself between my thighs, his cock teasing me.

When he doesn't push inside right away, I open my eyes and meet his gaze. It's full of pained concern, almost fear. "You're *completely* sure about this?"

"Blake, I don't want anything else in the world, right now. Just you."

He connects our mouths and pushes himself inside me at the same time. It's amazing how he fills me. The friction, the passion, the connection. It's all so much and so wonderful. He doesn't even begin slowly. Knowing how much I need him, Blake thrusts into me.

His relentless, powerful hips have me coming almost instantly, but he doesn't stop. He pumps into me again and again as I continue to tighten around his erection in what seems like endless orgasms.

I can tell he's putting two months' worth into this by the strained grunts coming out of him and I know he needs release. But he won't relent until he knows I'm satisfied. How he can't know, I have no idea, but I need to tell him somehow.

I grab his shoulders, digging my nails into his skin, and wrap my legs around his waist. Hooking my ankles together, I pull myself up so my lips are against his ear. "Fuck me harder, Blake."

It's all over at my words. Blake groans and speeds up his thrusts for only a minute before succumbing to his own orgasm. He pulses inside me, nearly collapsing, but catching himself on his elbows. As he hovers over me, his hot, ragged breath cascades down my neck before he rolls to his side and pulls me to him.

I slide to my side, putting my back against his chest, and melt into him. Wrapped in Blake's embrace, with his chin on top of my head, I allow my heart to rest. His torso expands as I feel his heartbeat return to normal. All is right again.

"Maggie?"

Wouldn't be completely right if he didn't say something, though. "Hm?"

"Are you okay?"

"I'm perfect, Blake. How are you?"

"Oh, I'm fine. More than fine, actually." I feel his Adam's apple bob against the back of my head. "But can you tell me what made you want to do this?"

"I need a reason to want to have sex with my boyfriend?"

His fingers start drawing circles on my hip. "No, you don't, but you've been so distant lately. This kind of came out of left field. What's been going on?"

Tears well in my eyes, but I blink them away and run my hand up his forearm. "I had to feel you. Had to know you were still here."

"I'm here, Maggie." He tightens his grip. "I'm not going anywhere."

I sniffle and pull away, rolling over to face him and splaying my hands across his chest. "But what if it's the last time?"

"What are you talking about?"

"Before I texted you, I was talking to Michelle about how annoying your messages were."

"Ouch."

"Sorry, but I've been listening to that chime every day for almost a month, knowing exactly what the message will say, knowing exactly what my response will be, and it became tedious."

"So, you being annoyed with me led to you wanting some afternoon delight?"

"Yeah, I guess." I chuckle, but close my eyes. "When you texted today, I placated myself with the idea that in a week, they'll stop. Then, I was reminded of what happens in a week." I open my eyes to meet Blake's and watch realization wash over him.

"Next week is when–"

"Yes. It is." I choke on the tears rolling down my face. "And I started thinking about how, if I knew five years ago what was going to happen, I would've relished every minute with Charlie, and I should be doing that with you now."

Blake reaches up, wrapping a hand around mine and pressing our hands to his chest.

"I should be over the moon you even take the time out of your day to check on me. You've been so patient these last few weeks, and a lesser man would've left me by now. But not you. You're still here, and I should cherish the moments we have."

Blake runs his hand over my head before pulling me into his chest. "Maggie, can I stay tonight?"

I bite my lip and my toes wiggle under the sheet.

"It's just... I want to hold you. It's been killing me being apart from you. I haven't slept very well, to be honest, and all I want is to fall asleep with you in my arms."

"Blake, I don't–"

"Before you protest, I know the kids will be here. You don't have to worry, though. I just unleashed two months of pent-up, um, tension, so I'm good. For a day or two."

I laugh, my toes going still.

"But seriously, Maggie, all I want is to have you next to me. Honest."

"Okay."

"Really?"

I nod. "But you have to be here for dinner, too."

"Absolutely." He rolls over to look at the clock. "The kids will be home soon. I'm going to go home and get Oscar, and I'll be back at six, okay?"

"Bring pizza."

He laughs this time, and kisses the top of my head. "Of course."

After the pizza is gone, Sydney and I sit on the front porch to watch Blake teach Dylan how to skateboard. Really, it's Blake showing Dylan all the things not to do. Dylan has been practicing every chance he gets, and he's able to stay on the board most of the time. He also has all the pads and the helmet, but poor Blake has nothing and his butt is hitting the pavement left and right.

My fingertips tingle with the anticipation of giving him a massage later.

When the sun has dipped all the way below the horizon, the four of us head inside, where Dylan promptly drags Blake into the basement for some "guy time" and video games. Sydney and I settle in to watch a movie. Even though we aren't in the same room, I feel Blake with me every second. Knowing he's treating my son like his own, gives me an overwhelming sense of satisfaction, and sitting here with my daughter, enjoying a movie together, makes my heart so full it's bursting at the seams.

When the movie ends, it's nearly ten o'clock. I hear the light click off in the basement and Blake's heavy footsteps on the stairs. He comes through the doorway with a sleeping Dylan in his arms. Blake juts his chin toward the kitchen and disappears through it and up the stairs.

I sigh, letting out a huge breath. Maybe Syd was right. Maybe Blake does want to be their dad. Am I okay with that? They seem to be, and he's doing a wonderful job of it. I wonder what he thinks about the idea.

"Blake is pretty cool, Mom." Sydney's voice startles me out of my adoration.

"He really is, isn't he?"

"Keep him around, okay?"

I turn to Sydney, my eyebrows furrowed. "You think I have intentions of letting him go?"

"You never know, Mom." And with that, Sydney gets up and heads upstairs to her own room. I hear her and Blake exchange goodnights on the stairs before he rounds the corner and crosses the room to sit next to me.

He scoots closer and wraps an arm around my shoulder. "How was the movie?"

"Good. And I really enjoyed sharing it with Sydney. It's been a while since she and I had some time together, just us. How was video games?"

Blake laughs. "So much fun. But I spent too long on my turn, because when I finished, Dylan was asleep. I must have bored him, I guess."

We both share a laugh, but mine turns into a yawn.

"And now I'm boring you?" Blake asks with a smirk.

I nudge him with my shoulder. "You're never boring."

"Bedtime?"

I nod, and he scoops me into his arms. Once inside my room, he lays me in my bed, but I get up to wash my face and brush my teeth. He follows suit, as he has kept a toothbrush at my house for months now, though it hasn't been used in a while. We exchange glances in the mirror as our toothpaste foams in our mouths, each making faces until the other can't take it anymore. I win, and he practically spits toothpaste all over the mirror.

Wiping the white foam from his beard, he pinches my waist as he leaves the bathroom. "Cheater."

I try to scoff, but with a mouthful of toothpaste, it sounds like I'm choking. Once I'm finished, I meet him at the bed. He's already stripped down to his boxers, and I'm breathless. Even after all these months, and after the wild afternoon we had, he still drives me crazy with desire.

I swallow it down, though, as my children are right down the hall. Crossing the room to my closet, I undress with my back to Blake. As my shirt comes over my head, I hear him groan. Nice to know I still affect him as much. I throw on a sleep shirt that hits above my knee and come back to the bed.

Blake looks me up and down, his eyes darkening. "You are so incredibly sexy."

I giggle. "Even in this?" I grab the hem of my pink, oversized sleep-shirt covered in numbered sheep jumping over fences.

"You're sexy in everything," he says, and lifts the blanket up for me to crawl in.

He pulls me against him, my back hitting his chest and his chin resting on the top of my head. My favorite position. For sleeping, anyway. His fingers lightly brush up and down my arm, graduating onto my hip and running across my ribs. As they make their way back down, they slip under the hem of my shirt and travel back up my body.

He pauses at the bottom of my ribs, his fingertips tickling my skin, before continuing up to cup my breast. His thumb runs over my hardened nipple, and I tip my head back against his throat to feel his Adam's apple bob up and down.

I arch my back so my breast is pressed fully into his warm palm. He hardens against me, and I moan.

He lets out a strained groan, dipping his head down to nibble my ear. Taking the lobe between his teeth, he whispers, "If you can be quiet, I'll make you come before bed."

My panties instantly soak and all I can do is nod.

Blake's hand leaves my breast and travels down to settle between my thighs. He parts my legs and slips his fingers inside me, thumbing my clit as he does. I'm moaning and groaning my pretty little head off when his arm I'm laying on extends.

His hand covers my mouth, holding my head against his shoulder. "I told you to be quiet." The growl in his voice has me moaning louder and his hand presses harder.

This is hot.

Blake's fingers continue their movement, but speed up, making me buck against his hand. He's rock hard and part of me feels bad he's not getting anything out of this, so I reach back and grip his cock. He shudders, but allows me to release him from his boxers.

As my hand pumps him faster and faster, his fingers work harder to get me off. All the while, his hand is clasped over my mouth. I wish I could yell his name. I wish I could say all the things on my mind, but I know my kids wouldn't appreciate the commotion.

Blake reads my mind, because he puts his mouth back to my ear. "Come for me, Maggie." The gravel makes its appearance, and I pump him harder. "Fuck, you feel so good."

I moan into his hand.

"Quiet, naughty girl."

His cock gets slick, and I know he's close.

He nips at my ear. "I want you to come on my fingers."

All my resolve is gone, and I'm reduced to a puddle in seconds. I tighten around his fingers, and he pulses in my palm, releasing his orgasm against my back, but he doesn't stop. His fingers keep moving, slow and steady with my crest until I'm finished. Once done, he tips me onto my stomach and goes to the bathroom, returning with some tissues to clean me up.

He puts his boxers back on and climbs into bed. Pulling me against him once again, he kisses my temple and whispers, "Goodnight, Maggie. I love you."

CHAPTER THIRTY-THREE

The week following Blake's sleepover goes so well I'm scaring myself. I feel more in control than I've felt in years. I have more energy, and am happier overall. My nightmares have even stopped again, and Blake's messages have gone back to being cute with me looking forward to them.

So, when my phone rings on Thursday afternoon, I'm actually disappointed when it's Michelle.

"Hey," I say.

"Hey, how are you?"

"I'm doing really well, thanks for asking."

"Really?" The disbelief in her voice is palpable.

"Yes. Why is that so hard to believe?"

"It's not. I just didn't expect–" She pauses, like she's contemplating something. "You know what? It doesn't matter. Good, I'm glad to hear you're doing well."

"Is this a wellness check, or did you have a point?"

She huffs. "My *point* was to offer you something."

"Ooh, a present? You have my attention. What is it?"

"Tomorrow, after work, I'll come pick up the kids and they can stay with me Friday and Saturday night. I'll bring them home Sunday."

"Michelle, you don't have to do that."

"I know, but I want to. A: it's been forever since they stayed with me, and I miss them."

"You and Tom should've had kids. Then you wouldn't have to use mine." I laugh, because Michelle knew in her early twenties she didn't want to be a mom. She likes kids, but she knew it wasn't what she wanted with her life.

"Yeah, but then I wouldn't be able to give them back." She pauses a moment, letting the humor in the conversation pass. "And B: I want you to be able to do what you want this weekend. If that's staying inside and drowning in pizza and wine, then so be it. If it's being with Blake and drowning in him, even better."

I bite my lip. That doesn't sound half bad. "What if I wanted to be with my kids?"

"Listen, Maggie. I know those kids are your everything, your heart and soul, and you love them more than life itself, but everyone needs a break from their fucking kids every now and then."

"You make a good point. Okay, I accept. And thank you."

"Of course. I'll text you when I leave work."

I hang up and my head is swirling with options. I have an entire kid-free weekend. This happens... never. I have so many ideas of what I could do with my time, but I decide it's best to wait until tomorrow to see how I'm feeling before deciding.

The next morning, after breakfast, I tell Sydney and Dylan the plans and they both light up at the idea of spending the weekend with Aunt Michelle. It has been ages since they did this, and even though Sydney tries to hide it, she's as excited as Dylan. I have to practically beg them not to pack their things before sending them off to school.

My day goes by smoothly. No intrusive thoughts. No negativity. Just me and my quiet house. My only anxiety is centered around whether to tell Blake about Michelle's offer. Normally, yes, I'd tell him right away so we can spend every second of the weekend together. But this weekend will be different. Tomorrow is... Well, tomorrow is the most difficult day of the year, and I don't know what is best for me.

Every year prior to this one, I've been alone. My kids may or may not be in the house with me, but I'm holed up in my room, usually crying my eyes out. But this year feels completely different, and I have Blake to thank for it.

I should use this time to thank him... properly.

A smile overtakes my face and I grab my phone. As I do, a message comes through, my phone dinging with the now endearing chime, letting me know Blake is thinking of me.

BLAKE: *Hey. This is your everyday check in message. How you doing?*

ME: *I'm doing fine. It's been a good day.*

BLAKE: *Good to hear. Need anything?*

ME: *No. But I do have something for you.*

BLAKE: *Me? Go on I'm listening.*

ME: *Michelle gifted me a kid-free weekend and I thought what better way to spend it than in the arms of my favorite man.*

BLAKE: *So, where do I come in?*

ME: *Ha. Ha.*

BLAKE: *Lol. Sounds awesome. Are you sure?*

ME: *Of course. But I want to spend the weekend at your house. Ok?*

BLAKE: *Whatever you need.*

ME: *I need to get out of the house and waking up with you will make it better.*

BLAKE: *Ok, sounds good. I'll let you know when I'm home and showered.*

ME: *Thx.*

I spend the next few hours getting ready. I take a long shower, making sure to shave every inch of myself. I take the time to do my full makeup, something I don't do very often and certainly not to this degree. The only time Blake has seen my full face is at the handful of parties we've been to. My hair is not only washed, but it's also curled so it falls softly around my shoulders.

I won't change clothes until after the kids are gone, but I've got my outfit planned. A baby blue top with split sleeves so my arms are exposed, but it hugs my middle, and paired with my favorite skinny jeans, my curves are accentuated perfectly. My shoes are tan flats, because although heels would make this outfit better, I'm not walking to Blake's in those.

The kids come home and tell me about their day over an afternoon snack. We get to spend a decent amount of time together before Michelle texts me she's on her way. The only instance she leaves work on time. Dylan all but runs to the window to watch for her, even though it's going to be a good thirty minutes.

I laugh and shake my head, lifting it to meet Sydney's gaze. She's smiling at me. "What?"

"Nothing. You look nice. And happy."

"Thanks. I feel happy."

"I hope you and Blake have fun tonight."

My cheeks heat at the idea of what Blake I will be doing for fun tonight. "How did you know I'd be seeing him?"

"Oh, come on, Mom." Sydney rolls her eyes so hard I'm surprised they stay in her head. "You never do your makeup like that. If you weren't seeing Blake tonight, I'd think you'd gone crazy."

"Thanks for your confidence."

"I'm just saying, you look good, and I know Blake will think so, too."

With a full heart, I pull my wonderful daughter in for a tight hug, thankful I have her to ground me. If I didn't have her, I might be crazy by now.

The thirty minutes flies by, though Dylan would disagree. Michelle comes in for a quick minute to chat while the kids grab their things. Then it's a hug and kiss and they're out the door while I'm left to wallow in boredom while waiting for Blake to get home.

Now I know how Dylan felt.

When my phone finally dings, I practically jump out of my skin, I'm so antsy. Blake is home, showered, and ready for me. I grab my things and have to exercise some serious self-control not to run down the street. As I stand on Blake's porch, I take a second to run my hand through my hair and adjust my shirt so it's hanging just right. Then I knock.

Blake opens it within seconds, his eyes lighting up and then darkening as he looks me over. "You look... amazing."

"Thank you," I say, flipping my hair. "Can I come in?"

Blake blinks himself out of his stupor and swallows as he steps aside. I giggle, making sure to brush against him when I pass. He sucks in a breath, and I giggle some more.

He shuts the front door, and Oscar immediately starts barking in the back-yard. Blake groans. "Sorry. The neighbors behind me got a cat and it's been teasing Oscar. Let me go get him."

I follow Blake into the kitchen, where there are about a dozen take-out menus scattered across the island.

"I'll let you pick what's for dinner while I get Oscar inside. And I don't know if you're in the mood, but there's beer in the fridge." He juts his chin over his shoulder, then disappears through the back door.

A beer sounds great. It's Friday, after all.

I spin around to open the fridge, grabbing a brown bottle and twisting it open. Before I take a drink, I turn the bottle to look at the label and my stomach sours. My heart stops and my head spins.

Charlie's beer...

The room around me fades away, darkness closing in as I stare at the label, my focus going in and out. I'm vaguely aware of Blake coming back in at that moment and ushering Oscar across the room to the garage. I don't see him enter the kitchen as much as I'm simply aware of his presence.

"What did you decide for dinner?" He pauses, waiting longer than I'm sure he thinks is normal for a response before asking, "Maggie, you okay?"

"The... beer," is all I can manage.

"Yeah, I thought it would be a nice way to honor Charlie. And it's the first beer we ever shared, remember?"

I can't stop my chest from heaving; the air around me is too thin. This is how it started.

"Maggie?"

I keep my eyes focused on the bottle, but things around me begin to clear, and I blink. "You stole Charlie's beer."

"I can assure you, I paid for it." Blake chuckles, but it's stilted, nervous.

"You've stolen everything." I finally raise my head to find he's staring at me with his mouth turned down. "You're trying to replace him."

Blake doesn't move, doesn't do anything except breathe, and I hear it shaking.

"It started with the beer. This beer was mine and Charlie's, and now you've made it *yours* and mine, just like everything else."

"Maggie," he says, quietly, his jaw quivering. "I'm not trying to replace Charlie."

"Aren't you, though? You've not only inched your way into my life, but my kids', too. You're doing all the things Charlie should be. I mean, Sydney even thinks you want to be their dad."

Blake lays his hand on his heart, his features softening. "Syd wants me to be their dad?" An easy grin spreads across his lips, but he shakes his head. "Maggie, I'd be honored to take on–"

"See? There it is! You'd be taking Charlie's role."

He throws his hands in the air. "I don't want to take anything! I'd be happy to be a dad to them because I fucking love those kids, Maggie!" He huffs before planting his hands on his hips and hanging his head. "And it sounds like they're okay with it."

"They just don't see what's going on." I fold my arm across my chest.

"And what is going on?" He lifts his head, meeting my eyes with a fiery gaze. "What have I done that's so horrible, huh?"

My chest heaves as my eyes dart across the floor. All of our time together flashes behind my eyelids with each blink. Every single moment I've felt unsure or uneasy about something, Blake has found a way to talk me into it.

"Maggie?" Blake takes a step forward, but I back away.

"Don't touch me." I take another step back, wrapping my arms around my middle. "You've been coaxing me into things from the beginning. Things I didn't want to do."

"Like what? Everything we've done has been your decision. I may have come up with the ideas, but I always made sure you were okay with them."

"I've done things with you, Blake, I never would have done. But the one I can't believe I let happen, was last weekend when I let you..." My gaze drops to the side. "When you talked me into having sex while my kids were home."

"First of all, we didn't have sex." The irritation in his tone is hard to miss. "If you remember, it was all hand stuff. Secondly, I made sure you wanted to. You could have told me no and I would've backed off."

I jerk my head up, a fire building in my gut. "It's kind of hard to say no when you're already feeling me up!"

Blake runs his hand through his hair, tugging on the roots as he stares at the floor.

"I made it clear I didn't want to have sex when the kids were home, and you ignored my wishes."

His head whips up, locking his burning gaze with mine. "Did anything happen, Maggie? No. The kids had no idea. They didn't need you because they're not as fragile as you think they are. This belief that something bad lurks around every corner cannot dictate your life." He licks his lips, biting his bottom one before continuing, "I know Charlie's death traumatized you, but it's been five years, now. Don't you think it's time to stop living in so much fear?"

Hyperventilation threatens my lungs. I squeeze my eyes shut, gripping my shirt in my fists at my sides. The heat rising in my core is so unbearable, it makes me lightheaded. I stumble to the side, my shoulder hitting the fridge, and I sag against it.

"Shit, Maggie." Blake closes the gap between us in an instant, his hands gripping my arms and holding me up. "Maggie, open your eyes. Look at me."

When I do, I meet his beautiful brown irises, and my heart slows.

"Let me ground you," he says softly. He looks like a frightened puppy, but I'm not letting the softness of his gaze manipulate me anymore.

I rip away from his embrace, my head still spinning and my stomach on the verge of upheaval. My legs wobble, but I stand tall. "I don't need your help."

Blake reaches for me, but drops his hand. "That's all I want, Maggie. To help."

"I've let you help, and you've taken yards when I've given you inches. You want me to forget Charlie and only think about you. But I won't. I won't let him go."

"Maggie, that's never been what I'm doing and you know it. Deep down, you know I've always respected what you and Charlie had and–"

"HAVE! What Charlie and I have!" My shouting even scares me.

"Dammit, Maggie!" Blake slams his fist on the island, the take-out menus flying across it. "Do you hear yourself, right now? You sound insane." He stands straighter and runs his hand through his hair. "Charlie is gone, Maggie. But I'm here. I'm here trying to help you, but you can't get past your drama and let me close to you."

I clench my teeth. "How dare you call it drama! You don't know what kind of pain I'm in. You have no idea."

Blake's fists clench and release as he groans. "Only because you won't tell me. All this pain and suffering you're going through is entirely brought on by you, Maggie. No one else. You don't let anyone help you when you need it." His shoulders relax and his tone softens. "It's okay to ask for help. That's what rule number two is for. What *I'm* here for."

His accusations make my blood boil. "You may be here, but I'm stopping that, right now."

Blake pales. "Maggie, what are you saying?"

I raise my chin, standing tall. "I'm saying we're done. I'm going home, Blake. Don't follow me, don't text me, don't call me. Leave me alone."

I stomp out of the kitchen to the front door, but Blake catches me by the wrist before I can get outside. "Maggie, please don't go. We can fix this, I know we can." His jaw quivers. "I love you."

I turn to him, my heart shattering at the sight of his tear-stained face, and I struggle to keep my resolve as I rip my arm from his grip. "Sorry, Blake." My voice is low and cold.

As I walk home, I know he's watching me, but I don't turn around. Not once. Instead, I keep my head high all the way to my house. Once I'm inside, I collapse against the door and sob until I fall asleep.

At some point during the weekend, I make it to my bed, and I don't leave it. I'm still in it on Sunday afternoon when the front door opens.

"Mom! We're home!" Sydney's voice rings out. I hear three sets of footsteps on the tile in the foyer. "Mom?"

"Mags?" Michelle echoes.

Great. I roll my eyes at the oncoming interrogation, and pull the covers over my head. The door to my room opens, the sound of feet padding across the carpet is faint, but noticeable.

"Mom?" Sydney pats the blanket. "Are you okay?"

I groan, mumbling the word "yes," but don't roll over.

"Mags, what's up?" The bed dips down with Michelle's weight.

"I'm fine."

"Then why are you still in bed? Blake's not under there with you, is he?" Michelle asks, poking at the blanket, and I hear Sydney giggle.

"No," I choke out through my constricted throat.

"Then what gives?" Michelle puts her hand on my leg and shakes it.

"It was a long weekend."

"Oooooh. Gotcha." Michelle's probably winking at Sydney. "Well, then my work here is done. Syd, take care of your mom. Let her get some rest and she'll be okay. Come on, walk me out."

Then they're gone, and I'm alone.

But not for long, because Sydney returns shortly after I hear the front door close. "Mom? What's really going on?"

Nothing gets past her. I roll over and uncover my face. "It was a long, difficult couple days. I'm okay, sweetheart."

"You still seem sad. I know it takes a day or two before you get back to normal, but the sadness is usually gone. What's going on?"

She's going to find out sooner or later. "Blake and I broke up."

"What!?"

"We had a fight."

"Like the one last Christmas?"

I nod. "This one was worse, though. In the end, I decided it was for the best."

"Best for who? I can't imagine Blake agreed with you."

"Sweetheart," I say, putting my hand on Sydney's knee. "There's a lot about relationships you don't know, and can't understand yet."

"But Blake is really cool, Mom. Dylan and I like him. A lot."

"I do– I did, too, but having a good relationship is more than just liking each other."

Sydney furrows her brow, almost scowling at me.

"You'll understand when you're older, Syd."

"I don't know if you even understand." She gets up from the bed, leaving me speechless, and exits the room.

CHAPTER THIRTY-FOUR

Two weeks later, on a Tuesday evening, I'm lying in my bed, staring at the empty spot next to me. It may only be big enough for one person, but it's missing two people. Charlie, and now, Blake. The only difference being the latter is completely my fault.

I'd be lying if I said I didn't miss him. We spent the better part of a year together, so it's only natural I feel an emptiness without him around. It's for the best, though.

My chest caves in. I may be able to say those words, but believing them is another thing.

When there's a knock at my door, I call out, "Come in," but don't move from my curled-up position.

"Hey," Michelle says quietly.

I roll over and sit up. "Michelle? What are you doing here?"

"At the request of your daughter, I'm here to find out what's wrong with you." She steps inside, shuts the door, and crosses the room to take a seat on the end of my bed. "So, what's wrong with you?"

"Nothing. I'm fine." I pick at the edge of the blanket, not looking at Michelle.

"Well, that's bullshit. Anyone can see that. If you were fine, you wouldn't be hiding in your bed."

With a groan, I ask, "What did Syd tell you?"

"That you've been sleeping a lot, and you don't ever want to do anything, and you've been moody. Why does she sound like the mom and you're the teenager?"

I let out a small, self-deprecating chuckle. "I guess this year was harder than I thought it would be."

"It's been over two weeks since Charlie's... Since the 24th. It never takes you this long to bounce back. Why is this year so much harder?"

My throat tightens and my jaw quivers. I blink back the tears as I whisper, "I broke up with Blake."

"What!?" Michelle practically leaps off the bed, standing up with her hands thrown to her sides. "When? Why?"

"The Friday you picked up the kids. It was all too much."

"Mags, you were supposed to let him mend your heart, not tear it apart again." She takes her seat on the bed. "What happened?"

The thought of reliving that night causes my body to shake, but once I start telling Michelle the details, I can't stop. The story comes spilling out of my mouth so fast, I can barely keep up. By the end of it, my blanket is soaked with my tears and Michelle stares at me.

"And I haven't heard from him since."

"Mags..." Michelle reaches over and takes my hand. "You're the biggest idiot I've ever met."

My head whips up. "Excuse me?"

"You broke up with Blake over a beer? A *beer*, Mags?"

I rip my hand from hers. "It wasn't just the beer. It was the fact Blake was making it his favorite when it was already Charlie's."

"Jesus Christ, people are allowed to like the same beer. I love margaritas, but you don't hear me telling everyone else they're mine and mine alone."

"I know it sounds silly, but it was the catalyst for everything else. Blake was taking over all aspects of Charlie's life. It started with the beer, then suddenly Blake was my date to all the neighborhood functions. He was giving my kids presents and helping celebrate our birthdays and holidays. He even wanted to go on family vacations. Charlie was being replaced and I finally saw it."

Michelle looks at me with loving pity in her eyes. "You wouldn't know a good thing if it came up and slapped your ass, would you?"

"What?"

"Those things Blake's been doing are because you're in a relationship! Why do you think he wants to do all that stuff? He's only trying to be a part of your life. Let's look at the facts, shall we?" Michelle scoots onto the bed, crossing her legs beneath her. "Blake is what? Twenty-nine, right?"

I nod.

"And the man is downright gorgeous. Mags, he could be drowning in pussy if he wanted to be."

I scoff at Michelle's lewdness, but she has a point.

"But he's not. He chose you. A thirty-seven-year-old, single mom of two kids. Who, by the way, he treats like his own, does he not?"

A dull ache forms in my chest as I think about Blake interacting with my children. How he naturally fell into the role of the dad with them. Spending time with them, speaking to them like people instead of juveniles.

"And those kids love him. That's got to mean something, too. You wouldn't be with someone your kids hated, would you?"

I shake my head vehemently.

"Okay. Then there's the fact he never once asked you to put Charlie on the back burner. You may think that's what he was doing, but he never expected you to put him ahead of Charlie. Did he?"

I think very hard about this one. There were so many instances when Blake took Charlie's place, did things Charlie should be doing, and I never saw it for what it was. They were subtle, unassuming moments. My throat closes up as I think over each one, berating myself for letting Blake take them over.

It started with the garbage disposal. Then, it was movie night, which led to us having sex on his couch. Possibly setting off a string of the best sex I've ever had, but that's just another way he manipulated his way into my life.

Did he, though?

Blake was always the perfect gentleman. He never pressured me at all. If any-thing, he over checked his boundaries, and confirmed I was okay with everything we did. That's part of the reason I fell for him.

Then, there's all the time he spent with the kids. Playing video games with Dylan, attempting to break Sydney out of her shell, helping with homework and school projects. In the past almost year, Blake has done some amazing things for me and my family, and they were never about him. He never made himself the center of attention.

Except when he stripped in my living room.

My cheeks heat, but I swallow down the emotion and focus on Michelle's question. Blake never asked me not to bring up Charlie. Instead, he would listen intently when I told stories, or relived a memory. He never expected me to stop talking about my late husband, in fact, he gave me a gift to commemorate my marriage.

I glance at the river rock on my nightstand and my eyes well with tears. Then, a funny thing happens; Charlie's voice echoes in my mind, *Magpie, be happy.* I close my eyes and I can almost feel him with me, my heart fluttering.

"And lastly, Mags, Blake loves you. The man has thrown himself into a relationship with not only you, but your kids. You told me how he would stay the night and not pester you for sex because he knew you didn't want to with the kids down the hall. Hell, the guy spent two months without you because you told him you needed your space. Which was a bad call, by the way."

"I know." I open my eyes, meeting Michelle's gaze.

"You are never going to find another guy who treats you and your kids so well and looks that good while he does. Trust me."

The tears bubble over and spill onto my lap. "I miss him so much, Michelle."

She crawls across the bed and wraps her arms around my shaking body. "I know you do. I'm sure he misses you, too. But you have to ask yourself if you're ready to fix this. Are you?"

I shake my head and sniffle. "I don't know if I can. The damage is done. I told him to never speak to me again, and if I know one thing about Blake, he's a good listener."

"Well, if I know one thing about Blake, it's he's undeniably, irrevocably, in love with you, and he won't let you go that easily." She loosens her grip, pushing me back to look me in the eye. "Now, is there some way we can run into him by 'coincidence'? Like a neighborhood get together, or something?"

"The next one will be the Fourth of July, but Blake won't go to it. He hates that party."

"And it's too far away. We need to fix this now." Michelle bites her lip, dropping her chin into her hand.

"His birthday is Friday. His thirtieth."

Michelle's eyes light up. "Perfect. Do you know what he's doing? Where he'll be?"

"He's not doing anything."

"What? It's his thirtieth birthday. Why wouldn't he do something?"

"Because after he did such a wonderful job on my birthday, I asked him what he wanted for his. All he said was 'You, Maggie.'" I recall the depth of his voice and the flash in his eyes as he said it, and my stomach flips.

Michelle lets out a shaky breath. "Yeah, we got to fix this now. I won't let you lose a man with lines like that. Tell you what. I'll come over on Friday and stay with the kids, so you don't worry about them. You can go find Blake and make up. Don't come home."

Friday afternoon, I'm standing on Blake's porch, wearing the sundress I wore on our first night together. I've chewed off all my fingernails, licked the lip gloss clean from my lips, and swallowed a million times, trying to quench my dry throat.

But I can't work up the courage to knock. What if I do and he slams the door in my face? Or worse, what if he doesn't answer at all?

My heart pounds in my chest. At least if he slams the door on me, I'll know he's done. But if he doesn't answer? I'll be left wondering if I should do this all over again. I'd never get over it.

I shake my head and don't give myself another second to think about it before knocking on the door.

Silence.

I ring the bell. Three times.

Still, nothing.

My pounding heart sinks, turning to ice. I turn to shuffle away, when a thought hits me. Oscar didn't bark. If Blake is home and ignoring my knocking, Oscar would have barked at the door. Realization smacks me in the face.

He's not home.

I think hard for a minute about where he could be. The bar? Getting drunk and drowning in pussy, as Michelle so eloquently put it?

No. That's not who he is.

Then where would he be? It's Friday afternoon, so it's possible he's still working, but he told me he took the day off. Plans change, though.

I wrack my brain until I come up with the answer. I run back up the street, dashing into my house to grab my purse and car keys, completely ignoring Michelle's and my children's questions before racing out to my car. Peeling down the road, my hands grip the wheel so tight, my knuckles are white.

Since I don't have a park pass, I have to pay to get into the reservoir, but it's worth it. Blake is worth it.

I pull into the parking lot and hike to Blake's favorite spot. *Please be here.* As I round the bend, I get a small glimpse of Blake sitting by the water's edge before Oscar jumps all over me.

Blake whips his head around at the commotion. His face lights up for the briefest of moments, before falling back into defeat as he turns away.

I kneel down, settling Oscar with an ear rub. "Guess there's no sneaking up on you, is there?"

"What are you doing here, Maggie?" His tone is heavy, not at all like the deep, gravel I've come to love. Now, it's laced with anger and hurt, and it stabs me in the gut.

"I, uh–" I step forward, my eyes locked on Blake's hunched shoulders. His breaths are getting deeper. I can tell by the way his torso expands with each one. "I wanted you to know I started seeing my therapist again. Had my first appointment last week, and I'll be going every Tuesday."

He turns his chin over his shoulder. "That's really great. I'm glad you're going again, but did you come all the way out here to tell me that?"

"No." I inch closer, and my eyes fall to the drawing pad and pencils sitting on his other side. My mouth curls into a smile.

"Then why are you here?" He turns back to the water, its gentle lapping keeping the silence between us at bay.

"Because I– I–" I can't bring myself to say the words I don't even know he'll accept. I bite my lip and wring my hands in front of me, my jaw quivering as I turn my gaze to the beautiful sunset shining on the water. I turn back to him. "I'm sorry, Blake."

He turns his head to me, his eyes full of pain locking on mine, and he scoots over to offer me a seat. I hesitate, but sit down on the blanket next to him. We sit in silence for several minutes, watching the sunset and listening to the lake, but we don't touch. Though we're inches apart, I feel his heat burning my arm and it's devastating to know he's no longer mine to hold.

When he doesn't speak, I get nervous, thinking he didn't hear me. So I repeat, "I'm sorry."

"Don't." The harshness of the single syllable word puts knots in my stomach.

I sniffle, and my mouth opens to explain further, but Blake doesn't let me. "Don't give me your sorries, and your explanations, unless it's the last time."

What? "Blake, I don't–"

"Maggie, you threw me out after our fight at Christmas, only to come back and apologize. And I accepted that, because I knew what you were going through was tough. I gave you all the space you needed for two months while you figured out what you wanted and dealt with your baggage."

Indignation flares in me at his use of the word "baggage", but I swallow it down to let him finish.

"When you called me to suggest we spend the weekend together, something told me it was a bad idea, but I was starving for you, so I agreed. I thought maybe it would be a turning point for us, and things would go in a different direction." He swallows deeply. "I never thought that direction would be apart."

"I know, Blake. I didn't either. I was–"

"Let me finish, please."

I press my lips together and nod.

"My heart has been torn apart twice now, and I don't think I could handle it again. So, if you're here to give me an apology, it better be permanent." He turns his head, locking his glossy eyes with mine. "Because once I grab onto you again, I'm never letting go."

A shaky breath escapes me as a tear streams down my cheek, and I turn my gaze back to my lap. "I do have a birthday present for you."

He reaches over and wipes the tear from my face, his touch radiating through my body. "I don't need anything except you."

I turn my head and am met with those soft, shining brown eyes that melt my soul. "Well, then it's your lucky day, because that's exactly what I'm giving you."

His eyes widen a moment, before his brow furrows.

"I love you, Blake Averson." As the words leave my lips, my entire body feels lighter. I've been so afraid to say them, thinking that if I did, my world would implode, but now, I can't believe I waited this long. "I'm done pretending I don't. I'm done being afraid of what loving you means, because I lost you for the last few weeks and it's been Hell." I swallow as I watch Blake's face twist into happy relief. "So, this is the last time I'll apologize for my insecurities, because I'll never let them come between us again."

Blake throws his hand behind my head and pulls my mouth to his. He wraps his other arm around my waist as I grab onto his shoulders. The kiss deepens, like our souls are connecting and, for the first time in years, I know I'm right where I need to be.

Epilogue

"**H**appy birthday, Blake!" Dylan yells as he wraps Blake in a bear hug.

"Thanks, Buddy. I love it." Blake holds up a new Rockies baseball cap. Dylan hand-picked it after he saw Blake eyeing it at the game they went to together.

My heart swells watching how incredibly well Dylan and Blake mesh. It's like they were always meant to be friends, just separated by too many years.

Blake slides his new hat onto his head. "How do I look?"

"Thirty-one looks good on you," I say with a wink.

"I meant the hat, not the age." He crinkles his nose, and I giggle.

"When do we get cake?" Dylan chimes in.

"Geez, Dylan. Calm down," Sydney snips without looking up from her book. She's nestled into a chair on the other side of the table, a book in one hand and the other massaging Oscar's head in her lap.

"It's okay, Syd. We can have cake now." I take a look at everyone's plates. They're all finished with the wonderful meal Blake grilled for us. Even on his birthday, he's still taking care of everyone else.

"Yay!" Dylan yells as I enter the house.

Pulling the cake from the fridge, I slide it onto the counter and gather the candles. I bought a three and a one. I'm not about to fill Blake's cake with thirty-one individual candles. Though it would be funny.

As I'm putting the candles into the creamy frosting, I start thinking about where we were a year ago. Blake and I sitting by the lake, the tension between us palpable as he poured his broken heart out. My heart and stomach fluttering in unison as I listened, but didn't know what he would decide.

In the end, everything turned out the way it should. Blake and I made up, several times that night, and not long after, he sold his house and moved in with me and the kids. It's been a crazy adjustment, but living with him has been better than I could have ever imagined.

Especially after this past April and May. The year before, I was terrified of having him too close, and this year, I can't imagine how I ever survived without him. Blake was there to hold me every night, whether or not I was crying, and he was there to listen to my ramblings about Charlie, no matter how happy or sad I got. I made it through those two months completely intact. Because of Blake.

"Mom!" Dylan's muffled voice through the sliding door startles me back into reality.

"Okay!" I yell back, picking up the cake.

One of them slides the door open, and I'm so focused on not dropping the cake as I step through the doorway, I hardly notice I'm the only one singing "Happy Birthday". I raise my eyes from the cake to find Sydney, Dylan, and Oscar all flanking Blake as he lowers to his knee.

Oh my God!

"Maggie," he starts, but has to clear his throat. "I love you. I love you and the kids more than anything. This last year made me realize how happy and how lucky I am to be a part of your lives. I want to press my luck and ask you something, but only if you say 'yes'."

I stifle a laugh as my eyes well with tears.

"Mags. Maggie. Margaret." The way he says my full name gives me a chill. He's never called me that. "You are my everything. You and the kids have made me happier than I've ever been in my life. I'm honored to be part of your lives, to be able to play the role of Dad, but there's one thing missing."

I pull my bottom lip between my teeth, my toes bouncing.

"I'd like to make you my wife. Will you do me the honor of giving me the best birthday present I could ask for, so I can call you mine forever?" He pulls a small box from behind his back, presenting it to me as he opens it to reveal a beautiful ring. Large enough to be noticed, but not ostentatious, in a simple setting between two smaller diamonds. "Marry me?"

My jaw quivers with my answer, but my throat has run dry.

"Say yes, Mom!" Dylan shouts, and we all laugh.

"Well, how can I say no now?" I look at Blake and, for a moment, concern covers his face, but he quickly recognizes my joke and smiles. "Of course, I will marry you, Blake Averson."

The smile grows as he stands to put the ring on my finger, but I pull away a bit and drop my gaze to the cake still in my hands. The candles are melting, wax pooling at the bases.

Blake takes it and slides it onto the table before glancing down at Dylan. "You blow them out, Buddy." Turning back to me, he locks his brown eyes on mine, happiness flooding them. He slides the ring on my finger. A perfect fit. "I've already got my wish." He tugs me toward him and plants his lips on mine.

My children cheer as Oscar weaves himself in circles between us. The world melts away. I have two happy, healthy kids, a rambunctious dog who can't be controlled, and the love of a man I don't deserve. Everyone always said Charlie would want me to be happy, and now, at last, I am.

The End

Preview of Love Hops

The following is an unedited excerpt of an upcoming novel.

Chapter 1

Happy birthday to me, Lena thought as she watched the clouds move slowly across the blue sky.

Laying on her back in a canoe with a bright orange life vest strapped to her chest while she nursed a cheap bottle of Pinto Noir was not how she pictured her 40th birthday. She was supposed to be on a luxury cruise, sailing the Caribbean with a fruity mixed drink in her hand, not drifting across a man-made reservoir in Aurora, Colorado, alone.

At least it's fairly quiet.

Other than the children's laughter from the swim beach behind her, all Lena could hear was the hum of jet ski engines in the distance. She propped up against the canoe's back and flung a leg over the side. Her toes dipped into the cool water. Watching a group of men jet skiing out in the middle of the reservoir, Lena's adrenaline pumped as they sped across the water's surface, making sharp turns and narrowly missing each other.

You'd never catch me on one of those dangerous things. She took another swig of her wine, leaned her head back and closed her eyes.

With a deep breath, she flooded her lungs with lake-scented air. She took another drink. This may not have been her first choice of birthday celebrations, hell, it wasn't even her fiftieth choice, but it was all she had.

A cloud passed over the sun, giving her a quick reprieve from the heat. Mid-May in Colorado was plenty warm and the sun was doing a good job of baking her olive skin. She would tan nicely. With another swig of the wine, she swished it around in her mouth a bit before swallowing.

This is a rocking party.

There was never anything truer than in that moment.

As soon as she thought it, the hum of the jet skis became a roar. The water lapped at the canoe and it rocked back and forth as someone yelled, "Watch out!" The next thing Lena knew, she was under water.

She kicked her legs furiously, flailing her arms around until her head popped above the surface. Lena sucked in a breath, coughing and spitting lake water from her throat. With her eyes shut tight, her hands searched for the canoe. They came up empty.

Lena's heart pounded in her chest. She employed what little swimming knowledge she had to tread water. The life vest was doing its job, but if Lena stopped kicking, it rose up, smooshing her face so her cheeks puffed up like a chipmunk. It was terribly uncomfortable.

Right as Lena felt the urge to scream, the canoe bumped into her hand and she gripped it tighter than she'd ever gripped anything. Now that she was stable, Lena rubbed her eyes, blinking them open.

"That was a mighty spill you took," a man's deep voice said. "You okay?"

Lena whipped her head up, her long, black hair flipping into her face, to find a man, a few years her senior, leaning from his jet ski to hold onto the other side of the canoe. His bright, blue eyes stayed trained on hers, and Lena's breath caught in her throat.

From the lake water in it, I'm sure. "Uh, I'm okay. Thanks."

The man's mouth curled into a smile behind his dark beard peppered with graying hairs. "Well, that's good to hear. Sorry about that. Apparently, my son needs more lessons."

"No, I'd say he handled that jet ski fine," Lena said as she climbed back into the canoe, peeling her wet hair from her face. "He didn't crash into me."

"I meant lessons about watching where he's going so he doesn't endanger the lives of pretty ladies such as yourself, miss...?"

Lena's cheeks flushed slightly as she fought a flattered smile. "Lena, Lena Bouras."

"Nice to meet you, Lena. I'm Del." They stared at each other a moment until Del cleared his throat, letting go of the canoe and straightening up on his jet ski. "What were you doing floating aimlessly around in a canoe?"

Lena licked her lips before pulling her bottom one between her teeth. She turned her gaze away from Del. "Celebrating my birthday."

She heard Del chuckle. "Well, happy birthday, though you have interesting ideas on celebrations."

A smile crept across her lips and she lifted her gaze to his once more. The warm smile on his face made her stomach flip, but she chalked it up to her adrenaline starting to settle. Del wasn't Lena's type.

He was handsome in his own right. A man in his mid-to-late forties with a full head of salt and peppered hair that matched his thick beard was nothing to laugh at. Del was certainly what one would call a silver fox, as he sat perched on the jet ski, his shoulder and bicep muscles rippling from under his life vest. He just wasn't who Lena usually went for.

"Would you like a tow?" he asked. "Or are you planning on drifting along some more?"

Lena chewed on her lip and checked the sun. It was getting lower and now that she was dripping wet, she'd be cold when sunset came. Plus, her wine was almost gone.

Oh no! Her eyes darted around the canoe. She reached under her seat and blew out a breath as she felt the bottle on her fingertips, but her cheerful face dropped when she pulled the bottle out. It was empty. Lena hung her head and said, "A tow would be great, thanks."

Del hummed a laugh through his closed lips, shaking his head as he took hold of the canoe and pulled it across the reservoir to the dock. He tied it to the pier before beaching his jet ski. Lena watched as he dismounted, his swim trunks straining dangerously tight across his ass, and her heart rate rising. When he took off his life vest, Lena snapped her mouth shut to keep from gaping. The man was cut, and that was being conservative.

She averted her eyes as he walked down the dock to extend a hand to her. Lena swallowed and stood, but the rocking canoe proved to be a worthy adversary. She nearly tumbled back into the lake, and she would have, had it not been for Del's strong hand wrapping around her wrist.

"Whoa, careful," the rumble of his deep voice made her throat run dry. He helped her onto the dock, where the world spun, making her trip on a splintered plank and falter. Del caught her, but not before she crashed into his firm chest. He cocked an eyebrow. "How much of that wine did the lake get?"

Lena pushed away from him, straightening her posture before she shrugged. "Only like a quarter of the bottle."

"You know, if a ranger would've caught you, you'd have gotten a hefty fine."

"Honestly, that was the least of my concerns." She ran her hands up her arms, shivering in the breeze. "Thank you for the tow."

Lena took a wobbly step, but Del leaned into her space, stopping her in her tracks. "Did you eat before you went out on the lake?"

"I had lunch, but I haven't eaten since."

Del pursed his lips and eyed her from head to toe.

Not wanting to squirm under his intense gaze, Lena removed her life vest. As she fought to keep from swaying, she noticed Del staring. She worried he was judging her for being intoxicated, but when she met his gaze, she saw something warmer than judgment.

A soft understanding lingered in his eyes, and he turned his head over his shoulder to look at the parking lot where several food trucks were parked. "How about you eat something before you try to drive home?"

Lena thought for a moment. She really wasn't in the best shape to drive just yet, and her stomach was beginning to grumble. With a nod, she followed Del up to the reservoir parking lot.

"What do you like?" Del asked.

Lena eyed the Mexican food truck, her mouth watering. "Tacos."

"Perfect." Del strode up to the truck, pulling his wallet from a zippered pocket in his swim trunks.

Lena skipped to catch up and put her hand on his forearm. "I can get my own."

Del smiled, warm and genuine. "Call it a birthday present." He winked and Lena turned her face away to hide her pink cheeks. There was a quick gust of the breeze, sending a chill through Lena. "Why don't you go change clothes while I get the food? Otherwise you'll be freezing your butt off out here. Just tell me what you want."

"Okay, thank you. Um, can I have two veggie tacos, please?"

"Sure thing."

Lena hurried off to her car where she had extra clothes tucked in her backpack. She scanned her surroundings quickly. There wasn't another car anywhere near her, so she crawled into the trunk of her Honda CR-V, and changed clothes. Stripping off the wet tank top proved arduous inside the cramped space. It was form fitting already, but now that it was sopping wet, it stuck to her like glue.

Too bad there wasn't a wet t-shirt contest.

Lena smacked her forehead. Del hadn't been staring at her because he was judging, he stared because of the wet shirt. Her chest had probably been staring at him first. Embarrassment flooded Lena for not realizing what was going on, but it turned into flattery the more she thought about it.

With her chin raised a bit, Lena finished changing. As she stepped out, now wearing a snug fitting long-sleeve tee and shorts, she felt more comfortable. She slipped into her flip flops as she fixed her hair into a ponytail, and headed back to the food trucks as her stomach growled mightily.

She found Del sitting at a picnic table, still in his swim trunks but with a sweatshirt on, too. Their food was set out in front of him and a bottle of water next to her basket. A smile crept across her face. "Thank you," she said and took a seat.

"No problem. Happy birthday."

Lena dug in, the delectable flavor of grilled peppers and onions mingling with lime and cilantro tantalizing her tastebuds. Maybe it was the best taco she'd ever had, or maybe it was just the overwhelming hunger that had crept up on her, but Lena devoured the first taco in an instant. As she swallowed the last bite and wiped her mouth, she lifted her head and met Del's smiling face.

Her cheeks flushed. "Sorry."

"No, it's cool. Glad I got you a decent birthday gift." He winked and the heat in Lena's face grew.

She took a deep breath and opened her water. Although the cold liquid did well to quench her dry throat, it did very little to ease her overheated state. Lena pushed her basket a few inches away, wanting to take a break and not look like a wild animal. She met Del's gaze again, but flicked her eyes away. Silence had settled at the table, and Lena was hard pressed to think of conversation.

"So, Lena, what do you do?"

Her heart leaped into her throat, but she swallowed it down. "Um, nothing actually." She dropped her hands into her lap and picked at her fingernails. "I lost my job a few weeks ago, and I haven't been able to find anything."

Del's face fell sympathetic. "Sorry to hear that. What were you doing?"

"I was an interior designer. I worked at a firm that did renovations for hotels and office buildings." Lena's shoulders slumped. "I'd been there for almost ten years."

"Wow, that's a long time. And they fired you?"

"More or less."

Del furrowed his eyebrows, pursing his lips as if deep in thought. "Well, maybe my son tipping your canoe was more than an accident."

"What?" Lena crinkled her nose.

"It just so happens, I have an employee leaving soon and I'll have an opening." His pursed lips relax, spreading into an easy grin.

There's no way this guy owns a design firm. Is there? "And what do you do?"

Del rubbed the back of his neck. "I own a brewery. One of my bartender's is having her baby any day now and she wants to be a stay at home mom. I'm happy for her, but I'm less one bartender, so if you need a job…"

Lena fought the laugh attempting to burst from her. "That's awfully kind of you, and I appreciate the offer, but that doesn't sound like my area of expertise."

"I know it's not anything like design, but it pays and has steady hours," his tone held something resembling hope.

"Del, I don't want to feed you some line of crap and tell you I'll think about it, or even keep it in mind, because I won't. No offense. I don't even drink beer."

He laughed, hanging his head a moment, and Lena exhaled with relief. "Okay, that's fair."

"Hey, Dad. Where's your jet? We're gonna load everything up." A young guy with shaggy blond hair ran up, patting Del on the shoulder and leaning down.

"Hey, Johnnie. It's down at the west dock." Del pointed behind Lena, but flipped his hand so his palm is up and motioned to her. "And I'd like to introduce Lena Bouras." He turned his head with a stern look. "The woman whose canoe you flipped."

Johnnie swallowed and gave a sheepish grin. "Sorry about that."

"Thanks. I survived, though." Lena chuckled.

"Lena, this is my youngest son, Johnnie."

"Nice to meet you." Johnnie turned back to Del. "Key?"

Del reached in his pocket and held the jet ski key in the air, but snatched it away as Johnnie reached for it. "Let Jack back the truck down the ramp."

"Okay, fine." Johnnie rolled his eyes, took the key, and ran off to the dock.

Del watched his son disappear down the hill before pulling his gaze back to hers. "Twenty-one years old, and still such a kid."

"You said he was your youngest. How many kids do you have?"

"Three. All boys. You?"

Lena shook her head vehemently. "None."

Del nodded with pursed lips and silence took over the table once again. Lena, picked up her other taco and took a big bite. At least that would give her a moment to think of something to say. When nothing came to mind, she took another bite, and another until the taco was gone and she still had no topics for conversation.

"Well," Del said, getting up from the table. "I should go supervise to make sure the boys don't drive my truck into the lake. It was nice meeting you, Lena, and I hope you enjoyed your birthday."

Lena nodded, confused by why she was disappointed for Del to leave. "I did, thank you. I'll have to remember the name of this food truck."

"There's an easy way to do that."

"And what's that?"

"Just take the paper in your basket home. It's got their name printed on it." Del nodded at the basket in front of her. "Goodbye, Lena. Drive safe."

"Bye," the word came out almost inaudible as Lena felt her heart sink watching Del walk away.

The sun was kissing the horizon, turning the sky orange and pink and Lena didn't want to drive home in the dark. She grabbed her basket, prepared to crumple the greasy paper liner when Del's suggestion to keep it echoed in her mind.

She chuckled, shaking her head, but as her eyes fell to the basket in her hand, her breath caught in her throat. There, scribbled on the corner was a phone number. The words "think about it" were written above the numbers and "Del" was signed underneath. *Was that there the whole time?*

A flutter ran through Lena.

It dissolved quickly, though. Del's kindness and charm didn't negate the fact he wasn't Lena's type. *Besides, he's probably married.*

The thought hadn't struck Lena until then. Sure, there wasn't a ring on his finger, but he'd been on the lake so he probably tucked it away someplace safe. With three kids and looks like that, of course he was married. The phone number was merely in case she changed her mind about the job.

Which she wouldn't.

But it's the first good lead I've gotten.

Lena swallowed her pride, tore the greased stained part of the paper away, and tucked Del's phone number into her pocket. It was always a good idea to keep one's options open, and right now, Del was the only option she had.

Coming Fall 2023

Also by Christine Layne

Love Hops – https://a.co/d/f0Ro6N4

Mud, Love, and Chemistry – https://a.co/d/aCLFP83

Acknowledgments

The process of not only developing and writing this story, but also publishing it was humbling, to say the least. I could not have done it without the help of many.

To my loving, supportive husband:

Thank you for continually listening to me rant about my story ideas, but mostly, thank you for believing in me every step of the way. From reading my "smutty romance", to not batting an eyelash at the price of self-publishing, you were with me from start to finish, and I love you every day for it.

To my children:

Thank you for understanding that mom needed quiet time to work. Even though I tried to keep my working hours to school hours, there were times I had to work while you were home, and you were both respectful of my needs (most of the time).

To my awesome critique partners, Shayna Astor and Tara Brodbeck:

Where do I even begin? Between your constructive criticisms, and your friendship, I couldn't ask for better writing partners. Without the two of you, Because of Blake wouldn't exist, and the multitude of stories in my head would never see the light of day. Your belief in me and my writing always gives me the strength to continue. I can't thank you enough for reading, and rereading, my work. Also, thank you for letting my think out loud, answering *all* my questions, and talking me off the ledge when I got in my head about things. You are both spectacular.

To my wonderful writing group:

Thank you for continuing to meet with me even though all I ever talked about was Because of Blake and the process of publishing it. I promise I will have new material at some point to discuss!

To my fantastic editors, Mackenzie and D.P.:

Thank you for all your hard work on this project. You have not only made this book better, but you have made me a better writer, as well. Thank you for not only helping me through this process, but also for keeping my voice my own.

Thank you **Coffin Print Designs** for my beautifully stunning cover!

To my ARC team:

Thank you for taking the time to read my book before it was available to the public, and for leaving your fantastic reviews.

And, most importantly, to my readers:

Like the old adage, "if a tree falls in the forest, and no one is around, does it make a noise?", an author is not an author if no one reads their work. From the bottom of this new author's heart, thank you for taking the time to read my book. Writing started as a hobby, became a passion, and now that I'm published, sharing my stories with you is the icing on the cake.

About The Author

Christine Layne is a romance author who loves to tell
stories about people falling in love against the odds. Though writing is her
passion, Christine also enjoys painting, spending time with her children, or
watching movies with her husband, as long as she has a cup of tea in her hand.
Follow me for the latest updates, teasers for upcoming
novels, giveaways, and more!
Instagram @christinelayneauthor
Twitter @ChrisLayneLove
Facebook Group: Christine's Creations

www.ingramcontent.com/pod-product-compliance
Lightning Source LLC
Chambersburg PA
CBHW022104310726
48972CB00007B/1877